JILL SHALVIS

has been making up stories since she could hold a pencil. Now, thankfully, she gets to do it for a living, and doesn't plan to ever stop. She is the bestselling, award-winning author of over two dozen novels. She's a Waldenbooks bestselling author, is a 2000 RITA® Award nominee and a two-time National Reader's Choice Award winner. Jill has been nominated for *Romantic Times*'s Career Achievement Award in Romantic Comedy, Best Duets and Best Temptation.

DAY LECLAIRE

and her family live in the middle of a maritime forest on a small island off the coast of North Carolina. Despite the yearly storms that batter them and the power outages, they find the beautiful climate, superb fishing and unbeatable seascape more than adequate compensation. One of their first acquisitions upon moving to Hatteras Island was a cat named Fuzzy. He has recently discovered that laps are wonderful places to curl up and nap—and that Day's son really was kidding when he named the hamster Cat Food.

In Name Only

Jill Shalvis

Day Leclaire

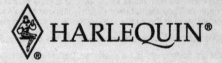

HARLEQUIN®

TORONTO • NEW YORK • LONDON
AMSTERDAM • PARIS • SYDNEY • HAMBURG
STOCKHOLM • ATHENS • TOKYO • MILAN • MADRID
PRAGUE • WARSAW • BUDAPEST • AUCKLAND

ISBN 0-373-23015-X

IN NAME ONLY

Copyright © 2003 by Harlequin Books S.A.

The publisher acknowledges the copyright holders of the individual
works as follows:

THE BACHELOR'S BED
Copyright © 2000 by Jill Shalvis
ACCIDENTAL WIFE
Copyright © 1996 by Day Totten Smith

This edition published by arrangement with Harlequin Books S.A.

Visit us at www.eHarlequin.com

Printed in U.S.A.

CONTENTS

THE BACHELOR'S BED

Jill Shalvis

_____ **Prologue** _____

"YOU FORGOT to take the cash I left out for you."

At the low, unbearably sexy voice in her ear, Lani hugged the telephone closer. They weren't strangers, not by a long shot, but neither were they familiar enough with each other for her to joke about what the mere sound of his voice did to her insides. Shakily, she let out a breath. Her heart raced, and to combat the funny, weightless feeling that such a severe attraction caused, she leaned back in her squeaky office chair, lifted her tired, worn-out feet up to her desk and closed her eyes.

"Ms. Mills?"

"Yes, I'm here." He couldn't know she'd recognize his voice anywhere. She sighed and opened her eyes as she straightened. It wasn't right to fantasize about a client, no matter how much that client occupied her thoughts. Truth was, he probably occupied the thoughts of every woman in this small mountain town of Sierra Summit. Not that there wasn't plenty to do in the quaint, lovely place, but Colin West was such absolutely perfect fantasy material.

"Your money for your house-cleaning services," he repeated patiently. "You left it on the counter."

"I know. I'm sorry," she said, embarrassed. At the time, she'd been flustered because he'd been watching her with a silent intensity that she didn't understand as she'd prepared to leave his house.

"No need to apologize, they're *your* earnings."

Again, that quiet yet steely tone. She was intelligent, she knew she couldn't love someone she didn't really know, but she could lust.

He was a man who knew what he wanted and how to get it, and if rumors were to be believed, he rarely ever let anything get in his way. "Ruthless and aggressive" was what they said about him, but Lani believed it was only a front.

To her, he wasn't frightening or even dangerous, but he *was* magnetic and passionate and fiercely private.

He also intimidated the hell out of her.

They'd known each other for one year. Lani had provided services for him once a week since they'd met, and though she had hoped their relationship would have risen above this stilted awkwardness by now, it was clear she was the only one who wished it so.

Sighing again, she shoved back all her secret yearnings and desires. "I'll pick it up when I come next week," she said. "Thank you."

"You're welcome." The husky timbre of his voice deepened, and for just a second, Lani thought that maybe it did so with equal yearning, but that was silly.

She was a nobody to him, less than a nobody. What she made in a year, he considered less than pocket change. Her office was smaller and more cramped than the walk-in closet of his huge bedroom.

He probably didn't even remember her first name.

"Next week then, Lani," he said softly.

She hung up the phone, stared out the tiny office window at the Los Angeles Crest Mountains and smiled dreamily.

He *did* know her name.

"Next week," she whispered to herself.

THE FOLLOWING WEEK when Lani drove up to Colin's house, it looked dark. Disappointment filled her.

She'd rearranged her crazy schedule even though she could have had a rare day off, just to get a peek at him. It was all for naught.

She was an idiot. A lust-bitten idiot.

She walked into the kitchen and saw an envelope with her name on the counter. Inside was her money, for both this week and last.

"You won't forget this time."

Lani nearly leaped out of her skin at the unexpected, silky voice.

He stood in the doorway, filling it with his tall, dangerous-looking presence. She wasn't afraid of him. She didn't know why really, except that she knew all his dark beauty covered pain, not meanness. His gaze, as always, was inscrutable and measured, and every nerve inside Lani went shy. "I won't forget, thank you."

"You should charge more."

"I get by."

"You're worth far more." Colin said this sincerely, even as he remained against the doorway, cool and collected. Distant.

It didn't matter. She knew that was a defense, and she of all people understood defenses. But he'd noticed what a good job she'd done, and while it shouldn't mean so much, it did. Oh, it did. She smiled.

He stared at her, not returning the smile—she'd never seen him smile—his eyes for once readable. In them she saw confusion, which in turn confused *her* because he was always so sure of himself.

Apparently he didn't like the feeling, because he grabbed his keys, said a quick good-bye and vanished.

Lani watched him go, wondering at the flash of vulnerability she'd seen.

SHE DIDN'T SEE HIM again all month, though he always left money for her services. Twice he left her notes, complimenting her on her work.

She saved them and wondered how long it would be before he allowed them to run into one another again. Wondered also if he felt the connection between them, and if it unnerved him as much as it did her.

1

COLIN WOULDN'T HAVE SAID desperation was a personality trait of his, but he felt the cold fingers of it now. Frustrated, he stared at the calculated mess in his office. The building was deserted except for him. Even the downtown streets beyond the darkened windows were quiet on this late-summer evening.

His favorite time to work.

If he could, he'd work all night. Every night. Whatever it took to finish this project, he would do it, it was *that* important.

But he had to go home, had to ward off trouble.

It wasn't often he felt so helpless, and he hated that. There was only one thing to do—fight it.

Fight *them*.

The *them* in this case wasn't some terrorist threat or even a horrific viral infection, but something far worse.

It was his mother and her two meddling sisters.

The three of them had come together in their mutual campaign to ruin his life.

They wanted him married and they wanted him married yesterday, and to further this mission, they had sent woman after woman to him. They'd created parties, blind dates, "surprise" visitors, chance meetings, anything and everything to drive him insane.

He had no idea what the latest plan of attack was, but they'd been too quiet since the last one, when they'd sicced Ms. Mary Martin, the town librarian and closet nymphomaniac, on him. She had made his life a living hell for a month, smiling wickedly every time she ran into him, which had been disturbingly often. When she had goosed him in his office elevator one night, practically stripping him before he managed to separate himself from her, he had drawn the line.

No more interference by his family.

They had to be stopped.

LANI'S CAR barely made it, but that was little surprise. The poor clunker had been threatening to go all year and since she'd just recently put her cleaning business into the black for the first time, transportation had taken a low priority to other things, such as eating.

Carmen glanced at her with a raised eyebrow when the car lunged and jerked.

"Hey, it got us here," Lani told her worker as she shut it off. *Barely.*

Carmen read her lips, looking not so much grateful as doubtful. The woman was sixty years old and deaf. She also had a bit of an attitude and didn't do windows—not exactly perfect maid material.

But Lani was so short-staffed that she, too, was out in the field cleaning today. Not that she minded since this was *his* house.

In fact, for a glimpse of *his* rugged, athletic body she'd clean every toilet in the house. With his dark, thick hair, even darker, fathomless eyes and full, sexy mouth, Colin West was truly the stuff secret fantasies were made of.

Sometimes she pretended that he noticed her for something other than the weekly maid. That he wondered how he could have employed her for a full year and not seen her mind-shattering beauty, her sharp wit. But in the end that was a cruel fantasy because he was perfect and she was...well...not.

Still she never stopped wishing, because someday she was going to take her great-aunt Jennie's advice—she was going to stop living life so carefully and purposely, she was going to jump up and take a risk and not worry about getting hurt.

Carmen sighed theatrically at the delay while Lani daydreamed. Lani knew she was going to have to stop hiring people just because she felt sorry or responsible for them. But it was a difficult habit to break. Besides, Carmen could be sweet.

The older woman stared at the huge house they were to clean and shook her head sharply, glaring at Lani. She huffed with indignation, which made Lani laugh. Okay, not *sweet* exactly. But she was company, which was nice.

It's going to be a scorcher of a day, Lani thought as she tugged and yanked at the heavy bucket in her trunk, panting a little under the weight of it. The mountain air was supposed to make a person strong, but Lani had lived here all her life and she was still on the puny side of petite.

Sierra Summit was located at the base of the Los Angeles Crest Mountains above the sprawling Los Angeles area, but still the July hot spell penetrated the altitude.

Lani swiped at her sticky forehead and hefted the bucket higher while Carmen watched, probably relieved she hadn't been asked to carry anything. The bucket was filled with sponges and cleaners and Lani wrinkled her nose when the strong aroma of pine and lime caught in her throat.

She had nothing against cleaning—it was her liveli-
hood. But if Colin wasn't going to sweep her off her
feet, which she had to admit was highly unlikely, then
she might as well be back in her small but cozy office in
town, working on her very-behind bookkeeping.

A sponge bounced from her bucket to the ground.
Lani nearly killed herself in the juggling act she had to
perform just to get it back in.

Carmen simply watched.

"Hey, don't worry, I've got it." Silence met this dry
statement, and Lani found herself yearning for someone, *anyone*, to speak to.

The blast of unexpected self-pity was startling. She
never allowed it, so why was she wallowing in loneliness today? "Because I just had my twenty-sixth birthday," she realized, speaking out loud.

Carmen watched her speak then snorted her opinion
of that.

But, twenty years after losing the family that had
been her entire life, Lani was just realizing something
disturbing. Despite her inherent sunny disposition, despite her determination to live her life as though each
day was precious, she had never again fully opened her
heart to another. Guilt stabbed at her because she did
have Great-Aunt Jennie, who'd taken in a traumatized
six-year-old Lani instead of enjoying her retirement
years. But still, Lani ached for something that continued to elude her.

Truth was, she wanted more from life. She wanted to
follow Jennie's advice and take a chance, lower her
guard. *Risk.* And if, in the process, she managed to have
a hot, wildly passionate love affair with a man as
dreamy as Colin, then so much the better, because she

had to face facts—orgasms were but a blissful figment of her imagination.

Cleaning bucket in tow, Lani followed Carmen up the long, bricked walk of the upscale home, the early morning sun beaming down on her. She should be used to waking up on one side of the tracks and working on the other, but she still stopped to gawk at the incredibly beautiful home.

Her own place was a tiny modest apartment in an older part of town. Not seedy or even dangerous, just...cheap. She lived there for nearly nothing because Jennie owned the building and never let Lani pay what she charged everyone else.

But Colin's two-story, sprawling house took her breath away. The cedar siding had aged to the color of expensive whiskey. There were no less than three chimneys to conjure up the imagine of hot, crackling winter fires. Decking surrounded the bottom floor. Lani could close her eyes and imagine the swing she'd place where Colin would draw her down and whisper husky promises in her ear on warm summer nights. Then, beneath a sliver of a moon, he'd make good on those promises, using his hands, his tongue, his body until she was limp....

In the real world, she plowed into Carmen, who'd also stopped short to admire the house.

Icy liquid flowed down Lani's front, cooling her off.

Carmen frowned down at her own splattered tennis shoes and worked her lips in what Lani was certain was a colorful Spanish oath.

"Sorry," she muttered and, ignoring her wet shirt, kept moving, her gaze back on the fabulous house. She knew that Colin never used the fireplaces. He hadn't placed a swing on the deck either. His work was his life, and while Lani appreciated and understood his dedication, she wondered if he didn't sometimes yearn for more, the way she did.

As she came to the back door, she felt a strange thrill in her belly.

Would she see him? Would she catch a glimpse of his deep mysterious eyes? Would she hear his low, mesmerizing voice, the one that turned her inside out?

She hoped so because he was the highlight of her week. He was incredible. Okay, maybe a little dark and moody, but positively magnificent. Maybe he'd be wearing those soft, faded jeans again, the ones that fit him like a glove, emphasizing...

Carmen tsked deep in her throat and Lani jumped guiltily, knowing her thoughts had been plastered across her face. "Oh, like you don't think it, too."

Carmen made the equivalent of a grumpy old woman's laugh and wagged her little finger at Lani. Then she wiggled her ample hips suggestively, pausing in her dance to shake her head. Lastly, she gestured to the cleaning supplies.

"Yes, yes, I know." Lani rolled her eyes. "We're here to clean. Clean, clean, clean. No hanky-panky. You know, it's amazing how well you can communicate when you want to. Maybe while you're in the mood, you can explain to me how you have the energy to make fun of me, but the minute we get inside you'll suddenly tire and let me do all the hard work."

Angelic now, Carmen smiled with a lift of one shoulder and a vague shake of her head. *No comprende.*

Right. Lani shook her head in disgust at the both of them. Every woman, young and old, within thirty miles sighed over the thought of Colin. He was rich, amazingly intelligent, gorgeous and, most importantly, he was single. That he kept his distance from people only fueled the constant rumors about his love life. It was said that he went through a different woman every day of the week—but that only made Lani all the more morbidly curious.

He invented *things,* for lack of a better term—electronic robotics. She knew nothing about that.

It didn't matter. She didn't need to understand to appreciate him. Colin worked hard, a good quality in anyone. He was driven and successful. His dark, dangerous fallen-angel looks didn't hurt, either.

Too bad he was so involved in his work. But unlike some of her other clients, who preferred to pretend that their maid was invisible, Colin West always nodded politely to her, spoke easily, and never made her feel less than the woman she was. They'd had many pleasant conversations over the months, and she could remember every one of them.

Enough, she told herself firmly. Ignoring the overwhelming heat, she headed quickly up the steep walk to the kitchen entrance, leaving Carmen huffing far behind.

Just as she reached the door, it whipped open, sending blessedly cool air into her damp face. Standing there before her in all his somber glory was Colin, looking unexpectedly wild, rumpled and just a little desperate.

"Thank God it's you."

"Instead of?" she asked in surprise.

"One of your non-English-speaking employees or, God forbid, the older woman who can't speak at all, the one who always sticks her tongue out at me."

"Well..." She thought of Carmen making her way up the walk right this very moment.

"Come in," he said a bit impatiently, his voice deep and rumbling. His dark, wavy, collar-length hair was more disheveled than usual and standing on end as if he'd been plowing his fingers through it. His eyes, so deep blue they looked black and fathomless, shimmered with what she might have suspected was nerves, if she didn't know better.

From what she'd seen, Colin West never suffered from nerves.

So why was his tall, well-built frame—which she couldn't help but notice was beautifully packed into a well-worn T-shirt and those snug old Levi's she loved—so taut with tension?

Lani opened her mouth to speak, but it fell shut again when his huge, warm hand closed over the heavy bucket she held. He set it aside as though it weighed no more than a penny.

His mouth was grim.

"What's the matter—" Lani squeaked in surprise when he pulled her the rest of the way into his kitchen, slammed the door and, with a gentle but inexorable force, pressed her back against it.

She should have spared a thankful thought for the deliciously cool house. She should have thought about Carmen, who was going to wonder why Lani hadn't waited for her, but her attitude-ridden helper was the last thing on her mind at the moment.

"Mr. West!" she gasped, even as she closed her eyes to fully enjoy the sensation of his incredibly hard body against hers. After all, if this was a dream, she didn't want to wake up. "Did I forget my money again?"

"No."

Lord, she felt good against him. *He* felt good. "So...this is to thank me for the job I did last time?"

"No." For a brief moment he pressed closer, and the almost-embrace spoke of a desperately needed comfort. She lifted her hands to his waist and squeezed reassuringly, trying to remember that he was a client.

"She's not going to let up," he said gruffly. "And I can't take it, not now, not in the middle of this project. It's too damn important."

Reluctantly, Lani opened her eyes because a *she* definitely ruined the fantasy. "Who won't let up?"

"It's enough to drive me insane." His voice was low, edgy and spine-tinglingly rough. "Only one way to stop her and—damn, you're wet!" His dark brows came together in a sharp line as he jerked back, staring down at his T-shirt, now clinging damply to his broad chest.

"I spilled. I'm...sorry."

"It doesn't matter," he said, still staring down at himself.

Lani stared too, because wow, with his wet shirt pasted to that fabulous chest, the blood rushed right out of her head, which made thinking a tad dangerous to her health.

"It's the project that's so important."

She concentrated on his words with effort. "Project?"

"I'm designing a laser-surgery process," he said, pulling at his shirt. "It's so close."

"Laser surgery. They already have that."

"This is different—better." His voice told her how important this was to him. "Less cutting," he said earnestly. "Less time under anesthesia. It'll revolutionize the way surgeries are performed."

And would help countless numbers of people. Lani's save-the-world heart squeezed.

Her crush on him tripled.

"You'll save so many lives," she marveled. *A modern day hero*, she thought.

"The surgeons will save the lives." He moved close again, his eyes flashing with passion, and though she knew it wasn't directed at her, it made her dizzy anyway. Capturing her head in his big, warm hands, he tipped it up to stare down into her eyes. "But I can't finish, they won't leave me alone. No one will leave me alone. They want me out socializing, dating, spending the money I don't care about. I need help."

"You do?" With his long, powerfully built body against hers it was hard to imagine him needing help from someone like her.

"I need a fictional fiancée." His gaze held hers captive. "I know how this sounds, Lani, but will you marry me? For pretend?"

The situation finally overcame Lani's sensory pleasure. Yes, she was plastered up against the door, held there by the fabulous body she'd fantasized over for months, but had he just really asked..."M-m-marry you?" She hadn't stuttered since kindergarten, nearly twenty years before, but suddenly her tongue kept tripping over itself. "B-b-but..."

At that moment, Carmen finally made it to the back door and knocked with enough pressure to wake the dead.

Lani ignored her. "Did you really just ask me to...?"

"Yes." Colin drew a deep, ragged breath. "I've thought about it, planned it all out. I know this is a huge imposition, and I promise to compensate you...." At her soft sound of dismay, he hurried on. "I'm not trying to insult you, but I'm aware of what I'm asking and that it's an inconvenience, to say the least."

She couldn't help it, she laughed.

He frowned. "This isn't funny."

"No, it's not," she agreed. *An inconvenience to be married to him?* Not likely.

"It won't be easy, but I've watched you all year now. You're smart, funny and, best yet, even-tempered. We can do this."

He'd watched her all year.

At her expression, he hesitated. "You understand, this is *pretend*. I just need the *pretense* of being engaged while I finish my project." His hands were still on her face. Rough skin, tender touch. "Lani?"

Maybe she ought to vow to risk more often because, holy cow, this was more like the thrilling life she'd dreamed about for herself since she'd been a young girl remembering her happy, romantic parents. During those first painful years she'd wondered what kind of man would eventually sweep her off her feet. She'd wondered as time had gone by as well, even as she put up mental barriers to avoid the intimacy she so feared.

Now Colin wanted her.

No, she corrected, he *needed*, not wanted. There was a difference and she would do well to remember it. His proposed arrangement was too easy to romanticize. Colin needed time for his laser project, which would save countless thousands. She could be a part of that altruistic cause by helping him out.

And be married to him at the same time.

Carmen pressed her face against the window in the door, ruining the moment, glaring over Lani's shoulder as she tried to see. When she caught sight of Colin wrapped around Lani, her eyes widened comically.

Lani turned her head and concentrated on the warm male pressed against her.

"I just need your agreement," Colin urged in that rough yet silky voice.

It wasn't that she wasn't paying attention, she was. Yet she couldn't help but wonder—how did an inventor get such a great body? She'd seen plenty of great bodies before, but she so rarely had one held against her this way. It made thinking curiously difficult.

"I know this is really sudden, and a big decision, but I can't work like this." Colin dropped his forehead to hers. "I have to have more peace and quiet. It's crucial."

"I understand." His mouth was close enough to kiss if she just leaned forward a fraction of an inch. Her heart raced.

"It's urgent we resolve this before—" The phone rang, echoing strangely in his large house. "Damn."

It rang and rang, in tune now to Carmen's persistent and annoying knocking.

Colin's eyes seemed even more wild, more desperate, and because she'd never seen him anything less than completely put together, it startled her.

"Will you help me?" he asked.

"Well..."

"We're not strangers."

"Uh...no. But..."

"And you know I'm not a mass murderer," he urged. "Or a criminal of any kind."

"Yes. But..."

"Lani." He stepped close again, but didn't touch her. "I'll give you anything in my power, just name it. Money?"

"No!"

"A trip somewhere?"

Lani knew her eyes had lit up; she'd never had the

chance to go anywhere. "I would never accept such a thing."

"Hawaii," he said rashly.

Hawaii. A personal fantasy of hers. "No. No, thank you," she added gruffly, knowing she was going to regret this in the deep dark of the night.

"I'll do *anything* for you in return," he assured her. "Your business...could you use another client?"

Only desperately. "Sure."

"Then please, add my downtown building to your client list. Daily."

Just like that, he'd upped her income. Not only upped it, probably tripled it. He could have no idea what that meant to her, and though she knew it was a pity that he felt he had to offer a bribe, she shamelessly took it, thinking of the extra hours she'd be able to offer her employees. "That's...very generous. Thank you."

"Will you do it?"

Despite her little fantasies, Lani was commitment shy, always had been. She was intelligent enough to realize that most of what made her life so good was the fact that she concentrated on others rather than on herself. The town of Sierra Summit was fairly small, only about seven thousand people in all, and she mothered, sistered and babied a good many of them. Her business was struggling constantly to break even, but only because she didn't charge enough and hired people who needed her more than she needed them. Her business handled mostly industrial work because there weren't too many residents who needed or could afford a housecleaner—Colin being the exception, of course. It wasn't much of an effort to keep everyone happy and satisfied, and Lani genuinely cared about them all, but even so, she still managed to hold everyone at a distance.

This came from a deeply ingrained fear of getting involved, of getting hurt. Whether it went back to losing her family so young or to something much more simple—her own basic shyness, for example—she didn't know and didn't often try to analyze. Colin had said this would be just for show, but she didn't fool herself, it would be complicated, and as a rule she didn't do complicated well.

Stalling, she offered a crooked smile as he once again pulled his wet shirt away from his body. "I don't really know you," she said finally.

The phone rang again and Colin cursed under his breath. His shoulders sagged and his eyes went even more wild.

Carmen knocked.

Colin growled and yanked the door open. In contrast to the tension pouring from him, he spoke slowly, distinctly, and appeared surprisingly calm, considering how white his knuckles were on the knob. "I need another moment with your boss," he said through his teeth, which were bared in a mockery of a smile. He waited until Carmen read his lips and nodded reluctantly. "*Alone,*" he added firmly when Carmen would have entered.

The older woman's eyebrows disappeared into her hairline, but she backed off the threshold. As she turned away, she stuck her tongue out at him.

Lani held her breath, but he didn't seem to notice.

Colin shut the door. His gaze whipped back to Lani, and there was no mistaking his recklessness now. "It's not all that difficult an issue," he assured her. "I'm an open book. Truly."

Lani let out a little laugh, for he was the most closed-mouthed person she'd ever known. And also, something else bothered her—why *her?* Surely he could have asked anyone and got a resounding *oh boy, pretty please, yes!*

Her silence must have scared him. "All right." He plowed his fingers through his hair as he turned in a slow circle. "You want to know me." He faced her and shrugged. "It's simple, really. I'm...technically inclined. I don't drink or do drugs...I like fast, sleek, sexy cars...and I'm fairly certain I don't snore."

When the phone rang yet again, his words came faster. "I like classical music, smart dogs and spicy Mexican food. And I always put the seat down. *Now,*" he added tightly over the annoying phone, "will you agree?"

Lani would never know what came over her, whether it was the unexpected flash of loneliness she'd experienced that morning, or just the deep, inexplicable yearning she felt for this man.

Risk, she reminded herself.

Help him with his great project. *Help him help you out of the rut your life has become.* "Okay," she whispered. Because that sounded weak, she licked her lips and simply, confidently said, "Yes."

Surprise flitted across his features and he held himself very still, clearly unsure if he'd heard correctly. "Did you just say yes?"

"Yes." Oh, God, she couldn't believe she was going to do this. "I mean, what the heck. I love spicy Mexican food, too. Let's do it."

2

THE TENSION DRAINED from Colin's shoulders and while he didn't quite smile, some of the strain left the lines around his mouth. "Well," he said, obviously relieved.

"Yes. Well." Lani grabbed her broom and laughed again, a little giddily. "I feel swept off my feet."

"For pretend," he clarified, eyes sharp on hers. "You feel swept off your feet for *pretend*."

Darn, she had a pesky habit of forgetting that. "Right."

He opened his mouth to say something, but Carmen stuck her face against the glass again, looking like a troll doll as she scrunched up her features to see better. Colin held up his finger for another minute.

Carmen rolled her eyes and disappeared.

"Um...Mr. West?"

He smiled at Lani for the first time, and wow, it was a stunner. "I think under the circumstances," he said, "you can call me Colin."

"Okay." Lani smiled back, feeling a little dazed. What had she done? Had she really agreed to marry this wild, untamed creature just because her life needed a boost? "I should clean now."

"Okay." He frowned, plucking again at his wet shirt. "Ouch."

"Yeah, the cleaner is starting to burn a bit," Lani admitted regretfully, shifting uncomfortably herself. "I'm sorry."

Without another word, Colin pulled the shirt over his head and tossed it aside.

Oh, man. *Oh, man.* He was perfect. Wide sinewy shoulders, hard chest, flat belly, lean hips, and the most amazing eyes that drew her right in... She was getting light-headed, and it most definitely wasn't from the cleaner fumes.

Colin ran a hand over his bare chest with obvious relief. "Better."

Better, Lani agreed silently. There was a solid thunk behind her. Carmen had banged her forehead on the glass attempting to get a better look.

The phone rang again and Colin sighed resolutely. "I have to get that." He looked as though he'd rather face a firing squad. "But I'll be back. We have to go over some things."

Lani nodded, wondering if some of those things involved her wifely duties.

Now why did just the thought of that give her a heady rush of anticipation? She wasn't promiscuous, not by a long shot, but somehow, with a man like Colin, she thought she might learn something about being a woman.

Yep, the chemicals in the cleaning stuff she used were most definitely going to her head—and really starting to burn her skin. Too bad she couldn't rip her shirt off, too. At the thought, she let out another laugh.

"Lani?" Colin dipped his head down a little so he could see into her eyes. "Don't leave yet."

Did he honestly think she'd disappear now? He didn't know much about her if—

What was she thinking?

He knew *nothing* about her. Still speechless, a truly unusual state for her, she shook her head.

She wouldn't leave.

He looked at her for a long moment, and she wondered what was going through his mind, what he saw in her.

Again, the enormity of what she'd agreed to do staggered her. What was she going to tell Great-Aunt Jennie, who was likely to be so excited to have wed off her old-maid niece, finally? She'd have a heart attack!

It was just pretend, she reminded herself. No real heart involved. Walk away when the project's done.

Lani watched her half-naked boss—and, good Lord, her future husband—as he walked out of the room.

Another unstoppable giggle escaped and she slapped her hand over her mouth. Giggling wouldn't do, it didn't become the future Mrs. West. "Oh, my God."

Quietly, and since her knees were very weak, quickly, with a wide, silly grin on her face, she sank to the nearest seat, which happened to be the floor.

THE PHONE had stopped ringing by the time Colin got to his home office, which suited him.

Everything was good, he thought with relief. He had his fictional fiancée, and now, finally, he could concentrate on his work.

All other troubles faded away as he did just that, with a hyper-focus born of necessity. Nothing intruded, not the Institute's hurry for his completed laser, not the fact he still had to talk to his well-meaning if meddling mother, nor that he had conned his cleaning lady into a pretense she clearly wasn't prepared for.

His fingers raced over the keyboard of his computer,

his mind locked deep in the complicated equations he was formulating. He was so close to perfecting his compact mini-laser, all he needed was time, *uninterrupted* time.

Turning to the console behind his desk, he lifted part of the scale model of his invention. He worked on many projects at a time for various conglomerates and institutions all over the world, but he had also incorporated himself. Generally he worked out of a large converted warehouse downtown, but this home office allowed him the privacy he sometimes craved.

The laser component hummed when he activated it. A miracle, and the miracle lay in the palm of his hand. Finally, after months and months of work, everything had begun to gel. Just as he let out a rare smile in response to the thrill of that, the phone rang, startling him from his intense concentration.

Blowing out a breath of frustration, he grabbed the phone.

"Darling, you haven't returned a single one of my calls," said his mother before he had a chance to open his mouth.

Thirty-two years old and that tone could still plant a headache between his eyes as fast as lightning. "I know. I—"

"How are you? I hope you're good, you work too hard. Listen darling, I'm in town for the night only. I'm at the Towers with Aunt Bessie and Aunt Lola."

Oh, God, all three of them at once. They were just women; petite, innocuous, elderly. But together, this team of New York, Italian, Catholic-raised siblings had guilt-laying and conformity-forcing down to a science. Colin was convinced that together they could have conquered Rome in a day.

And now they were in town. He rubbed his temples, knowing they cared about him beyond reason, which made it all the more difficult to hurt them in any way. "I thought you were going to be traveling all summer."

"We are, we're just back to check on things."

Namely, *him*.

Since his mother had been the only sister to have a child, the three of them felt they co-owned him. Growing up, Colin had been raised by committee. His father had bowed out under pressure; after all, he was only one man. As a result, Colin had been fiercely watched over, fiercely disciplined and fiercely loved.

He was *still* fiercely loved, he had no doubt.

He just wished they would do it from a greater distance. Jupiter, maybe.

"I wanted to remind you," his mother said. "Muffy is expecting you tonight." She paused, then delivered the coup de grâce. "I've confirmed that you will attend."

"Now wait a minute...."

"We want to see you, darling. How long has it been?"

Only two months, he thought desperately. Had she and his aunts only been on their annual shopping trek in Europe for eight short weeks? He struggled for patience, in short supply on the best of days and this wasn't one of them. "We've spoken every week," he reminded her firmly but gently, not pointing out that even from a distance of thousands and thousands of miles, she still tried to run his life. "And I'm not going to the auction."

"*Charity* auction," she corrected him. "It's expected, Colin. It's why we came back into town. Everyone will be there."

Gritting his teeth to bite back his comment, he

opened the delicate machinery in front of him and adjusted the micro-module with one of his tiny precision tools. "I can't. I have a—"

"Oh, Colin, I do so love you."

His heart softened. "I'm still not going."

"Please? Do this for me. Honey, I don't want to be a hundred years old before you make me a grandmother. I—"

"Stop!" He managed to interrupt and let out a short laugh. "Stop with the old. You and your sisters are the youngest old biddies I know."

"Oh, you." But his mother laughed, too. "This is the second time you've disappointed Muffy. Take a break from building those robot thingies and come out with us tonight." Her voice gentled. "Have a social life, darling. You need to get married again and do it right this time. Please? For me."

He might have laughed, if she were kidding. But she never kidded when it came to this—seeing her only child taken care of in what she saw as matters of the heart.

"Please don't hurt my feelings on this," she said in that quietly devastated voice all mothers have perfected.

Guilt. *Dammit.* "You made the plans without consulting me."

"Because you won't make plans for yourself! Your divorce has been final for five years, Colin. *Five* years. Move on. Please, darling. For me. Move on."

The pain that slashed through him had nothing to do with his ex-wife. Lord, he needed a major pain killer. A bottle of them. Instead, he lifted another part of his advanced scale and ran a knowing finger over the trouble spot—the laser shaft. Complex plans for repair tumbled in his head.

"I'm simply trying to better your life."

He could think of several ways to do that, starting with leaving him alone. Especially since with or without this project he was currently obsessing over, he would never again "better his life" with another female. "Save yourself the trouble, Mother."

"But I want to die in peace."

He rolled his eyes. Great. Now the death speech, when she was healthier than anyone he knew and likely to outlive him by thirty years.

"Just one night," she urged. "That's all I'm asking. Maybe she's the one..."

"No." He stretched his long, cramped legs over the top of his cluttered desk. No one was the one. No one ever would be again. "I've been trying to tell you, I have a good reason for not wanting to date."

"Oh, no," she whispered, horrified. "I knew it! I knew it wasn't safe to let you play with dolls when you were younger!"

"Mother..."

She groaned theatrically. "Oh, no. *Oh, no!* How am I supposed to get grandkids now?"

He wisely contained his laughter. "No, Mother, that's not it. I'm...engaged."

The silence was deafening.

"Mother?"

"To whom?" she asked weakly.

"Her name is Lani Mills."

"What does she do?"

"She runs her own cleaning business."

"Oh." She thought this over. "Does she love you?"

Colin wasn't sure he knew the meaning of the word.

Still, he remembered how wide- and wild-eyed his little cleaning lady had got when he'd removed his shirt. He hadn't thought he could be sensual standing in his own kitchen doused in cleaning fluid, but the way she'd looked at him had certainly put a spin on things. "She's...crazy about me," he said.

"Colin, are you sure? Really, really sure? I mean if she doesn't totally love you, then—"

"I thought you wanted me married," he teased.

"Well now I have a fiancée, so no more dates! In fact, no more calls about dates. No more making *other* people call me about dates. Okay? Tell everyone."

"She's the one for you? You're sure? How do you know?"

Lani was quirky. Sweet and kind and exceptionally patient. After knowing her for one year, Colin knew she was a positive ray of sunshine that he usually tried to avoid at all costs, because to see someone so happy...it hurt in a way he didn't quite understand.

They were polar opposites and therefore, no, she was most definitely not the *one* for him. But he had to do this, had to be left alone to finish the project. His work was everything, it meant the difference between life and death to others.

It also meant a lie to someone he cared about, his mother. "I'm sure," he said quietly.

"But..."

She wasn't going to let this go and he knew this was because she blamed herself for his own last failure. He couldn't let her do that again. "I'm sure because—" he glanced out his window and saw Lani's small car parked there "—we're staying together," he improvised.

"You mean you're living together?"

"Yes," he said, sealing the lie with yet another, hating how he felt about the deception. "I have to go."

"Wait! I want to meet her. Your aunts will want to meet her, and, oh, damn, we've got a flight out in the morning. No problem," she said, quickly reversing herself. "We'll cancel. Your father can wait. We have to come stay with you, of course, for at least two weeks, that's how long we'll need to get to know Lani, and— Colin, *don't you dare hang up on me.*"

Two weeks, good Lord. "Gotta run, Mother. I'll let you know when Lani and I set a date."

"Colin! You hang up on me and I'll come right now, I swear."

The threat wasn't an idle one, he knew she'd do it. "Mother...Lani and I need time alone, to..." To what? How was this backfiring when he had it all planned out? "We need to get to know each other," he said quickly.

"Fine. I'll give you two days, I really can't just stand your father up, he'll pout. But I'll be back after New York." Excitement made her voice shrill. "I'm so thrilled—we have a wedding to plan! Can you imagine the fun? See you in a few days!"

Colin stared at the phone when it clicked in his ear.

Irene West was coming here. In two days. For two lifelong weeks.

Suddenly it hit him. His fictional fiancée had just become—he had to swallow hard to even complete the thought—a *real* fiancée.

The implications were mind-boggling. Lani would have to stay here, pretend to love him.

Sleep in his room.

He couldn't imagine she'd be willing, which brought

him to another thought. Why *had* she agreed to this in the first place?

It wasn't as though they were friends, he hardly knew her.

Oh, God, his mother was coming.

This hadn't just backfired, it had blown up in his face.

COLIN CLICKED AWAY at his keyboard, pretending he didn't have time to face the mess he'd created.

Which he didn't.

"Sorry to interrupt." Lani poked her head in the door. She looked at him with those huge baby-blue eyes, framed by a golden halo of hair precariously perched on her head. "I'd like to get in here to vacuum and dust, if that's okay with you."

Colin found himself staring rudely, but he couldn't seem to help it. It was as if he was seeing her for the first time, though it'd only been an hour since he'd asked for her help. She was lovely, startlingly so. How could he not have noticed before?

She'd also saved his life.

What kind of a person was so willing to help?

He didn't know another soul who would have done so. Uneasy with that thought, and irritated that he'd needed her help in the first place, Colin stood and walked around his desk to meet her. "You're not interrupting. But there are some things we should go over, if you don't mind." *Some* things? It was laughable.

How to ask her if she was willing to put the entire charade on yet another level and attempt to fool the nosiest, most meddling, well-meaning mother that had ever lived?

Lani's eyes widened slightly as he moved toward her

and Colin slowed, realizing she probably considered him a certifiable nutcase.

He would just insist he pay her extra, over and above her cleaning fees, which had always been surprisingly low anyway. He'd yet to encounter a woman not susceptible to his money.

"You...didn't put on another shirt," she announced breathlessly.

He'd forgotten. He still smelled like pine, but then again, so did she. Her gaze was plastered to his chest. Her cheeks reddened, but she didn't stop in her curious perusal of his entire body.

He felt curious, too, though it wasn't as easy for him since she was fully dressed. A strand of her long hair hung in her still-flushed face. The baggy, shapeless, drab-colored clothes she always wore completely hid her figure, but judging from the lack of meat on her arms, she was a bit scrawny.

Definitely not his type, he thought wryly. Thank God. To have been attracted to her would have made this whole situation all the more impossible to deal with. "I have a bit of a problem," he said.

She blinked, stopped staring at his chest, and went still. "You don't need me anymore?"

"Ah...not exactly."

She shot him a smile then, and it was a stunner. At the impact, he lost every thought in his head and then had to reassess the whole not-being-attracted-to-her thing.

"We need to set a date?" she asked.

"Worse." He braced himself. "We need to live together."

"Before the wedding?"

"It won't get that far," he said fervently.

"No...wedding?"

Uh-oh. She sounded shocked...disappointed. "This is just for pretend," he said slowly. "Remember?"

She laughed and quickly turned away, hiding her face. "Of course. It's just that I thought...never mind. Excuse me...I've got...something to do."

"Lani?"

"I'm sorry. I've got to go." She ran out of the office.

3

COLIN STARED at the empty doorway of his office. What had just happened? No way had Lani misunderstood. He'd made it clear that this engagement wasn't real.

Hadn't he?

Running back through the conversations in his mind, he went still. Yes, he'd made it clear it was all for show, but had he let her think there would really be a wedding?

Swearing, Colin went after her, grabbing a shirt on his way, but he was a split second too late. Both Lani and Carmen were gone, speeding down the driveway in her noisy car. Colin grabbed his keys and raced out into the searing heat after them.

Having no idea where Lani lived, he broke several traffic laws trying to keep up with her. And when they crossed the train tracks, bringing them into an undesirable neighborhood, Colin hoped Lani was just dropping off Carmen. She was, but as he again followed Lani, he realized she also lived in this area.

He waited until she'd gone into a rundown fourplex, then followed her. He knocked softly on her front door, which was ajar, but she didn't answer so he let himself in. Her place was stiflingly hot. Colin didn't know how people lived in Southern California without air-conditioning, and he hated that Lani had to.

But once he was inside the apartment, he found it

much lighter and roomier than he had expected. There wasn't much in the way of furniture, but the small living room was clean and appealing.

He found her in the tiny kitchenette and when he said her name softly, she jumped, a hand over her heart.

"You need to lock your door," he admonished. "For safety..."

"I'm safe here." She turned away and tossed a sponge into the sink. For a brief second, before she flipped on the water, her small, calloused hands gripped the counter tight. "Why did you follow me?"

"You left before we were through."

"I didn't see what else we had to discuss."

So hurt. Dammit. "Lani—"

"What a fool I am, huh? I mean I knew it was going to be for pretend, but I thought we were going to actually *do* it, for pretend. How dumb! It was ridiculous to think—" She let out a painful laugh.

God, he hated the helplessness that swam through him. "I'm sorry. I didn't mean to hurt you."

"You're so far out of my league, I should never have—" She broke off and her shoulders sagged. Strands of wild, curly hair hid her expression, but he could picture it well enough. Devastated. Humiliated.

Leaning around her, he turned off the water, his mouth forming explanations and apologies. In the confinement of the tiny kitchen their bodies brushed against each other. His arms surrounded her, whether he intended them to or not. It couldn't be helped. The insides of his biceps grazed the sides of her breasts and, completely without logic, his body hardened.

Silence reigned.

Lani faced him at last, her hands behind her, gripping the counter tight. Now their bodies no longer touched, but a mere inch was the only thing keeping them from an embrace. If she so much as breathed, Colin knew Lani would feel his illogical response to her. The pine scent coming from the bib of her wet, baggy overalls was overpowering, but beneath that, he caught the scent of Lani, sweet and sexy.

"I always prefer to be alone when I'm making a fool out of myself," she said so quietly he had to dip his head close to hear her. "Maybe you could just go away and pretend today never happened?"

"You're not the fool, *I* am," he assured her grimly, tipping her face up so he could torture himself with her hurt eyes. "I *did* ask you to marry me, I just never intended to actually have to do it. It sounded so simple in my head," he said, bewildered. "I have no idea how it got so crazy."

"I see."

No, she didn't. She couldn't. "I told you how I wanted you to pretend to be my fiancée to placate my family and well-meaning acquaintances so they'd leave me alone to work."

"Yes."

It seemed so ridiculous now, and feeling a little embarrassed himself, he offered her a small, tight smile. "I told you also that they have a habit of matchmaking. If they thought I was taken, they'd have to stop. And then I could finish my project."

"Yes, I understand."

"You do?"

She smiled tentatively, which gave him pause. It was one thing to recruit a woman to lie for him, quite another to tease one. He dated only occasionally, and he consistently chose women who were looking for no more, no less than what he was willing to give.

Somehow, he couldn't picture this little waif of a housecleaner being interested in a quickie affair with him. She seemed more like the kind of woman who played for keeps.

And while he wanted everyone off his back, he absolutely did not want to be playing games with someone he could inadvertently hurt. *Had* inadvertently hurt. There could be no attraction between them, none at all.

"So you *do* still need a fictional fiancée?"

"Yes," he said.

She nodded slowly. "But no wedding date."

"God, no."

"I see." A light eyebrow raised. "You wouldn't want to get stuck with the hassles of a *real* relationship."

Not ever again, he thought with a shudder. "It's not necessary in this case. But..." he sighed, "I just found out my mother is coming in two days to meet my fiancée. She'll want to stay at my house and get to know the woman."

"Oh. So now you need a *live-in* fictional fiancée."

"Yeah."

"Well." Lani flashed him a hundred-watt smile, which quite frankly dazzled him blind and left him decidedly unsettled.

This was a business arrangement, he reminded himself. No reason for her smile to alter his pulse. Hormones had no place here.

"I understand now," she said.

"Will you do it?"

She looked at him, surprised, then reached out and

squeezed his hands. "You can wipe that frown off your face, Colin. I don't go back on my word."

The easy forgiveness startled him. So did the physical contact. Not only because she was surprisingly warm, but because he wasn't used to being touched for absolutely no reason at all.

He came from a family of firm non-touchers.

His father had never touched him, unless of course he had been tearing the hide off Colin for taking apart an appliance or blowing up the garage with his biology experiments. His mother wasn't a toucher, either, she had been too busy running everyone's life or traveling.

As a result, Colin himself rarely touched anyone, certainly not for no reason at all. Which didn't explain why he'd done exactly that earlier when Lani had first arrived at his house.

Suddenly Lani danced away, frowning and shifting uncomfortably, plucking at her clothes. The air hissed out between her teeth and she looked pained.

"I've really got to get out of this shirt."

Before he could blink, she unhooked the two shoulder straps of her overalls and shoved the bib to her waist. She was still amply covered in that shapeless, huge T-shirt. Colin didn't blink. After all, he knew exactly how that cleaner felt against skin. It hurt like hell.

No problem that she appeared to be stripping down in front of him, in a kitchen so small he couldn't breathe without nearly touching her. He wasn't attracted to her, not in the least.

Besides they were going to be living together. He could handle this.

"Darn it," she murmured, still wiggling and rubbing her chest, bumping into him with every little shimmy. "Darn it all." And with that, she ripped the T-shirt over her head, revealing a tight, cropped tank top. She closed her eyes with a dreamy sigh. "Yeah, that's better. Whew! That stuff burns after a while."

Colin opened his mouth to speak, but nothing came out. Her elbows brushed his chest as she lowered her arms, her thighs bumped into his. Now his jeans were beginning to cut off circulation, belying his self-assurances that he didn't find her attractive.

How could he have known that beneath her awful, huge clothes, his cleaning lady/fictional fiancée had been hiding a body to die for?

"I think I burned my skin in a couple of spots." With her head bent, her silky hair slid over his arm as she stared down at herself.

Colin stared, too. She was slender yet wildly curved, and he wished she would pull her overalls back up.

She drew a deep breath and opened her eyes, smiling at him in relief. "You didn't tell me how much better that felt!"

Speech was impossible. Her overalls had dropped to just below her waist, so he had a front-row view of her smooth, very flat stomach, her slim but curved hips, the outline of her firm, high, unencumbered breasts.

Good Lord. No doubt in his mind, he *was* attracted to his cleaning lady.

To his fiancée.

She flashed that brain-cell-destroying smile again. "You okay?"

He wasn't sure. He couldn't think. He remembered a bawdy joke he'd been told, about how men had both a brain and a penis, but only enough blood to operate one at a time. He believed it now. "Uh-huh. I'm fine."

"So we're going to live together to prove we're a loving couple."

A loving couple. Damn, but that was terrifying. Unable to help himself, he looked at her again, and felt his body's surging response. She was one of the sexiest women he'd ever seen. And he was going to live with her. "We have to fool my mother, never an easy thing," he said a bit hoarsely. He cleared his throat. "She has eyes in the back of her head, and..." at her questioning look, he sighed again, loudly, "she thinks we've been living together already."

Her gaze widened briefly, then ran over his body once before she swallowed hard. "Well," she said.

"Yeah. *Well*."

They stared at each other, awkwardly. Colin couldn't get past her easy forgiveness, her willingness to want to help him. Or her huge, expressive eyes.

"It's certainly not going to be a hardship to live at your house instead of here," she said finally. "You have air-conditioning."

That wasn't the hardship he was worried about. This was pretend, this whole crazy scene, and it would be over as soon as he could finish his project. Lani would leave, and in spite of the fact that he was discovering an attraction, he wouldn't hurt her by letting her think there was more involved here.

"My work won't change," she said, almost as a question, touchingly uncertain.

"No, I don't want to disrupt your work. Lani...I have to know... Why are you doing this?"

She tilted her head, a small smile about her lips. "Your project," she said simply. "It's unselfish and hopeful and full of promise. I want you to finish it. If I can help, then it makes me feel useful and a part of it."

"Is that the only reason?"

A flicker of unease crossed her face, then disappeared. "Of course."

He didn't know what to make of her, she wasn't like any woman he'd ever met. And they were going to live together. Her razor in his shower. Her toothbrush on his sink. Her panties in with his whites. His head spun at that last thought.

He wondered if those panties were as revealing as the teeny, tiny, little top she wore now. And oh boy, sometime in the past minute or so, she'd gotten cold. Her nipples, rosy and mouthwateringly perfect, were pushing at the thin cotton, straining for freedom.

"So we're on?" she asked innocently.

He was a dead man, but they were on. "Yes."

She laughed, dove at him and flung her arms around his neck.

"What the—"

She squeezed him close, pressing against him all those warm curves in a spine-breaking hug. Before he could lift his arms to push her away—and he most definitely would have pushed her away no matter what his hormones were screaming—she stepped back.

"I have work to do," she said with a laugh. "I can't be hugging you all day long."

He had work, too. Didn't he? He opened his mouth to say so, but Lani shimmied past him to hold open the door, her body and smile rendering him deaf, blind and dumb.

How in the world had he fooled himself into thinking this was a good idea?

IT WAS A BALMY, sticky evening, the kind only midsummer could bring.

Colin wolfed down a quick bowl of soup for dinner,

preoccupied with some critical adjustments he needed
to make on his project. Forgotten soup bowl at his elbow, he sat at his kitchen table, furiously scribbling
notes. He'd used up nearly the entire tablet when he
heard the car.

It was hard to miss as it backfired, sounding like the
fourth of July.

Then Lani was at his back door with a duffel bag and
a smile that lit up the hot Southern California night.

Something within him warmed to match it.

He opened the door and she moved in, invading his
space with her cheerfulness, her bright eyes, that sexy
scent of hers.

At least she wasn't wet anymore, or cold, thank God.

But then again, it was hard to tell in the shapeless
summer dress she wore. She'd layered it over a loose
T-shirt and high-top tennis shoes, and if he hadn't seen
her incredible body earlier, he could never have imagined it.

Before he could move away, she gave him a quick
hug, which so startled him he froze.

At his reaction, she froze, too, and pulled back.
"So..." She bit her lip, looking a little unsure of herself.
"You did want me to come back tonight, right?"

His mother wasn't coming for two days. But Lani
was looking at him with those unbelievable eyes and he
didn't know what to say. And was she always going to
touch him for no reason?

If so, it was going to be a hell of a long engagement.

He had originally approached this whole fictional fiancée situation as he would anything—management by
objectives. It wasn't something he looked forward to,
but it had to be done. And how hard could it be? They'd
already known each other a full year.

Except, she was unpredictable. She was also too... *happy*, a definite personality disorder in his book.

She tugged at his hand to get his attention, and just that small connection had a current of awareness shooting through him.

Oh, yeah, he was in big trouble in the hormone department.

"I thought we should practice," she said. "You know...being a loving couple?"

Never mind that he'd thought so, too, before; it was no longer a good idea.

When he didn't say anything, she ran her teeth over her full bottom lip. "I don't know about you," she said, "but it's not something that comes naturally to me." She blushed. "I mean—"

"I know what you mean." He had to let out a dry laugh. "It doesn't exactly come easy for me, either." If she only knew he'd been there, done that and bought the T-shirt. But if he was ever stupid enough to marry again, and if his wife had the body of his pretend fiancée, he thought he just might attempt to learn how to be loving.

"I'm not that great an actress," she admitted. "I think I'll need a couple of days."

A couple of days would kill him. He had no idea if he could keep his hands to himself that long. "I don't think—"

"Oh, but I do." She smiled angelically. "We have to be convincing, Colin."

"Yes." His mother could detect trouble five hundred miles away.

"We should also put an announcement in the paper."

Wait. This was becoming far too...real. "Why?"

She looked at him with that kind smile, the one she

seemed to reserve for when she was intent on getting her way. "You want people to stop bothering you. There's no way faster to do that than to put the engagement in print."

"But..." But what? She was right, she was *always* right, he was beginning to suspect. And why was she so sweetly disagreeing with him on everything? *Dammit.* "Okay. Fine. An ad is fine."

Lani dropped her gaze, looked around at the kitchen she'd seen a thousand times. Almost nervously, she glanced out into the hall and up the stairs.

She was wondering about the sleeping arrangements.

"Come on," he said with another heartfelt sigh. "I'll show you where the spare bedrooms are. You can pick one."

She looked relieved and disappointed at the same time.

He could understand.

LANI PICKED the bedroom at the far end of the hallway from Colin's. Not because she found him offensive, but because she didn't trust herself.

Her natural, easy affection seemed to terrify him. He'd nearly leaped out of his skin when she'd hugged him hello. Just a simple hug, an affectionate hug, but he'd hated it.

He'd made sure not to come within five feet of her since then. And when they'd climbed the stairs, he'd shown her the bedrooms as far from his as he could get.

She didn't know what she had expected—that he would have suggested his own bed? That wasn't his style.

Still, she couldn't help but wish, as she followed his

tall, lean, oh-so-watchable frame, that in this one aspect, their engagement was real.

He dropped her duffel bag on the bed that would be hers. "Let me know if you need anything."

Did he mean it? She doubted it. He had that expression on his face, the one that assured her he'd rather be at the dentist having a tooth extracted. Without drugs.

Well he wasn't alone in that. She had so many reservations about this farce they were undertaking! She could tell herself she'd agreed to help because she believed in his project—and she did. But she knew the truth, that it was far more than that. And she was scared.

Colin West was driven and focused, and if she believed the rumors, he was cold and aloof as well.

But it wasn't true, she knew this with all her heart. No one with eyes so deep and heated could be cold. All year she'd been drawn to him on some deep, primal level and while she might not understand it, she couldn't ignore it. Any of a million things could have happened to make Colin the very private man he was, and she understood that better than most, because for all her bubbliness, she herself was incredibly private.

What she didn't get was the sudden need she had to please him, to be with him. To make him happy.

"I'll be fine," she said quietly, and decided to face the music with a brave smile. "So what are we going to do to get to know each other?"

Given the way his eyes flared, she'd gotten his attention. In response, her insides heated and they both stared at each other like idiots.

It drew a laugh out of her, because they were both so obviously thinking about only one thing. She reached out and stroked his arm. "This is silly, you know. We're adults."

He stared down at her hand on him. "Yeah, adults," he agreed, those intense eyes of his heavy and shuttered.

Her inner warmth spread, pooling in areas she hadn't felt heat in for some time. "Maybe we'd better sleep on it tonight," she suggested. "We'll think of something. Like Twenty Questions, or another game."

He blinked and looked as if he'd rather face a firing squad, which made her laugh. "This was *your* idea, you know," she teased.

His mouth quirked, though he didn't actually smile. "I'm trying to remember that."

From outside came a distant clap of thunder. Lani jerked, thrown by the harsh sound. "What's that?"

"A summer storm is moving in." He glanced out the window. "We'll get some rain I hope. And some relief from the heat."

Lani had an aversion to storms, one that went bone-deep. Goose bumps rose on her skin as the sky lit yet again. A twenty-year-old fear goaded her. In the guise of saying good-night, she wrapped her arms around Colin and hoped he'd hold her back.

He didn't.

"'Night," she whispered, gripping him tightly as a crack of thunder hit.

Letting go of him was difficult, for he'd felt warm and strong and wonderful, but she could feel how rigidly he held himself. Trying not to take it personally, she backed off and plopped down on her bed, just managing not to flinch when lightning flashed again. When the following thunder boomed and the windows rattled, she nearly jumped out of her skin.

She really hated storms.

Colin hadn't breathed, not once since she'd touched him.

She swallowed her silly fear. "Colin?"

"'Night," he muttered finally. And then he was gone.

4

THE STORM came and raged, and Lani tried to be strong.

She dreamed, long haunting visions of things best forgotten. Her mother, warm and loving, smiling as she placed Lani's hand on her rounded belly, letting her daughter feel the little sibling just waiting for his or her time. Her father, laughing with delight as he twirled her around and around on their lawn.

In her sleep, Lani sighed and smiled.

And then came the images of their sightless faces after the car accident that had killed them both, twenty years before in a wild, unexpected summer storm.

Thunder rattled the windows. Lightning bolted. Lani lurched up, a scream on her lips, but it died, replaced by a gasp of shock at the shadow that sank to her bed.

"What is it?" came a deep voice.

Colin. He'd come. He was rumpled from sleep, hair tousled, eyes heavy. Chest bare.

Offering comfort.

And she needed it just then, oh, how she needed it. Before she could speak into the dark, chilled room, he lifted a hand and touched her face gently.

It came away wet from her tears.

"Lani?" he murmured, bracketing her hips with his strong, corded arms as he leaned over her, his face close to hers as he tried to see her expression. "You okay?"

In answer, she slipped her arms around that warm,

hard body and tugged, needing him close, swallowing her last lingering sob as he resisted.

Staring down into her eyes, he shook his head slowly. "You were dreaming."

Thunder resounded again and unable to control her whimper, Lani squeezed her eyes shut and tried to disappear.

With a low, wordless sound of concern, Colin gave in and his wonderful arms gathered her close. "Just a storm," he said quietly, stroking her hair as she curled into the warmth of his embrace. His rough jaw scraped lightly over her cheek. "It can't hurt you. You're safe here."

She knew that, but her fear was irrational, as was her need for him.

The rain hit the roof with a drumming, driving force. Wind howled and shook the windows. The temperature had dropped, cooling the air. More thunder came, and lightning, too, but Lani, locked in the security of Colin's arms, sighed. His mere presence soothed, drove back any lingering part of the nightmare.

It was all in the past, gone, and it could no longer hurt her. Colin was here in the present, bending over her, whispering words meant to ease and soothe, and they did. But his husky, still sleepy voice also aroused and, despite the storm beating against her windows, Lani reacted to that. She needed him and yearned to feel needed in return. Without conscious effort, her hips rocked to his.

Colin went utterly still.

She should be mortified, at least sorry, but she wasn't. His heat seeped into her chilled body. He was dressed only in soft, flannel pajama bottoms, slung low on his hips. Their bodies were connected from chest to legs and it was such an erotically shattering position that Lani did it again, that little uncontrollable movement with her hips.

"Lani."

Just that, just her name, in a gruff, warning tone that wavered slightly with his own, very clear, need.

Her heart thundering, she pulled him closer, feeling that if he didn't kiss her, if he didn't put his hands on her and make love to her right then, she would die. "I want you, Colin," she whispered, lifting her face to his.

His arms tightened around her.

"Please want me back."

In the dark, he let out a groaning laugh as they both felt the evidence of his own wanting. "This isn't how to assuage a bad dream," he said.

"We're engaged."

"For pretend."

"It feels real enough right now, doesn't it?" She tucked her face into his warm, wonderful smelling neck and licked his skin.

He shuddered and groaned, and again his arms convulsed around her. "I've never felt anything more real," he admitted.

A gust of wind battered the windows on the outside, while inside the tension came from the heat of their bodies. She winced at a flash of lightning.

"Lani—"

He was going to stop her, tell her why this wasn't a good idea and she didn't want him to. "We could start now," she suggested quickly. "You know, getting to know each other."

"What happened to the game of Twenty Questions you suggested earlier?"

"Okay—if you want a question, how's this?" She

nuzzled his chest, seeking, then finding a small, hard nipple, which she kissed. "Do you like that?"

"Lani—"

Warm flesh, inflexible muscle—he felt so good, so indelibly male. His heart thundered beneath her cheek. Her insides clenched at the delightful contrasts of him and she lifted her hand, cupping his rough jaw, drawing a finger over his wide, sexy mouth. Her other hand touched his hip to urge him closer still.

"Lani, this can't be real between us, you know that."

"I don't know any such thing."

"Look, you're no longer frightened," he said a bit desperately. "I should—"

Her fingers slid over his lips softly, halting his words. "You make me feel safe. Comfortable."

He closed his eyes and she brushed her lips lightly, so lightly, over his. "Please," she whispered. "Don't go." She felt at home in a way she hadn't felt in so long. Too long. She held no illusions about the man poised for flight above her. He was caught, locked in a battle between regret and arousal, but to her, it felt right. She had to convince him. "Colin."

"I shouldn't have come in here," he said finally. "You're scared and vulnerable."

"Why *did* you come?"

His forehead furrowed as he searched her gaze. "You needed—"

"*You*. I needed you."

"You were having a dream, anyone would have done—"

"Not anyone. *You*."

"I can't believe that."

This breathless, weightless, needy sensation was utterly new for her, but Colin wasn't in a place to believe that. She'd have to show him. Her nipples were hard, with excitement not cold, and she arched up until her chest just barely touched his.

Colin sucked in a harsh breath. In the pale light, his eyes darkened. "Lani."

"Touch me."

She could hear his ragged breath, could feel his struggle for control. Rain slapped against the windows as he lifted his head and looked deep into her eyes. His face held a mixture of need and confusion. "It wasn't supposed to be like this," he murmured. "It was supposed to be uncomplicated. Easy."

"I know," she murmured, sinking her fingers into his thick, silky hair. "I know."

"It's going to make it harder."

"Well, I *hope* so," she whispered.

His lips curved then, and he set his forehead to hers. "I'm the one complicating this, aren't I?"

"Yep." To prove it, she wriggled and squirmed until she was solidly beneath him. Slowly she drew up her legs and wrapped them around his hips.

At the unmistakable invitation, he groaned and dipped his head, touching his mouth to hers.

"Finally," she whispered on a soft breath, which he promptly claimed as his own.

Finally was right, was all Colin could think. He'd wanted a taste of her since she'd appeared at his door earlier this evening, though he would have continued to deny himself.

There would be complications, he knew, but as he kissed the corners of her soft, giving mouth, then her lips, he knew whatever would happen could wait until this storm that raged both inside and out passed.

It wasn't going to pass quickly or quietly, that was

certain, not with all the heat being generated between them. The soft covers plumped around them, cozy, enticing. The kiss deepened, hot and wet and unbearably arousing. Beneath him, Lani's sweet body writhed, and the heat devoured him.

Before Lani, he hadn't given enough thought or care to kissing, it had always seemed so intimate, and he'd shied away from anything remotely related to that.

He was beginning to see how wrong he'd been.

The only sounds in the room were the rustling bedcovers, the rain against the window. And then deepening silence as he slowly pulled back to gaze, shocked, into Lani's face.

The room went bright as day with a bolt of lightning, followed by a boom that rattled the entire house.

Lani jerked.

"It's okay. It's getting farther and farther away."

"I know." But she swallowed hard. "I'm not afraid anymore."

Those huge eyes of hers were full of secrets that he didn't know. He didn't want to know, or so he told himself.

She took his hand in hers and placed it over her racing heart. His long fingers skimmed over warm, giving flesh and curves, and he groaned. He liked the helplessly aroused sounds escaping her throat, the way she'd plastered her delectable body to his. He liked—

He liked *her*.

And no amount of distancing himself was going to change that.

"Colin—" She tried to wrap him closer.

He was losing himself in her, unable to remember why this shouldn't happen.

"Now," she whispered in a voice that told him exactly how much she needed him.

In response, he found himself raining open-mouthed kisses down her slim neck, over her collarbone, nudging her plain white T-shirt up as he went until he got to...ah, a ripe, warm curve, just begging for his touch.

She gasped. "More. Hurry."

"I'm exploring," he muttered around her heated, sweet flesh. "Don't rush me."

Her arms slipped from around his neck, down the taut muscles of his back. Unable to keep still, he undulated his hips, thrusting against the soft core of her, caught up in a rhythm as old as time.

And suddenly, he wanted to hurry every bit as much as she did.

Lani gave him everything, her lips, her tongue, her passion. He'd expected an awkwardness, that first-time ineptitude. Bumping noses, grinding teeth, but with Lani, there was none of that, nothing except for a horrifying feeling that this was exactly as it was supposed to be.

He'd had women before, even women he knew less well than he knew Lani, but never had he felt as though he'd been given so much. It made him want to give in return, as her hunger fueled and fed his own. Both tenderness and savagery tore through him, equally mixed. He should have known it would be this way with her.

He kissed her again. His hands danced over her body. Her legs were bare. Beneath his fingers, her body quivered.

"Colin..."

His name had never sounded so sexy before. Her eyes drifted closed, but they flew open again, dazed and unseeing, when his hands cupped her breasts.

"Colin!"

He thought maybe he could get used to the way she cried out his name, all throaty and full of yearning. In fact, he wanted to hear it again, so he held back, just palming her warm curves.

Her fingers clenched and unclenched on his chest, her head tossed on the pillow and, when his thumbs rasped over her tight, puckered nipples, she again gasped his name.

He smiled in satisfaction. "Is that what you wanted, Lani?"

She made some unintelligible sound that turned him on even more. This was like a project, he thought with hazy delight, only better, much better. He wanted to take her slowly apart and watch her explode, then help put her back together again.

"Lani?" He pulled her T-shirt all the way off, exposing her to his gaze. She was perfect, beyond perfect. He bent over her, his mouth hovering as he let his fingers tease. "Does this feel good?"

She squirmed beneath the torment. "Yes!" she gasped, reaching for him. "More. Please, more."

"Like this?" He drew a taut, aching peak into his mouth, laving the very tip with his tongue, switching sides in tune to Lani's soft, seductive moan. "And this?" he wondered. "Are you sure—" his tongue swirled over her, then he sucked strongly "—this is what you wanted?"

Her hips were rocking against his and he knew she was nearly mindless. He didn't know what had come over him to tease her like this, he himself was dying, hot, and so unbelievably hard. It had been so long for him, and he'd thought all he wanted was to plunge into her and seek the oblivion that sex always provided. But he realized he wanted more. He wanted her to take that wild journey with him.

"Colin..."

His name again, in that breathless, sexy, hoarse, needy whisper. "I'm right here," he promised.

She reached up to pull him to her.

"No, no stay like that," he whispered. He didn't think he could take her touch, not yet, so he held her hands above her head for a moment until he knew she would keep them there. "Let me...Lani, let me..."

And he slid down, down her body, delivering hot kisses over every inch he passed until he was kneeling between her legs, gazing down at her gorgeous, straining body. In the pale glow of the night, her skin was creamy and lustrous. "You're...stunning," he whispered thickly, unbelievably close to the edge and she hadn't even touched him. He was going to lose it, just staring at her.

He jerked when her fingers brushed against the taut skin low on his belly, and he gripped her hand in his. "No," he whispered, knowing if she touched him again, it would be over in one second, maybe two. "Don't, Lani." He held her immobile, staring deep into her hungry eyes. "Don't move."

5

LANI LAY STILL with an effort, aware of how exposed she was, of the way Colin was looking at her while she lay spread and vulnerable. It was nothing less than thrilling—with his nostrils flaring, his chest rising and falling rapidly, all that power and passion within him barely leashed.

Heat suffused her, and it wasn't embarrassment, but need, sharp and unrelenting need.

His hands cupped her face, surprisingly gentle. "You're beautiful, Lani."

She'd never been told that before, much less even thought it, but Colin's soft, genuine voice made her believe it.

His fingers trailed slowly, ever so slowly, down her throat, around her breasts, lingering, then over her belly. He met her gaze as he drew her panties down past her thighs, her calves, then finally off, tossing them over his shoulder as he rose up, towering over her. He touched his mouth to her neck, sucking and nibbling. Then he kissed her, long and hard, drawing the need out, intensifying it.

"Colin...touch me."

He merely smiled against her skin and dragged his mouth down to a nipple, where he spent another long moment.

She was going to die. "More!"

Keeping his mouth to her breast, he trailed a hand up her trembling, restless legs. "Where?"

He wanted her to tell him? In words? She didn't know if she could. Yes, somehow she'd lost every ounce of inhibition she'd ever had, but to actually tell him what pleased her....

"Here?" he wondered, stroking behind her knee.

Her hips thrust upward impatiently and he let his fingers trace higher and higher, circling ever so close, but not quite close enough.

She nearly screamed. Her body arched, her eyes closed tightly and she reached for him, stroking him through his pants once, twice before he managed to stop her. "Not yet."

It was his turn to gasp when she ignored him and stroked again. "I'm ready!" she whispered impatiently. "I am!"

"Hmm. Maybe after this...if you're good." He scooped her hips in his hands and brought her to his mouth, where he introduced her to yet another sort of delicious torture.

His talented, greedy tongue dipped, slid, probed and languidly lapped, coaxing an earth-shattering climax out of her. When she floated back down to earth, the rain had lightened.

No more thunder or lightning.

Her fear of it was long gone.

And she was cuddled in Colin's arms, against his rock-solid chest. His face was buried in her hair.

She realized *he* was the one trembling, his big body taut as a bow. "You didn't—I mean, don't you want—" The words tumbled awkwardly to a stop. "Colin?"

He kissed her, pulling away when she would have

deepened the connection, backing from her when she tried to tug him over her.

"We can't." He groaned when she wrapped her fingers around the huge, hot, throbbing part of him that assured her that he still wanted her, very much.

She didn't understand. "You changed your mind?"

"Not likely." He rose, regret lining his face. "I don't have any protection."

"*Oh.*"

"Yeah, *oh.*" Tension outlined his every muscle. "I think we're better off in our separate bedrooms."

Her body was still on fire. She needed him inside her. "How could you not have...*you* know?"

At her disbelief, he let out a little laugh, but it held no mirth. "I'm not really in the habit of needing any," he admitted.

"You...*really?*"

"You sound so amazed." He lifted a shoulder. "It's been a long time for me, Lani."

She had no idea why, but the thought was endearing and her heart warmed toward him even more. She watched as he untangled his limbs from hers. Without any sign of self-consciousness, he adjusted his pants up and over the biggest erection she'd ever imagined, and grimacing a little, he walked to the door.

She called his name softly.

He stilled, the long, sleek lines of his back glimmering in the dark. After a second, he glanced over his shoulder at her. His eyes were still smoldering, ensuring her it would be a long, sleepless night for him, too.

She smiled, feeling almost shy, which was ridiculous after what they'd just shared. "It's been a long time for me, too," she whispered.

He smiled and it stopped her heart.

Then he was gone.

IT MIGHT NEVER have happened—the nightmare, Colin's magic touch, any of it, except that her body tingled knowingly at just the sight of him.

Lani pressed her hands to the butterflies dancing in her belly and, pretending she really belonged there, she let the swinging kitchen doors shut behind her as she walked in.

Colin sat at the table, expression intense, head bent over a cup of steaming coffee and a newspaper. His dark hair was wet and pushed off his forehead as if he had no time for such things as picking up a comb. The black shirt he wore looked soft and incredibly masculine, especially given that he hadn't yet finished buttoning it up. His skin was smooth and sleek and rippled with strength.

Her fingers itched to touch.

His long legs were stretched out in front of him, covered in slate-gray trousers, tailor-made to show off every exceptional inch of him. His feet were bare.

"Colin." The name floated off her lips in a tone of longing before she could stop herself, and he lifted his gaze, holding her hostage with nothing more than his eyes. He nodded at her, managing to hold all his thoughts safe and sound, giving nothing of himself away, and again, Lani had to remind herself that last night had *not* been a dream, but a hot, welcome reality.

He *had* touched her. He *had* shown her an unrestrained passionate side of him that until now she'd only fantasized about.

There was no further sound, nothing except for the little squeak Lani could have sworn her heart made at the cool, distancing look in his eyes.

Pushing his coffee away, he rose. He towered over her, all elegant, male grace as he moved to the door, clearly unwilling to spend even a moment with her.

He was probably afraid she'd beg him to touch her again, she thought, blushing, because she held no illusions, she *had* begged him last night. Still, she pushed her chin in the air, not having to force the spurt of fierce pride. "You forgot to take your cup to the sink."

He stopped, his hand on the door, and looked at her, clearly surprised. "What?"

Ah, he *could* speak in the morning. Granted it was a rough and gruff sort of voice, assuring her he'd not been long out of bed, which only increased the fluttering low in her stomach because he sounded so irrationally sexy. "I'm not your maid today," she reminded him. "Only once a week, remember?"

His eyes darkened and she knew he was remembering last night, too. She certainly hadn't been the maid then, had she?

"You're right. Excuse me," he said and went back to the table. He grabbed his cup and took it to the sink, though he didn't rinse it or put it in the dishwasher, just set it in the sink. When he turned and caught her eye, he lifted a brow as if in a dare.

She said nothing. She knew he rarely took care of his dishes in the morning because whenever she came to clean, there was always a stack in the sink. If he thought he was going to get a nagging pretend fiancée, he was in for a surprise.

Instead she called out cheerfully as she opened the door. "Have a good day!"

He hesitated, body stone still, and she couldn't resist adding, "Nice talking to you, Colin. You're so sweet and chipper in the morning."

He turned and faced her. "I'm never sweet and chipper."

"I hadn't noticed." She bit her lip. "We're not going to talk about it, are we?"

His eyes went wary. "Do we have to?"

"It might help."

"I doubt it."

"We're supposed to be getting to know each other. Glaring at me over your morning coffee as if you can't remember why I'm here isn't going to solve your problem."

He drew in a deep, ragged breath and let it out slowly. He ran his fingers through his drying hair. The scent of him drifted to her, woodsy soap and a hint of clean, healthy male. "I remember why you're here," he said.

How could he forget, Colin wondered, when he was still feeling her skin beneath his fingertips, still tasting her on his lips?

After he'd left her, he hadn't slept a wink. It had been impossible with his body aching and needy, his mind unable to forget the image of Lani in sheer bliss.

"Colin."

He nearly leaped out of his skin when she came close and set her hand on his. The top of her head barely met his chin. Her eyes were compassionate and full of things that made it hard to look at her, but he couldn't tear his gaze away.

"Don't, Lani. Don't say it. This is my doing, I know it."

She shook her head, her eyes warm and soft. And dammit, she continued to touch him in that comforting yet madly arousing way. It wasn't difficult to imagine how it would be between them if he said the hell with his decision not to mislead her or hurt her, if he pulled her body to his and slowly stripped off those ridiculously ugly overalls until she wore nothing but a hot, needy look on her face and his name on her lips.

"It'll work out," she assured him with a little pat. "You'll see." Her fingers ran up his arm and then to his chest.

He captured her wandering hand, but not before the sizzling connection aroused him. He'd slept that way, and after touching her, after watching her come in his arms, he just might sleep in that uncomfortable state for the rest of his life.

Her sweet, beguiling smile never wavered. "I'll put the ad in the paper announcing our engagement today."

How the hell had he done this to himself? he wondered, looking down into her eager-to-please eyes. "Lani, I don't think—"

"Now, I have to get to work, but don't worry so much," she soothed, gently pushing him out of the kitchen, dismissing him with an ease that was startling. "Being so stressed will give you wrinkles."

Wrinkles. He was about to blow the zipper off his pants and she was worried about wrinkles.

"If you'd like, after work I'll cook dinner. We should sit around and talk."

"Talk."

"Yes." She seemed amused. "We have to get to know each other, remember? Your mother is coming tomorrow. And I'm not trying to criticize you here, but you really don't have the look of a man madly in love. We'll have to work on that."

He closed his eyes.

"It's fine," she insisted, again touching him, slipping

her hands around his waist. "Everything is going to be fine."

He remembered those hands, remembered how they'd encircled him, driven him to the very edge with those slow, sure, mind-blowing strokes—

His own groan vented the air.

"Colin—" She hesitated and he opened his eyes, looking over his shoulder to meet her unsure gaze. "Thanks for being there for me last night. You know, after my nightmare."

He'd worried about that, too. What haunted her? He hadn't wanted to spend any more time than absolutely necessary thinking about her, but nothing had gone as planned so far—he shouldn't have been surprised by the depth of his concern. "Do you have them often?"

"Dreams? Yeah. My favorite is the one where I get to go to Hawaii and snorkel."

"The nightmares, Lani."

She bowed her head, studied her fingernails which were short and unpainted. "Not too much anymore."

"What are they from?"

Her head tipped up at that, and amusement crossed her face. "What's this? Genuine curiosity? Hmm, maybe you're going to be better at this than I thought." Her smile faded. "Are we going to share a bed when your family comes?"

She looked suddenly unsure, vulnerable. He wouldn't hurt or lead this woman on, not for anything, not even to save his sorry hide. "That wasn't part of the original deal, was it?"

"No," she whispered.

"I don't want to make you uncomfortable. Ever."

"You won't," she said quickly. "And we really *should* share a bed— I mean bedroom. For your mom's sake."

He cleared his throat around the knot of desire there. "Yeah."

"Are you...um..." A red flush worked its way up her face. "You know, going to the store to get...what you need?"

It took him only a second to realize what his sweet little fiancée wanted to know. "It's not a good idea."

"I see." She backed away from him, her smile wavering. "Well. Have a great day, Colin. See you tonight."

Tonight. God, tonight. How could he continue to resist her? Having a condom would be little protection against the true danger—her worming her way into his heart.

After she was gone, Colin stared at the swinging door, the image of her expressive eyes imprinted on his mind. They'd held honest affection when she'd looked at him. Warm compassion. Humor. And hope.

It was that last emotion that was going to be the hardest of all to resist.

GREAT-AUNT Jennie tossed back some of her sparkling cider, heavily liberated with her not-so-secret stash of whiskey, wheezing when it went down the wrong way.

Lani shook her head with a shudder when her aunt offered her the jug. "No thanks."

"Let me get this straight." Aunt Jennie took another swig and gasped, pounding her chest. Her curls, the silver burnished ones she'd been paying Verna at the Body Wave Salon weekly for for the past forty years, bounced as she set down her drink. "You're finally engaged."

"Yes," Lani said. "But—"

"Engaged to the most eligible bachelor in town."

Great-Aunt Jennie grinned and slapped her knee. "Imagine that!"

"But—"

"Hold it right there." Jennie, who was eighty-two but didn't look a day older than sixty-five, held up a hand. She knew her niece well. "Honey, why is it with you there's always a *but?*"

Lani let out a reluctant grin. "And this *but* is a biggy."

Jennie sighed. "You're going to ruin this for me, aren't you?"

"It's likely," Lani admitted. Her great-aunt had not been the most conventional of guardians. She'd held séances, had traveled extensively, whipping Lani out of school on a whim, and had never followed any of the rules. She hadn't joined the PTA, had never made easy friends with the other parents or driven in the carpool.

But she'd been there for Lani when she'd had no one else, and for that she was grateful. Lani might have grown up differently than most, but Jennie had done the best she could and Lani would never forget it.

But she was well aware that her aunt's greatest wish was to see Lani taken care of. Jennie took it personally that Lani had a deep-rooted fear of emotional attachments. She wanted Lani to go the route of the very normal and expected marriage, no matter how abnormal Lani's upbringing had been. She wanted Lani's future secure, and she wanted that because she loved Lani with all her slightly off-kilter, wacky heart.

Realizing that brought both a lump to Lani's throat and a shoulder-load of shame about the façade. She had to tell Jennie the truth about the engagement, had to make her understand that marriage, a true marriage, was just not in the cards.

At that thought, Lani's heart sent up a little protest,

but now was not the time for self-reflection. "The truth is, it's just pretend, Aunt Jennie. Colin needs me to *pretend* to marry him, that's all."

"Pretend."

"That's right."

They were in Jennie's house, just a few blocks from Lani's apartment. It was run down on the outside, but the inside was a treasure trove, decorated with things from all over the world that Jennie had collected on her various travels.

There was not a speckle of dust, Jennie wouldn't allow it. Not on her things. She was Lani's toughest, hardest-to-please client, and also her favorite.

To get her thoughts together, Lani moved around the room, touching those things now, unable to sit still.

Jennie had gone quiet, but now she had a question. "What exactly do you mean, *pretend?*"

"Colin needs to finish a very important project he's working on, but he's being hounded. He thought a fiancée would help."

"What's the matter with him that he can't get a real fiancée? Is he ugly?"

Lani thought of Colin's piercing eyes, of the lean rugged body that had left her breathless. "No," she managed to say. "Definitely not ugly."

"Is he mean?"

No one could hold her the way Colin had last night and be mean. "No."

"Uh-huh." Jenny's brilliant green eyes sparkled. "I get it. You just want to live in sin without people bothering you. That's okay, honey, I understand a healthy sexual drive. I lived through the sixties, remember?"

"It's not like that—"

"Hormones aren't easy to deny," Jennie went on

blissfully. "Why in my day, we didn't even try. We just married young so it was all legal."

"It has nothing to do with hormones," Lani said weakly, grabbing for the jug of cider when the older woman reached for it. "You've been reading too many of those romances, Aunt Jennie."

"They give a woman a better sex life." At Lani's startled laugh, Jennie smiled and nodded. "I read that somewhere."

"Can we get back to my engagement?"

"Sure. What you're trying to tell me is that you're not really marrying him." Aunt Jennie studied a box of open cigars on the low table in front of her couch before choosing one. She didn't dare light it, not with Lani within reach, so she just clamped her teeth around it.

"What do you think of the whole thing?" Lani asked.

"Well, I think it's a damn shame, honey. Make him earn it. Don't give it to him for free."

"He has nothing to earn," Lani insisted, blushing in spite of herself.

"Of course he does. I hope he's going to at least cook, or do the grocery shopping."

"No, you don't understand. It's for show. All of it."

Jennie's jaw went slack and the cigar tumbled out into her lap, making Lani thankful Jennie's doctor had given her strict orders not to light up. She was a danger to society.

"*All* for show?" she repeated in disbelief.

"Well...yes." Mostly.

"You mean you're not...?"

"No."

Her great-aunt sadly shook her head. "Oh, honey. I taught you better than that."

LANI DIDN'T KNOW what she expected that night. Certainly that she and Colin would spend a considerable amount of time talking, gathering facts and coming up with a common story.

Colin was a planner, she knew that much. She knew how important it would be to him to have this all analyzed and prepared for his mother and aunts.

But she was alone, pacing Colin's large, eerily empty house. The house itself was beautiful; old, airy and full of character. The inside should have been a delight. But though Colin had been there a number of years, he had hardly furnished it. Most of the glorious rooms remained practically empty.

Lani wondered why. Her sneakers squeaked on the wood floor of the wide hallway as she paced.

She knew so little about him.

Why was he so private? What secrets did his dark, mysterious eyes hold? Did he ever share himself? What made him so leery of physical affection?

He might like to think that his cool, aloof front would keep people at bay, but not Lani. Oh, no. It only made her all the more curious.

Lani thought of last night and smiled. He certainly wasn't leery of passion, he'd been hot, earthy and completely uninhibited. That he'd made her feel those things, too, shouldn't have surprised her, but it did. She'd never felt so out of control in her life.

She had liked it very much.

So where was he?

She glanced at the clock for the tenth time in as many minutes. It was nearly 9:00 p.m. and it was becoming more and more clear that her reluctant fiancé wasn't coming home.

It wouldn't do to get annoyed. All she'd accomplish

would be to raise her blood pressure because she did understand Colin. He didn't want to be tied to her, didn't want the commitment.

Neither did she, Lani reminded herself.

But Colin had been backed into a corner. He had no choice and, whether he realized it or not, he was rebelling. Pushing him now would be a big mistake.

Besides, his nonappearance could be an innocent mistake. She couldn't imagine Colin would ever hurt her on purpose, but she could imagine him in his downtown office, working frantically, completely into what he was doing, oblivious of the passing time.

Without stopping to consider the wisdom of interrupting the lion in his den, Lani grabbed her keys and was out the door. Typical of a Southern California summer, the night temperature hadn't dropped to a comfortable level, despite the recent storm. It was over eighty degrees and unbearably muggy.

It didn't stop her. Truth was, nothing could. She was driven to help Colin, and she wouldn't give up.

The building Colin owned and worked in was one she'd admired often. It had once been an old warehouse, but Colin had remodeled it to suit his own needs. It was made of an intriguing mix of brick and glass, and exuded character and charm, proof that Colin possessed both.

The reception area was deliciously cool. So much so that Lani stood there a long moment, absorbing the breathable air. Then she followed a dim light that shone from down one of the two hallways. She came upon an office where a young woman was hunched over a set of books. Wearing faded denim, no makeup and a scowl, the woman was obviously not happy about her hours or her work.

"Hello," Lani said softly, not wanting to startle her.

Too late. The woman let out a squeak of surprise.

"I'm sorry," Lani exclaimed as the woman put a hand to her chest and took a deep breath. "I didn't mean to scare you, I'm just looking for Colin."

"Who are you?"

"Lani Mills, his—" *cleaning lady* came to the tip of her tongue, but she was much more. Wasn't she? "I'm his fiancée."

The woman blinked. "Colin *West?*"

The disbelief was understandable. Not only was Colin the most eligible bachelor around, he wasn't exactly known for having long-lasting relationships, much less an engagement. "Yes. I think he's working—"

"He's *always* working." The woman still looked stunned and Lani couldn't blame her, she herself was still reeling over the strange, unexpected turn of events.

"Yes, well...he's incredibly dedicated." Lani smiled. "I admire that."

The woman sighed and stood, shoving her huge glasses higher on her nose. "*Engaged.* Hard to believe. Well, I'm Claudia, his overworked, underpaid, not-quite-appreciated secretary." She stuck out her hand. "Maybe women will stop calling him now?" she asked hopefully.

"Women will definitely stop calling him now," Lani answered firmly. "You're working pretty late yourself."

"Special project and I'm behind on the books." Claudia stretched her back and yawned. "But I'm outta here. He's all yours." Her look said she wasn't sure why Lani would want him.

Lani should have left well enough alone. She knew

better than to interfere, really she did, but she couldn't seem to help herself. She had a streak of loyalty a mile wide, it was deeply ingrained. She protected those she cared about, and she cared about Colin. "Colin is just very involved with his work, it's important to him."

"I hadn't noticed."

Claudia's soft sarcasm only made Lani all the more determined. "He's a wonderful man. He deserves employees who think so, too."

Claudia had the good grace to blush. "I'm sorry. I do respect him, greatly. He pays fairly well and the work is steady. I even get benefits. It's just unnerving to work for someone who can render any female stupid with just a look and remain so unaware of it, you know?"

Lani was afraid she did.

"He's so...well...distant. Remote." Claudia hesitated. "Look, we're both women. I feel compelled to ask you. Do you have any clue what you're getting yourself into?"

6

AT CLAUDIA'S WORDS, Colin came to an abrupt halt outside the office door. He'd been walking down the hallway toward the coffee machine. But now he stood rock still, waiting with a strange breathlessness for Lani to come to her senses and run like hell.

"Yes, I think I have a good idea what I'm getting into," Lani said quietly, her voice sure and strong.

Colin drew a deep breath and leaned against the wall. The emotion pounding through him didn't bear thinking about.

What would he do if she reneged?

Claudia let out a little laugh. "Well if I were you," she said. "I'd think twice about marrying a man too gorgeous and rich for his own good."

"Those aren't sins, you know." Lani sounded amused.

Still unseen, Colin cursed himself for not giving the still-pouting Claudia the new computer she'd asked for. Clearly, she wasn't going to forgive him easily.

"No, not sins," Claudia said, agreeing with Lani. "But he's not exactly an easy man to be with. He can be selfish as hell, and from what I understand, he's not very good at the marriage thing."

Colin went very still. It was all too true, so it seemed silly to be insulted.

He fully expected Lani to back out of their bargain,

and found himself tense and straining, waiting for the damning words.

The silence was deafening.

What was taking her so long? Any second now, she'd let him down.

Nothing new.

It happened a lot, he reminded himself. Plenty of people needed him, counted on him, but in return there wasn't anyone *he* needed, no one *he* could count on.

Lani was going to disappoint him, and strangely enough, it was going to hurt. He'd thought himself immune to that kind of pain long ago, but apparently he'd been wrong because his insides were twisting.

"Oh, I know *exactly* what I'm getting."

At Lani's soft but certain voice, some of Colin's warmth returned.

"And he's exactly what I want," she went on. "He's not what you've described. Not at all. He's a wonderful man. Maybe a little wary, but can you blame him? He's hounded night and day by people wanting something from him. It'd make anyone uncomfortable."

"Look, I'm not trying to talk you out of it, I just want to make sure you know what you're doing."

"I know what I'm doing. His aloofness doesn't scare me. Not when beneath that is a warm, passionate, beautiful man. And I feel lucky to be marrying him."

Colin was stunned at Lani's conviction, to say the least. Her unwavering loyalty shocked him, especially when he'd done nothing to deserve it.

What would she want from him in return?

Pushing away from the wall, he stepped into Claudia's office. Ignoring his secretary's flush of shame, he met Lani's gaze, which turned joyful at the sight of him.

"I was hoping I'd find you here," she said, rounding

the desk and coming toward him. With that unnerving habit she had, she touched him, reached for his hands. She came up on tiptoe and, as if they were alone, she brushed her lips over his.

At the touch of her mouth, his body jerked in surprise. And instant arousal.

But beyond that was another confusion. There were no recriminations from her. Not a word about the fact that he'd stayed at work to avoid her, and yes, that's exactly what he'd done.

She was smiling at him, just a sweet, simple smile. No tears, no pouting, nothing to indicate she was annoyed at him for disappointing her.

Shelly, his ex-wife, would have skinned him alive for far less.

"Will you come home with me now?" Lani murmured, looking deep into his eyes. She cupped his face, stroked his jaw with her long fingers, all in front of an avidly curious Claudia. "It's late, and I want you all to myself for this last night before your family comes."

He stared at her, having trouble putting thoughts together with her hands on him, her gaze holding his, promising things that he couldn't remember why he didn't want. "Lani—" She'd forgotten again, dammit, that this was all pretense. "Lani, this isn't—"

"You're absolutely right," she said smoothly, smiling as she stepped back and shot Claudia a laughing, sheepish look. "This isn't the place to talk like that. I'm sorry Claudia, sometimes we get carried away."

"That's okay," Claudia said, gaping.

"I'm going to take my future husband home now, for a little privacy."

Claudia shut her mouth carefully. "Well. Have a good night."

But as Lani took Colin's hand and led him out of the office, Claudia shot her boss a reassessing sort of look.

Colin wasn't sure if she was shocked that he'd let Lani lead him away, or if it had been the kiss.

Definitely the kiss he decided, rubbing the heart that was still threatening to explode out of his chest.

With her hand still holding his, Lani tugged gently, not saying another word or even looking at him as she opened the front door of the building and brought him out into the warm night.

Above them stars twinkled in the sky. The storm of the night before might never have happened. He might never have held this slight, charming, far-too-cheerful woman in his arms.

But he had, and the knowledge of her sweet, delectable body would be with him forever.

"Will you follow me back to your house?" she asked, apparently oblivious to his discomfort.

Forever.

"Colin." Lani shook her head at his silence. "This is difficult."

He shook off his reverie. "What?"

"You trying to figure out if I'm acting or if I've forgotten our deal."

"You kissed me."

"For Claudia's sake. Remember? She doesn't miss much and she needed to know we're crazy about each other."

"You were pretending?" He couldn't possibly be disappointed. Could he?

"That's the idea, right? Pretend?"

The kiss, the one that had both wowed and warmed him, hadn't been real. He laughed a little at his own stupidity. "Uh…yeah. Pretend. That's the idea."

"I came to get you because this is our last night, and we have stuff to go over."

"I know."

"I wasn't sure if you remembered."

"I remembered."

She nodded, dragged her teeth over her lower lip. Despite the warm air, she wrapped her arms around herself and stared at the mountain peaks surrounding them. The moon was nearly full, and it bounced a silvery light over the dark night. "I'm sorry," she whispered, staring at the sky. "This is awkward and I didn't want it to be. I know you overheard my conversation with Claudia."

"I'm everything she said I was."

She whipped around to face him, her eyes fierce. "You're not! You're kind and decent and sweet—"

"I think you're confusing me with Mr. Rogers and his friendly neighborhood."

Anger shot off her in waves as she lost the temper he didn't even know she had. Hair wild, eyes sparking, she came close enough to stab him in the chest with her finger. "Just because you're a private man doesn't mean you're a selfish, cold, hardhead."

"I don't remember Claudia calling me a selfish, cold, hardhead."

Some of her temper faded. "Maybe I added that."

He had to laugh.

She sighed. Shoved at her hair. Stared at him. "Tell me about you, Colin. I feel so in the dark."

"There's nothing to tell."

"Why are you such a private man? Who hurt you?"

"No one."

"I know someone did," she said softly. "I can see

flashes of anguish behind that aloofness you show to everyone else. Won't you tell me about it?"

This was why he wanted everyone to think he was engaged, so he wouldn't have to ever talk about, or even *think* about, what had happened to him.

"I understand pain," she whispered, stepping close again, but instead of stabbing him with her finger, she slid a hand over his chest, down his arm to his hand, which she held in hers. "You could tell me anything."

"No. I can't." Not only was it stupid, it would be as embarrassing as hell to admit the mistakes he'd made. He'd like to think he would never do it again. And though that meant not ever trusting another woman in his life, when this woman had such pretty, trusting eyes, it was a decision he'd made out of self-preservation. He wouldn't change. "Your knowing isn't necessary for this charade of ours."

"Sharing parts of each other has nothing to do with the charade. It's part of being friends."

God, no. Being friends meant caring, genuine affection. A closeness he couldn't handle. "I'm not sure being friends is a good idea."

She stared at him for a moment, then with all traces of warmth gone from her eyes, she nodded. "I see."

It was over. He'd gone too far. But she didn't say anything. "Still want to go through with this?" he forced himself to ask.

"Yes, I do." She managed a smile at his start of surprise, though it held little mirth. "I told you, Colin, I won't go back on my word. Maybe one of these days you'll believe me. Can we go home now? It's late and I have a long day tomorrow."

Home. Their pretend home. Suddenly Colin wished,

just for a second, that she was coming home with him for real. Coming to his bed. To his open arms.

"Colin?" She was waiting. "Okay?"

"Yeah." He sighed and shook off the strange yearnings. They had no place in his life. "Let's go."

THE NEXT DAY, Lani's mind wasn't much on work. Because of that, she was thankful to have a complete staff. She never left her office.

Things were good, or they would have been, if her mind hadn't kept wandering, gravitating, toward the tall, dark, enigmatic man she had agreed to help.

It wasn't Colin's fault that she wanted more. She had no one to blame for that but herself.

To combat her restlessness, she worked like a fiend, catching up on bookkeeping, phone calls and scheduling.

But she never stopped thinking about what had happened the night before.

Or rather, what *hadn't* happened.

Colin had slept in his room and she in hers. She had lain there in her big, empty chilly bed, staring at the ceiling all night, hoping the stubborn man down the hall was getting no more rest than she was.

She wondered what made him so damn unyielding. So incapable of giving in to the yearning in his heated eyes? He could deny it all he wanted, but she'd seen it for herself when she'd come out of the bathroom dressed for bed in nothing more than a plain T-shirt that hung to her thighs.

Cool, inscrutable Colin had taken one look and come to an abrupt stop. His gaze had run slowly down the length of her, lingering in spots that had made him swallow hard before dragging it back up to meet hers.

There'd been such hunger there, Lani's knees had quivered and, never one to hold back, she had actually taken a step toward him. But before she could say a word, Colin had spun on his heels and shut himself in his bedroom. Alone.

She shut off her computer now and looked out the narrow window her office afforded. It was late enough in the afternoon that she could pretend the day was over. The heat would be intense, but Colin's house was cool.

He'd be there today. He would have to be, to let in his mother and two aunts. Just thinking about it made her sweat. They were pathetically unprepared. They'd accomplished little in the past few days. Fact was, she knew no more about Colin now than when she had started this farce.

Oh, he wanted her, she knew that much about him.

She hadn't mistaken the look in his eye, the almost palpable attraction radiating between the two of them.

But for whatever reason, he refused to act on it, or even acknowledge the existence of their chemistry.

It wasn't much to go on as far as engagements were concerned.

Apparently it would have to be enough.

IT WASN'T DIFFICULT to talk herself into running errands before going to Colin's house. Lani wasn't too eager to face his mother and lie about their engagement.

She drove through town, melting in the heat, going to the bank, the gas station, the library, any place she could think of.

Then she drove to her apartment, where she grabbed her two plants. By the time she'd set them in her car, along with a few more changes of clothes, she was a sticky wreck and wishing she'd had her car air-conditioning fixed instead of paying down her credit card bill.

Out of errands and with nowhere else to go, Lani crossed the train tracks. Immediately the quality of the houses improved. Within two minutes she was heading up the steep grade that led to the hill above the town where the wealthy residents lived.

At the top of the hill, she pulled into Colin's driveway and took a long moment to admire the beautiful place. She could only imagine how wonderful it could be if Colin turned it into a real home. She glanced down at her plants. "You'll be a start," she decided. "A good start."

She let herself out of the searing hot air and into the soothing coolness of Colin's kitchen. Because her nerves were suddenly leaping, she called out jokingly, "Hi honey, I'm home!"

Juggling her plants, her purse, a bag of clothes and a smile, it took her a moment to realize she was the only one grinning.

Colin was standing at the open refrigerator, a dark eyebrow cocked. "*Honey?*"

"It's supposed to be funny."

"Ah. Well, they're in the living room, you can drop the show." He shut the refrigerator and came toward her, looking far more handsome and cool and relaxed than any man with a panicked fiancée in one room and a nosy mother in another should. He wore those jeans that made her light-headed and a dark knit polo shirt, untucked. Simple clothes. Complicated man.

Lani set down her things and took the bottled water he handed her, gratefully running the bottle over her hot forehead. *What was she going to say to his family?*

Would she convince them? "Thanks," she said lightly. "Whew, it's a scorcher, isn't it?"

"What's all this?" He looked at her plants as if they held the plague.

"I know they're drooping," she said a little defensively, stroking one sagging leaf. "But they're just hot. I thought your kitchen window would be perfect for them. All that empty space."

That unsettling gaze of his switched to her, and for once he wasn't so difficult to read.

He was afraid she was forgetting again.

"You know," she said evenly, holding on to her temper. "That's getting annoying."

"This is just—"

"*Temporary*," she finished for him, rolling her eyes. "Look, are you going to remind me of that every single moment of every day?"

"Just until I'm sure you remember," he murmured, taking the water bottle from her fingers and opening it for her. Gently he brought it to her lips where she took a long, grateful sip. "You look hot."

"I brought more clothes. Is that going to scare you, too?"

"I'm not scared of you."

The heat really wasn't good for her disposition. Nor was looking at him all calm and collected while she was still sticky as hell and feeling as though she was dissolving. "Could have fooled me."

"Lani, my mother is *here*. In the next room. Are you going to do this or not?"

That was it. She didn't know if it was the temperature or just Colin annoying her all to hell, but her patience was gone. "I keep telling you I'm not going to back out! Jeez, you think you can't trust anyone."

His eyes flashed with warning, but she was good and hot and hungry, all things which had her spoiling for a fight. "No matter how grumpy and difficult you are, Colin—"

"I'm not grumpy, *you* are."

"Let's not go there, all right? I'm not going to leave you hanging. Got it?"

"Fine," he bit out. "And I'm ever so grateful." At her rough laugh, he gritted his teeth. "But if you're not going to back out, why do you keep baiting me?"

"Because you're easy."

He stared at her. "I'm— What the hell does that mean?"

"Nothing." It was irrational, but desire flooded Lani at Colin's frustration. He honestly didn't understand, or trust, her loyalty. It was infuriating. "You might have come up with a solution to your problem, Colin, namely, *me*. But I'm not some puzzle you can solve and then just forget about."

He blinked. "Are you speaking English?"

She threw up her hands. "You're impossible."

They were nose to nose now, and Lani had to admit she was enjoying the sparks flying from his eyes, because while they'd started out full of temper, they'd gone to something much hotter.

"I have feelings," she whispered. "And you have the singularly annoying ability to hurt them."

He put his big hands on her shoulders, squeezed lightly and drew her up close. "I have feelings, too."

"I never meant to hurt you." Her voice had lowered, gone husky, but she couldn't help it. The very tips of her breasts brushed his chest and suddenly she was much, much hotter.

So was he, given the low, harsh breath he let out.

"Colin...about the other night."

"When you had your dream."

"Yes." She licked her suddenly dry lips. "I don't suppose it's asking too much to know if you...uh, if you've...you know, changed your mind about going to the store?"

"For?"

"Supplies?"

He actually blushed.

"*You're* embarrassed?" she asked, shaking her head. "I'm the one that can't even say...*you know.*"

"Condoms?"

Now she blushed. "Yeah."

He ran his thumb over her lower lip, mesmerized at the movement. "I went to the store."

All sorts of wicked, inappropriate thoughts danced in her head. Anticipation tingled through her body, but he sounded less than thrilled. "You didn't want to."

"No, but it wasn't my brain doing the thinking at the time."

As he spoke, their bodies touched and an electrical current ran through them.

"Is that a bad thing?" she asked. "Not thinking with your brain?"

He made a little sound, a growl of both frustration and reluctant pleasure. "It's damn suicidal. We're so attracted to each other, Lani. It's out of control. It's crazy." He sucked in a hoarse sigh when she toyed with the sensitive skin behind his ear. "Stop it." He captured her hands in his and held them between their bodies, his expression nearing pain. "It is hot in here, dammit. The air isn't working."

"It's *us*, Colin. I'm making you hot, just as you're doing the same to me. Why can't you admit that?"

"Pretend. The key word here, remember? This is supposed to be pretend."

"Well you can't plan everything, every little detail, for your entire life. Some things just don't work that way." He still held her hands captive. But he looked so miserable, so baffled by what was happening between them. She just had to touch him. She reached up and nipped at his jaw with her mouth.

He groaned. "Dammit, stop."

She couldn't, she felt different when she was with him. She felt good. Happy. And she knew he could feel the same way if he let himself.

What held him back?

She dragged an open-mouthed kiss down his neck, inhaling deeply his wonderful, masculine scent.

Again, he let out a rough sound of desire and helplessly pressed his hips to hers, hard. "Lani."

"Don't fight it anymore, Colin."

He stilled, then lifted his head and looked at her. His struggle to control his feelings was obvious. He harbored some secret pain and she wanted to share it.

"What the hell am I going to do with you?" he wondered.

Keep me, was on the tip of her tongue. "Kiss me," she whispered instead, leaning closer. "Kiss me like you did the other night."

He let out a rough groan and dropped his forehead to hers. "That's going to make it worse."

"I don't see how."

"Lani, don't you get it? I don't want to want you."

"Well that's a fine thing to say to your future wife."

Colin groaned again as his mother came into the kitchen.

7

IRENE WEST was a cool, calm, beautiful, five-foot-tall sophisticate. She wore expensive-looking black tailored trousers, a matching blouse so fine and shimmery smooth it had to be made of silk, and squeaky-clean, bright white tennis shoes. The latter immediately endeared her to Lani's heart.

Irene had elegant features and very chic blond hair, cut artfully to chin length. She looked unapproachable, until she smiled like a pixie.

Lani decided she was going to like her.

And what Irene said next sealed that fact.

"Kiss your fiancée, Colin," Irene instructed. "Don't make her ask you twice, it's not gentlemanly."

Lani grinned and tipped up her face.

Colin let out one concise, pithy word, shoved his fingers through his hair and glanced upward as if hoping for divine intervention.

"With sentiments like that one," Irene said disapprovingly, "you'll lose her before you ever get down the aisle. And I'm very much looking forward to that so don't blow it for me. Introduce us, Colin."

He sighed heavily, but did so, after firmly setting Lani away from him. Lani watched him slip his hands into his pockets and knew a surge of satisfaction.

He didn't trust himself not to touch her.

Even if that urge to touch was really a need to strangle her, she'd take it as a good sign.

Without a shy bone in her body, Irene smiled warmly at Lani. "I'm so happy to meet you." Her eyes held exasperated affection when she turned her fond smile on Colin. "I was becoming more and more certain I would never have the pleasure."

"You weren't going to give up until you did," Colin said dryly.

"Well somebody had to see to your happiness. I would have labored until doomsday, if needed."

Colin shot Lani a look that said, *see why we're doing this?*

Lani smiled. She thought it was cute and touching how important Colin was to Irene. But she was also beginning to understand Colin's desperate measures to ensure his privacy.

She waited for mother and son to hug, but strangely enough, they didn't. This disturbed Lani, because one of the things she remembered and missed most about her family was the physical affection.

Moving close enough to grasp Irene's hand, Lani wrapped an arm around the woman and gave a light squeeze. "Very lovely to meet you."

"Oh," Irene whispered softly, touching Lani's face gently. "You're so sweet."

Colin frowned.

Irene ignored her son and the silent, unmistakable tension between him and Lani, her sharp yet eager eyes frankly devouring her future daughter-in-law.

Feeling a little bit on display, Lani was painfully aware of the picture she made. Self-consciously, she stroked her wild hair, trying unsuccessfully to tame it, wishing she'd combed it through. She wore little or no makeup and grungy clothes. She'd not dressed for this. For one thing, she didn't have anything suitable. And secondly, she hadn't thought of it. Why hadn't this scene occurred to her? In all her justifying of *why* she was helping Colin, in all her denials that this was nothing more than wanting to see his project completed, she'd never pictured an actual meeting with his family.

Somehow, she'd thought she would have more time. More preparation.

Actually, Lani admitted, she hadn't wanted to think about it, hadn't wanted to wonder if she'd be accepted, if she'd fit in.

Would his mother approve? After all, Lani was nothing more than a housecleaner, without social standing. She knew Colin had grown up with class and money. He'd probably had a maid, a nanny, a cook, and she'd had nothing but her great-aunt Jennie and the occasional séance.

Uncomfortable, she tugged at her ragged T-shirt, stroked a hand down her rough overalls. And wished with all her might for elegant sophistication.

"Did you work today?" Irene asked her politely.

The woman's gaze easily met Lani's and, though there was no censure there, Lani still felt it. She knew Irene was far too cultured to let her true feelings show, and certainly she had to have feelings about her son marrying someone like Lani. For the first time in Lani's life, shame filled her at her choice of a career. "Yes, I did."

Irene's features softened. Her smile was warm. "Well then you must be very tired. And here I am keeping you on your feet."

Surprise hit Lani first, then such an overwhelming gratitude she felt her eyes sting. How easy it would be to pretend this *was* real, that she really cared about what Colin's mother thought of her. But it wasn't, and it never would be. She had a job to do—convince this woman that she loved her son. Then get out of Colin's life. He would be free of hassles and she would be free to get on with her own life, happy and secure in the knowledge that she'd both helped mankind and had taken a risk for the first time in too long.

But the pathetic truth was she *did* care, about both Colin *and* what his mother thought. There was nothing she could do to stop it, not when her heart had already made the decision.

Irene pushed Lani into a chair and softened the wordless demand by saying kindly, "Would you like some iced tea?"

Colin was watching her, his eyes back to their inscrutable depths. What was he thinking? she wondered wildly. Was he worried she would fail?

Was he sorry he'd ever recruited her in the first place?

"Yes, please," she said to Irene. "But I can get it."

"No, please, let me," Irene insisted.

She looked at Colin when his mother turned her back to get the tea, fussing at her clothes, pushing at her hair, desperate for a sign that she was doing okay.

Colin's long arm reached out and gently, almost tenderly, he tucked a stray strand of hair behind her ear. His lips softened, so did his eyes, and he whispered for her ears alone, "I like the way you look, all flustered and mussed up."

Torn between pleasure at his words—*he liked the way she looked?*—and horror that she looked mussed, she bit her lip.

Colin laughed softly. "Stop it. You look..."

Their gazes met.

His breath caught.

So did hers. "I look...?"

"So pretty," came his soft, husky voice, so silky and light it felt like an embrace.

Startled, Lani blushed. "I...do?"

"Lemon in your tea, Lani?" Irene whirled back from the refrigerator. She smiled at the sight of Colin clearly doting on Lani.

"Please," Lani managed, her gaze never leaving Colin's. "Lemon would be great."

Colin didn't smile. His eyes gave nothing away except for that flash of recognition of what stood between them.

She wanted to touch him again, assure herself he was really there and for a little while, hers.

What was happening? This wasn't just a physical yearning, it went much deeper. And suddenly, the truth hit her. She wasn't capable of making up the feelings that he required for this silly pretense, not when the feelings were becoming real.

As if he could read her disturbing thoughts, Colin's eyes shuttered against her. He leaned back against the counter, his rugged body moving with easy, economical grace.

Oblivious to the arrow-taut tension between them, Irene was a study in movement, never standing still as she got a tray, some glasses, sliced a lemon and continued to talk without a breath. "I can only imagine how overwhelming this all is to you, Lani. Getting married! My, there's just so much to do, so much to think about. I hope you'll let me and my sisters help you, we just can't wait."

Colin, still watching Lani, finally let a smile touch his

lips. "Did I mention how wildly enthusiastic my mother would be? Let's hope she tells the entire world so everyone will be sure to stop calling and telling me I need a date."

"Oh, you," Irene shook her head. "Stay out of this. I'm having a talk with my future daughter-in-law."

Maybe it was the title, or it might have been the sincere, warm, fondness in which Irene spoke, but at his mother's bubbly happiness, Colin's smile slowly faded.

It was replaced by worry, guilt, regret. And Lani felt every one of those emotions as well.

"I've so looked forward to this," Irene said, laughing.

Colin actually winced at that, and, at his obvious misery at having to lie, Lani's heart ached.

She reached for his hand. At the touch, he jerked in response, but he didn't pull away. She considered that great progress. "It's lovely that you came to visit, Mrs. West—"

"Oh, but you mustn't sound so formal! Please, call me Irene." She tossed a grin over her shoulder and looked twenty years younger. "Or Mom, if you think you can manage."

Mom. How many years had she wished for such a woman in her life? To be so freely given one now, when it was all just a hoax, seemed cruel. Sitting there between Colin, the man of her dreams, and his mother, a sweet, kind woman so full of heart, Lani wasn't sure she could pull it off.

"It's almost too good to believe." Irene was watching them closely. "Are you sure you're going to marry my son?"

"I—" Startled by the question, Lani looked at Colin. *She'd promised.* This predicament was her own doing now. But to out-and-out lie.... She'd not imagined how it would make her feel. "Yes, I want to marry your son," she said, and to Lani's relief, Irene accepted that.

"Good." Satisfied, Irene turned back to the counter.

It was hard to think with the weight of the lie dragging at her. Some of her happiness drained. Colin lifted her chin with a finger, looking deeply into her eyes with gratitude, and for the life of her, she couldn't turn away.

"Mom," he said quietly, still watching Lani, "I know you just got here, but I really need a moment alone with Lani."

"Oh! Of course." Irene smiled slyly as she wiped her hands on a towel. "She just got home and you haven't seen her all day. What was I thinking? I understand what young love is like." With a dramatic sigh, her expression turned dreamy. "And I can't tell you how wonderful it is to know that you've found that kind of true passion, Son."

The remorse and sorrow on Colin's face matched that in Lani's heart. How could they continue to do this? How could they lie to this woman?

"Well at least I know I can stop trying to help you find it," Irene said. "I can't tell you what a relief that is to me."

"Or me," Colin murmured.

Irene backed to the door, watching them with such affection that Lani felt like slime. "I'll just run upstairs and tell Bessie and Lola you're here." She grinned again. "My sisters are dying to meet you."

"Can you hold them off a few minutes?" Colin asked. He gestured to Lani. "I need—"

"Oh, Colin." Irene sighed wistfully, her hand over her heart. "Just to hear you say it. That you *need*. It's so beautiful. I've never known you to need anyone at all, not me, not your father, not friends or even a woman. You've always been so self-sufficient."

And alone, Lani thought. Could she fix that for him? Could she teach him the joys of true love, even when she didn't know them herself?

Irene turned to Lani. "In just a few short moments, you've given me such pleasure, you'll never know."

"I'm glad," Lani whispered, guilt tugging at her.

"Oh, we're going to have the most wonderful time." Irene's eyes lit up. "We'll throw you an engagement party next weekend. Of course, everyone will come."

Colin looked decidedly *not* excited. "Wait a minute—"

"No, don't thank me, darling." She grinned. "I insist." Then she was gone.

The silence in the kitchen was deafening.

Colin made no move to break it. Feeling awkward and uncertain, Lani moved around the table. She lifted her pathetic-looking plants and arranged them in the window.

Silly as it was, the kitchen instantly seemed homier. Happier. She hoped they lived.

Behind her, Colin still didn't speak.

The quiet grew until she couldn't stand it. "I'm sorry," she said finally.

"She's going to get hurt. *Dammit.*" Colin paced the length of the kitchen, eating up the wide open space with his long, restless legs.

"Well, what did you think would happen?"

When Colin whipped around to face her, his dismay and shock evident, she shook her head and laughed. "Come on, Colin. You must have thought about what would happen after your project was finished. About how we'd end this. How she'd feel when I go back to my life."

Back to her life. Just the words brought a melancholy she didn't want to face.

Colin looked stunned.

"You didn't," she breathed. "You, Mr. Planner, Mr. Organization. You never thought about the end."

"I only thought about getting left alone." He looked disgusted with himself. "And having the phone calls stop. Ending the parade of blind dates." He swore softly before looking at her miserably. "This can't go on. I can't do it. Not to her and not to you."

"I'm okay, Colin."

"It's not fair."

He was going to call it all off. And she'd have to go back to being...without him. "You can't tell her now," she said much more casually than she felt. "It's too late. She'll get hurt either way, Colin. You might as well finish your project."

"I'm so close," he said wistfully. "So close."

Though she was beginning to understand that there would always be a project for Colin, each more important than the last, she accepted that. "The pretense is set," she said quietly. "You need time for yourself, and now you've got it. I'll keep them busy while they're here over the next few weeks. You just work as hard as you can, and get your project done. We'll face what happens afterward later."

His eyes were like the sea, black and fathomless. "Are you really up for this?"

He was talking about *them.* About what they would have to do to pull it off. "I'm ready if you are."

A rare laugh escaped him. "Oh, I'm ready," he assured her. "But not for my project."

"No? What then?" Was that her voice, all breathless?

"The supply of condoms I bought. They're waiting upstairs by my bed."

"How many is a supply?"

He laughed again, a wondrous sound. "I got the huge economy box, thinking even that couldn't possibly be enough for the two full weeks."

Heat spiraled through her. "Oh."

"Are you sure, Lani?" His voice was low, thrilling. He came close, but didn't touch her. "Because if you're not, you'd better tell me now so I can come up with some reason why we'd be sleeping in two separate beds. I thought I could lie next to you and sleep, but I was fooling myself. We're like fire together, one touch from you and I'll go up in flames."

His voice alone was turning her on, making her tremble. "Colin, you're making my head spin."

"Well, you should see what you're doing to me."

She looked, then blushed furiously. "Oh, my."

"I've been like this since your nightmare."

Oh, my. She lifted her hands in a helpless gesture. "I haven't a clue what to do with you."

"Well that makes two of us."

LANI MET Aunt Bessie and Aunt Lola and was immediately charmed by their nosy, meddling, sweet, imposing ways. They were funny, wild, brutally honest and impossibly curious about the woman who had agreed to marry the nephew they all thought of as their own.

They ate together, and immediately afterward, Irene invited Colin to leave so he could go and work.

He hesitated, clearly torn between his unwillingness to leave Lani alone in their clutches, and the wonderful draw of his work.

But Lani knew he felt hopelessly behind on the project, so she took mercy on him and waved him off.

Besides, how was she going to learn more about him from his family while he listened to every word?

Irene, Bessie and Lola obliged her curiosity, regaling her with hysterical and interesting tales of Colin's youth.

And yet she found her attention wandering.

Would he really make love to her tonight? She wondered, glancing up the stairs in a state of high anticipation.

Oh, she hoped so.

They sat in the air-conditioned living room, a room that definitely needed a homey touch, Lani thought. There was elegant, expensive furniture, but just the bare minimum. A couch, a lamp, two chairs that looked sophisticated but uncomfortable. Not a comfy touch in sight.

She could easily fix that, with just a few plants, a nice rug, a couple of pictures.

"So you've snagged our Colin." Aunt Bessie—a four-foot-ten dynamo with the soft sweet voice of an angel and the ferocity of a protective momma bear—smiled, drawing Lani out of her reverie. "We're so thankful, darling, really we are." She leaned forward conspiratorially. "But do you think you could tell us *why?*"

"Why?" Lani blinked. Had she missed something?

"Why you want him."

Eager, Lola and Irene leaned forward, too. "He's such a pain in the tushie," Lola commented, her voice full of exasperated love. "We just want to know how you bullied him into it again."

It took her a moment to switch gears from putting warm, soft touches on the house to... "*Again?*" Lani straightened, her full attention focused now. "I'm sorry. Did you say, again?"

"Why, yes." Lola didn't move. She was the tallest at five foot two, and skinny as a rail. Her voice was husky, deep and loud. "We're dying to know how you convinced him to try again, when for five years we've been so unsuccessful."

"I see." Lani nodded calmly while her head spun. "He's been married before."

"Uh-oh." Bessie sat back and bit her meddling lip. "Oh, dear. Dear, dear, dear. Irene...?"

Irene glared at both her sisters. "Now you've done it." She turned to Lani with a worried smile. "Lani—"

"He's been married before," she repeated like a parrot. All the signs had been there, of course. His reluctance to share himself. His fear of being hurt. Still, devastation rocked her.

"Damn!" Lola cried. "We blew it!"

"*We?*" Irene demanded, sitting upright with dignity. "I am not going down for this. No way. I should have left the two of you in New York!"

"Well how was I supposed to know she didn't know?" Lola asked. "Somebody tell me that."

"We should have known," Bessie decided. "Colin always has been so closed-mouthed. It's natural that he wouldn't tell her about his single-most devastating failure."

"Wait a minute." Lani tried again to soak this all in. "Give me a minute here. Colin's been...*married*." She looked at them, feeling weak. "How could I not have figured that out by now?"

But the argument between the sisters was in full swing.

"I knew better than to bring the two of you with me,"

said Irene. She glared at her sisters. "I told you, *let me handle it. Let me check out the fiancée for myself,* but no, you both had to come. You had to interfere. Now look what you've done!"

"No offense, Sissy," Bessie interrupted stiffly. "But I was more Colin's mother than you ever were, so I had the right to meet Lani first."

Irene stood, then, quivering with indignation. "Now, just a minute—"

Bessie stood, too, glaring. "Yes?"

Good Lord, the three of them, these elegant socialites, were going to brawl. "Ladies..."

"You might think Colin belongs to you, but he's mine. *Mine,*" Irene emphasized. "That means Lani is mine, too!"

"Okay, that's it. *Stop.*" Lani stood up from the circular sofa, where they were perched in front of the lovely fireplace she'd had such high hopes for. "It's true then, he's really already been...married?"

Silence fell while all three older women shifted uncomfortably.

"It's really a very simple question," Lani said calmly as if her heart hadn't just cracked. She had a terrible feeling she now had the answer to the secret anguish swimming in Colin's eyes.

Was he pining away for a woman who'd left him?

Had the ex broken his heart, causing him never to trust another?

And how in the world could Lani compete with such a memory? The answer was simple. She couldn't. "Please tell me."

Irene sighed but looked right at Lani. "Yes, Colin was married before. I'm sorry you didn't know. Even sorrier that you had to find out like this, from us."

It took Lani a minute to collect herself; she felt such sorrow, both for her and for Colin. But she wasn't a selfish person by nature, and after the first fling of self-pity had passed, she hurt only for Colin. To know how much he must have loved his ex-wife, so much that he couldn't allow himself to have a real home or family now, was unbearably sad.

Somehow she managed to excuse herself.

They let her go, their eyes sad and worried, but she couldn't reassure them. Not yet.

She went straight to Colin's office upstairs, planning on opening her arms and her heart, wanting to tell him how sorry she was about his past. She wanted to share whatever comfort she could. Surely she could help, now that she understood.

But he was gone.

She assumed he had gone to his other office, the one in town. Disappointed, she climbed the stairs, walked into his bedroom and got ready for bed. She'd wait.

Feeling a little bit like Goldilocks, she climbed into his huge, soft, welcoming bed.

And waited.

The sheets smelled like him. The room looked like him. She felt him all around her. She daydreamed about what would happen, how she'd help heal him and, in return, he'd take her to ecstasy.

Sighing, imagining his body, his hands, his mouth, all on her, she sank down into the covers and waited some more.

And waited. And waited.

Only, Colin never came, and finally, exhausted, Lani fell asleep, his pillow hugged tight to her body.

8

GETTING LOST in his work was the last thing Colin had expected to do, especially with thoughts of Lani dancing through his head, but by the time his thoughts switched from work to life, it was 2:00 a.m. How had that happened? Hours had passed.

Lani would be waiting for him.

She'd be warm and inviting, he imagined, *smiling as she lifted her arms to welcome him.*

Wrong.

It was the middle of the night. She'd be asleep, and if she wasn't, she'd be mad as hell. Rightly so.

Racing home, he found her pretty much as his wildest fantasies had dictated, sprawled on the bed. There was one difference however. She wasn't hot and bothered, instead she was fast asleep with her arms squeezing his pillow close to her heart.

Damn, he'd really blown it. He had to have hurt her feelings again, and he hated that. Much as he loved his work, right then and there he experienced a first—a spurt of genuine anger at how it consumed him body and soul, to the point of such forgetfulness.

He had to make it up to her, had to at least apologize. "Lani?"

It didn't help that the sheets and blanket had become tangled in her legs, below her hips. She wore a tiny white camisole that looked soft and silky, and even tinier panties. Her skin was pale and creamy and glowed in the faint moonlight.

She took his breath away.

Helplessly drawn to where she lay, he kneeled on the mattress. "Lani?"

In her sleep, she frowned, and from deep in her throat came a low sound of irritation.

Still Colin leaned over her, hand outstretched, hoping to wake her, planning on starting with sweet, sexy promises.

But then he was stopped cold, frozen by the tracks of dried tears on her cheeks.

THE NEXT MORNING Colin was back in his office downtown, unable to concentrate on a damn thing except Lani and how she'd looked in his bed.

As if she belonged there.

The long restless night on his floor, listening to Lani's soft, deep breathing, hadn't improved his disposition.

"Line one's for you." From the door, Claudia thrust her chin at his phone. "The Institute."

"Great," he said, meaning anything but. He had nothing new to report. He still wasn't finished and wasn't sure when he would be. "Claudia?"

She'd turned away and was halfway out the door when he said her name. She stiffened, but didn't look at him. "Yeah?"

"Next time you want to scare off a woman for me, can you check and make sure it's one I want scared off?"

"God." She winced and turned back to face him, her expression full of guilt. "I'm so sorry! I'm so used to trying to chase off everyone your mother sets you up with, I didn't realize she was the real thing."

The real thing. His stomach hurt. "Has word gotten around?"

She smiled. "Oh, yeah. Women from all over the county are having a wake in honor of your lost single status. You're the talk of the town. So is Lani." A slight frown marred her face. "She's really wonderful, you know."

He was beginning to realize that. "I know."

"Loyal, dedicated. Sweet, too, and very kind."

"But?" Colin pushed away his work. It held little appeal at the moment. "I'm sure I heard one at the end of that sentence."

"Well..." Claudia sent him an apologetic look to soften her words. "Truth is, I think she's *too* wonderful for you. She'll want more than you'll give her, Colin."

"And what would that be?" he said, amused now. "I have more money than I know what to do with, a huge house with every amenity she could ever want. There's nothing missing. I can give her whatever she needs."

Claudia's look turned pitying. "See? That's *exactly* what I mean. You don't have a clue as to how to keep a woman like that." She gave him a long look that made him squirm. "Or maybe you do, and you just don't want to see it."

"I have a call," he said, conveniently remembering. He picked up the phone, almost forgetting that this whole thing was just a sham. That he didn't have to justify anything to his secretary. That it didn't really matter what anyone thought because what he had with Lani was just temporary.

Temporary.

But before he pressed in the phone line, he watched Claudia shake her head in disgust, watched her leave...and knew she spoke the truth.

He didn't have a clue as to how to keep a woman like Lani. *Any* woman.

And he had an ex-wife to prove it.

COLIN GLARED at his office phone. He hadn't been able to reach Lani all day, either at the house or at her office.

Had she bolted, tired of the charade?

He couldn't blame her, but hoped not, and not because he'd have nothing to tell his interfering mother and aunts. He just couldn't leave things between them as they were now.

It was only three in the afternoon, an hour of the day he rarely saw because he usually had his head buried in work, but he actually got up and left his office. At the moment, he couldn't have buried himself in his work to save his sorry life, and he had Lani's huge, expressive eyes to thank.

He couldn't get them out of his mind. How was she feeling about last night?

All he'd ever wanted was peace and quiet. He'd never wanted to hurt anyone; not his family and certainly not Lani.

How he had managed to get himself in such trouble was beyond him.

He drove up to her apartment, once again struck by the differences in their life-styles. He walked up the cracked, crumbling driveway, wishing he could get Lani a better place to live. But he knew she'd never accept such help from him.

She worked so hard. It didn't seem fair that this was all she had to show for it.

"She's not here."

He turned and was surprised to see an old woman speaking to him. She was tiny, at least eighty years old, and dressed in hot-pink-and-red spandex. "Excuse me?" he said politely.

"Lani. She's who you're looking for, isn't she? Your...fiancée?"

"You know Lani?"

That made her laugh until her rust-colored curls bounced. Well, actually *cackle* would be a better word for what she did. She bent at the waist, slapped her knees and let loose. Finally, sniffing, she straightened. Still grinning, she nodded. "Yep, I know her." Grabbing a rake, she leaned against the fence of the small garden.

For the first time, Colin realized that while the apartment building itself looked as though it had seen better days, the garden was full and lush and well tended.

"The question is," the woman asked. "Do *you* know Lani?"

She was missing some marbles, Colin decided. "I'm sorry. You're...?"

"Ah, no doubt you're right. Where are my manners? We've not been introduced. Strange, wouldn't you say, since I'm Lani's great-aunt Jennie?" She eyed him shrewdly, acknowledging his surprise with a lift of a gray eyebrow.

Lani had a crazy woman for an aunt?

"I raised your soon-to-be-wife," she told him. "But, of course, you knew that, since you're engaged to her. You know everything about her. Right?"

Somehow he'd managed to step into an episode of the "X-Files."

Great-Aunt Jennie winked, then leaned close and whispered conspiratorially, "Nice to meet you, Mr. Pretend Fiancé."

She knew.

Unperturbed by his silence, Great-Aunt Jennie made herself comfortable on a wooden bench and tapped the spot next to her.

Colin sat.

The old woman smiled, her pink-and-red workout suit glittering in the relentless sun. "Next to you, I'm all Lani has," she confided. "But you knew that already, too, right?"

He should have. That message came loud and clear.

"She loves flowers, did you know that?" Jennie asked. "She also loves loud music, kids and has a serious weak spot for kittens. And Lord, does that girl have a sweet tooth. It's amazing how good a figure she has, given what she eats. Did you know she has a particular thing for white chocolate?"

A real fiancé would know these things, and more, about the woman he loved.

He would also know where to find her on any given day.

"And I don't have to tell you her dislikes, namely vegetables and exercise," Jennie said easily. "Or that she fears violent thunderstorms because her parents died in one."

Colin remembered Lani's fear well. Terrified, she'd clutched at him every time thunder had hit. "I didn't know that," he admitted.

"You should have."

"Yes." He most definitely should have.

Sadness was etched in Jennie's every movement as she stood and dragged the rake across a few fallen leaves. "I'm sorry. I love her and I'm upset. I'm taking it out on you, and that's very unkind of me. Inexcusable actually. Please forgive me. It's not you I'm mad at, but my darling, huge-hearted, idiot niece."

"Lani's parents—"

"Died when she was six." She lifted her head and met his gaze with her own steady one. "I'm her mother and her father now and her best friend. I'm certain you're not good for her, but one of these days, I'll learn to let her make her own mistakes."

Colin could not dispel the image of Lani as a child, frightened and alone, facing her parents' death at such a young age.

"And don't bother to ask me anything else. I won't tell you." She lifted a stubborn chin, sharing a strong resemblance to Colin's equally stubborn fiancée. "Whatever you want to know, you'll have to ask her yourself."

"I will." Soon as he could find her. He stood, intending to do just that.

"Lani told me about you." When he pivoted back around, startled, Jennie set the rake aside and pierced him with sharp blue eyes. "She told me you were smart and compassionate and wonderful."

Colin blinked in surprise, but Jennie only nodded. "She's a very generous soul, my Lani."

Pride tasted like hell, but Colin swallowed it anyway. "Do you know where I could find her?"

"Depends why you want her."

Because I miss her. But because that was a ridiculous thought, he shook his head to clear it. "I'd like to talk to her."

Jennie just looked at him, smiling. Silent. Smug.

Dammit. "Okay, I hurt her feelings. I have to see her, try to talk to her about it."

She was silent for so long, Colin thought she'd fallen asleep leaning on her rake.

"She's working," she said at last. "Too hard, if you ask me."

Again, another message. But Jennie didn't understand how complicated this was. Under their present terms, Lani would never allow him to help her financially, no matter how much he'd like to. "I called her office already," he said. "She wasn't there."

"Of course not." Jennie's expression made it clear that she thought *he* was the crazy one. "She doesn't spend all day sitting behind a desk, Mr. Pretend Fiancé. Not like other people. No, she's out there working her fingers to the raw bone, cleaning *rich* people's places because they don't want to do it themselves."

Well he had to hand it to the woman. In the space of the few minutes that he'd been there, she'd made him feel ridiculous, selfish, greedy and now guilty.

But Lani liked her work, didn't she? God, he didn't know, he'd never even asked. "I just want to talk to her. We have a lot to work out. Most of which is a direct result of my own stupidity, if you must know."

Jennie laughed loudly. "Nice to see a man admit it."

"Can you tell me where to find her? Please?"

Jennie hesitated a long moment, and Colin knew he was being seriously measured. He had no idea what Lani had told Jennie about him. Hell, up until now, he'd had no idea who made up Lani's family.

How could he not have known that? How could he not have asked?

"She'll be cleaning Dr. Morrow's offices today," Jennie said finally. "On Main Street."

"Thank you," he said sincerely, but something had him hesitating, and it took him a second to realize he wanted this woman's approval. For Lani's sake. *For his.*

The feeling was so alien, he didn't know what to do with it, but he found himself saying, "I won't hurt her."

"Of course you will." Her smile was sad, and she suddenly looked much older than she had before.

When he opened his mouth to protest, she lifted a hand with a sharp shake of her head. "Don't make promises you can't keep, Colin. I know this engagement isn't real, at least not to you."

She didn't have to tell Colin what she thought of that, it was all over her face.

"Lani has talked herself into believing she's helping you," she said. "And maybe she is, but believe me, she'll get hurt. I'm not happy with you for that."

She walked back into her house, leaving Colin to his own miserable thoughts.

COLIN HAD NO TROUBLE finding Dr. Morrow's offices on Main Street. He had no trouble parking, no trouble at all walking into the building, the one with a brightly colored sign announcing that today was Dr. Morrow's day at the local hospital.

What Colin did have trouble with was figuring out what the hell he was going to say to Lani.

Or what the hell he wanted from her.

He entered the empty waiting room, figuring he'd find Lani on her hands and knees, slaving away in shapeless clothes that hardly fit her. Or maybe she'd be up on a ladder brushing away at dust bunnies, her face streaked with sweat and dirt, her hands worked red and raw.

Certainly she'd be solemn and upset over the night before.

Whatever he'd expected, it certainly wasn't to find her rosy and screaming with laughter, pointing a squirt bottle filled with water at his aunt Bessie, who was squealing in response, also wielding a water bottle like a weapon.

Behind them both, shouting like a crazed banshee, came his aunt Lola, waving yet another squirt bottle. She had a handkerchief wrapped around her head. "Duck or you die," his oldest and most dignified aunt yelled, grinning widely from ear to ear.

"What the—" he began, only to find himself the target of three wild-looking women. He registered the change in their eyes, saw the exact moment the target of their fun game switched from each other to him.

Him.

"Now wait just a minute," he said, backing up as all three women advanced on him. "Just—"

It was all he got out before Lani—not looking even close to devastated—took the lead and sprayed him full in the face.

From the couch came a strange, muffled sound. It was Carmen, working hard at reading a magazine, holding her hand over her mouth as her shoulders shook with silent laughter.

Water dripped off Colin's nose, down his ears, into his collar. Both his aunts found this absolutely hysterical. Bessie was so overcome she had to sink to one of the couches. She rolled back and forth, laughing as tears ran down her face.

Lola took one look at her and snorted in a most unladylike fashion, which sent Bessie and Lani back into fresh fits of giggles.

Colin gawked at Lani. Tears of mirth streamed down her face, along with a good amount of water—one of his aunts had obviously gotten her good. Her hair was out of control, rioting around her face, her eyes were bright, her skin positively glowing.

Nope, no matter how hard he looked, he couldn't find an ounce of solemnity about her.

She squirted him again.

"What was that for?" he sputtered as he wiped cold, wet drops from his face.

"Well..." She grinned. "You looked hot." Her smile mocked him and his all-day misery.

The urge to haul her to him and kiss away all frustration came on incredibly strong, but he couldn't be sure he wouldn't strangle her. He actually reached out to grab her, but at the last minute remembered his avidly watching, meddling aunts and slammed his hands into his pockets instead.

She'd sprayed him, right in the face! He couldn't believe it, couldn't believe how shock had turned into something else, something far more base. If he didn't kiss her right here and now, he would just explode.

The primal, savage urge startled him. He'd never, ever, felt this way over a woman. Over work, yes. But never another human, and it shook him to the core.

She wore jeans today, and while they were several sizes too large for her, hiding the figure he knew could alter his blood pressure, they had holes all over, including one high on her right thigh that revealed enough skin to have him swallowing hard.

Where was his distraught, depressed fiancée?

"What are you doing here?" she asked sweetly, as if she hadn't attacked him with a squirt bottle only a second before.

"What am *I* doing here?" He let out a sound of amazement. "I've been going crazy looking for you. What are *you* doing here?"

"It's not too difficult to figure out." She smiled innocently, gesturing to her cleaning supplies, lying useless and unused on the floor. She seemed without a care in the world. As if she hadn't given him a second thought. *She probably hasn't.* The thought was curiously deflating.

"I'm working," she said. "Very hard."

"Oh, yeah, I can see that."

Lani turned slightly to glance at his aunts, and when she did, Colin's eyes nearly bugged out of his head. The back of her jeans were even holier than the front. There was a slice through the denim so high on her left thigh he could see a flash of hot-pink panties.

Had he really once thought this woman not sexy? How had he been so blind?

With Lani giving them some silent but meaningful looks, Bessie and Lola finally managed to control themselves and straightened.

"Better get to work," Bessie said cheerfully, nudging her sister. They beckoned Carmen, who with a sniff of disdain, took her magazine, rudely stuck her tongue out at Colin, then disappeared down the hall.

Colin's aunts then grabbed a bucket full of cleaner and sponges.

"What are you doing?" he asked.

Lola and Bessie, both old enough to be grandmothers, both world travelers and grand sophisticates of the small educated, high-brow population of Sierra Summit, grinned wildly.

"Lani's short-handed today, poor thing," Lola said. "She could never get everything done all by herself so we're staff today. I'm going to clean the bathrooms."

"And I'm on vacuuming and dusting detail," Bessie said proudly.

Colin couldn't believe it. "But neither of you have cleaned a toilet or worked a vacuum in your lives."

"Always a first time, hon." Bessie's smile turned wicked, and Colin knew enough about his aunt to know he wasn't going to like what she had to say next. "And speaking of first times," she continued sweetly, "we're really short-handed here, and on a time budget since Lani pays by the hour. I think since she's your fiancée, you should help."

"*What?*"

"Grab a sponge, darling," Lola said, nodding her approval. "Let's see you prove your worth to this wonderful girl here. Give her a hand."

Colin turned to stare at Lani. "Are they kidding?"

She looked at his aunts with laughter and affection in her gaze, but when she turned back to him, she said somberly, "Nope. I don't think they are."

He thought about what he'd learned from her greataunt Jennie, how hard she worked. How loyal and caring she was. How she'd lost her family so early.

How she feared storms.

He was beginning to realize the extent of Lani's depth and inner strength, and though he admired her very much for it, a much more basic emotion pushed to the surface.

Protectiveness.

"Unless of course, Colin, you can't spare the time for her," Bessie said evenly.

Lola shifted the bucket in her arms like a pro. "Or maybe you think pushing a sponge isn't your kind of work."

He couldn't believe it. These two women supposedly loved him as if he was their own child. Why were they giving him hell?

But they were right. He'd always put work ahead of everything else, and he'd always thought himself far above cleaning.

Guilt and shame were new to him, and he didn't like either. "I'll help, dammit." He grabbed a sponge, but then Lani was there with a hand to his chest, her eyes soft and apologetic.

"They're just teasing you." She wiped a drop of water off his jaw. "I'm fine, I don't need you to stay."

"I said I'd help."

She looked into his eyes and apparently saw she couldn't convince him otherwise. "All right, then," she said quietly. "Thank you."

He unbuttoned his cuffs and shoved up his sleeves. "Where's my mother?"

"Florist shopping." Lani chewed on her lip in the gesture he now knew was a nervous habit.

"For the wedding," Lola added. "She's so excited. And the engagement party is completely under control. You two are going to love it."

It was all too much, and he could see in Lani's eyes she felt it, too. "We really don't need an engagement party," he said. "I wish you wouldn't go to the trouble."

"Of course you need one." Bessie rubbed her hands together in delight just thinking about it. "It'll be spectacular. Flowers, candles, music for dancing. So romantic."

"An engagement party," Lani whispered to herself, the sweet look of longing on her face tearing at Colin.

She wanted it to be real, with all her heart. Knowing that, he felt overwhelmed. What had he done to her? Hell, to *him*. For a moment he couldn't even remember why he had chased her all over town and back. He should have left it alone.

Lani was staring at him. "What did you just say?"

"Nothing."

"No, you most definitely said something." She stepped closer, studying him intensely. "You said you can't remember why you were worried about me."

Great, had he really said that out loud?

"Why were you worried, Colin?"

"You're hearing things."

"I don't think so." She was right in front of him now, smelling like pine cleaner and shampoo and he wanted badly to haul her close and show her exactly what all this insanity did to him.

"You chased me all over town? Really?"

"So?"

At that statement of brilliance, Lani let out a little smile, as if she found his rare petulance very funny.

He didn't find anything even remotely humorous about it, and this time when she took another step toward him, he backed up.

This made her eyes warm, though he had no idea why, and now in addition to the humor he could see so plainly on her face, he also saw affection and more emotion than he knew what to do with. He was painfully aware of their audience when she asked him softly, kindly, "Did you need me for something?"

He stared at her. "Yeah."

"Can you tell me what?"

"Not in mixed company."

Bessie and Lola snickered in delight and left them in peace. Finally.

Silence reigned.

With both his aunts gone, Lani's bravado seemed to

fade. She clasped her hands, studied her feet, then played with a spec of dust on the floor with her toe.

"Lani..." But nothing else came out. Now that he was here, with her right there within his reach, he hadn't a clue as to what to say or do.

She solved that for him. "I'm sorry your marriage didn't work out, Colin." Her voice was quiet, full of sorrow. "I know you must have loved her very much if you haven't wanted to be in another relationship since. A *real* one anyway."

9

LANI HADN'T MEANT to just throw it out like that. She'd really intended to bring up Colin's marriage much more gently. She'd wanted him to understand that she was very sorry he'd gotten so hurt, that she understood how much he must have loved his wife.

And if irrational jealousy pounded through her, she would keep that part to herself.

But after her statement, Colin had carefully closed his mouth, grabbed a sponge and disappeared down the hallway of the medical building.

Lani had let him go. This was neither the time nor the place to hash it out, no matter how much she wanted to comfort him, wanted to encourage him to give love another shot with someone who would never hurt him, with someone who would cherish him until the end of her life.

And if she was thinking that that someone could be her, if she had conveniently forgotten she wanted no more of an emotional tangle than he did, she would live with that.

"You're an idiot," she whispered to herself, shoving her hair out of her face. In one of the private patient rooms, she swept the floor with a vengeance.

"Who told you?"

She nearly dropped her broom.

"I want to know how you know," Colin said, standing in the doorway, quietly furious.

"It doesn't matter." Her heart ached because only a deep, unrelenting pain would cause him to be so upset. She knew first-hand how much damage that kind of anguish could cause. "I'm sorry you got hurt by it, Colin. I'm sorry your heart was broken."

His jaw tightened. His eyes went hard. "I absolutely don't want to talk about it."

"But—"

"Never, Lani."

"It's not a crime to still love her."

The laugh that escaped him was short and hard. "You've got it very wrong."

"Then tell me."

"Just leave it the hell alone."

She leaned on the broom and studied him. "You could tell me about it, you know. I'd listen and maybe you'd feel better."

"I've got a better idea. Let's talk about you. About why you never tell me anything about yourself."

"You've never asked."

"Tell me about your family."

"All right. I have only my great-aunt Jennie. It's been just us for a long time."

"Does the reason for that have anything to do with your nightmares?"

She paled, felt the blood drain right out of her face. "Yes."

"It's also probably the reason you're alone now. Just like me, you're not interested in more hurt. Am I right?"

She crossed her arms, chilled. "I don't think I want to talk about it."

"Well then, we're even, aren't we?"

Damn him for turning this around. It wasn't about her, it was about *him*. He'd never see that, not right now. "I have work."

"Yes, well so do I." And he vanished.

He'd go back to his work, she thought wearily, and bury both himself and his anguish in it, and it would be all the harder to reach him.

She figured he'd done exactly that, so when she heard the crash from the next patient room, she assumed it was Bessie, Lola or Carmen.

She went running, imagining all sorts of things, only to skid to a halt in the doorway.

On his butt, on a very wet floor, surrounded by a spilled bucket and a mop, sat Colin.

He wore a disgusted expression. Lani covered her mouth, but a laugh escaped anyway, making his frown all the more fierce.

"I suppose you think this is funny," he growled.

"Are you all right?"

He shoved to his feet. "Physically? Fine." He patted the seat of his drenched trousers. "Though my ego just took a hell of a beating."

"I'm sorry."

"Yeah? Then why are you grinning?"

Lani shook her head, but ruined it with another laugh that she quickly swallowed. "It's relief that you're okay. Honest."

"Right." He pulled at the material clinging to him.

"I thought you'd left."

"I told you I would help, dammit, and I'm going to help. I just don't want to talk while I do it."

"Then why did you come?"

"You disappeared, I was worried."

"I was working," she pointed out gently.

"I didn't know. I thought maybe you were upset or mad. Maybe you'd decided that—" Swearing, he broke off and looked away. "Never mind."

Her stomach twisted. "That I would leave? I won't, Colin. I told you that."

But she was going to have to prove it, she realized. Not only prove it, but give him the time to accept it as well. She could do that. For him, she could probably do anything.

"People don't always do what they say they're going to do," he said.

"I do." She smiled at his noncommittal grunt. "Oh, Colin. You don't have to follow me around and mop and—" she gestured with her hand to his very wet backside "—do the slip and slide just to keep me."

His eyes narrowed on her, and the laughter she'd been barely holding back escaped.

With a suddenly wicked gaze, he came slowly, purposely, toward her. "You're laughing at me, Lani. Again."

"Now, Colin—" She backed up, right into the door, which shut behind her. She held her broom between her hands like a shield. "I wasn't laughing *at* you...just *with* you."

"Uh-huh." He kept coming, this big, sleek male animal. This big, sleek, wet, *annoyed* male animal.

"It's that you're so cute," she said quickly. "Coming here, wanting to help me—"

He was there in a flash, moving far more quickly and gracefully than she'd expected, sandwiching her between the door and his body.

"I didn't realize how nice it would feel to have you care about me," she managed. Oh, he felt good, so very good, against her. "You gave up your own important work today to come here and fall on your butt—"

He held her head in his big, gentle hands, his body imprisoning hers. "Stop it."

"But it's such a great butt, Colin." She burst out into renewed laughter at his expression.

"Lani? Be quiet." Reaching around her, he flicked the lock on the door, and with a loud, metallic sound, it slid home.

The amusement backed up in her throat, immediately replaced by a searing, heated excitement. "Colin..." Did he have any idea what that look on his face did to her insides? "Your aunts..."

"...will no doubt be listening so you'd better keep it quiet, hadn't you?" She was flattened to the door, between the hard wood and his even harder body. Gentle but inexorable fingers found the rip in the front of her jeans and played with the soft, giving skin on the inside of her thigh.

Her heart thundered in her chest. "I know you're upset because I probed into your personal life..."

Now his other hand slid around to the back of her, toying with the larger rip back there, stroking the flesh just beneath her panty line. "This has nothing to do with anyone else," he informed her, his fingers shifting slightly, playing with the elastic on her hot-pink panties.

Lani forced herself to remain absolutely still, when what she really wanted was to arch into his hand. "Then you're embarrassed about that little pratfall you took." She gasped as he slowly traced the line of the material. "But you don't have to be."

"This isn't about the fall either," he assured her roughly, slipping beneath the material now to cup her bare bottom in his hand. He kneaded it gently, sighing at the connection. "It's about before that. It's about last night and this morning and the fact I can't get you out of my head."

The words broke through her haze of passion, and they meant so much she could hardly speak. "Really? You think about me?"

"Yeah. Really."

"You don't like it."

"Not much," he admitted. "But that doesn't seem to stop me." Abruptly, he backed away from her. Shoving the bucket and mop aside with his foot, he grabbed her wrist and hauled her across the room, to the full-sized hospital bed that Dr. Morrow used to treat his patients. "Lani, I have to touch you."

"You *were* touching me."

"More then."

She couldn't breathe. "Colin, I was thinking—"

"I was, too. You should be quiet now."

She nodded. "Okay."

With a none-too-gentle push, Colin pressed her down on the mattress. The bed groaned when he followed her. Seizing the broom she still held between them, he flung it across the room.

Then his mouth took hers, hot and demanding.

The connection sizzled. Dizzy with it, Lani could only cling to him. Her heart had already been aroused, from the very moment he'd stormed into the office looking for her, so it didn't take much more than a stroke of his tongue to bring her startlingly close to completion.

He tore his mouth away and stared at her. "You're driving me crazy."

"The feeling is mutual." She had gripped his shirt in

fisted hands, holding him close. She couldn't bring herself to let him go. "You were going to touch me, Colin. Why aren't you?"

He settled himself between her legs, spreading them farther to accommodate his body. He rocked against her with a slow, building rhythm that had her moaning, gasping for more, a slave to the motion.

She couldn't keep a thought in her head as her body raced desperately. Colin gripped her hips in his hands, arching them up to better meet his, his erection nestling tightly to the aching flesh between her thighs, and the friction was so delicious she could hardly stand it. His mouth trailed over her jaw to her ear. The sound of his ragged, uneven breathing assured her he was every bit as wild as she. Still fully dressed, she was going to climax, with nothing more than his hips sliding against hers.

"I don't know what's happening," he whispered, bewildered. She writhed against him and he moaned. "This was supposed to be fake, dammit."

Only a few strokes away from blessed orgasm, Lani could do nothing but hang on for dear life. "Don't stop," she begged.

"*Fake,*" he repeated hoarsely, still rocking against her in perfect harmony.

Her body tightened, she couldn't see, could only feel, she was so close. He captured her mouth again, the kiss deep and urgent and so needy Lani's entire heart melted. And just to make sure she lost the rest of her head completely, he stroked his hands over her body, molding and pressing and coaxing, then slowing to kiss her again, until she was whimpering and begging and writhing beneath him.

"Lani, let me, let me—" Rearing up, he unbuttoned

her cotton work shirt, letting out a groan when he found her bare beneath it. He dipped down, nuzzling first, then taking a tight, waiting nipple into his mouth. His hands went to the buttons of her jeans and while he fumbled there, she attacked his shirt, shoving her hands beneath it.

"This is crazy," he muttered, slipping his warm, rough hands into the back of her jeans. Scooping her hips up, he thrust against her again, rubbing her with the hard ridge of his erection. He let out a dark, needy sound and dropped his forehead to hers. "I can't get enough of you, I need more...."

"More," she agreed breathlessly, nearly crying in relief when she heard the rasp of his zipper. He shoved his jeans down, freeing himself. The back of his hand grazed the part of her that was hot and wet for him. Just that light brush of his knuckles was enough to send her once again skittering to the very edge. She tossed her head back as her limbs started to shake. Heat spiraled through her and she grabbed his hand, needing just one more touch to send her over, just one more little touch....

The knock at the door had them both freezing. Hot, unseeing gazes locked on each other.

"Darling?" came Bessie's voice. "We're finished in the front room. Is Lani in there with you?"

Lani loved Bessie, really she did, but at that moment, she wanted to scream and stamp her feet. She wanted to throw a full-blooded tantrum at the fate of Bessie's bad timing.

It wasn't fair! She'd been so close, so very close, that her entire body was damp and trembling and still rocking helplessly.

Above her, a solid mass of taut, quivering sexual an-

imal, Colin growled. His shirt was shoved open, thanks
to her desperate fingers. His zipper was down, his hair
wild, his eyes were beyond description. His chest was
hard and slick, his belly flat and rippled with strength.
Below that...oh, my. He was magnificent.

And furiously aroused.

"Hello, Colin?" Bessie called. The doorknob rattled,
making Lani thankful for the lock.

Colin hadn't moved, and Lani could understand. She
could hardly think. She licked her lips and cleared her
throat, but still her voice sounded weak and trembly.
"We're both in here, Bessie," she managed. "Fighting
some nasty dirt, too." She glanced at Colin. He hadn't
moved or blinked. She could feel him between her
spread legs, hot and throbbing. "We'll...we need a moment," she said weakly.

"No problem," Bessie called cheerfully. "We'll
wait."

She let out a choked laugh. "They'll wait," she whispered up to Colin, who shook his head and groaned.

"Great," he said through clenched teeth. For a moment, he sagged over her, bracing himself on his fore-
arms. His eyes were already shuttered, hiding himself,
so it surprised her when he leaned close and brushed
his lips over hers in one quick, hot, hard kiss.

"Oh, Colin," she murmured against his mouth, holding him tight.

"I know."

"I can't stand it."

"I'm going to kill them," he assured her. "*They'll
wait*," he repeated with disgust, pushing off her and
yanking his shirt back up over his shoulders. "Damn,
they've got timing."

Lani didn't respond.

Colin turned back to her and groaned. She was still sprawled on the bed, clothes awry, hair everywhere, lips wet from his mouth, looking mouthwateringly beautiful.

He struggled to close his zipper over his still raging erection.

Lani lifted an eyebrow. "Careful with that."

He laughed, then winced as he finally got his pants closed. What was it about her? She made him smile, made him laugh. When was the last time anyone had done that for him?

She also made him ache.

He went to her, gently took her hands and pulled her upright. The movement shifted her shirt open again, and her warm, full breasts spilled out. When he drew the material closed, he let his knuckles brush over her one last time.

She pressed against him. "I didn't want to stop," she whispered, burying her face in his neck. "I was so close!"

Carefully he sucked in both his breath *and* the urge to haul her to him. He searched hard and deep, but from nowhere within himself could he summon up the need to flinch from her affection.

He didn't understand it. They weren't having sex and yet he still wanted to hold her. It was a very new concept for him.

And a scary one.

She hadn't moved, other than to burrow into him. "Come on," he whispered, taking her shoulders and straightening her. "We have to pull it together, Lani."

"No." She let her shirt fall open again and when his eyes crossed with lust, she hummed with satisfaction, drawing him back to her. "I don't want to pull it together, I want to come apart. With you."

His hands were full of hot, sexy, needy woman, the first woman to actually attract him in far too long. In light of that, he couldn't believe he was holding her away from him, begging her to stop. "Lani, please."

"Yoo-hoo!" Lola tapped cheerfully on the door. "Lani, honey, where's the—"

"We'll be right there!" Colin bellowed. "Hurry," he whispered, drawing Lani to her feet and yanking up her jeans. "Snap them," he urged while he attempted to tuck in her shirt.

"That's the last time I ask them for their help." Irritation swam in her voice as she finally—thankfully—fastened all her clothes, hiding that gorgeous, mind-numbing body from view.

Colin smiled, not an easy feat in his condition. "I thought you liked them."

"Well, I changed my mind!" She had turned away, but glanced at him over her shoulder, her eyes still smoldering with heat and unfed passion. "Colin?"

He ran his fingers through his hair, knowing it was hopeless. They both looked as though they'd been well loved.

Loved.

Oh, no. "Yeah?" he asked warily.

"Sometimes people make mistakes, you know? Especially in marriage and affairs of the heart."

"Lani—"

"I know you were hurt the first time around, and I'm so, so sorry. But for whatever reason, you're alone again." She touched him gently, slid her hand over his heart. "Maybe you could give love another try sometime...you know, with the right woman."

She thought he was still pining over his ex-wife. Nothing could be further from the truth, but how could someone like Lani understand? His wife had not only destroyed his belief in everlasting love, but she'd slept with his ex-partner as well, then had taken them both to the cleaners financially. He couldn't care less about the loss of that first fortune. Or even the marriage. But dammit, he still to this day mourned Max, with whom he'd been friends all his life.

He hadn't had a friend since, not a real one.

There had been no emotional attachments for him. He'd wanted nothing to worry about. Nothing to hurt over.

And now Lani was looking at him with those sweet, caring eyes, the ones that told him she was quickly becoming much more than a temporary situation in his life.

It scared him. It wasn't supposed to be like this.

"I would never hurt you, Colin," she whispered. "I'd be careful with your heart."

"Don't," he said hoarsely, rubbing a hand over his eyes. "I can't do this."

Something flickered in her expression. Hurt, and even more devastating, disappointment. But she nodded and turned from him.

She reached for the lock, then hesitated, staring at the closed door for a long moment. "You'll have to try sometime, you know," she said softly to the wood. "You can't hide forever."

Watch me, he thought, hardening both his mind and his heart before he followed her out.

LANI CAME to Colin's house that night, her car loaded with ammunition.

Ammunition to make the house a home.

She had four more plants, two lovely watercolors painted by a local artist who was a casual friend of hers, and a framed picture of Colin she'd got from one of the recent newspaper articles written on him.

Her heart was armed, too, with compassion and patience. She hoped it would be enough.

Colin wasn't home. No surprise. Most likely he was still at his office, attempting to hide from what was happening between them.

She knew she was doing it again, pretending that this wasn't pretend. She could get seriously hurt that way and she knew it, but somehow she couldn't seem to help herself.

She couldn't explain it, this strange elation she felt, but for the first time in twenty-odd years, she was prepared to give her heart away. Hell, she was prepared to *toss* it away, hard and long, straight at Colin.

She couldn't wait until he was willing to catch it, but she didn't fool herself, she had lots of work ahead of her. Colin was no more ready to accept what was happening between them than she'd been only days before.

She had come to a rather startling realization. She wanted a real relationship. Not the superficial ones of her past, where she could, and did, walk away before any attachments occurred. She'd been doing that nearly all her life.

It was far too late to walk away from Colin.

How he would panic at her thoughts. He'd hate that she was thinking of a future beyond the pretense. What had happened in his marriage to make him so leery?

How could Lani convince him that it was okay to have loved and lost, but that he *had* to try again? Convince him that without love his heart would wither and die? That she knew this firsthand, and that together they could help one another?

While the house was quiet, she spread out the plants and the pictures, attacking the living room first. The other rooms would follow, gradually, and she could hardly imagine how wonderful the house would be when it was homey and warm.

But for now, she'd start with this room. It was crying out for attention. The floors were bare wood, beautiful but…well, bare. The walls were a sophisticated, cool cream, and also far too stark. The brick fireplace was empty, too, and she had just the picture to hang over it.

Standing on a stepladder, she climbed high, hammer in hand. A dreamy smile crossed her face. It would be so lovely in the winter, she thought, with a fire blazing. Pretty pictures on the walls, some thick rugs tossed here and there. She and Colin, together, enjoying it.

Her dreamy smile grew into a full-fledged grin. She couldn't wait.

Since the stepladder wasn't quite tall enough, she got up on the very tippy top of it, where a bright orange sticker warned her against doing that very thing.

She stretched with all her might, the hammer precariously balanced in one hand, a nail in the other. She was still grinning, ridiculously happy, anticipating the long, hot night ahead in Colin's arms.

"What the hell are you doing?"

At the unexpected, angry voice—Colin's voice—Lani jerked.

And fell.

10

IT ALL HAPPENED too fast. One moment Colin was staring at Lani and her hammer, the next she was far too still, in a terrifyingly crumpled heap on the floor.

Colin hit his knees on the stone hearth beside her, his hands cupping her face. "Lani!" *Oh, God, she didn't move.* "Lani!"

His heart was in his throat. She was lying too quietly. Quickly, he ran his hands over her body, but he didn't find anything broken.

Then he discovered the already huge bump on the back of her head, and let out one concise oath. "Lani? Come on, baby. Open your eyes."

She did, slowly, blinking in confusion and Colin took his first breath since he'd watched her tumble off the ladder.

"Don't get up," he demanded when she tried to sit. He held her down. "Don't move yet."

But she shifted, and at the movement her skin went green and pasty. "Nope, you're absolutely right," she said weakly, wincing. "No moving." And she closed her eyes.

Panic scampered up his spine. "Lani!"

"Shh." She groaned. "Please, don't...don't talk. My head is going to explode."

"Okay, that's it. Come on." As gently as he could, he scooped her into his arms.

Her head lolled against his chest and she moaned softly, lifting her hands to hold it still. "Put me down." Her voice was a thready murmur and Colin clenched his teeth at her obvious pain.

"We're going to the hospital. I think you have a concussion."

She blinked at him, clearly disoriented, and his alarm escalated.

"No hospital."

"You hit your head too damn hard on the stone hearth. We're going to get it checked out."

"No." But the protest was feeble, and her color was even worse now, her skin so light it was nearly transparent. "I'm...okay," she whispered. "Really."

Like hell. "Better safe than sorry. I want to make sure." He strode to the door, the warm, hurting bundle in his arms breaking his heart.

His fault, dammit.

"No doctor," she protested. "I told you...I'm fine."

"Let's prove it."

"Your mom and aunts...they think I'm cooking dinner while they're getting...manicures."

He could tell talking was difficult, and her words were slurred, making him walk even faster while trying to keep her cradled against him. "They can fend for themselves." He had her in the foyer now but the summer evening had chilled.

"They can't cook, Colin."

She was worried about his family when she should be concentrating on herself. It wasn't a stretch to express his fear for her in anger. "Look, if they can learn to clean toilets, they can cook." Hoisting her closer, he grabbed his denim jacket from the closet with one hand and tried to toss it over her, but she jerked in his arms.

"Down!"

"You're going to the hosp—"

"Colin—" She looked horrified and had gone pea-green. "I'm not fine anymore."

He'd never felt like this—so full of fear over another human being. "I know, sweetheart, I'm just going to—"

"*Down*," she cried, shoving at him until he practically dropped her.

The hand she held frantically across her mouth finally clued him in and as she stumbled past him into the kitchen, he went after her, wrapping a securing arm around her waist as she leaned into the kitchen sink and threw up.

"Go away," she told him halfway through, when he was trying to hold back her hair and wipe her forehead and support her all at the same time.

He didn't, but stayed right with her, fretting, panicking, wondering if an ambulance would be faster.

When she was done, she sank to the floor and glared at him.

He braced himself for recriminations. He deserved it, whatever she said to him. He hunkered down beside her, the better to see into her hurting eyes.

"How could you call me sweetheart when I'm too sick to enjoy it?" she demanded, smacking him lightly on the chest.

He stared at her. "I did not call you that."

"Yes you did." She leaned against the cupboard and shivered. "I heard it."

"I— You're mistaken."

"No." Energy drained, she sighed wearily, a sound that pulled at some elementary core of him.

He pulled her close to him. "Any better at all?"

"Some." But she closed her eyes. Her body still

shook, small tremors of shock that made *him* feel ill. "How many fingers?" he pressed, holding up two.

"Too many." Miserable, she looked at the mess she'd made. "I just cleaned this kitchen."

Then, still in his arms, she fainted.

THE GOOD NEWS was that Lani's concussion wasn't serious.

The bad news was that they kept her overnight in the hospital.

Or maybe that was the good news in disguise, Colin thought grimly, as he showered the next morning. He'd spent a long, miserable night in a chair beside Lani's hospital bed watching her breathe.

Under different circumstances, she would have been in his arms, beneath him, writhing, sighing...coming.

Damn. He needed sleep.

It was really ironic, he decided, yanking a towel around his hips and studying his dark expression in the steamed mirror of his bathroom. Ironic that he hadn't been sure sleeping with Lani was the smart thing to do, and yet now that he'd decided differently, he couldn't manage to arrange it. He was getting a little tired of the constant erection he had going.

Like some lust-struck teen, he was mooning over a woman who had put her life on hold just to help him out. Her smile lit up his day and made him smile helplessly back. One affectionate touch from her could make his heart soar.

Truth was, he thought about her all the time when he was supposed to be concentrating on his project.

She made him laugh, made him think, made him want to please her, and in return he'd given her nothing but heartache and trouble.

He'd *yelled* at her, dammit. She'd been trying to warm up his house with her world, and he'd yelled at her.

She was going to be okay.

Gripping the edge of the sink, he bowed his head and squeezed his eyes shut. She was going to be fine, she could come home this morning. The doctor had said so, both hers and the one he'd hired for a second opinion.

He closed his weary eyes, but then he had to relive in slow motion the sight of Lani falling, her huge eyes wide in terror, before her head cracked against the stone hearth.

In that first moment of horror for Colin, when she lay still, pale and unresponsive, he'd thought that if anything happened to her, he would die.

Then her eyes had flickered open.

He didn't want to go through anything like that ever again. Lani didn't remember the fall, but the doctor had assured them both that was normal.

Normal.

His Lani wasn't a normal woman, she was bright and sunny and almost painfully easy to love.

Love.

That had been his first, instinctive thought, and it was enough to have his blood pressure rocketing. He didn't love her, he *couldn't* love her. Couldn't love anyone.

He repeated this to himself as he raced through dressing. Then he broke three national speed records to get back to the hospital before Lani awoke and found herself alone.

But he didn't love her.

LANI WASN'T SLEEPING and she wasn't alone. She had both Lola and Bessie by her side telling her stories of Colin as a child.

They were wonderful, warm women, and hearing about Colin was heartwarming, but Lani could neither smile nor laugh. Her head throbbed. She was queasy, dizzy and tired.

And she wanted Colin.

Can't always have what you want, she told herself firmly, and forced her attention back to Colin's aunts. They were talking about the time Colin had taken apart the engine on his father's brand new BMW Sedan.

Colin had been twelve at the time.

She knew how smart he was and how precocious a child he must have been. She also knew how much his family loved him and wanted him to be happy.

Which was why, of course, they were doing their best to entertain her. She could tell they didn't quite understand what she saw in Colin, but they were grateful and relieved that she saw something. Since loyalty was everything to Lani, it endeared them to her.

"I'm going to be okay, you know," she told them. "You don't have to be here."

"Oh, honey. We *want* to be," Bessie said.

But both Bessie and Lola glanced for the hundredth time at the hospital door, and it made Lani smile even as tears burned her eyes. "I know what you're doing."

They tried to look innocent. "We're just watching over you," Lola said casually.

"You're afraid if you don't stay and guard things, namely me, that I'll leave Colin."

Their guilty faces said it all.

"I made a promise," she told them. "And to me, promises are sacred." They didn't have to know that the promise wasn't to love and cherish, but to lie.

Closing her eyes didn't shake the strange sense of melancholy, not when she kept reliving that moment just before her fall. The one she'd told Colin and the doctor she couldn't remember.

What the hell are you doing? Colin had demanded, the anger in his voice unmistakable.

She really was an idiot. A sentimental one, but an idiot all the same. How could she have thought he'd appreciate what she'd been trying to do to the house? *His* house.

Obviously he was so angry with her that he couldn't stand to see her. She'd been half out of it when he'd first brought her to the hospital and asleep by the time X rays had been finished. She'd slept fitfully all night in her darkened room, awakened every few hours by a nurse asking one silly question after another. She hadn't even bothered to open her eyes, but she hadn't heard Colin, not once.

It was morning now and still no sight of him.

Oh, yeah, she'd definitely blown it.

"The doctor said you're going to be fine enough to enjoy your engagement party," Bessie said now, quietly, "but if you don't think you'll be up to it, we'll understand."

They were so looking forward to it. And secretly, she had been, too. She may have had intimacy issues, but she was only human. A very female human at that. She had fantasies about her wedding, her real wedding, with a flowing white dress, a beautiful cake, an exotic honeymoon.

A huge, elaborate engagement party sounded so thrilling. If only it were real. "I'll be fine."

"Oh, good, because we're so excited. Look, I brought you something to read," Lola said, handing her a brightly colored bag. Lani pulled out a book with a red satin ribbon tied around it. *"How to Sexually Please a Man So That He'll Never Leave You?"*

Bessie gasped. *"Lola!* That's...that's pornography!"

"Not porn," Lola corrected with a dignified sniff. "Erotica." She exploded into giggles. "And it's very interesting reading, I'll have you know."

Lani flipped through the illustrations. "Wow!" They were graphic and definitely designed to titillate. She tipped her head to study a particularly interesting full-page photo. "Just...wow!"

Both sisters crowded close to see over her shoulder.

"Thought you might find something useful in there." Lola grinned. "Look at that. He's awfully good."

"Honestly, Lola." Bessie shook her head. "What's the sense in being a closet erotica reader if you're going to tell everyone?"

"Hey, I didn't tell her we read the book already." Lola blushed and bit her lip. "Oops."

Lani smiled around the pounding behind her eyes. "Thank you." She was surprised to find herself close to tears. "It means so much to me that you'd share."

"Oh, honey." Equally touched, Bessie smiled with suspiciously bright eyes.

Lola wasn't quite as sentimental, but she cared, too, and Lani knew it.

Lani fell asleep soon after, holding the book close to her heart.

WHEN COLIN came in a short time later, his aunts had been kicked out by the nurse. Lani was asleep, her expression tight from pain, her skin far too pale.

Fear stabbed him, even though her doctor had just signed her release. He whispered her name softly, not wanting to disturb her if she was sleeping deeply. She didn't budge. Gently, he touched her hand, the one holding a book close to her chest.

He took one look at the title and his eyes nearly bugged out of his head. "*How to Sexually Please a Man?*"

Lani's eyes flew open. "Colin!" She slipped the book under her blanket and tried to look casual.

"Interesting reading material."

She blushed wildly. "I don't know what you're talking about."

"Uh-huh." He tugged at her blanket until it came free. In her hands was the incriminating evidence.

Caught, she lifted her chin. "Your aunts gave it to me."

He started to laugh, then realized she was serious. "You're not kidding?"

"No."

He opened the book, and his eyes widened at some of the wilder illustrations. He pictured Lani reading it, getting ideas, and became aroused just at the thought. Slowly, he handed the book back to her.

Her eyes were shiny and aware and...hot. Very hot.

"You've read it," he said, his voice gravelly with the desire that never seemed to be far beneath the surface around her.

"A little," she admitted, dropping her gaze. "I wanted to know if it was true."

"If what was true?"

"If I sexually pleased you, would you never be able to leave? Or to ask *me* to?"

He stared at her. "I don't think you feel good enough for this conversation. You're pale and shaky. The doctor said—"

"Chicken."

"All right, fine." He didn't hedge, couldn't, not while pinned by the heat in her eyes. Rising from the uncomfortable chair where he'd spent the night, he sank to her bed, put a hand on either side of her hips. "I think you know that you sexually please me, Lani. In fact, we're so hot together, I'm surprised we haven't spontaneously combusted."

Her eyes smoldered.

He knew his did, too. "But I think you also know that what's happening to us is more than sex. Much more."

"And it's not what you wanted," she concluded, searching his face carefully.

"I never wanted such a connection, no," he admitted.

"I made you mad last night." Lani reached for one of his hands. "I was putting things in your house without asking, and now you don't want me anymore."

No. God, no. "I was mad at *me* last night, because when I walked in and saw what you were doing, and how right it all seemed, I panicked. I've been very busy, Lani, trying to avoid you and what you make me feel. My temper's frayed. All control is gone, flat gone." He studied her hand in his and sighed. "My project isn't getting done because I can't concentrate on work. That's never happened before. And when I look into your eyes, I see the terrifying truth."

"What truth?"

He grimaced, stood and walked the length of the hospital room before turning back to her.

Everything about her in the big white room seemed so vulnerable. Her pale features. Her narrow shoulders. Those expressive eyes.

"Colin, what truth?"

"I accused you of forgetting this was all pretend. But

the truth is, it's me that keeps forgetting." He turned and stared grimly out the window.

Behind him, on the bed, Lani remained silent. "I'm sorry, I'm so damn sorry you got hurt," he said. "I sat there by you all night crucifying myself because it's my fault, but I can't go on like this. It has to be pretend between us, Lani. That's all it can be."

"You sat by me the entire night?"

He turned and saw the stunned surprise on her pale face. "Did you think I would leave you here alone?" But he saw that's exactly what she thought. He swore softly. "That's not very flattering."

"But it's just pretend between us." She repeated his words, slightly mocking. "What else would I think?"

"I care for you," he said carefully. "More than I want to. I've always been honest with you."

"Yes," she agreed, rubbing her head. "You're right. You've been honest. Don't worry, Colin, I don't blame you. There's no reason for all that guilt I see on your face."

"You're free to leave here," he said quietly, coming close. "But you need rest and to be taken care of. Will you let me bring you home?"

"Are you worried I'll renege on our deal?"

"No," he lied.

Lani let out a little laugh, which made her wince. She tossed back her covers and stood shakily, pushing his hand away when he tried to help steady her. "I'm fine, I don't need taking care of. Just a little headache, that's all." Her eyes were unusually cool, even as she weaved a bit on her feet. "And yes, I'll come with you. I gave you my word, remember?"

He remembered. And hated himself for it.

"HOW LONG are you going to be mad at me?" Colin asked.

Lani was sprawled in his bed. He couldn't help but notice she was wearing a T-shirt, *his* T-shirt, and she looked so damn good he had to stay at the door so that he could be sure to control himself.

She didn't answer him.

Her face was pale. Her eyes were lined with delicate purple shadows. His heart hurt just looking at her. "Lani?"

She leaned back against his pillows, her face inscrutable. "I'm going to be mad for a while. Probably." She looked away. "Well, for at least a few more minutes."

"Isn't there anything I can do to change that?"

"Sure." She met his gaze again, her eyes daring him. "Tell me about the ex-wife you still love."

"Lani."

"That's what I thought. Too chicken."

How was he supposed to tell her that he wasn't nursing that kind of pain, but a deeper one, the betrayal and loss of his best friend? It humiliated him, shamed him. "I'd rather talk about that fascinating book." He gestured to the erotica sitting on his nightstand. It was open, and when he moved closer he saw the chapter she'd been reading was titled, "Pleasure Him Every Night and You'll Never Regret It. Here's How."

"Did you finish that chapter?" he asked, his voice thick.

"Maybe." Her lips quirked, and in that moment, he saw a flicker of the warm, loving Lani he'd come to care for so much.

Unable to stop himself, he smiled at her. "That looks good, that almost-smile on your face. I missed that."

"Oh, Colin." She melted, all ice gone. "You drive me crazy, but I miss you."

"I'm right here."

"That's not what I meant."

He knew what she meant, and he was helpless against the pull of the promise in her voice. But there was lingering hurt there, too, hurt *he'd* put there.

She was willing to listen to his past. His hurts. And suddenly, he wanted to tell her everything. "I don't still love my ex-wife. And I'm not pining away for her, either. It's not what you think."

"Then tell me."

"It was a long time ago. I thought we were happy, even though I knew she'd married me for my money—"

"Oh, Colin."

"It's true, and it's okay," he told her, hating the pity, knowing there'd be more before he was through. "I wanted her, too. She was beautiful and elegant and everything I thought I'd need. We were young, just out of school." He lifted a shoulder. "I worked a lot, and she hated that. She needed attention, lots of it, and I didn't give it. I couldn't—the truth is, I didn't see what the problem was. So, out of boredom, she struck up a friendship with my partner, my best friend, Max. She started off trying to convince him to have me work less. She ended up convincing him to—" Unable to stand still, he walked the length of his bedroom to stare out the picture window. "You know, I've never said any of this out loud. I've never been able to tell anyone."

"You can tell me," said Lani quietly from the bed. "You can tell me anything."

"I know." He drew in a deep breath and concentrated on the garden beyond his window. "She seduced

Max, stole all my money and left town. Six months later I received divorce papers in the mail."

"How long ago was this?" she asked gently.

"Five years. I guess you could say I've not let a lot of people close to me since then."

"I think that's a fair assessment."

There was so much compassion in her voice he couldn't look at her. "I still blame her for Max," he said roughly. "We'd been friends all my life." He tried to be distant and tough, willing Lani to understand, to somehow help him resist her. "I promised myself I'd never get involved again. *Ever.* And I meant it."

"You're blaming the wrong person," she said quietly.

"I'm not blaming you."

"I meant yourself. It wasn't your fault. And it wasn't all hers, either. Your friend betrayed you, too, not just your wife. You were hit twice, hard, and I don't blame you for remaining hurt all this time. But Colin, not all women are so weak. Not all of us will betray their vows, and break the law while they're at it."

He shook his head. "I don't blame all women. That would be silly."

"Very," Lani agreed. "But I just realized, I haven't been as patient as I could be. I'll try harder, and maybe you will, too." Scooting to one side of the bed, she lifted his own covers, wordlessly inviting him in. "We're in a situation neither of us are easy with, but I think we can still salvage something and make the most of it, don't you?"

His heart was suddenly in his throat.

"Won't you hold me?" she asked. "Hold me as we've both wanted for too long now?"

He was there, doing exactly that, with no recollection of kicking off his shoes and diving into the bed.

With a slow touch, she smoothed his hair back and ran her fingers over his face. She cupped his jaw, studying him.

"What do you see?"

"You." She smiled. "There's not much of the successful inventor here right now." She looked pleased at that, and laughed when he frowned. "Don't get me wrong," she assured him. "I like that man. But this one—" her thumb slid over his lower lip and his entire body tightened in response "—this man is so much more. He's warm and loving and incredibly handsome. Colin..." her voice went husky with emotion "...you're the most wonderful thing in my life."

He knew he was staring at her with a dopey look of wonder on his face, and for once he couldn't master the control to mask it. She looped her arms around his neck and kissed him softly, then less softly. Then with her tongue.

"Must have been a hell of a chapter," he said, gasping when they broke apart for air.

She let out a slow, sexy grin that had him grinning back in return. "Yeah, it was." She snuggled close, pressing all those warm, lush curves against him. "Want to know what I learned?"

Before he could answer, she had snaked her hands beneath his shirt, touching him with eager, seeking hands. She unbuttoned his shirt, then shoved it off so she could touch his chest. Not stopping there, she slid the zipper on his pants down, then looked up at him. "If anyone stops us this time, I'm going to hurt them."

He let out a laugh that ended up as a groan because

she'd slipped her hands inside and touched everything she found, and she'd found plenty.

Desire pumped through him as he buried all ten fingers in her cloud of blond hair, and holding her to him, seared them both with a long soul-searching kiss. It surprised him, this desperate need he had to keep that connection, that special, hot, wet mating of tongues. "Was this in the book?" he asked.

"No, I made all that up. Here—" She laughed breathlessly as she cupped him in her palms. Her fingers moved on him and he nearly lost it. "*That's* in the book," she whispered, breathing heavily in his ear. "And so is this..."

He moaned under her greedy fingers.

He wanted her skin to skin, wanted her legs entwined with his, wanted, wanted, wanted *everything*. It had been so long for him, and with all their aborted attempts at lovemaking over the past days, he was painfully aroused, so much so that his bones ached with it. "I want to see you," he murmured, and pulled off her shirt.

She wasn't wearing anything underneath.

Enthralled, he watched his fingers on her pale breasts, mesmerized by the way her nipples hardened when he tormented them with the tip of his tongue. He untied her sweatpants and slowly slid them down her smooth, toned legs.

She wasn't wearing anything beneath them, either, and he groaned at the sight stretched out before him. "Oh, baby," he whispered. "You're something. I've got to taste you."

She gripped and ungripped fistfuls of the sheets, writhing beneath him, panting his name as he traced over her with his tongue. When she shattered, crying and shuddering, he held her, rocked her as she slowly came back to her senses. Then he started all over again.

"I want you..." she managed when she could "...inside me."

He couldn't breathe, couldn't think beyond doing just that. He reached into his drawer by the bed, into the box he'd put there and tore open a foil packet while she watched, her eyes heavy and full of promise.

He came back to her, letting out a shuddery breath at the feel of her beneath him. "Open for me," he whispered. "Yeah..." he moaned as he sank in deep "...just like that."

She sighed his name.

"Wrap your legs.... Ahh, Lani." He buried his face in the softness of her neck, surrounding himself with her. He could never get enough, never. He felt her muscles start to shake as he slowly pulled back, then again sank into her.

Her head tossed back and forth on the pillow.

He thrust again. And then again. Because he had to, he gathered her close and watched as her eyes glazed, as she gripped him tight and sobbed his name.

His last conscious thought before he followed her into paradise was that if she read the rest of that book, she just might kill him.

11

HE OVERSLEPT. A shock, because Colin never overslept. His inner clock was as reliable as any alarm...or had been until this morning.

He was sprawled on his stomach, and given the chill hitting his bare butt, the covers were long gone. Groggy, he lifted his head and groaned when he saw that it was nearly nine o'clock.

His staff would get a big kick out of this since he knew Claudia had made certain each and every one knew about his engagement.

He'd get those sly looks, the ones that said they knew *exactly* what he'd been doing all night long.

They'd be right. He cracked open another eye and saw the empty foil packets scattered on the floor. He grinned. Oh, yeah, they'd made a considerable dent in his supply.

He felt insatiable. Unable to stop grinning, he rolled over, ready for more.

But he was alone.

Lani was gone. There was an indentation on the pillow where her head had been, giving him hazy images of how they'd finally slept, limbs entangled, faces close, but the sheets were cold now.

His heart constricted. No reason for panic, he told himself. It had just been sex.

Really *great* sex.

Then he saw the note on the nightstand.

Colin,
Had to work. Couldn't bring myself to wake you, you looked too cute.
Looking forward to sharing the next chapter in the book.

Love, Lani

Cute? He wasn't cute. But just thinking about the next chapter brought his early morning hard-on to new levels of *hard*.

He hit the shower, closed his eyes to the hot, pounding spray and pretended that the "Love, Lani" part of the note didn't mean what he knew it did.

He had nearly convinced himself it was nothing, just a way of signing a note, when he walked into his kitchen. He was still barefoot, his shirt unbuttoned, a tie hanging loose around his neck in anticipation of a meeting with the Institute's founder.

Had Lani eaten? he wondered.

The thought stopped him in his tracks. He wasn't her keeper. She'd been managing to take care of herself for some time now without any help at all. He shouldn't worry.

But this strange protective possessiveness was startling and not a little uncomfortable. "It'll pass," he assured himself, coming to an abrupt stop.

Sitting at his table were his mother, Bessie and Lola, wearing wide, knowing grins.

"What?" he grumbled. "You've never seen a man desperate for coffee before?"

"Is that all you're desperate for?" Lola asked sweetly.

"In my books, a man's in bad shape when he talks to himself," Bessie decided. "And can't even properly dress himself for company." She tsked at his appearance.

Scowling, Colin started to button his shirt. "Since when are you company?"

"Darling." His mother looked at him with tenderness. "You seem a bit...well, unlike yourself."

"I'm late." He moved to the counter.

"We're here because we love you, you know that."

"I thought you were here to torture me." The last button at his neck felt like a noose.

"No, that was before you got engaged. The point is, we're here for you." His mother was hedging a bit, which was very unlike her. "By any chance," she asked, "is there anything—anything at all—that you'd like to talk to us about?"

He laughed. "I know all about the birds and the bees, Mother, thanks."

"Oh, you." But she laughed, too. "You know what I mean."

He thought about thanking his aunt Bessie for giving Lani such delightful reading material. Thought also about thanking them for the previous interruptions because last night had been the most incredibly passionate night of his life.

"I'm fine," he said instead.

"And in love," Lola added.

Whoa. All three women were watching him now, waiting breathlessly on the edges of their seats.

"Right?" Bessie pressed. "You're totally, one-hundred-percent, can't-live-without-her, irrevocably, head-over-heels in love?"

He shook his head. "Okay, what's this really about?"

"We saw Lani this morning," his mother said. "She practically floated down the stairs. She's lovely, Son, and so special. I love her already."

"But?"

"But if you're just toying with her to get me off your back, I'll never forgive myself."

"Frankly, Colin," Bessie interrupted, "we're not sure you deserve her."

"What?" He couldn't believe it. "You've been hounding me to get married, and now—"

"If you hurt that dear, sweet child..."

"Believe me, she's not a child," he informed his mother.

"Colin!" Lola gave him the evil eye. "Don't forget, we brought you into this world, and trust me, we can take you out again."

Colin managed to laugh. "This is a joke."

His mother stood and came close. She reached for his hands, touching him for the first time in a long time. "Colin, I love you. I want you to be happy. I think you could have that with Lani, but I don't know if you're going to let yourself do it. If you don't, or can't, you're going to hurt her. I feel responsible for that."

"Well, don't."

Her smile was sad. "I can't help it. Let go, Colin. Let go of your painful past and move on. That's all I want for you. I'd like to see you let yourself love with Lani."

"How do you know I'm not?"

"I know."

"I don't have time for this," he decided, pulling away. He grabbed his keys from the counter. "I wish the three of you would make up your damn minds. You want me married, you don't want me married...you're driving me crazy. I have work."

But it wasn't work he thought about on the drive into town; it was a sweet, blue-eyed blonde.

COLIN PARKED and entered his building. Just being here made him feel better.

Today he'd be able to work. *Had* to work. He had some great ideas he wanted to start on right away.

Claudia stood when he came to her desk. Her face was pale and she looked as if she had a terrible secret.

His stomach fell. "What's up?"

"Here's your messages." She handed him a small stack of notes.

"Claudia, what's the matter?"

"Maybe you should get some coffee before you head to your office?"

"No, I need to get started. Are you all right?"

Again she dodged the question. "Your cleaning crew is still in there."

Lani. His heart leaped. "Okay."

"Um..." She hesitated, then shook her head. "Never mind."

With one last look at her, Colin walked down the hallway, thinking Lani shouldn't be working, not so soon after her concussion. She should be in bed. Maybe he'd put her there himself.

Yeah, he liked that idea.

Then he stood in the doorway to his office, staring in horror at the crushed mess of metal and delicate laser model laying on his floor. Above it, tears in her eyes, stood Lani.

Carmen stood quietly next to her, looking both defeated and afraid. Refusing to acknowledge Colin's presence, she stared at her clenched hands.

He gritted his teeth. His ruined prototype looked like a cheap two-dollar toy.

"I'm so sorry, Colin," Lani said quickly. "It was a terrible accident. Carmen was dusting and—"

"It's ruined."

His eyes were dark, angry and colder than Lani had ever seen them. "Yes, I know. I'm so sorry."

"I'd like to talk to you alone," he said in a terribly quiet voice.

"But—"

"Now."

Lani could hardly move she was so upset. Awkwardly, she made a few signs, and for once Carmen didn't pretend to not understand.

With one last furtive glance at Colin, the older woman escaped through the door.

It was the first time she'd left Colin's presence without sticking out her tongue.

Despite Lani's best efforts not to cry, two tears squeezed out, slid down her cheeks. "God, Colin. I feel sick."

"That's because you shouldn't be working today, dammit."

"Not from the concussion. From what I've done! Tell me the cost of the damage."

"It's irreplaceable, Lani."

It was his tone that got her, that distant tone that told her she was nothing to him but an irresponsible maid. "Everything can be replaced for the right amount," she said. "Tell me the cost and I promise to somehow—"

He laughed. *Laughed.* "You could work for the rest of your life cleaning and still not make enough."

The implication of that sank in. She knew he was angry, he had a right to be. She had made a horrible, heart-breaking mistake and she would do anything she could to rectify it.

What couldn't be rectified was her pride. "Are you telling me there's nothing I can do to make this better?"

"Firing her would be a great start."

"Carmen?"

"Who else?"

"I..." She didn't understand why he would ask such a thing, but she thought of Carmen's three grandchildren, the ones that Carmen struggled to raise by herself. Lani could never live with herself if she fired the woman, but that was beside the point. She would never choose the welfare of four lives over the value of one thing, no matter how important that one thing was. "I can't believe you can ask me to do that."

"I'm not asking, I'm telling."

"I don't follow orders well," she warned him, her voice shaking. "Not even for you."

"You'd keep her after this?" he asked incredulously. "After she broke the laser prototype?"

Now she understood and was overwhelmed with sadness for his quick judgment. "Carmen didn't break the model, Colin. *I* did."

"No."

"I tried to tell you, you didn't want to listen. Carmen was dusting and saw a spider. She made a funny strangled noise and I jerked around. When I did, my elbow bumped the laser. It shattered before I could catch it."

His eyes were hard and shuttered. "You're covering for her. You wouldn't be so clumsy."

The sorrow spread through her veins, killing her spirit. "Then you don't know very much about me. Certainly less than I thought if you think I'd fire Carmen over my own error."

"I know you better than you think. You have a save-the-world-heart. You're trying to save Carmen, and she doesn't deserve it."

"I'm telling you, it wasn't her fault."

He stared at her, clearly unable to believe she could be so loyal. But then again, he hadn't had a lot of loyalty in his life. She tried to remember this and looked for a sign of the warm, loving, passionate man she'd been with the night before.

He was completely gone, hidden behind a mask of grim, unforgiving anger.

But she did see a flicker of something that looked suspiciously like fear, and it made her heart hurt. "You're using this as an excuse to push me away," she realized. "Did last night scare you that much?"

A tightening of his lips was her only answer.

"It was the real thing and you can't take it." She let out a hurt little laugh. "I'm right, aren't I? You can't trust me enough to give me your heart. You woke up and panicked. You needed a reason to be hard and ungiving, to back off and tell yourself you were right in doing so. I just gave you that excuse. Well, damn you, Colin West. After all we've shared, you still can't do it. You can't let yourself love me."

"You're forgetting again, dammit, that this is all pretend."

"Oh, no. It stopped being pretend the moment you first touched me, and you know it. And even if you somehow didn't, then last night should have proved it to you once and for all."

"No." But his voice was hoarse. "You agreed to this, Lani. I knew I was asking a lot, but you agreed to play house. It's all a show."

He was right, but that only made her feel worse. She

wrapped her arms around herself for comfort. "I realize this is the last straw for you, Colin. You see your project set back even further now. You see me having to stay longer. You see your peaceful, quiet existence permanently in your past. I understand. I'll back out of this office job. And out of the deal, if you'd like. But don't you dare lie to my face and tell me you never had feelings for me."

He dragged in a ragged breath and admitted nothing.

She looked at him, hoping to find a piece of the man she'd fallen for, but there was no one but the successful, rich, disdainful inventor, the one who could and would trust no one.

"I was there last night," she said urgently, trying one last time to reach him, knowing this was her last chance. "I saw your face when we made love, I saw the wonder and the affection and the heat swimming in your eyes. You can't tell me it was fake. I won't believe you."

Colin had no idea what to say to her, not when his head was spinning with the need to run away, far and fast. Yes, he lusted after her, deeply. But lust wasn't love.

He didn't do love.

He simply couldn't allow himself to fall for this woman who had turned his life upside down without trying. Couldn't allow himself to get in that deep because he wouldn't be able to take it when it was over.

"Obviously you're not ready for this," she said, pinching her lips together. He thought he saw more moisture fill her eyes, which was like a knife to his gut, but she blinked, clearing it away.

Gently, she scooped the shattered laser onto her

dustpan, then very carefully set the entire mess on his desk. "I'm very sorry, Colin," she said quietly, straightening. "I'd do anything to be able to take it back. I know I can't. I only wish that you'd understand I'd rather rip out my own heart than hurt you."

He didn't say a word when she came close, smelling like sweet summer rain, looking strong yet vulnerable in a way that made him want to throw everything he'd said out the window. With an incredibly light touch, she set her hands on his shoulders, bracing herself so that she could reach up on tiptoe to kiss his cheek.

"Good-bye," she whispered.

Then she was gone.

Colin stood there, still frozen. He had been blown away by her intense determination to break through to him, by her fierce loyalty to Carmen, by her need to make him understand. That she had walked away now, when he knew damn well how much his business meant to her own, caused a deep, piercing ache.

He was an idiot. A big, dumb jerk. He was taking his frustrations out on her and an old woman for God's sake.

For an encore he'd have to go beat up some orphans.

Disgusted with himself, he walked to his desk and took a good long look at what he'd put before everything else. Pieces of metal, nothing more.

Shattered, like his heart.

He looked at the closed door, certain he'd just let the best thing ever to happen to him get away.

IT WAS PAST MIDNIGHT before he allowed himself to go home. He was heavy-footed and bleary-eyed.

And just maybe exhausted enough to crawl into bed without missing Lani.

The house was dark, a good thing because no way could he face his mother and aunts and admit his failure. Or that the engagement party, scheduled for tomorrow night, was pretty much a moot point.

He turned his shower on boiling hot and stood under it for a long time, but the tension inside him didn't drain away. Naked and wet, he padded out of the bathroom into his dark room, hoping to fall into the oblivion of sleep.

"Hey."

It was the sweetest, softest, sexiest "hey" he'd ever heard, and it had come from the vicinity of his bed.

"Hey back," he said, so ridiculously relieved that his voice sounded like gravel. He peered into the moonlit dark and saw the shadow of Lani sitting cross-legged on his bed.

"I thought you'd never get out of that shower."

Her voice held a touching mix of affection and nerves. He'd never been so happy to see anyone in his life, even though he couldn't exactly *see* her. He came closer to make sure he wasn't dreaming. His knees touched the bed. "I thought you were gone."

"You fired me from the cleaning job," she said slowly, touching his arm when he reached for the lamp. "Not yet, Colin. I'll say this better in the dark." She drew in a ragged breath. "You didn't say anything about this, about our agreement, so I didn't know, but...I didn't want to go back on my word. I still want to help you, if you want me."

He didn't deserve her.

"I'm so sorry, Colin," she said quickly before he could say a word. "I'm so, so sorry about your work, about what I did to the laser. Please forgive me."

God. He'd yelled at her, been a complete jerk and she was apologizing to him. He was slime.

Worse.

And completely incapable of keeping his distance, not tonight. Hell, he couldn't even remember why he'd ever wanted to.

"Colin?" She was still worried, still half braced for his rejection.

He had to see her. He overrode her hand on his arm and flipped on the light, thinking only that he *had* to look into her gorgeous eyes.

Her startled gasp filled the room and he remembered...he was totally nude.

"Colin..." Her eyes feasted on him, feeding the heat and hunger that were already nearly out of control. "You're so beautiful," she said dreamily.

"Not like you." His gaze never left her face. She could have been wearing a potato sack for all he cared. "Not like you, Lani. You're the most beautiful sight I've ever seen." Slowly he lowered himself to the bed, then dragged her close. Banding his arms around her, he bent his head to hers.

"Does this mean you forgive me...?"

"Don't," he begged. "Don't ever apologize to me for today. I can't believe how I talked to you, how you looked when I did. I know that you've lost too many people in your life—"

She went utterly still.

He cupped her face, made her look at him when she would have pulled away. "You never told me about it. About your family."

"I...couldn't. It was a long time ago, it doesn't matter now."

"It still gives you nightmares, it matters. I'm so sorry, Lani. I will never forgive myself for how I treated you."

"I will," she said simply.

Unable to bear hearing the words that came straight from her heart, when his own was so overflowing and confused, he kissed her. Blind, obsessive heat consumed them but it was different this time, different from anything he'd ever known.

It was soul-searching, earth-shattering and incredibly tender. The urgency was there, but suddenly they had all the time in the world, at least all night, and knowing that, Colin was hopelessly caught by every little nuance, the whisper of a kiss, the slightest touch, a promising glance.

It started again before it was over, the passion, the hunger, and while the initial desperation was gone, the need remained.

He needed her, and he knew without a doubt that she needed him, too.

Nothing in his life had ever felt so...right. So perfect, though even that word didn't do justice to what they shared in those magical hours between midnight and dawn.

"I love you, Colin," Lani whispered at one point, the pale moonlight highlighting her lovely features. "I'll love you forever." Then she kissed him, halting any words or panic, and for the rest of the long, dark night, he lost himself in her.

12

THE NEXT DAY Lani literally danced down Colin's hallways.

It wasn't pretend anymore between Colin and her, it couldn't be. Not with all they'd shared the night before.

Deliriously happy, she danced right to work, starting with Colin's house. She had lots to do—too much, given how behind she'd gotten yesterday, but she didn't mind.

Work was great. Life was great.

She was great.

And tonight—her engagement party.

Hugging herself, she grinned with excitement. Then got to work, starting with the downstairs. She was in the room next to Colin's office, very carefully dusting the bookshelves, concentrating intensely. The last thing she wanted to do was break something else.

In the next room, she heard Colin's office phone, heard his rich, deep voice answer and greet Claudia.

Lani tried to ignore what the mere sound of him did to her. She sprayed furniture polish on her cloth and turned her attention to the shelf.

Through the wall came the low, sexy timbre of Colin's voice. She didn't listen to the words, that would be eavesdropping, and Lani respected his privacy too much for that.

But she wasn't above losing herself in the simple

sound of him. She'd done the same last night, listening to his husky whispers as he'd made love to her. Just the thought of some of those wicked suggestions brought a heat to her face now. For a dark, driven man, Colin was earthy, uninhibited and amazingly sensual.

She loved it.

Then she heard the word *wedding* from the other side of the wall and she stilled.

Wedding? He was talking to Claudia about a wedding? It was wrong to listen, she knew that, but she couldn't tear herself away.

"I realize you just want to help," he was saying. "But it's not necessary."

Lani put a hand to the wall to steady herself. There was going to be a wedding? *Theirs?*

"No, Claudia. You don't understand." He spoke more quietly now, so that Lani had to strain to hear. And strain she did, plastering her ear to the wall.

"It's not necessary," Colin said. "Because there isn't going to be a wedding."

The rag and polish can fell from Lani's hands to the thick carpet as her raging emotions went from a sudden high to an all-time low.

It's all right, she told herself, scooping up her supplies. They'd not discussed anything yet. There was plenty of time.

And she should walk away now, before she heard something she shouldn't.

"I didn't want to tell you about it for this very reason," came Colin's voice. "I knew you'd react this way— No, listen to me, Claudia. I'm not trying to shut you out of being involved. It's not like that at all. My engagement to Lani? It's not real. It never was."

His voice was so calm and certain. So mundane, as if he were discussing dinner plans.

Lani staggered away from the wall. *Shouldn't have listened*, she chastised herself, but it was too late. Her heart was processing the words her brain had heard, and it hurt. God, it hurt.

Colin made a disparaging sound. "Yes, that's right. It was all a sham, designed to let me work. There's not going to be a wedding. Ever." His certainty was unmistakable.

Lani's heart broke.

Colin had never dropped the pretense. The realization wasn't an easy one. Last night—oh, last night—she covered her hot face. She'd been so free with herself, so into the beauty of what they'd shared, and it hadn't been real.

She should have known. After all, he'd been careful to make her no promises. She had no one to blame for the anguish she felt now, no one but herself.

Facing the truth was a humiliating experience, and far more painful than she could have believed. No matter what she had told herself, no matter what she'd thought she'd seen in Colin's eyes, she had been the only one to fall.

Lani just barely managed to scoop up her bucket and get out of the room without falling apart. Her vision hampered by bright, hot tears, her throat clogged with stinging hurt, her head down so that she could concentrate on getting her feet to cooperate, she escaped.

And ran directly into Irene in the hallway.

"Darling?" Irene frowned with worry.

Lani's heart was at her feet, crushed, and she was seconds away from self-destructing. Irene's sympathetic smile nearly killed her.

"Are you all right? What's the matter?" Irene wanted to know.

What was the matter? Her heart was broken. She wanted the man of her dreams to fall in love with her. She wanted him to need her above all else. She wanted, oh, how she wanted, to be a *real* bride. For Colin.

"Lani?"

"Nothing," she answered quickly, her chest hitching with pain. "It's nothing." She let out a little laugh to mask her quiet sob. "I just got a dust fleck in my eye, that's all. Excuse me—"

But Irene gently took her arms and held her still. "You don't have to hide from me. I can see what's happened plain as the nose on my face."

"I doubt it."

"My son hurt you."

"Oh, no. He would never—"

"Not physically," Irene agreed. "Of course not. But he hurt you all the same. No need to rush to the rat's defense."

Lani cleared her throat and swallowed her tears, hoping she sounded normal. "He's a wonderful man, smart and—"

"Lani—"

"—and responsible and strong and—" Her voice cracked when Irene's sad smile threatened her control.

"Oh, Lani. I know what Colin's good points are. Believe me, I know. But I also know the man's faults, and one of them is an inability to open his heart to another."

The tears Lani had been holding back betrayed her and several spilled over. "It's not his fault," she whispered. "He's been hurt." She sniffed and wiped her face. "He's afraid."

"And now you're paying the price." Irene made a

small noise of distress. "I shouldn't have pushed him into this. I'm so sorry."

More than anything in that moment, Lani needed love, desperately. She needed a hug, needed to feel the warmth. It seemed natural to surge forward and hug Irene tight.

It took Irene only one second of hesitation before she wrapped her arms around Lani. "I'm sorry. So, so sorry," she murmured, her voice rough with her own unshed tears.

The affection from a woman very unused to such things made Lani cry harder, but it was worth it. For one last special moment, she held onto a part of Colin's life. A life she'd wanted for herself with all her heart. "I have to go," she whispered, knowing if she hung around now she'd make a fool of herself.

Irene straightened away, her own eyes suspiciously damp. "Where? What will happen?"

"I don't know."

Irene's gaze was still hurting, but searching, too. "Truth, Lani. Was this engagement ever real?"

Only for herself. It'd been all too real. And short.

"Damn him," Irene breathed when Lani didn't answer. "How could he have done this to you? To me? To the entire town? It's unthinkable."

"Don't judge him too harshly," Lani begged. "He had his reasons and they were unselfish ones. He didn't want to hurt you or anyone else."

Irene nodded, looking thoughtful. "Yes, I see where he thought he was doing the right thing. Maybe there's hope for him then."

Lani couldn't imagine it; she'd given him everything she'd had and that hadn't been good enough. She had nothing left but her pride, and she was taking that home. "I'm sorry about tonight." The thought of her engagement party seemed...obscene. "Will you be all right?"

"Don't you dare worry about me." For the first time since they'd met, Irene made the first move of physical affection. She reached out and clasped Lani's hands. "Are you sure you have to leave? There's nothing left?"

There was plenty left. Too much. It was why she had to go. "I have to leave, Irene. For me. Do you understand?"

"I don't want to, but of course I do. Lani, darling..." her eyes filled again "...take care."

And so, for the second time in her life, Lani lost a mother. She wanted to hate Colin for that alone, but couldn't. Not when she understood him so well.

She managed to walk away, but it was the hardest thing she'd ever done. Remembering his last words helped.

It's not real, he'd said. *It never was.*

By leaving, she was breaking her word to Colin, something she'd sworn never to do, but it could no longer be helped.

It took her a pathetically short amount of time to pack—less than three minutes. She left the cool house and stepped out into the simmering heat. She got in her car, rolled down her windows and drove off while Colin was still in his office, probably still on his phone casually denying everything she had believed in.

Risk.

She'd wanted one, and in the bargain had gotten far more than she'd counted on. Oh, well, it was done. She wouldn't regret it.

She headed down the hill and crossed the tracks.

COLIN HEARD the front door shut. Between himself and Lani, and now his family, he heard the sound many times a day.

But for some reason, this time his head came up. His heart clenched. A very bad feeling filled his gut.

Something was wrong.

Claudia was still talking in his ear so he shook off the feeling and made a new attempt to listen to her listing his messages. They were important, he knew this, but he couldn't concentrate.

Not when inside him there was a sudden, terrifying aloneness. "I'm sorry, Claudia, I've got to go." He hung up the phone, then went still as he tried to place his sudden uneasiness.

The house was silent as it hadn't been since...since before Lani had come into his life. He got up and left the office.

The living room was empty. So was the kitchen. His unease grew. "Lani?" he called out.

Nothing. No sweet voice, no musical, contagious laughter.

Spurred on by a strange fear, he raced up the stairs. She wasn't in the bedroom, where he'd left her soundly sleeping only a little while before. He remembered how she'd looked when he came out of the shower, sleeping so peacefully, looking heart-wrenchingly at home in his huge bed, wearing nothing more than his sheets and a contented expression.

Now she was gone.

Probably at work, he assured himself.

But the panic persisted. He looked in the bathroom.

Her toothbrush was gone.

So was her hairbrush and her small bag of makeup.

Heart racing, palms damp, Colin raced back into the bedroom, but there was no mistake.

All her clothes were gone.

She'd left him.

She'd broken her promise and—

"Well, Son, you finally did it," said his mother from behind him. "Chased away the best thing ever to happen to you."

"She's...gone," he said, stunned. His thoughts raced back to last night, to their incredible night of passion. Had she been upset, even as he'd held her, touched her, tasted her? Remembering her soft cries, her not-so-soft demands for more, the way she'd held him clenched tight to her, he knew she hadn't been holding back, harboring any resentment.

She was too honest for that.

But was he honest enough to see the truth? He knew she loved him, knew that he hadn't been able to say those words back to her.

And he knew, dammit, he knew that eventually what he'd given her wouldn't be enough. She'd want the pretense dropped once and for all.

She'd want him for real.

Why hadn't he given her that? Why had he held on to his fear in the face of the most incredulous, giving love he'd ever received? "She's really gone," he said again, bewildered, sinking to his bed. He looked around him as if she might materialize out of nowhere. "Gone."

"Yes," his mother said.

"She promised." He had no idea why he said it, it just popped out, and he wouldn't take back the words because suddenly pride meant nothing. "She *promised*."

"Promised what?"

No, dammit. He couldn't pin this on her. This was his fault, all his fault. "What happened?"

"She came out of the room next to your office, looking like she'd seen a ghost..." She paused. "Or maybe she heard something? Something that would hurt her?"

Colin closed his eyes, knowing what he'd done. What she'd heard, and how it would have crushed her.

Claudia had been so eager to help, so eager to rush him down the aisle, and he'd balked.

But even as he'd done so, he'd known in his heart he wanted to throw the deception out the window and hold Lani to him forever. *Forever.* And that meant vows.

So why had he been so adamant with Claudia? Stubbornness, pure and simple, and Lani had been on the other side of the wall, unable to see the truth in his eyes, hearing only what he had said to his secretary.

It's not real, it never was.

He'd said that to Claudia and Lani had heard him and believed it. Why wouldn't she? He'd certainly said it enough.

Just another lie.

He swore.

"Oh, yes, it's a mess," his mother agreed solemnly. "And you only realize the half of it."

"What are you talking about?"

"In less than eight hours everyone that knows you is converging here for the engagement party of the year. It's going to be unpleasant without a fiancée, Colin."

"That's the least of my problems at the moment." He sighed and looked into his mother's hurt eyes. "I'm sorry."

"I don't think I'm the one you should be apologizing to."

"No, you're wrong about that. I tried to fool you. I lied to you."

His mother gave him a sad, forgiving smile. "I might still have been furious, but Lani pointed out that you had good reasons and even better intentions, and I have to agree with her." She sat next to him. "You're a wonderful man, Colin. You can run your own life perfectly well and I shouldn't have tried to interfere. I hope you'll forgive me for that."

· She startled them both by giving him a fiercely loving hug. "You'll do what's right now," she whispered, squeezing him close. "I have faith in you."

Then she left him alone.

It was the emptiness that scared Colin the most, the deep, ripping loneliness already filling his heart. That he had caused Lani to feel the same way was unforgivable. She deserved so much more.

He wanted to give it to her, if only she'd let him.

Having no idea how he was going to make this all better, only knowing he had to try, he went after her.

SEVERAL HOURS LATER, in the thick, repressive heat, Colin had to admit failure.

Lani had vanished.

She wasn't at her office, wasn't on a job, wasn't in her apartment.

He'd got a fulminating look from Great-Aunt Jennie, one that should have withered him on the spot, but he was already so miserable she couldn't possibly make him feel worse.

He had fallen hopelessly and irrevocably in love, only he'd been stupid enough to let it sift through his fingers.

He drove by every one of Lani's jobs. Nothing. Eventually he made his way back home, only to be confronted with the frantic, last-minute preparations for his fake engagement party.

Faced with only a few hours until guests were due to arrive, dinner in various stages of preparation and the house more like a home than he could ever remember it being, Colin came to a decision.

He stood in his foyer and stared down at a plant on the floor. It had a blue ribbon around it and several white flowers blooming. He had no idea what kind of plant it was, but it looked very at home.

Just another visual reminder of Lani. Somehow it strengthened his resolve. "I'm not going to give up," he told the plant. "I love her and, dammit, she's going to hear it."

"Well, it's about time."

Grimacing, he turned to face an unusually quiet Bessie and Lola.

"Fix this," Bessie demanded of him, poking him with a finger. "Because I got to tell you, Colin West, that Lani was a definite keeper."

He managed a smile. "I know." God, how he knew. "The party—"

"We'll worry about the party, you worry about your fiancée," Lola said much more kindly than her sister, patting his arm. "Just go fix this mess, darling."

He turned to leave, but suddenly Carmen was there blocking his way. She'd been hired for the day to help prepare for the party, and though she didn't look friendly, at least she hadn't stuck her tongue out at him.

Her eyes told him she thought he was one stupid man for letting Lani go. They also told him something else, and hope surged within Colin for the first time in hours.

"You know where she is," he said, trying unsuccessfully to rein in his excitement. "Tell me."

She gave him a sardonic gaze.

Damn, she couldn't talk. "I have to know, Carmen." She peered deeply into his eyes for so long he nearly yelled in frustration.

The more agitated he got, the calmer she appeared. She pointed to her ring finger, then looked at him with her eyebrows raised.

"I'll buy her a ring," he promised, but she rolled her eyes, disgusted.

What then? He would have gone running for paper and pen, but she grabbed his hand and pointed to his ring finger.

"Yes," he said urgently. "I promise, I want to marry Lani for real. I want the party tonight to be real. But I can't do any of it unless I find her. Tell me, Carmen, please, where is she?"

She searched his eyes, and he hoped to God she found what she wanted there because he had to know. Time was running out. "Tell me."

She nodded, then backed up to give herself space and started to…gyrate?

Bouncing, shimmying and shaking her bootie, she turned in a slow circle. Colin just stared at her, certain she'd cracked. "Uh…Carmen? We were talking about Lani?"

Irritated, eyes flashing, she stopped and glared at him with her hands on her hips.

"Okay, okay! Try again. I'm watching."

Again she started to writhe. No…she was hula dancing? "She's taking…dancing lessons?"

Carmen sighed loudly and shot a glance heavenward. Then she started again, definitely doing the hula for all her heavy, sixty-something-old body was worth. Colin stared at her in amazement. "She's...oh, damn. She's going to Hawaii!"

Carmen pointed to her nose and nodded triumphantly.

He was right. Lani had apparently said the hell with life and had taken off for a well-deserved vacation.

Colin hoped he could catch her or she was going to miss her own—*real*—engagement party.

13

LANI HADN'T TAKEN a vacation in...well, forever. She owed herself one, she decided.

Now seemed as good a time as any. Hawaii was calling.

In less than an hour she had a bag packed and had notified everyone that she was taking two weeks off. In another hour she was at the airport, staring at the departure screens, wondering which flight to take.

The airport was a bundle of activity around her. Voices, laughter, shouts, people rushing, walking, sleeping. Even the smells: coffee, leather, people, diesel, they all made her think of exotic places.

She was standing in front of a ticket counter before she knew it. The next flight left in minutes. If she was quick, she could be in Oahu for a late dinner. She'd lie on the beach watching the sunset, sipping pretty colored drinks.

She'd enjoy herself.

She would.

"Ma'am?" A friendly ticket agent smiled at her. "Are you next?"

She could be. With a flick of her poor, abused credit card she could be gone. Outta here. Away from any memory of the man who'd broken her heart.

But that heart didn't want to run. It wasn't the answer, no matter how tempting, and she had to face the truth.

Yes, she'd fallen in love with a man who couldn't give that love back to her. But that wasn't a crime, nor was it his fault. He'd never misled her, not once.

Not only was she acting childishly, she'd done the one thing she'd promised she wouldn't—she'd broken her promise.

She'd let him down.

It hurt, just thinking it. How could she have done that to him?

At this very moment, Colin's mother and aunts would have staff racing madly through his house, preparing for their engagement party, the party she'd agreed to attend.

But her heart was breaking, dammit. To stand at Colin's side and pretend to love him, when she really did, would be the hardest thing in the world.

"Ma'am?"

"I'm sorry." Lani smiled apologetically. She stepped aside. "I've changed my mind."

If she lived through this heartache, she promised herself, *then* she'd travel. She'd go to Hawaii and maybe, just maybe, never come back.

But she didn't move away, not yet, just stood there and gazed blindly at the black screen high above her, where the flight she had nearly gotten on started to blink.

They were boarding. Without her.

Then her neck was tingling, her heart racing, and slowly she turned. Standing there, chest heaving as though he'd been running, his face drawn and pale, was Colin.

"Lani."

Just her name, but he put such a wealth of feeling into it, she closed her eyes against the new onslaught of pain.

She felt his hands on her shoulders. They slid up, cupped her face, tilted it up. "Thank God, I found you in time."

Lani hadn't imagined this, what seeing him again would do to her heart.

Funny, but around them everything was normal. People rushing like ants toward their gates, hugging good-bye, laughing, smiling.

And her heart was breaking all over again.

"Please," Colin said, his voice low and raw. "Don't go. I'm so sorry I didn't understand everything sooner." His hands slid down her arms, clasped her hands tight, and in a heartrending gesture, he brought them to his lips. "Please, Lani, don't leave me."

He thought she was going.

She glanced down at her packed-to-bulging bag. She still stood in front of the ticket counter. In one of her hands tucked in his, she held a brochure she'd picked up at the airport entrance, one that could have been mistaken for a plane ticket.

He believed she could leave him.

"I know I don't have the right to ask," he said urgently. "But if you could listen to me, just give me a few minutes, maybe I can change your mind."

She owed him. She had made a promise she had no right to break simply because of her feelings for him. She pulled her hands free and stepped back. She needed to be able to think, and she couldn't do that with his hands on her. "Colin, I'm not going—"

"I know I hurt you," he said in a rush. "I'm sorry for

that, too. You're the last person in the world I wanted to hurt."

"I'm not—"

"But you threw me, Lani. You were so...real. So loyal and trusting and sweet." He came close again but didn't touch her. "So absolutely—"

"Colin, I'm not going." *It wasn't his fault*, she reminded herself. *You fell on your own, knowing he couldn't return the feelings.*

"Lani, I love you."

"I'm not— *What?*" She grabbed his shirt, hauled him closer. "What did you just say?"

"I love you."

There was a new line forming at the ticket counter behind them. It was a noisy group, but Lani managed to make herself heard. "That's a low blow, Colin," she whispered furiously. "I said I'm not going anywhere. I'll be there for your damn engagement party. You don't have to tease me by telling me—by saying— *You know!*"

He blinked at her, opened his mouth in shock, but she whirled, intending to stalk off, madder than she could ever remember being.

How dare he throw her words back in her face just so that she would come back, especially when she had already made up her mind to do so on her own.

A firm but easy hand settled at her elbow, drawing her back against the hard, warm chest she'd know anywhere. "Lani, wait."

She actually had little choice since Colin wasn't about to let her go anywhere with such a huge misunderstanding between them. Her bag fell on his foot, but he ignored the pain because it took two hands to hold her still.

The people in line seemed interested in the tussle between them but Colin didn't care.

All he cared about was keeping Lani.

Too dignified to struggle, she went limp in his arms and glared at him. "Let me go," she snapped. "I said I'm not leaving. I'll come back with you and play house, dammit, now let me go."

"You think I was toying with you," he said in disbelief, staring down into her hurting eyes. "Lani—" A frustrated growl was all he could make for a moment, he was so surprised. And hurt. "Listen to me. I've never said those words before, to anyone. *Never*, Lani. Do you understand what I'm saying to you? God, the last thing I would ever do is fling it around like a joke."

Her eyes filled, not with hope or joy, but with hurt, and he felt sick. "Am I too late?" he whispered, pulling her tight to him just to feel her body heat. "I can't be, I won't let it be too late. I love you, dammit. I'm sorry I was so slow about it, but you scared me to death."

One tear fell, but she remained silent.

Behind him, in line, several women muttered to themselves about men and their stupidity.

"No," he said fiercely, forgetting everyone that surrounded them, most of them blatantly eavesdropping now, as he hauled her closer yet, banding his arms tightly around her. "Don't cry, I'm so sorry."

"Say it again."

He pulled back slightly and stared at her.

"Say it again," she demanded.

The small crowd pressed closer, listening.

Colin's pride was gone, he had nothing left to lose. "I love you, Lani. With all my heart and soul."

But the woman in his arms didn't move a muscle, not

a one, and fear filled him. Why wasn't she saying something, *anything?*

"You have to believe in me," he said, desperate now. "I'm a slow learner but once I catch on, it's for keeps. I know now what I've been missing in my life and it's you."

Several women in the crowd let out a collective sigh.

"I know you've had it rough," he said, ignoring their audience the best he could. "I know deep down you're just as afraid as me, that you have been ever since you lost your parents so cruelly. But I can love you that much, Lani. I already do, all I need is the time to prove it to you. We can start over and make our own family."

She dipped her head down to his chest so he couldn't see her expression but he felt her shaking. God. He'd made her cry again. "I'm rushing you, I'm sorry—"

"*Rushing* me?" She lifted her head now and he saw that she hadn't been shaking with tears, but with joy. It blazed from her eyes, lighting her face and his heart.

"Colin," she said with a laugh. "I've loved you forever. You couldn't have fallen fast enough for me. *Rushing?*" She laughed again, the sound contagious.

The crowd grinned unabashedly.

"You just finally caught up with me," she said to him softly.

"Does this mean—" He didn't know, didn't have a clue and he was dying. "You're okay with... I can—"

"Promise me forever, Colin," she whispered, looping her arms around his neck.

"I'll promise you forever and a day if you promise to marry me. Fill my heart with joy and love for the rest of our lives."

She went still. "Really?"

"Marry me, Lani. For real this time."

Lani smiled, her heart overflowing. "Oh, yes," she agreed. Her future husband leaned down and kissed her, a soft, sweet, giving kiss full of love.

Above them on the departure board, the plane bound for Hawaii left the gate.

ACCIDENTAL WIFE

Day Leclaire

PROLOGUE

Park Slope in Brooklyn, New York

NIKKI leaned back against the wall and closed her eyes, fighting for control. Her sister's voice continued—relentless and sincere, inflicting wounds as painful as they were unintentional.

"I'm sorry," Krista repeated. "I don't know why you bothered to phone when you already know my answer. I can't. I owe Nikki. I won't desert her now."

Why hadn't she realized? Nikki wondered in anguish. Why hadn't she noticed that Krista's needs were no longer the same as seven years ago?

"She's my sister, that's why!" Krista's voice rose in anger. "She gave up everything to take care of me. What do you want me to say? Thanks. You saved my life but now I'm out of here? I've decided to move in with my girlfriend?"

Saved her life? Nikki shook her head. She'd done so little. Offering a home when Krista's husband had died had seemed the only logical option. She'd been pregnant. What other choice was there? Family came first. Family always came first.

"Well, I can't and that's the end of it! After all she's sacrificed for me, the least I can do is be there for her now. Keli and I are all she has. And we're staying until she doesn't need us anymore."

Nikki didn't wait to hear the rest of the conversation. Silently, she retraced her steps down the hallway and entered the small room she used as a secondary office. Crossing to the desk, she opened the top drawer and removed a thick, gold-embossed envelope. It weighted her hand like a lump of lead, and yet the elegant ticket inside was anything but. An engraved wafer of gold metal, it offered a solution to all her problems.

She had prayed she wouldn't need to resort to such a drastic alternative. A choked laugh escaped before she could prevent it. She'd purchased the ticket because the situation at work had grown so untenable. It had never occurred to her that she'd have a dual reason for going ahead with her plan. Unfortunately, overhearing Krista's conversation had closed all avenues but one.

Slowly, she withdrew a white velvet pouch from the envelope. Inside the protective casing, the ticket shimmered as though alive, flooding the room with a brilliant, golden promise. For many people, the ticket would represent a dream come true.

Before she could control it, a lone tear slid down her cheek.

So why did it feel like a nightmare?

Chicago, Illinois

"Oh, Jonah, thank heaven you came." Della Sanders flew into her son's arms and hugged him fiercely.

A hint of amusement lightened Jonah Alexander's grim expression. "Did you doubt I would?" he responded, wrapping his mother in a gentle embrace.

She was a tiny creature, brimming with passion and

energy and emotion. She was also a woman who inspired unwavering devotion. Jonah had spent a lifetime watching as she charmed those around her with unconscious ease. Some singular quality reflected in her soft hazel eyes and shy, welcoming smile could win over even the most hardened cases. And in her second husband's line of work, hardened cases were the rule rather than the exception. Hell, she'd won over Loren Sanders—a steely, confirmed bachelor— in five seconds flat.

Della peeked over her shoulder at her husband and offered an apologetic smile. "Loren wasn't certain you'd be willing to bail Eric out of this latest mess." Her breath escaped in an exasperated sigh. "And to be perfectly honest, I wasn't, either. He's really gotten himself into a pickle this time."

Reaching around his mother, Jonah offered a hand to his stepfather. "You shouldn't have waited before getting in touch, Loren. Family always comes first with me. You know that."

It had ever since Jonah had been a tough, angry ten-year-old who'd unexpectedly found himself graced with a stepfather who'd appealed to both his intellect as well as his emotions. Loren had become an unconditional friend. And the deep and enduring love he'd given Della for the past twenty-five years sealed Jonah's eternal support and gratitude.

"You've always been a good brother to Eric," Loren said. "But the European operation keeps you so busy, we hated to bother you with this. Besides, we didn't realize how serious it was until recently. I just hope we're not too late."

Jonah released his mother and crossed to the floor-to-ceiling windows. The Sanderses' Chicago condominium commanded a stunning view of Lake Michigan—a view that under normal circumstances he'd have taken the time to appreciate. "Tell me about it," he requested, turning his back on the expanse of tinted glass.

"Eric's fallen for a married woman," Della announced starkly. "An *older* married woman."

Jonah lifted an eyebrow. Not the smartest thing Eric had ever done, but hardly the most reprehensible. "And?"

"And she works for us," Loren explained. "This…relationship is interfering with both her performance and his. Between them they almost lost the Dearfield account."

Jonah swore beneath his breath. It must be bad if Eric had put this woman ahead of their most important client. What the hell could he be thinking? Obviously, handing over the New York branch of the business to his half brother hadn't matured him any. "Do I know her?"

"Her name's Nikki Ashton. She's—"

"Head of Special Projects. Yes, I've heard of her. I don't think we've ever met, though." Jonah ran a hand across his nape, forcing himself to focus despite his exhaustion. "You hired her right after I left for London. What's she like?"

"She's a stunning woman, one of those leggy redheads."

"Loren," Della rebuked, "you know how much I hate it when you reduce people to the superficial."

He fingered his salt-and-pepper mustache and gave an apologetic shrug. "Sorry, darling. Old habits die hard."

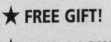

GET 2

HOW TO GET YOUR
2 FREE BOOKS AND FREE GIFT!

1. Peel off the MIRA® sticker on the front cover. Place it in the space provided at right. This automatically entitles you to receive two free books and an exciting surprise gift.

2. Send back this card and you'll get 2 "The Best of the Best™" books. These books have a combined cover price of $11.98 or more in the U.S. and $13.98 or more in Canada, but they are yours to keep absolutely FREE!

3. There's <u>no</u> catch. You're under <u>no</u> obligation to buy anything. We charge nothing – ZERO – for your first shipment. And you don't have to make any minimum number of purchases – not even one!

4. We call this line "The Best of the Best" because each month you'll receive the best books by some of today's most popular authors. These authors show up time and time again on all the major bestseller lists and their books sell out as soon as they hit the stores. You'll like the convenience of getting them delivered to your home at our special discount prices . . . and you'll love your *Heart to Heart* subscriber newsletter featuring author news, horoscopes, recipes, book reviews and much more!

5. We hope that after receiving your free books you'll want to remain a subscriber. But the choice is yours – to continue or cancel, anytime at all! So why not take us up on our invitation, with no risk of any kind. You'll be glad you did!

6. And remember...we'll send you a surprise gift ABSOLUTELY FREE just for giving THE BEST OF THE BEST a try.

SPECIAL FREE GIFT!
We'll send you a fabulous surprise gift, absolutely FREE, simply for accepting our no-risk offer!

Visit us online at
www.mirabooks.com

® and TM are registered trademark of Harlequin Enterprises Limited.

THE BEST OF THE BEST™ — Here's How it Works:

Accepting your 2 free books and gift places you under no obligation to buy anything. You may keep the books and gift and return the shipping statement marked "cancel." If you do not cancel, about a month later we will send you 4 additional books and bill you just $4.74 each in the U.S., or $5.24 each in Canada, plus 25¢ shipping & handling per book and applicable taxes if any.* That's the complete price and — compared to cover prices starting from $5.99 each in the U.S. and $6.99 each in Canada — it's quite a bargain! You may cancel at any time, but if you choose to continue, every month we'll send you 4 more books, which you may either purchase at the discount price or return to us and cancel your subscription.

*Terms and prices subject to change without notice. Sales tax applicable in N.Y. Canadian residents will be charged applicable provincial taxes and GST. Credit or Debit balances in a customer's account(s) may be offset by any other outstanding balance owed by or to the customer.

If offer card is missing write to: The Best of the Best, 3010 Walden Ave., P.O. Box 1867, Buffalo, NY 14240-1867

BUSINESS REPLY MAIL
FIRST-CLASS MAIL   PERMIT NO. 717-003   BUFFALO, NY

POSTAGE WILL BE PAID BY ADDRESSEE

THE BEST OF THE BEST
3010 WALDEN AVE
PO BOX 1867
BUFFALO NY 14240-9952

NO POSTAGE
NECESSARY
IF MAILED
IN THE
UNITED STATES

"Get rid of her," Jonah recommended without hesitation.

Loren cleared his throat. "I'm afraid we can't."

"Why not?"

"The company needs her. For one thing, she's brilliant," Loren admitted. "And for another…she's just been nominated for the Lawrence J. Bauman Award. The ceremony's in six weeks. How would it look if we fired someone of that caliber?"

Jonah's mouth tightened. Unfortunately, they were right. Businessmen and businesswomen nominated for the LJB Award were the most sought after in the country. It would cause irreparable harm to International Investment's reputation if they were to dump a potential winner on some trumped-up excuse. "Have you spoken to Eric about the situation?"

"No," Della admitted. "We kept hoping it would all blow over. You know Eric. He falls in and out of love more often than the wind changes."

"But not this time."

Della shook her head, tears gathering in her eyes. "She must be quite a special woman to hold his interest this long."

Jonah turned to face the windows. He knew Eric well enough to suspect which qualities needed to be so "special" to snag his half brother's attention for any prolonged length of time. If Nikki Ashton was a tenth as brilliant as Loren claimed, she'd have figured it out, as well…and she'd have used her wealth of riches to bring Eric to heel. He'd have been easy prey for a savvy—not to mention leggy—redhead.

"What about her husband?" Jonah questioned over his shoulder. "Or doesn't Mr. Ashton care that Mrs. Ashton is having a fling with her boss?"

"We don't know anything about him other than he's been out of the country for the past year," Loren confessed. "I don't even think his name is Ashton. She married about the time she started with us, but kept her maiden name. I checked with Personnel and Nikki never gave them any details. He's not part of her insurance or benefit program, either." He shrugged. "I'm afraid that avenue is something of a dead end."

"A modern marriage. How convenient," Jonah observed drily. He swiveled to face them, folding his arms across his chest. "Okay, Loren. What do you want me to do?"

"Couldn't you try to reason with Eric?" Della suggested before her husband had a chance to reply. "Or speak to Mrs. Ashton? If their relationship is causing as much trouble at the office as Loren fears, perhaps we could transfer one or the other."

"We have to be careful, Della," Loren replied with a frown. "I need Eric in New York right now. Aside from this incident with the Ashton woman, he's become a real asset to the firm."

"I've seen the reports," Jonah commented. "I'd hoped it meant he'd finally gotten his act together."

"Until this latest indiscretion he had." Loren shot his stepson a look of grim warning. "We also need to handle Nikki with kid gloves. She knows a lot about the company."

Jonah's eyes narrowed. "You mean she could do us some real damage?"

"If that's her angle," Loren confessed unhappily.

"Would you fly to New York and find out what's going on?" Della pleaded. Worry etched fine lines between her drawn brows. "Perhaps we're overreacting."

Jonah shook his head. "If anything, you're not worried enough. If Eric is serious about marrying this woman, she could be the worst thing that ever happened to him. But what if he's not serious? What if he loses interest in her? Would she want to even the score?"

Loren visibly paled. "I hadn't even considered that possibility."

"You'll fly out in the morning?" Della questioned, clutching Loren's arm.

"I'll leave now."

"But you must be exhausted," she protested. "You've just flown in from London. You need to sleep and—"

"I'm tough, Mother. Nor do I believe in jet lag." A tight smile touched Jonah's mouth. "Besides, I want to get to New York before Eric realizes I'm in the country."

New York City, New York

"What do you mean Eric's not here?" Jonah fought a losing battle with his temper. "Just where the *hell* is he?"

Eric's secretary squirmed in her chair. "I'm sorry, Mr. Alexander. He's…left."

"Left." Jonah planted his hands on her desk. "Could you be more specific, Ms. Sherborne? Where has he gone? And when will he return?"

"He had to catch a plane." She risked a swift, upward glance. "But I'm fairly certain he'll be back by Monday."

"Monday," Jonah repeated. Had someone heard he'd returned from London and warned Eric? "Was this a sudden trip?"

"Very sudden. I guess…I guess he had business out of town."

Judging by the nervous quiver in the woman's tone and the telltale flush invading her cheeks, the chances of Eric's disappearance having anything remotely to do with business were next to nil. "Where is he, Ms. Sherborne?" he demanded coldly.

"Um…I'm not certain of the specifics." She cleared her throat. "But he booked a flight to Las Vegas."

"*Nevada*? What business does he have there? We don't have any clients or investments in Nevada."

It was obvious that the secretary would rather be anywhere than pinned beneath his arctic stare. "Perhaps Mrs. Ashton's secretary knows," she finally suggested, the idea of passing him on to someone else clearly appealing to her. "Her name's Jan and her workstation is right across the hall."

Jonah stilled, fury gathering in his hazel eyes. "Mrs. Ashton's secretary is more familiar with Eric's movements than you are? Why is that?"

"Oh, no," she sputtered in alarm. "You don't understand. You see, Mrs. Ashton went to Nevada, too. Mr. Sanders didn't say where he'd be staying and I thought…perhaps…since the two of them were going together…" She trailed off miserably.

Jonah stepped away from her desk, letting her off the hook. "You thought that since this was a *business* trip, Mrs. Ashton and Mr. Sanders might be sharing the same hotel, and that Jan would have the particulars. Is that right?" He made sure she caught the grim warning behind his explanation. One breath of gossip about this weekend tryst and her career at International Investment would come to an abrupt end.

Comprehension dawned in her wide eyes. Drawing a deep breath, she nodded. "Yes. That's exactly what I thought."

Without another word, he crossed the hall. Jan proved to be quite efficient. Although she didn't have any information about Eric's movements, she had all the pertinent details in regard to Nikki's. Within minutes, he had a copy of her itinerary and was booked on the next flight to Las Vegas. Which left one more vital chore, he decided grimly.

Ignoring Jan, he thrust open the door to Nikki's office and walked in, shutting it firmly behind him. The room was dim, the November sun fast becoming a chilly memory as the afternoon waned. It wouldn't be long before the Friday rush hour started in earnest. He didn't bother to check his watch to see how close he was cutting the drive to La Guardia Airport. He couldn't remember which time zone he'd set it for anyway. One thing he knew for certain—this little fishing expedition would have to be swift.

As he glanced around, a light floral scent assailed him, a perfume he'd never smelled before. It could only belong to one person. He inhaled deeply, feeling as though he drew Nikki's essence into his lungs. It wasn't the musky odor he'd have associated with a sultry redhead. Instead of black satin and lace, her perfume brought to mind a Victorian parlor filled with fresh flowers, sunshine and lemony beeswax.

He shook his head, amused. Clever woman. Something heavy and overtly sexual would have been too much of a cliché. Eric would have seen through that in a fast second. No, she was smart. Cloak a sexy package with an air of charming innocence and most men could be brought to their knees.

Crossing to her desk, he switched on a high-intensity lamp. It cast a blazing circle of white in the middle of the mahogany tabletop. Files were placed in neat, orderly stacks to one side, and just outside the pool of light stood a framed photo. Intrigued, he picked it up.

The picture of a young, laughing girl jolted him. He hadn't suspected that Nikki Ashton might have a child. Career women hot to marry the boss's son rarely came encumbered. He studied the photo. The girl couldn't be much more than five or six, her fine-boned features surrounded by a cloud of strawberry blond ringlets. She was held in the arms of a woman. Nikki? he wondered, curious. It was impossible to tell what the mother looked like. Most of her face was obscured by the child's flyaway curls. Only the woman's eyes and hair were clearly visible—china blue eyes brimming with laughter and her hair a shade or two darker than the little girl's.

It wasn't much to go on.

He returned the photo to its former position on the desk and glanced around, searching for any other personal touches that might reveal more about Nikki. But the desk—hell, the entire room—was practically barren, its decor austere and stark and unrelentingly tidy. His gaze came to rest on the one other jarring note to the office. A scraggly line of badly tended plants filled the window ledge. For some reason, the plants bothered him. A lot. They suggested some clue to her personality he couldn't quite pinpoint, but exhaustion and a relentlessly ticking clock kept the vital piece from taking shape. Later. He'd think about it later, when he had the time.

Besides, what could a bunch of half-wilted plants mean other than she had a black thumb and didn't care who knew it?

Finally, he turned his attention to the appointment book centered within the circle of light. He didn't hesitate to invade her privacy, but flipped rapidly through the pages. Tucked between Wednesday and Thursday he found a thick, gold-embossed envelope. It was empty except for a small rectangular card. He pulled it out, scanning it swiftly.

The Cinderella Ball, it read. *The Montagues wish you joy and success as you embark on your search for matrimonial happiness.* At the bottom was an address and the date of the ball.

It was today's date.

It didn't take long for the full impact to hit. Nikki had flown to Nevada to attend some sort of marriage ball. He thrust his hand through his hair. It could only mean one thing—Mrs. Ashton was now free of her unknown husband and available to marry. And Eric, without question, was her groom-to-be.

Jonah gritted his teeth. Well, not if he could help it. Because when he caught up with the beautiful, scheming Mrs. Ashton, she'd regret ever interfering with his family. He'd see to that.

Personally.

CHAPTER ONE

The Montagues' Cinderella Ball—Forever, Nevada

NIKKI ASHTON walked into the ballroom fighting to hide her apprehension behind a calm expression. There was no doubt about it. She'd clearly lost her mind.

How could she have believed that the solution to all her problems was marriage? And how could she possibly walk into this room full of strangers and find a man willing to play the part of her husband for the next few months? It was crazy. Insane.

And she'd never been so frightened in all her life.

She drew in a deep breath, then another and another. Ominous spots danced before her eyes.

"Hi," said a cheery-voiced woman.

Nikki turned blindly in that direction and discovered a waiflike pixie hovering at her elbow. "Hello," she said, amazed she'd managed to return the greeting.

"Care to sit with me for a minute?"

Afraid that if she didn't sit down, she'd fall down, Nikki sank into one of the clutches of seats lining the outer fringes of the ballroom. "Thanks," she murmured, dropping her purse onto the small table in front of her.

"I'm Wynne Sommers," the woman introduced herself.

"Nikki Ashton."

Bright green eyes peeked at her from beneath wisps of white blond hair. "Scared?" Wynne asked sympathetically.

For the first time in what seemed like ages, Nikki answered with the truth. "Terrified." She twisted her fingers together. "I'm not sure I can do this."

"But you have to, right? People are counting on you and this is the only option left."

Nikki stared at her companion in amazement. "How could you possibly know that?"

"I thought I recognized a familiar air of determination mixed with desperation." Wynne laughed. "It's the same for me."

"You *have* to marry?"

"I have two kids counting on me. If I don't marry, I lose them."

"I have relatives counting on me, too," Nikki found herself confessing. "Only I'm *trying* to lose them."

Wynne nodded sagely. "Some birds won't fly as long as Momma's there to feed them."

Nikki smiled in relief at the woman's instant understanding. "Something like that." She glanced around the crowded ballroom, pleased she could breathe again. "Have you been here long?"

"A couple of hours. The Montagues sure have a beautiful place. Have you met them yet?"

"When I first came in. They're a sweet couple."

"And their story is so romantic. Imagine being introduced to a complete stranger at a ball, falling madly in love and marrying that same night." Wynne sighed. "And here it is fifty years later and they're still every bit as much in love with each other as the day they met."

"I don't expect that to happen to me," Nikki insisted firmly. "I mean it's lovely of them to throw a Cinderella Ball every five years so others will have the same opportunity they did. And I'm sure there are plenty of people who find real love thanks to them. But it won't happen to me. I'm here for practical reasons. I have to get married."

"So do I. Still..." Wynne cupped her chin in her hand. "I don't know why we can't have it all. I'm sure going to try. And did you know there's also an Anniversary Ball?"

"A what?"

"An Anniversary Ball. The Montagues throw a one-year Anniversary Ball for everyone who marries tonight." She sighed. "I'd sure like to go to that."

"We have to get married first," Nikki reminded her. She gazed out at the glittering array of chattering men and women and fought the resurgence of her former panic. "I don't even know where to begin."

Wynne offered an encouraging smile. "The first few conversations are the hardest," she said gently. "After that, it gets easier. Honest."

"Have you had any luck finding someone?" Nikki asked hesitantly, glancing at her newfound friend.

"Oh, I have my future husband all picked out. That's him over there." She inclined her head toward a tall, fierce-looking man chatting to a hard-eyed brunette. "Nice, huh?"

Nikki shivered. "Not really."

"Don't let the tough exterior fool you," Wynne said with a quick laugh. "He wouldn't be much of a man if he didn't carry a bit of armor. He's a fighter, that one. Do you need a fighter?''

"He can't be a pushover, that's for sure," Nikki said, thinking of Eric.

"I'll tell you what. How about if you practice on my warrior? He won't mind. All I ask is that if it looks like he might be the one you want, give me the chance to talk him out of it. Okay?''

Nikki stared in astonishment. "Let me get this straight. You want to marry him, but you'll let me—''

"Have a go at him first. Sure." Wynne gave a careless shrug. "I don't think he's the man for you or I probably wouldn't offer. But he's a great icebreaker. He doesn't bother with a lot of social chitchat, just gets right to the point. Once he teaches you how to do it, the rest of the night will be a snap.''

"I don't know....''

Wynne reached out and touched Nikki's arm. "Is marrying important to you?" she asked seriously. "Is it the most important decision you've ever made? Because if it isn't, go home.''

"I can't," Nikki whispered. "I don't have any other choice.''

"Then focus on that. It'll help get you through the evening. Look. The brunette is leaving. This is your chance. Go introduce yourself.''

Nikki took a deep breath and stood. She couldn't say how or why, but in the past few moments, she'd regained control. She glanced down at Wynne. "Thanks," she said. "I owe you more than you'll ever know.''

"Just remember our deal.''

With a nod of agreement, Nikki headed toward Wynne's future husband.

*   *   *

Jonah glanced again at the card he'd confiscated from Nikki Ashton's desk, then at the cabdriver. "You sure this is the place?" he asked doubtfully.

"The Montagues' Cinderella Ball, right?" the cabby said in a bored voice. "That's where you wanted to go and that's where I've brung you. Just follow all those people. So's long as you stay on the walkway, you can't get lost."

Jonah gritted his teeth and tossed some bills onto the front seat before climbing out. Walkway or not, it would have been impossible to get lost. The damn place was the only building for miles around. It sat in the middle of the Nevada desert, outlined against the nighttime sky by colored floodlights and looking like some sort of giant platter stacked high with white-frosted cupcakes. He stared at the ridiculous architectural confection, then shrugged. What the hell did it matter? If it allowed him to get his hands on Nikki Ashton, he didn't care if it was built to resemble a bowl of whipped cream and cherries.

He worked his way through the crowd and into the mansion, pausing in the white marble foyer to get his bearings. A huge chandelier hung overhead, its soft light magnified by thousands of tiny prisms. Pine garlands embellished with twinkling fairy lights and white satin bows graced the massive Doric pillars that supported the thirty-foot ceiling. The flow of people continued around him and up twin, heart-shaped staircases. Taking a deep breath, he followed.

At the top of the steps he joined a reception line filing into the ballroom and only then realized that this ball required tickets for entry. He felt for his wallet, wondering if they took credit cards. Or perhaps he could bluff his way in. The throng moved steadily forward and within a few minutes he'd reached the head of the line. In front of him stood one of the most beautiful women he'd ever seen. She was tall and slender, her dark hair styled severely off her face. She held a basket of gold, waferlike tickets and offered a smile of greeting.

"I'm Jonah Alexander," he began. "Listen, I have a small problem—" But before he could utter another word of explanation, she suddenly focused on the next person in line. Her rich amber eyes widened in shock.

"Hello, Ella," a man's voice rumbled from behind.

Her face turned ashen. "Rafe," she whispered, and the basket of tickets tumbled to the floor.

Dropping to one knee, Jonah scooped handfuls of the heavy metal wafers back into the velvet-lined basket. With a muffled exclamation, Ella crouched beside him to help. "Are you all right?" he asked quietly.

"Fine," she insisted, though her trembling hands betrayed her. Gathering up the last ticket, she stood. "Thanks for your help."

"My pleasure."

He rose, too, and glanced pointedly at the man she'd called Rafe. He hadn't budged, but remained rooted in place as though he had all of eternity to wait. His cold gray eyes met Jonah's, leaving no doubt whatsoever that the situation with Ella was a highly personal matter. Still, Jonah wasn't one to back down from a fight. Using his height and breadth to secure his position in front of the woman, he turned his back on Rafe.

"Anything else I can do for you?" he offered deliberately, folding his arms across his chest. Unless she asked him to move, it would take a bulldozer to shift him from his stance.

Despair filled Ella's eyes. "I'm afraid not. Welcome to the Cinderella Ball. Enjoy your visit and we wish you a…" Her voice wavered, but she recovered swiftly. "We wish you a joyous future."

She'd as good as handed him his walking papers. And as much as he wanted to remain and help her out of whatever predicament Rafe represented, he didn't dare. He'd managed to gain entrance through sheer luck. He'd be a fool to push it. To his private disgust, he lingered anyway. Old habits, it would seem, died hard. "You're sure?" he asked softly.

Rafe stirred behind him. "Tell him to go, Ella. You know this is a private matter."

She gave Jonah a reassuring smile. "Rafe and I are old…" She hesitated, her smile turning bittersweet. "We're old associates. But thanks for your concern."

Jonah inclined his head. Sparing Rafe a final look of warning—and secretly amused at himself for bothering—he exited the reception line and plunged into the crowded ballroom. Despite the urgency of his own mission, if Ella had asked for his help, he'd have given it. He didn't have it in him to desert a woman in need. But since she hadn't asked…it was time to get down to business.

He had to find Eric and Nikki before it was too late.

Staring out across the packed ballroom, he realized what a monumental task he'd set himself. Finding his brother would be near to impossible—Eric wouldn't stand out among the multitudes, despite his slim height and gold-streaked hair. Jonah's eyes narrowed. But perhaps by zeroing in on the redheads, he could shake Nikki Ashton loose from the pack. And wherever he found Nikki, undoubtedly he'd find Eric, as well. Unwilling to waste another moment, he fixed on a possible candidate and began his pursuit.

Jonah leaned a shoulder against the wall and glared at the dancers twirling by. Damn it all! In the past ninety minutes, he'd waded through dozens of redheads in every shape, size and shade. And not one of them was Nikki Ashton. He stifled a yawn, struggling to throw off the exhaustion that dogged him. He needed more coffee—and he needed it bad. Check that. What he really needed was a few hours' sleep. If his mission wasn't so urgent, he'd call it a night and find somewhere to crash.

But it was urgent, and tired or not, he had to get on with it.

He took a deep breath, steeling himself to chase after the next redhead who floated by, when a tantalizingly familiar scent snagged his attention. It came from a woman several feet away. She had her back to him and was conducting an earnest conversation with a small, bookish individual. He hesitated, eyeing her upswept, Gibson girl hairstyle. She wasn't a bona fide redhead—at least she didn't have the brilliant sun-streaked red from the photograph. In fact, it didn't even come close. This woman's hair reflected the opulent darkness of polished mahogany, the color awash with vivid ruby highlights.

He started to dismiss her, but she shifted her stance, and her scent drifted by once again. If it wasn't the same perfume he'd smelled in Nikki Ashton's office, it was damned similar. Regardless, it roused his hunter's instincts and driven to act, he resumed the hunt.

"Ah, there you are," he interrupted her conversation with a lazy smile. "Sorry to take so long."

The woman turned abruptly, her gaze clashing with his. He'd made a mistake, he decided in that instant. This couldn't be the Ashton woman. Not only was her hair color all wrong, her eyes didn't match the china blue of the photo, either. Instead they were a velvety pansy blue, almost violet in their intensity. He'd accosted the wrong woman. Again. But this time he didn't give a damn. He was tired and angry and in desperate need of a ten-minute break—a break he intended to spend in the arms of a beautiful woman.

He slipped a hand around her waist. "You promised me the next waltz, remember?" he asked. Before she had a chance to argue, he inclined his head toward her companion. "Excuse us," he said without a trace of apology, and swung her onto the dance floor.

To his amusement, she didn't say a word, simply stepped into his arms as though she belonged. He was a tall man, but with her in high heels, the top of her head nestled just beneath his chin. Her scent wrapped around him and he closed his eyes, surrendering to the moment. She didn't pull away, but allowed him to mold her close, her lush curves settling into his as though they'd been specially made to fit. They danced in silence for several long minutes before curiosity drove him to look down at her.

Lord, she was a gorgeous woman. Her bone structure was exquisite, her creamy complexion bare of any freckles. She'd dressed all in ivory, the tailored jacket decorated with tiny seed pearls and crystal beads, and cut to accommodate her full breasts. She moved with ease, despite her short fitted skirt. But it was the glimpse of her long, shapely legs that caused a momentary qualm as he recalled Loren's description of Nikki Ashton. *She's a stunning woman, one of those leggy redheads.* Jonah frowned, eyeing his dancing companion speculatively. If he hadn't seen Nikki's picture, the woman he held in his arms could fit that description.

Then he caught sight of the wedding ring decorating her left hand and his gut clenched. Nikki was supposed to be married, too.

"This might be a good time to introduce ourselves," he suggested.

She shot him a wry look. "I assume that means we haven't met before, despite what you told Morey?" Her voice was as dark and rich as her hair, humor adding a musical note to her question.

"You caught me," he admitted, his mouth relaxing into a smile. "But it's an oversight I'm happy to correct."

"And I suppose that also means that I didn't promise you this or any other dance?" She glanced at him, amusement glinting in her eyes. "Did I?"

Those eyes intrigued him, the color an unusual blend of lavender and blue, the lighter portion of the iris ringed by a band of indigo. "Would you have forgotten if you had?"

She shook her head, a husky laugh escaping. "I suspect you'd be a hard man to forget."

It wasn't said flirtatiously, but with the cool candor of someone stating an indisputable fact. If he weren't so suspicious of her identity, he'd find her frankness appealing. "I'm Joe Alexander," he said, using the abbreviated name he'd assumed for the evening.

"Nikki Ashton," she replied.

It took every ounce of self-possession not to react, not to haul her off the floor and level her with accusations. The music ended just then, but his arms tightened around her. He hoped to hell Eric wasn't anywhere nearby or there'd be hell to pay. "One more dance."

Again she subjected him to that calm, assessing stare. "You aren't asking, are you?"

"No."

She hesitated, but before she could respond, the lights dimmed and the orchestra slipped into the next song. It was a slow, romantic one, chosen to encourage physical and conversational intimacy. Jonah gritted his teeth and molded her close, struggling to remain unaffected now that he knew who she was. She brushed against him as they drifted across the floor and his entire body clenched in response.

He wasn't the only one affected, he realized in the next instant. Delicate color tinted Nikki's cheeks and her breathing quickened. She wouldn't react to him like this if she were in love with another man came the furious thought. Unless, of course, she wasn't really in love. Curious to test his theory, Jonah slid his hand down the length of her spine, his palm settling into the hollow above her backside. The slightest amount of pressure set her tight against him.

And then he slowed their dance until it was no more than a pretext, a subtle form of foreplay. In the space of a few steps, it went from subtle to searing as her movements aligned themselves with his. He was practically making love to her right there on the floor—and she to him. Each step became part of a mating dance, her breasts crushed against his chest, her hips and thighs melded to his. She moaned, the sound barely more than a breathless sigh. But he heard it. He heard it and knew what she wanted.

"You feel it, too. Don't you?" he murmured.

"Yes."

The admission seemed torn from her. As though stunned by her own daring, she lifted her gaze to his, her eyes darkening like the sky before a gathering storm. But she didn't pull away, which only confirmed what he'd suspected. If she was in love with Eric, she wouldn't be responding to him. Not like this.

Determined to have final confirmation, he maneuvered her toward a dark corner. Their movements slowed until the gentle rocking motion was no more than an excuse to maintain as intimate a contact as possible. Her attraction was undeniable and impossible to ignore. Everything about her appealed—her full, lush mouth, her sunset-hued eyes, the rich auburn of her hair, the low, confidential pitch of her voice.

A small part of him fought to retain a clinical detachment. But as hard as he struggled to remember whom he held, that knowledge didn't change the intensity of his reaction. Whether he'd finally succumbed to jet lag or her allure outweighed his common sense, he couldn't tell. He only knew that he was driven by an instinct born in the male of his species millennia ago—an instinct urging him to abandon caution and take the object of his desire, by force if necessary.

Thrusting his hand into her hair, he tilted back her head and covered her mouth with his. He didn't ease into the kiss, didn't bother with preliminaries, but stamped his ownership in the most primitive way possible. She instantly yielded, offering sweet surrender in the face of his determined assault. It was that unexpected capitulation that almost sent him over the edge.

With an incoherent murmur, her lips softened, parted, encouraging him to plunder within. He didn't need a second invitation. He forged a union between them, mating his tongue with hers. She trembled in his arms, clinging to him as though he alone sustained her. And he, heaven help him, worshiped her with both hands and mouth. If they'd been anywhere but in such a public setting, he'd have taken what she offered with such unstinting passion. But he couldn't allow the burgeoning fire storm free rein.

Not here.

Not now.

Ultimately, it was that thought that restored his sanity.

With a muttered curse, he dragged his mouth from hers. He'd made a mistake touching her, he realized. Desire had given her beauty a wild edge and he couldn't help but wonder what she'd look like after a night of passion. Just the thought of her in his bed, her glorious hair spread across his pillows and her white, silken limbs entwined in his sheets almost destroyed his control.

Slowly, she opened her eyes and he saw then that she'd become a flame to his moth, a bewitching siren capable of enticing him to his doom. If his little brother saw them like this, he'd know what sort of woman he intended to marry. Whether she planned to line her pockets with Sanders money or she just hoped to advance her career, her reasons for marrying Eric had nothing to do with love. Jonah fought a surge of anger. The proof of that stood trapped within his arms, evidenced by the blatant desire reflected in a pair of pansy-soft eyes.

So where the *hell* was Eric? he wondered savagely. Why wasn't he here to witness the duplicity of his blushing bride-to-be?

His expression must have betrayed the violence of his thoughts. With a small murmur of dismay, she attempted to twist free. Jonah caught her close, not daring to release her. Not yet. Not until he decided what to do with her.

"Easy," he soothed, stroking her back. "Take it easy."

"Joe, please…"

There was a frantic note to the way she spoke his name and he knew what was coming. If he didn't act fast, she'd panic and run. And he'd never have the opportunity to uncover her plans for the evening. He slackened his hold, allowing her some breathing space while still keeping her within the circle of his arms.

"It's okay, Nikki. Just relax."

"Easier said than done." She drew a deep, shuddering breath. "Look, this was a mistake. Maybe—"

"Maybe we should make polite conversation for the next minute or two," he interrupted. "Would that help?"

She nodded in relief. "It might be wise."

"Fine. Let's see…" He fingered the cluster of pearls and crystal beads decorating her lapel. "You look stunning this evening. Very bridal." He used the word deliberately, hoping to guide the conversation toward Eric and their impending nuptials. To his surprise, her tension dissipated.

His increased.

Didn't it bother her that she'd just made passionate

love to a complete stranger while her fiancé waited somewhere in the vicinity? A muscle jerked in his cheek. Apparently not.

She gave a self-conscious shrug, her gaze darting to meet his. "Isn't that the idea?"

"To look bridal tonight?" His eyes narrowed as he assessed the implications of her remark. Then he caught her left hand in his and lifted it until the overhead light sparked off her gold wedding band. "Most brides aren't already married."

"Sorry," she said with a wry laugh. "I've worn it for so long, I forgot it was there."

"I don't imagine your husband has forgotten."

"I don't have a husband. That's why I'm here."

"To get married," he clarified.

"Well, of course."

"And where is your groom-to-be?"

She'd recovered her poise and offered a cool, mysterious smile, so at odds with her fiery looks. "I haven't found him. Yet."

"And when he shows up?"

"Then we'll marry." A small frown touched her brow. "Isn't that how it works?"

His mouth quirked to one side. "Damned if I know."

"Look…" She moistened her lips, drawing his attention to their swollen fullness.

He'd done that, Jonah realized, or rather his kisses had. Here she stood waiting for her future husband while the taste of another man lingered on her lips. The anger that had smoldered just beneath the surface caught fire. What sort of woman was she? And why hadn't Eric seen through her? As though sensing that something about their conversation had gone awry, she stepped clear of his embrace.

"Perhaps this would be a good time to become better acquainted."

A harsh laugh escaped before he could prevent it. "I'd say the past few minutes pretty much covered that. Wouldn't you?"

His sarcasm didn't go unnoticed. She wrapped her arms around her waist in a defensive gesture. "I meant... Would you mind if I asked a few questions?"

"About what?"

"About you."

He eyed her with suspicion. "What do you want to know?"

She shrugged. "Why don't we start with the basics? Where are you from?"

"Originally? Chicago."

"And more recently?"

"Abroad."

That caught her attention. "You've been living overseas?" she asked with a delighted smile. "That's perfect. Will you be staying in this country for a while or—"

"My plans are indefinite." Impatience crept into his voice. "I should be able to wrap up the situation here in a week or two."

Disappointment drained the animation from her face. "I'm...I'm sorry to hear that. Is there any possibility you might alter your plans?"

What the hell was going on? Did she hope to arrange some future rendezvous? He glared in frustration, knowing he couldn't ask without tipping his hand. But damn it all, what about Eric?

"What is it you want?" he demanded bluntly.

She stiffened. "Nothing that will fit in with your plans, I'm afraid," she said, retreating behind a remote coolness.

"How the hell do you know that?"

She took a quick step backward, distancing herself still further. Jonah grimaced in annoyance, aware their rapport dissipated with each passing second. He'd screwed up but good and didn't have a clue how to make a graceful recovery.

"I'm based in New York," she explained. "If you were willing to move there, perhaps we could work something out. But—"

Work something out? Rage made him blind to everything else. He caught her arm and yanked her close. "Lady, I'm going to ask you one last time. What is it you're asking me?"

Alarm flared in her wide eyes. "I *was* asking if you'd relocate to New York. But now I just want you to let go of my arm."

Slowly, he released her and stepped back. It had to be exhaustion. There couldn't be any other excuse for his behavior. "Sorry," he muttered, thrusting a hand through his hair. "I didn't mean to hurt you."

"Forget it," she retorted. "Now if you'll excuse me, I need to find my future husband." And with that she turned on her heel and walked away.

CHAPTER TWO

NIKKI swept across the ballroom, determined to put as much distance between her and Joe Alexander as possible. Never in her entire life had she lost control like that. She fought to draw a deep, steadying breath. What could she have been thinking? Control was everything to her.

And she'd lost it the instant he'd put his hand on her.

Lost it? Hah! She'd given it up without so much as a token struggle.

She shook her head. How could she have been so foolish? Since the day her parents had died, she'd been forced to take charge of her odd assortment of relatives—Krista and Keli, Uncle Ernie and Aunt Selma, her cousins.... They all routinely turned to her with their problems. And with cool, calm logic, she'd resolved every single one they'd dumped in her lap. Even when her work situation had turned problematic, she'd found a solution without asking anyone for help.

She was proud of that. Proud of the fact that no matter how desperate the circumstances, she'd never become emotional, never failed to choose a course of action and never, ever lost her cool.

Until tonight.

She risked a quick glance over her shoulder. Joe

stood where she'd left him—apart from the glittering crowd, his arms folded across his chest—watching her with a fierce green-tinged gaze. She looked away, shaken. What had just happened? One minute she'd been kissed to within an inch of her life, and the next he'd treated her as though she were beneath contempt. It didn't make any sense.

She balled her hands into fists.

More than anything, she wanted to forget him and move on to the next man. But she couldn't. Joe was too fascinating. From the moment he'd intruded on her conversation with Morey, she'd been utterly spellbound, walking into his arms as though she'd been born to do so.

Was it his eyes? she wondered. They were such an odd shade of hazel—flashing green fire one moment, before darkening to a crisp golden brown the next. Or perhaps it was the keen intelligence she'd glimpsed in his stare, the instinctive knowledge that he'd fought his way through every single one of the years marking his hard, chiseled face. Whatever it had been, it had ignited an answering spark in her. Even when a cold sharpness had settled in his gaze, he'd still managed to hold her captive.

"Excuse me," an earnest young man interrupted, tapping her shoulder. "Would you care to dance?"

Unable to concoct a plausible excuse for refusing, she reluctantly slipped into his arms. She'd have time for regrets later. But not now, not when she had business to attend to. It was growing late and she still hadn't found a suitable husband. Unfortunately, Joe Alexander had succeeded in destroying what little enthusiasm she'd managed to summon for the job. She suspected it would be a challenge to find anyone else who came close to matching him.

She glanced at her current partner and struggled to muster some interest. He was a handsome man. Very handsome. In fact, his features bordered on the classic. Best of all, his rounded jaw didn't so much as hint at an annoyingly stubborn nature. Nor did he have thick, winged brows that notched upward in silent demand for answers to unreasonable questions. He also lacked that penetrating stare that stole every thought from her head.

Instead, his nose was arrow straight—no intriguing little bump to suggest a barroom brawl. His lips were on the narrow side—no wide, sensuous mouth capable of stealing soul-altering kisses from unwary women. And he had a soft tenor voice—no deep, rumbling bass tones that echoed through her mind long after the words had died.

He was quite, quite perfect.

And quite, quite boring.

She sighed. This had to stop! She had to quit comparing every man she met to Joe. She risked another brief look at her current dance partner, determined to find something that appealed. His hair was a pleasant enough shade of brown, but a degree or two darker than Joe's and lacking the startling sun-bleached streaks. Nor did this man's height compare. At a guess, Joe stood several inches over six feet. Broad shouldered and built along rock-solid proportions, he eclipsed most of the men she'd spoken to so far that evening, including this one. She'd never met anyone who exuded quite such an air of power and authority.

So what in the world had gone wrong?

"My name's Dan Forsythe," her dance partner announced at length.

She broke off her analysis long enough to reply, "Nikki Ashton." Was it something she'd said that had annoyed him?

"It's a pleasure to meet you."

Something she'd done?

"Er...the song's ending."

Something she didn't say or do?

"Would you...would you care to talk for a few minutes? Nikki?" He stopped dead in the middle of the floor. "Ms. Ashton?"

She blinked. "The song ended."

He looked at her oddly. "Yes. And I thought we could take the opportunity to talk. You know. Get better acquainted."

Nikki released a quiet sigh as they left the floor. How different from Joe's more aggressive approach. But then, if Dan had swept her off to a darkened corner and attempted to kiss her, she'd probably have slapped his face. "What is it you're looking for in a wife?" she asked, deciding to be blunt.

"Children," he blurted with awkward enthusiasm. His gaze slipped from her face to a spot somewhere behind her and then back again. "Do you like kids?"

"I'm afraid I'm not ready to have a baby," she confessed gently. "At least not yet."

"Oh."

His focus continued to shift to a point somewhere behind her with nervous regularity. She refrained from turning around, but couldn't help wondering if he'd found someone more appealing. She cleared her throat to regain his attention. "The problem is, I have a career."

"Then kids are out, huh?"

She hesitated. *Forget Joe*! she told herself sternly. *Concentrate on the business at hand*. She'd known all along that certain concessions might be necessary to achieve her goal. Her problem with Dan mirrored many she faced at work—two parties with similar ambitions but with differing needs and objectives. She just had to find an equitable solution to their dilemma. "I wouldn't say children are out, precisely."

"Still, you're not interested in having any." He looked behind her again while at the same time edging backward. "Are you?"

If she didn't do something fast, she'd lose him. "Perhaps we could reach a compromise," she offered quickly. "If you were willing to wait a while to have children—"

"Forget it. I…I guess we're just not compatible. It was nice meeting you." And with that he vanished into the surrounding crowd.

She frowned. That was odd. Why had he kept looking behind her? He'd almost acted as if… Her eyes narrowed suspiciously. He'd almost acted as if he were intimidated by something. Or some*one*. She spun around, not in the least surprised to discover Joe standing nearby. He held a glass of champagne, which he raised in salute when their gazes clashed. Why, that dirty, rotten… Hadn't he done enough harm allowing her to believe he was interested in her when he wasn't? Why did he have to chase off those who might be sincere?

Snatching the arm of the closest available male, she offered a dazzling smile. "Care to dance?"

To her relief, he didn't flat out refuse. But the next ten minutes proved to be the most arduous of her life.

It didn't take any time at all to discover he was a pompous ass looking for a wife whose qualifications roughly equaled those of a maid. Worse, he danced in a tight little circle so that every few seconds she came face to face with Joe.

The instant the dance ended, she excused herself, determined to find a better scouting location—one that offered a suitable array of potential partners and yet *didn't* contain Joe Alexander. Unfortunately, she lost out on both counts. Over the next thirty minutes, her situation progressed from bad to worse. It didn't matter whom she spoke to or where she went—there was Joe. Several times he blatantly listened in on her conversation, making her so nervous she couldn't even string a coherent sentence together.

Finally, she couldn't take any more. Determined to put an end to his harassment, she excused herself from her latest disaster and crossed to confront him. She wouldn't give up control as she had before, she told herself. This time she'd take command of their conversation. And no matter what, she wouldn't allow him to touch her.

He greeted her with a lazy smile, a smile directly at odds with the hard glitter in his eyes. "Having fun?"

"No, I'm not. And it's all your fault. Why won't you leave me alone?" she demanded. "What do you want?"

"From you? Not a thing."

"Then why are you following me?"

"Curiosity."

"*Curiosity*?" She blinked in surprise. "But why? You had your chance to work something out between us. You blew it. So why can't you go away and let me find a husband?''

He stilled, eyeing her intently. "Is that what you're doing? Looking for one?''

"I'm trying! But you're making it rather difficult. You keep scaring them off.''

She could see him analyzing her answers, considering them as though they were puzzle pieces that didn't quite fit. His brows notched upward and she knew what that meant—another of his impossible questions. "Tell me this…'' He fixed her with an irritable glare. "Are you meeting your future husband here or not?''

"Yes, of course,'' she said. "Or I will be if you stop interfering.''

"When and where will you meet him?''

"How would I know that?'' she retorted, exasperated. "I'm not a fortune-teller.''

He frowned. "I'm a bit confused. I was under the impression that you were waiting for someone specific.''

She planted her hands on her hips. "I am. I have very specific qualifications, and for your information, you don't meet a single one.'' Honesty forced her to concede, "Well, maybe one or two. But not the important ones.''

The predatory gleam returned to his eyes. "Perhaps we should discuss the ones I do meet.''

"Forget it,'' she muttered.

Jonah came to a decision. He still didn't know whether or not she was waiting for Eric. Unfortunately, as much as he preferred the direct approach, he couldn't simply ask, not without revealing a suspicious amount of ignorance. But he needed answers.

And one way or another, she was going to provide them. "Arguing like this isn't helping either of our situations. We need to talk. Truce?"

She hesitated. "I don't know.... It's getting late and I can't afford to miss this opportunity. If we can't work something out, I've lost a lot of time."

"I won't keep you long." His hand settled on her shoulder. "Why don't we go outside and talk?"

He didn't give her a chance to think of an excuse, but opened a pair of French doors leading to the gardens and ushered her through. It was cool outside, though not uncomfortably so. Slate stepping-stones marked pathways that twisted in and out of exotic trees and shrubs, their presence an incongruous touch in the Nevada desert. Splashes of moonlight revealed tables and benches half-hidden in the leafy vegetation. Few were occupied, but Jonah wanted to insure their privacy and led her deeper into the garden.

In the far recesses, they approached a table tucked snugly beneath a tree covered in twinkling fairy lights. The couple who'd been sitting there were just leaving. The man tucked a set of papers into his suit coat pocket and planted a possessive arm around the woman. She peeked out from beneath white blond hair and exchanged a smile of recognition with Nikki.

"Good luck," she whispered before being whisked along the pathway toward the mansion.

"A friend of yours?" Jonah asked curiously.

"We met earlier in the evening," Nikki confessed. "I was a bit nervous and she sat and talked to me for a while."

"Why were you nervous?"

She shrugged. "This is a pretty big step, don't you think? I suppose I was having second thoughts about the wisdom of going through with this sort of marriage.''

This sort of marriage? What the hell did that mean? He waited until she sat down before joining her on the bench. Enough was enough. The time had come for answers and he intended to get them, no matter what it took. "This is a rather unusual party," he probed carefully.

"Until I read the article, I'd never heard of anything like it," she agreed. "Imagine throwing a ball for people who want to get married."

So he hadn't misunderstood the card he'd found on her desk. This *was* a marriage ball. Still, he suspected he hadn't quite gotten the full picture. For instance— where was Eric? "That's how you found out about it?" he prompted. "From an article?"

"Yes. It was in our local newspaper." Her smile glimmered in the darkness. "My sister showed it to me. She found it highly amusing."

"But you didn't."

Her smile faded. "No," she admitted. "It struck me as the perfect solution."

"Solution to what?"

An innocent enough question, yet it clearly hit a nerve. She clenched her hands, the fairy lights in the trees above ricocheting off her wedding band. "It's…it's a long story," she said at last.

"I have all the time in the world." He didn't exaggerate. He was determined to find out what the hell was going on, even if it took all night. "Talking about it might help."

She hesitated, and he could tell she was debating whether or not to answer. "I suppose complete honesty might be best…all things considered."

"I gather you don't always feel that way."

She turned her head sharply at the disapproval coloring his words. "Normally, I believe in honesty above all else," she asserted, her tone growing notably cooler.

"But whatever your story is—it involves a lie," he retorted. He didn't attempt to placate her. He couldn't. Not when she'd lied about something—something that might affect Eric's well-being.

She didn't hesitate. "Yes," she admitted. "It does."

"Tell me about it."

He endured another brief silence while she gathered her thoughts. Even in the short amount of time they'd spent together, he had noticed that quality about her—her control and precision, the care she took before speaking. She'd be a tough one to break, should it come to that.

"It's my own fault," she began in a low voice. "I never should have lied about being married."

Of all the possible confessions he'd expected to hear, this one didn't come close to making the list. "What did you say?"

She held out her hand, and her wedding band winked in the subdued lighting. "You asked me about this earlier. What I didn't explain is…it's pure decoration. I'm not married." A whisper of a laugh escaped. "I'd hardly be here if it were real, now would I?"

He was at a loss to answer that. Not until he found out more about this ball. "Then why the pretense?"

"The company I work for prefers married executives."

Who the hell had told her that? "So you decided to accommodate them?"

"I played with the idea. But not too seriously. At least not until—"

"Until?"

"There's a man at work. He's very sweet. Young."

"He's interested in a personal relationship with you?" Was that possible? Could Loren and Della have misunderstood the situation? Or was Nikki Ashton just a damned good liar?

"He's more than interested."

"I still don't understand. You faked a marriage because you couldn't tell him no? Isn't that a little extreme?"

"Not when the man in question is my boss."

He stood. The way she said it—with such detached candor—convinced him she spoke the truth. At least the truth as she saw it. *Damn Eric!* What the hell had he instigated? "Why are you here?" he demanded.

She tilted her head to look up at him and the silvery moonlight caressed the pale beauty of her face. Her expression appeared calm and serene. But her eyes gathered in the shadows surrounding them, their fathomless depths hinting at untold secrets. "I'm here for the same reason you are. To meet someone compatible enough to marry."

"Couldn't you do that in New York?"

"Possibly. But courtships are often lengthy affairs. By attending the Cinderella Ball, I can meet someone, we can marry tonight and return home in the morning. Problem solved."

He must have misunderstood. After almost thirty hours without sleep, it was a distinct possibility. His mouth tightened. He'd better have misunderstood, because he didn't like the sound of this at all. "The people attending this party…that's why they're here? To marry complete strangers? They meet, choose someone at random and marry—all in *one night*?"

"Of course," she responded, surprised.

"Of course." He realized then that she was serious. Dead serious. "If that's true, you people are in desperate need of reality checks."

She frowned, her brows arching in question. "Now *I* don't understand. Aren't you here because you want to marry?"

He had no intention of answering that one. "Let's focus on you right now," he suggested. "We can discuss my situation later." He didn't give her time to respond, but continued with his interrogation. "You're marrying because your boss won't take no for an answer. Is that about the size of it?"

"There's a personal reason, as well."

"Which is?"

Her lashes flickered downward, concealing her expression. "As I said…it's personal."

He fought to hide his impatience. "So because of this personal reason and because you can't handle your boss any other way, you're going to marry a complete stranger."

She inclined her head, the rich auburn tones muted by the darkness. "I know. It sounds insane. But you see, everyone already thinks I *am* married."

He folded his arms across his chest, a hint of sarcasm creeping into his tone. "And since they do, you're going to turn this fiction into fact. That makes sense."

"I have no choice," she retorted, stung. "I'm not interested in acquiring a husband. Ever." She drew back into the shadows, her voice low and pained. "At least not for something as illusionary as love."

That gave him pause. "If that's how you feel, then why go through with such a crazy scheme?"

"Because it's the perfect solution."

"That's open to debate."

Her temper flared again. "This isn't some half-cocked plan I've devised," she told him. "I've given this marriage idea a lot of thought. Aside from needing to resolve a private dilemma, I have a boss who thinks he's in love with me."

Jonah looked at her sharply. "And is he?"

"No. Eventually, he'll realize that for himself. But until he does, I need the protection of a real husband."

"How is this husband going to protect you from…" Damn, he'd almost slipped up. "What's his name?"

"Eric." She released her breath in a long sigh. "It won't be easy. I need someone sophisticated. Someone mature. Someone intimidating. Part of the problem is that I've told everyone that my husband has been out of the country for the past year. Unfortunately, it's left the impression that our marriage is in trouble."

"So you need a man who can dispel those doubts," Jonah said slowly. "With a real husband on the scene—someone who can act the part of a passionate spouse—Eric will realize there's no future in a relationship and get over his infatuation."

"Exactly."

"So where's the problem? If you're actually committed to going through with this crazy idea, why haven't you married already?"

Her laugh was half groan. "The problem is that no one I've met so far meets my qualifications. Either they're sweet, lovely gentlemen whom Eric would rip to shreds in no time or they're strong, independent types with their own agendas. And those agendas don't include moving to New York for the duration of our marriage."

"I can't believe that there isn't someone—"

"No? What about you?" She leaned forward, her gaze never wavering from his. "I can offer a home, a car and a modest salary. It doesn't even have to be a permanent arrangement. There was a man I met this evening who wanted a temporary wife. If you prefer, I'd be willing to agree to a short-term marriage, as well. I'll hire you to be my husband for whatever period of time is convenient, under whatever terms you deem fair, so long as my predicament with Eric is resolved by the time we get an annulment."

"Isn't this a little extreme? Can't you—" He broke off as a sudden thought struck him. "This Eric…is he harassing you? Has he said something—done anything—inappropriate?"

"No, no, nothing like that," she answered immediately. "He's…kind. Protective."

Jonah gave a short laugh. "Yes, I can see where that might be a problem."

"It's not funny! He's never touched me, at least not in any suggestive way. But I know how he feels." The iridescent seed pearls decorating the bodice of her suit jacket sparked with each agitated breath she drew. "I'm not imagining all this. I'm not!"

He held up his hands. "All right. I believe you. But tell me, how do you know it's personal? Isn't it possible you've mistaken friendly concern for something more serious?''

She shook her head. ''I wish that were the case, but it isn't.''

''Convince me.''

Her gaze flashed to his. ''I don't know why I should have to.''

''You're the one desperate for a husband. Convince me you really need one.''

Again she took her time considering his request. After several tense moments, she inclined her head. ''Very well. Can you tell when a woman is attracted to you?''

''Sometimes,'' he admitted. ''If she's obvious about it.''

''Well, Eric has been very obvious. Right from the start he signaled his interest.''

''What did you do?''

''I…I told him I didn't share his feelings and that mixing business with pleasure was always a mistake. Needless to say, he thought he could convince me otherwise, and that's when I made my first mistake.''

''You lied.''

''Yes. I said I was engaged. Afterward, he remained…hopeful.'' She shrugged. ''I guess he thought he could change my mind. So out of desperation, I showed up one Monday morning wearing a wedding ring.''

''Your second mistake,'' Jonah informed her caustically. ''Didn't the wedding ring slow him down?'' Unless his brother had switched personalities this past year, it should have.

''Yes, it did. He seemed to accept the futility of a relationship.''

"But something happened to alter that. What?"

"A company banquet. I came alone, claiming that my husband was out of the country. Eric went along with it for the next several weeks. He'd even tease me about my husband's prolonged absence. But as time passed and I never brought him to any company functions, Eric changed." She hesitated as though searching for the appropriate description. "He became indignant on my behalf, and later angry. I think the anger changed to suspicion when I didn't share his distress. He senses I'm hiding something, and I suspect he's hoping my marriage is on the rocks."

"That still doesn't mean—"

"There's more," she interrupted. "He confides in me, although I do nothing to encourage it."

Jonah tensed. "What does he talk about?"

"His family. Mostly his older brother—how much he admires and tries to emulate Jonah, how it feels to lurk in someone's shadow, how tough it is to live up to a legend."

"Sounds like he sees you more in the light of a mother confessor than a potential lover."

"I wish that was all it were. But if I get too close to him, I can see how he fights for control. And when he looks at me..." She shook her head. "I can't explain it, except to say that a woman is able to sense these things."

Jonah had heard enough. "So you see marriage as the only solution."

"I don't like it, but I have no choice. I have to find a way to correct the situation before it gets any further out of hand. It's starting to affect our work. We're both making mistakes and eventually someone is going to catch on. I can't afford to lose this job. It's too important to me." She stood and approached. "Joe, please help me. Will you…will you marry me?"

He knew how much it cost her to ask. But that didn't change his answer. "No."

"Why not?" Desperation crept into her voice. "What is it you want?"

"What I want isn't at issue right now. Look, Nikki, you have two choices. You can go through with this ridiculous scheme to marry or you can do the smart thing."

"And what's the smart thing?"

"Tell Eric the truth. Tell him you faked a marriage because you didn't want any romantic complications at the office. Tell him you're not interested in anything other than work and that you want him to leave you alone. Ask for a transfer."

She spun away, wrapping her arms about her waist. "I can't."

"Why not?"

"Do you really think it's so easy?" Her temper flared, stirring the passions she obviously kept under such tight control. "I'm supposed to waltz into work and make this big announcement, and then what?"

"Then you're off the hook."

"No, I'm not. By the end of the day, it's all over the office that I lied about being married because I couldn't handle the situation with my boss any other way. By the end of the next day, our clients have heard about it, and by the day after that, so have our competitors. It would do incalculable harm to my reputation, Eric's reputation, as well as damaging the credibility of our firm. We'd be a bad joke. Thanks, but no thanks. Anything is preferable to that, even marriage."

Her attitude toward marriage bothered him. A lot. Perhaps if he'd had time to sleep on it, he might have been in a position to offer a more palatable solution. But since he didn't have that luxury… "Come on." Slipping a hand beneath her elbow, he drew her close. "Let's go."

"Where?"

"To find you a man. If you're so determined to buy a husband, I'll help you shop for one."

She resisted the pull on her arm. "I don't understand. Why are you doing this?"

"Let's just say I'm a sucker for a hard luck story."

"But what about you?" she protested. "It's getting late. Aren't you worried you'll miss your chance to find a wife?"

"Believe me, finding a wife is the least of my worries." The very least. He stopped in the middle of the walkway. "What's the problem, Nikki? Having second thoughts?"

A momentary hesitation disturbed the even tenor of her expression. It was quickly masked by a steely resolve. "No. I'm not having second thoughts."

"Then let's go."

The next hour only served to prove Nikki's point. No one they approached quite suited her needs. Most Jonah dismissed as being too weak. She was right— Eric wouldn't see them as a serious obstacle to his pursuit. If anything, he'd think he was doing her a favor. And those who would have held him at bay had their own requirements—which meant a wife to fulfill their criteria, not the other way around.

"There's a guy over there I haven't spoken to yet," Jonah said without much enthusiasm. The man in question was too old, too fat and too desperate. Eric would make mincemeat of him. But time was growing short.

"Don't bother," she replied with a shiver. "How about—" She broke off, her face paling. "Oh, no!"

"What is it? What's wrong?"

She twisted around, practically throwing herself into his arms. "Quick! Hold me."

His arms closed around her automatically and he tucked her close. His hand skated down the length of her spine, molding her more firmly against him. She felt like heaven, soft and warm, her unique scent filling his lungs. If he hadn't believed in jet lag before, he sure as hell did now. There couldn't be any other explanation for his reaction. It was too intense, too surreal.

Her breath came in quick, panicked bursts and he lowered his head close to her ear. "What is it, Nikki? What's wrong?"

She lifted her face, her mouth inches from his. For a crazy instant he thought she intended to kiss him. Then he saw her expression. Stark disbelief registered in the pansy blue of her eyes. "Eric's here," she whispered.

CHAPTER THREE

"I CAN'T believe it," Nikki exclaimed. "How did he find me?"

Jonah grimaced. He had a fairly good idea. The all too efficient Jan seemed a safe bet. He chanced a quick look toward the reception area. Eric stood there, an earnest expression on his face, talking to the Montagues. Undoubtedly, he was attempting to charm his way into the ball. And knowing Eric, he had every chance of succeeding. Jonah swore beneath his breath. The situation was more serious than he'd suspected.

A lot more serious.

"Come on." He dropped an arm around Nikki's shoulders and swept her through the nearest doorway.

She'd turned ashen, her eyes huge and desperate. "What am I going to do now?"

Jonah set his jaw, trying to decide. He'd been a fool to drink even a single glass of champagne—particularly when he hadn't slept for a day and a half. Right now he'd kill for a hot shower and eight solid hours between the sheets. Maybe then he could figure out an appropriate course of action. But tonight his exhaustion made that near impossible. Not that there were many avenues available to them. In fact, he'd only come up with one.

"It would seem we're out of options," he informed

her. "If he's this determined, you need to marry someone he can't intimidate."

"We've canvassed just about everyone here." She scanned the assembly with an air of urgency. "Who's left?"

"Me."

It took a full minute for that to sink in. Astonished, she turned to look at him. "But you said—"

"Forget what I said."

"You're willing to marry me?" she asked in disbelief. "Why? I mean, don't think I'm ungrateful, but…" Skepticism gradually replaced her surprise. "Why would you be willing to help me now when you wouldn't before?"

"I ignored one damsel in distress this evening," he said with a hint of self-mockery. "It just isn't in me to ignore another."

"I won't claim to understand what you mean by that."

"That's a relief." He offered a bland smile and indicated a corridor leading to a back staircase. "Shall we get this over with? We'll need a marriage license. I overheard someone say they're being processed downstairs in the library."

A small frown puckered her brow and she shook her head, indicating she wouldn't be so easily persuaded. He almost laughed aloud at the irony. Here he risked alienating his entire family to resolve a problem *she'd* created—and she still wasn't satisfied. If she'd just told Eric no from the start, instead of concocting this whole ridiculous scenario, they wouldn't be in their present predicament. Now, if he wanted to ensure his brother's well-being, salvage the jobs of two of International Investment's key personnel, as well as straighten out their hopelessly muddled personal lives, he'd have to take serious action.

"I know I'm not in a position to argue," she was saying.

"That's for damned sure."

She rebuked him with a look. "I do, however, have a few concerns."

He released his breath in a gusty sigh. "Naturally."

"First…I expect you to convince Eric we're a happily married couple. Can you do that?"

His eyes narrowed as he absorbed the slight. The mere fact that she needed to ask underscored her lack of faith in his abilities. Not many could have offered such an insult and escaped without repercussions. "I'll convince him that if he approaches my wife with anything other than business in mind, he'll regret it." He allowed a hint of his displeasure to show. "Or don't you think he'll believe I'm serious?"

She held his gaze for a tempestuous five seconds before looking away, color sweeping into her cheeks. "He'll believe you," she concurred.

"Fine. Let's go."

She dug in her heels. "Wait a minute. I'm not through."

He ground his teeth. "Lady, I said I'd marry you. What more do you want?"

"I just need to make sure we understand each other."

He grimaced. "Trust me, I understand more than you realize."

"I'm talking about specifics. I don't want any dispute later on."

"Then you'd better talk fast because I'm giving

you precisely thirty seconds,'' he informed her tightly. ''After that, you're on your own.''

Apparently, she took his warning seriously. Without wasting any further time, she ticked her questions off on her fingers. ''Okay. You've already agreed to convince Eric we're a happily married couple. Second…you're willing to move to New York, right? You'll stay with me until the situation with Eric is resolved?''

''Yes.''

''Third…you understand that your actions mustn't put my job in jeopardy?''

''I understand.'' He folded his arms across his chest. ''Is that it? Are you through now? No fourth, fifth or sixth on your list?''

''Just a fourth.''

''Which is?''

If he hadn't caught the turbulent glitter in her eyes, he'd have thought her completely unaffected by their discussion. After all, she'd rattled off her points like some sort of human computer. But that flash of deepening violet gave her away. Whatever her final point concerned, it should have been first on her list, not last.

''I need to know your expectations.''

He lifted an eyebrow, surprised by her request. He'd anticipated something far more crucial. ''I expect to marry you, save your bacon and then send you on your merry way,'' he replied. At the same time, he'd protect International Investment from any further business debacles and allow Eric time to come to his senses.

''And that's all?'' She moistened her lips. ''You won't ask any more of me?''

Comprehension dawned, and with it came a purely masculine reaction, a predator's response to spotting its prey unprotected and vulnerable. He stepped closer, his attention drawn to the pulse fluttering frantically at the base of her throat. "Are you asking if I want to sleep with you?" he questioned deliberately.

She retained her cool, although he suspected it was a hard-fought battle. "Yes. I guess that's what I'm asking."

"I don't think it's worth discussing."

To his amusement, she looked relieved. Did she misinterpret all business discussions as badly as this one? he couldn't help but wonder. He'd have to speak to her about that. He couldn't afford to have the company put at risk because of her erroneous assumptions. "Now, have we addressed all of your concerns?"

"Yes."

"Then I suggest we get this over with before your boss succeeds in talking his way past the Montagues and tracks us down." He shot her a sharp glance. "He doesn't know the purpose of this ball, does he?"

"I don't think so. I told him I was flying out to meet my husband," she explained, then eyed him uneasily. "I don't know why he followed me. Maybe he was curious to meet you..." She released her breath in an exasperated sigh. "My husband, I mean."

"Or maybe he didn't believe you were really meeting anyone. Let's just hope the Montagues don't go into lengthy explanations about their reason for throwing this little shindig or we'll be up to our necks in it." He took her arm in an iron grip. "Let's find the library."

Footmen dressed in white and gold uniforms directed them downstairs to a county clerk who processed the marriage licenses. She wore a name tag that read, "Dora Scott." Discarded on one side of her desk was a sign announcing, "For faster service, feed me hors d'oeuvres." A short line had formed in front of her, but by the time they'd filled out the necessary applications, the room had emptied.

"Let's see who we have here," Dora said as they approached. She held out her hand for their forms.

Realizing he stood on the brink of disaster, Jonah hastened to introduce himself. "It's Joe. Joe Alexander." Nikki might not associate the abbreviated form of his name with Eric's half brother. But his given name was unusual enough that if Dora blurted it out, his identity would be all too evident. And he had no intention of revealing his connection to Eric until after they were safely married.

The clerk glanced at his application and chuckled. "Fine, *Joe.*" She examined the second form. "And Nicole."

"Nikki," the bride-to-be hastily corrected. She indicated the sign. "I'm afraid we didn't bring any hors d'oeuvres."

"Forget it. One more cheese puff and I'd probably pop. Okay, folks, let's get through this." Within minutes, Dora had typed up the necessary paperwork and handed them a thick blue-and-white envelope. "Marriage ceremonies are conducted in salons off the main ballroom. Give the envelope to whoever officiates. You get to keep the fancy-looking certificate inside as a souvenir. But it's not a legal document. That comes later in the mail." She glanced at them. "Any questions?"

"Not a one," Jonah responded.

Dora nodded. "In that case, I have one piece of advice. Take care of each other, hear?"

"Taking care of people is what I'm best at," Nikki assured the clerk.

"Funny," Jonah muttered. "That's what I was going to say."

"Swell. A pair of caring souls," Dora said with a laugh. "Get out of here, the both of you. You need to get hitched and I have work to do."

"We better make this quick," Jonah advised as they returned to the ballroom. "If Eric managed to talk his way in, I don't want to run into him at an inopportune moment."

Nikki paused outside the door to the first salon. "It seems we have a choice of ceremonies. What sort do you prefer?"

"The short-and-to-the-point sort."

He shoved open the nearest door and looked inside. Nikki caught a glimpse over his shoulder and made a small sound of disappointment. Not that he blamed her. The room was attractive, but very stiff and formal. Even when the judge beckoned him to come forward, he hesitated. For some reason, he found ice blue brocade, walnut furniture and artificial flowers a total turnoff. Besides, it wouldn't suit Nikki.

He backed out and closed the door. "Bad choice," he announced.

"What's wrong with it?"

"Too long a line," he lied, fully aware that from her angle she hadn't seen enough to dispute his verdict. "Let's try another."

Opening the door to the next salon, he nodded in satisfaction. It was perfect. Tiny and intimate, it had an old-fashioned, almost Victorian feel to it. A dainty Laura Ashley rose print covered the walls, and the overstuffed couch and wing chairs were finished in a deep ruby velvet with ivory lace arm covers. Centered along one wall was a cherry highboy displaying an ornate silver tea service. Along the other was a fireplace with a gold-leaf beveled mirror above the mantel that captured an overview of the entire room. Fresh flowers filled delicate Waterford crystal vases, the fragrance of roses offset by the smoky scent of hickory from a gently crackling fire.

If he could have chosen the perfect setting for Nikki, it would have been one like this.

She stepped into the room behind him and caught her breath in delight. "Oh, Joe, this is wonderful."

"It'll do," he agreed with a lazy smile, not quite certain why the setting for a temporary marriage mattered so much. He must be more exhausted than he'd thought.

A minister rose from a chair beside the fire and smiled at them, his thick white hair reflecting the leaping flames. "Welcome. I assume you wish to be married?"

"Yes, please," Nikki answered without hesitation. "Right away, if you don't mind."

The minister smiled indulgently. "Very well, my dear. But before I begin, I'm required to ask that you give careful consideration to what you're about to do."

Jonah nearly groaned. If he did that, he might come to his senses and back out. No, better they get this over with and fast. "Look, we've considered, we've decided and we're in a hurry." He thrust the envelope containing the necessary forms at the minister. "Could you just get on with it?"

The minister accepted the envelope and adjusted the wire-rimmed glasses perched on the end of his nose. "I'm afraid not," he replied, his gentle blue eyes turning somber. "You see, marriage is a serious commitment, not to be entered into lightly. So I ask that you face each other and look carefully at your partner. Make sure that your choice is the right one."

Cursing beneath his breath—but realizing it was the only way they'd get this show on the road—Jonah turned to look at Nikki, studying her with clinical detachment. At first, all he noticed was her appearance. Tall and beautifully proportioned, she was a stunning woman. Her translucent violet-flecked eyes met his without flinching. He liked that about her; he had from the start. Of course, there were other qualities he liked, as well.

Her mouth was the most kissable he'd ever encountered and her skin the softest he'd felt in an age. Even the deep auburn of her hair suited her to perfection. He half smiled in appreciation as he eyed her elegant topknot. Sometime during the evening, glossy tendrils had escaped to curl with fiery abandon about her temples and the nape of her neck.

And that's when he saw beneath the surface.

Her hairstyle mirrored her nature, he suddenly realized. She struggled to attain the appearance of severity and restraint, but couldn't quite achieve it. Equally, she fought an unending battle between the tempestuous aspects of her nature and the need for rigid control. On the surface, she appeared perfectly composed. But underneath smoldered an inferno that probably terrified her, that threatened the calm, orderly existence she'd built. With new insight, he looked at her again. And in the end it was those pansy-soft eyes that gave her away—betraying her uncertainty, her desperation, her passion, as well as her unwavering strength and determination.

He wanted this woman.

He wanted to feed those sparks of inner rebellion, to release the delicious fire she kept tamped inside and to be scorched by the heat of it. Keeping all those emotions bottled up couldn't be good for her, and he decided then and there to find a way to demolish her control. Hell, he'd probably be doing her a favor.

In the meantime, he had to find a way to alleviate her fears. As though in response to his thought, the scent of roses drifted to him again. He turned and crossed to the nearest vase, stripping a few sprigs of baby's breath from the arrangement.

"Come here," he ordered gruffly.

She crossed to his side, hesitating a few feet in front of him. He closed the distance between them and very gently arranged the baby's breath around the loose knot crowning her head. Her hands slipped across his chest to cling to the lapels of his black suit coat as she waited for him to finish. She wouldn't be happy when she discovered his identity, he realized with regret. But he hoped to convince her that what he'd done was in everyone's best interest.

At least, that's what he told himself.

Nikki stared up at Joe, scrutinizing the taut, uncompromising planes of his face. She hardly dared to breathe as he tucked the flowers in her hair. Satisfied, he looked at her, a reassuring tenderness glittering in his eyes. And with that one look, all her fears dissolved.

She'd been so nervous, the enormity of her decision almost overwhelming her. When the minister had suggested they reconsider the step they were about to take, she'd almost fled the room. Not even her desperation over Eric could have dissuaded her from backing out, even at this late hour. Only the memory of Krista—and that overheard phone conversation—held her rooted in place.

But looking into Joe's hazel-green eyes and seeing his confidence and self-possession went a long way toward easing her uncertainties. He must have known how close to the edge she'd come, for he leaned down, his breath mingling with hers.

"Don't worry," he whispered in reassurance. "I'll take care of everything."

Cupping her face, he sealed his vow, his mouth capturing hers in a gentle kiss. She opened to him, the last of her misgivings fading within the protective strength of his arms. It would all work out. With Joe at her side, she could solve all her problems.

Reluctantly, he released her. "Any more doubts?" he asked.

"None."

"Then will you marry me, Ms. Ashton?"

A tremulous smile teased the corners of her mouth. "Yes, Mr. Alexander. I will."

"Have you reached a decision?" the minister asked.

"Please begin the ceremony," Nikki requested, perfectly calm and collected. Perfectly willing. "And it's Joe and Nikki."

With a rakish grin, Jonah plucked a single rose from the nearest vase and handed it to her. At her questioning look, he shrugged. "A bride should have a bouquet."

The ceremony was surprisingly brief, as per their request. Just before the minister pronounced them husband and wife, he peered at them over his spectacles. "Would you care to exchange rings?" he asked. "We have them on hand. They're tokens, really. Just something to use until you're able to replace them with the genuine article."

"I already have a ring," Nikki told Jonah in a hesitant undertone. "Everyone would think it strange if I wore something different now."

"Give it to me."

She slipped it off her finger and dropped it into his outstretched palm. "What about you?"

"I'll need a wedding band."

The minister dutifully fetched a tray of rings. The third one Jonah tried fitted. To her surprise the design on his ring almost matched her own. In fact, if she didn't know better, she'd have believed it to be every bit as real. Even more real was the moment he slipped the ring onto her finger. It was a moment out of time, a brief instant in which their marriage attained a veracity and permanence she hadn't expected.

It isn't a permanent marriage, she tried to tell herself. *It's only temporary.* But the image of their exchanging wedding bands became fixed in her mind, an indelible snapshot that she knew she'd carry for a long time to come.

And as the minister pronounced them husband and wife, Nikki realized she was in deep, deep trouble.

It wasn't until they'd reached her rental car that Nikki's earlier doubts crept back. Had she done the right thing? Had she married the right man? *Had she lost her mind*?

"So where do we go from here?" Jonah asked once they were confined in the dark interior of the sedan.

"I have a room at the Grand Hotel. It's not too far from here." She fought to keep her voice even and nonchalant. "I...I thought we could spend the night there before returning to New York in the morning."

"My ticket's open-ended," he said with a shrug. "Flying out tomorrow is fine with me."

"Are you staying at the Grand, too?"

He shook his head "I wasn't sure what to expect tonight so I booked a room in Las Vegas."

He didn't know what to expect? That didn't make sense. Surely he expected to find someone compatible and marry her. "Why—"

"How about—"

She smiled at the momentary confusion, her tension easing. "Sorry. Go ahead."

"Since your hotel is closer, why don't we stay there?"

Filing her question away for the moment, she gave her attention to the matter at hand. "What about your luggage? Would you like to pick it up now?"

"I don't see the point. We can take care of it on the way to the airport tomorrow. In the meantime, I'm sure your hotel can provide me with the bare essentials. To be honest, what I could use more than anything else is a bed."

She hoped he didn't mean that the way it sounded. Reaching for the ignition, she cast him a quick, suspicious glance, but it was too dark to read his expression. "You must be tired," she commented pointedly.

He caught her hand before she could start the engine. "Don't let your imagination run away with you." Amusement rumbled in the deep tones of his voice. "As much as a wedding night with you appeals, sleep appeals even more."

"I knew what you meant," she snapped, annoyed that he preferred sleep over her—and even more annoyed that she'd find anything objectionable about that fact.

She started the car, the engine roaring as she gave it far too much gas. Damn it! Why had everything turned so awkward? If only she could pretend he was a difficult client. She'd always been assigned the tough ones. It was her métier and one of the primary reasons she'd been put in charge of special projects at International Investment. In every instance, she'd used her analytical skills to figure out what the client wanted, then cool, calm reason with a touch of charm to negotiate from there.

She gnawed on her lip. Unfortunately, Joe was her husband, not a client. And she suspected that neither charm nor reason would cut much ice with him if he decided to be difficult.

She pulled onto the road leading to the hotel, determined to remain in control of the situation. After all, she wasn't interested in him as a man, at least not sexually. Her reaction to those kisses could be explained away as purely hormonal. That was it. It could be chalked up to a normal, healthy reaction any overworked, stressed and desperate woman would have to a virile, violently masculine, wildly sexy male animal. It had nothing whatsoever to do with a growing emotional attachment. She'd learned her lesson the hard way in that particular arena.

Emotional attachment led to pain and disillusionment and financial ruin.

Logic and control kept her world safe and protected.

All she needed was a husband to help resolve her problems with Eric and Krista. Once they were settled, she and Joe could get an annulment. Then she'd be free—free to simplify her life and pursue her career. In fact, she'd be able to give her full attention to work and not worry about anything else. That would make her happy. Right?

"You okay?"

"I'm fine," she insisted with a too-bright smile. "I'm looking forward to starting a new life. Off with the old and on with the new and all that."

"Yeah, right."

She turned into the hotel parking lot and suddenly remembered his earlier comment. "I've been meaning to ask…why didn't you know what to expect?"

He shook his head as though to clear it. "What?"

"A few minutes ago. You said you'd booked a room in Vegas because you didn't know what to expect at the Cinderella Ball."

"Did I?" He gave a weary shrug. "I must be more tired than I thought. I don't remember saying that."

She pulled into a parking space and turned off the ignition. "You did. To be exact you said—"

"I guess I wasn't certain I'd find anyone who would suit," he cut in decisively. "I didn't know what sort of women to expect at the ball."

It wasn't until they were in the elevator that she

found the flaw in his response. "I still don't understand," she began.

"What don't you understand now?" He spoke calmly, yet she caught a betraying flash of autumn gold in his cool gaze.

"You didn't have any conditions."

He leaned against the back wall and folded his arms across his chest. "Come again?"

"Conditions." She frowned as the elevator panel blinked its way through the lower numbers. "I asked what you wanted out of the marriage and you didn't have a list. Every other man I spoke to had some requirement or request or need." She turned to look at him. "Except you."

"So?"

The door slid open and he gestured for her to proceed. "So...you're intelligent. And you're good-looking in an uncompromising sort of way," she itemized slowly. "That much would be obvious to most women who met you for the first time."

"Gee, thanks."

Recalling the passionate kiss he'd laid on her, she conceded, "Unfortunately, you're a bit on the aggressive side." Though he certainly knew his way around a woman's mouth. She glanced at him from beneath her lashes, deciding to keep that particular asset to herself.

"I'm a man, not a marshmallow. Aggression comes with the territory."

"You're also argumentative," she shot back. "But without a list, you're easy to please. That's your best quality, in case you didn't know. So why didn't you think you'd find someone to suit?"

"I guess I have a pessimistic nature."

"So do I, but I was still fairly confident I'd find *someone*."

He stopped in the middle of the hallway and held out his hand. She stared at it blankly. "The key," he prompted in dangerously soft tones. "For the door."

"Oh. It's a card, not a key."

His hand didn't budge. "The card, then."

Reluctantly, she dug through her handbag and gave him the thin strip of plastic. "What I'm trying to say is…you never showed any interest in other women after you danced with me. In fact, you spent the whole time helping me find a husband instead of looking for a bride."

"What room?"

"Eighteen-twenty. You spent all that money to attend the Cinderella Ball and you didn't find a wife."

Reaching the appropriate door, he slid the card into the slot. The light on the steel plate by the knob flickered from red to green and the lock snicked open. "I believe that wedding ceremony we just went through means I found a wife." He thrust open the door. "After you."

She hesitated. "But I'm not a real wife. And you never explained. Exactly why did you need to get married?"

A muscle jerked in his jaw. "You're a real enough wife as far as I'm concerned. And I didn't." He planted his hand in the small of her back and ushered her firmly across the threshold. "Need to get married, that is."

"You didn't?"

She spun around as the door swung closed. He stood in front of it, a large, impregnable barrier. For the first time, she realized that aggressive men could also be intimidating—especially when the man in question was her husband. Perhaps if they were in an office instead of a hotel room and it was a business meeting instead of her wedding night, she wouldn't have felt so nervous. But he had such a grim expression on his face. She clasped her hands together, aware that her confidence was rapidly ebbing.

She cleared her throat. "If you didn't need to marry, then why…?"

"I didn't *need* a wife," he repeated, stepping away from the door and stalking into the sitting area toward her. "Not everyone gets married because it's the only way out of a tight spot. Some people actually marry for more pedestrian reasons. Like companionship. Or children. Or even love."

She fell back several steps, her eyes widening. "Is that why you wanted to get married? For love?"

"Why the sudden interest, Nikki?" His question had an edge she didn't like, a raspy quality that spoke of exhaustion and frustration and anger. "We had all night to talk. You could have asked these questions at any point during the evening. But you didn't give a damn about anything except solving your own little predicament. So why bring it up now?"

The sitting area that had seemed so spacious when she'd first entered the room had grown dramatically smaller. "I…I just wondered why you married me."

"Because solving your problem solves mine."

"I don't understand."

He stripped off his jacket and tossed it over a nearby chair. "I don't expect you to. Yet."

Before she could question him further, he took a final step in her direction. Retreating an equal distance, the back of her knees hit the edge of the bed and she sat down abruptly.

"It's a king-size bed," she explained in a rush, scooting backward on the quilted cover. "When I realized the mistake, I tried to get two doubles, but the hotel's full. Every room's taken. I thought maybe the couch…" She gestured wildly toward the sitting area.

"You're not using the couch and neither am I." The mattress dipped beneath his weight. "We're husband and wife now, remember?"

He trapped her beneath him before she had a chance to roll away and she stared at him in shock. "But you claimed we wouldn't… You didn't intend…" Frantically, she searched her memory, struggling to recall his exact phrasing. "You said you didn't want to sleep with me!"

"I told you it wasn't worth discussing. And it's not. Certain issues are non-negotiable, and this is one of them." His eyes were a fierce green, glowing with blatant desire. "So no more discussion. No more negotiations. The time has come for action."

"No—"

"Yes, Mrs. Alexander. Most definitely, yes."

Framing her head with his hands, he stole a gentle kiss, confirming her earlier opinion. Dear heaven, but he knew his way around a woman's mouth. He also knew when to coerce and when to coax. And right now, he coaxed. Teased. Tempted.

Seduced.

Hot little flames flickered to life again, splashing across her skin, seeping deep within to weaken every muscle and sear every nerve ending. She tried to resist, to explain all her reasons for keeping their relationship platonic. But the words were lost, swallowed by a far greater need—a need that consumed all rational thought.

The buttons of her suit jacket fell open and his mouth drifted downward, following the length of her throat. She teetered on the edge of surrender. He was her husband. He was helping her resolve an untenable situation. And she wanted him. Heaven help her, she wanted him. Considering the circumstances, could making love be so wrong?

"Nikki," he muttered in a passion-slurred voice. "I'm sorry. I can't resist."

"I know," she whispered. "I feel the same way."

"Thanks for understanding."

His shadowed jaw rasped across sensitive skin and she held her breath, aware that she'd committed herself to folly. He cupped her breasts, nuzzling the curves above her lacy bra and then…

Nothing.

"Joe?" she murmured, shifting beneath his oppressive weight. He didn't respond, and as the seconds ticked by, desire waned. She moistened her lips, the return of sanity making her extremely self-conscious. "Are you sure about this?" she asked uneasily. "Don't you think we should wait until we know each other a little better? Joe? *Joe*?"

And it was then she realized he'd fallen fast asleep.

CHAPTER FOUR

NIKKI stirred, two disparate sounds bringing her to full consciousness.

One was the familiar hiss of a shower.

The other was a tentative knocking at the door.

Neither made any sense to her. But then, until she'd had two strong cups of coffee, not much did first thing in the morning. She rolled onto her back and blinked up at the ceiling, struggling to recall why the bedroom looked and felt so strange.

And then she remembered—remembered everything.

She darted a quick, nervous glance toward the far side of the mattress. Joe wasn't there, only a depression in the bedding confirming he'd spent the entire night beside her. That explained the sound of running water. Her—she swallowed hard—*husband* must be in the shower. Another knock sounded at the door the same instant as the flow of water stopped.

Confronting the unknown entity in the hallway seemed a safer bet than confronting the well-known entity toweling off after his shower, she decided. Kicking back the covers, she pulled on her robe and went to answer the summons. With luck, Joe had ordered breakfast before closeting himself in the bathroom. Thrusting an unruly tumble of hair from her face, she unlocked the door and tugged it open.

"Hi, Nikki." Eric stood there, an abashed grin on his face. "Surprise."

She whipped the door partially closed and ducked behind it, glaring at him through the remaining two-inch crack. "What are you doing here?" she demanded in a furious whisper. "Have you lost your mind?"

"Is that room service?" Joe's deep voice rumbled from close behind. "I'd kill for a cup of coffee."

"It's not room service," she replied without turning around. Speaking softly, she ordered, "Go away!"

Eric's jaw dropped. "I'm not going anywhere until you tell me what the hell my brother is doing here."

Her eyes widened in alarm. "Who? Where?"

"Right there behind you! My brother, Jonah. What's he doing in a hotel room with you? And dressed like that, no less!"

She spun around and literally went weak at the knees. Never in her life had she seen such an appealing sight. Joe stood in the middle of the room wearing nothing but a fluffy white towel. His skin was golden, his chest an endless expanse of dark brown fur, and he stalked toward her with the determination of a gladiator ready to join battle. Everything about him exuded power. From the resolute expression in his autumn-hued eyes to his wall-like shoulders to his solidly muscled legs, he approached with the grace and assurance of a seasoned warrior. And all she could do was stand and wait, uncertain of the rules of engagement in this particular war.

Reaching her side, he wrapped his arms around her. "Morning, sweetheart," he muttered in his distinctively raspy voice and nuzzled the side of her neck.

She gasped at the torturous pleasure his stubbled jaw kindled. "Joe, what is—"

"Don't say a word," he cut in tersely. He spoke close to her ear, his quiet warning conveyed with a harshness that stunned her. "Just play along or I swear you'll regret it."

She opened her mouth to protest, but as though anticipating that, he kissed her. It was long and slow and deep, stealing every thought from her head. Unable to help herself, she relaxed, her body turning pliant and eager within his embrace. How did he do it? the rational part of her mind wondered. With one kiss, he demolished every hint of resistance and turned her from a reasonable, logical, intelligent woman into a helpless puppet. How was it possible?

"*What the hell is going on here*?" Eric shouted.

Nikki started, having completely forgotten about his presence. But Joe—or was it Jonah?—didn't even twitch. Taking his time, he finished the kiss before lifting his head. He grinned down at her, flicking his finger across her rosy cheekbone.

Finally, he addressed Eric. "Hello, little brother. Here I manage to sneak off for a romantic weekend with my wife and you still find a way to track me down. How'd you do it?"

Eric fought to draw breath. "What— When—"

Jonah released a gusty sigh. "It was Jan, wasn't it? She spilled the beans." Shooting Nikki a reproving look, he ruffled her already-ruffled hair. "You've got to get better control over that secretary of yours, sweetheart. What could be so urgent that we can't have a private weekend without business intruding?"

"I—" Her mouth opened and closed like a stranded fish.

Without missing a beat, Jonah returned his attention to Eric. "And just what is it that's so urgent?"

"I didn't— I thought—"

"I'll tell you what," Jonah interrupted. "There's a restaurant downstairs. Order up a large pot of coffee while we dress and we'll join you for breakfast as soon as we can." He didn't wait for Eric's reply, but slammed the door shut in his brother's face.

"What the *hell*—"

Jonah cupped his palm over her mouth. "Wait!" he snapped in a curt undertone and cocked his head meaningfully toward the door. Hustling her to the sitting area at the far end of the room, he removed his hand. "Okay, finish."

"Is going on?" she concluded in a furious whisper. "Just who the hell are you?"

"Your husband."

"That's not what I mean and you know it! You're not Joe Alexander, are you?"

"No."

He folded his arms across his chest, drawing her attention once again to the corded muscles of his well-developed arms and the impressive width of his shoulders. Lord, he was gorgeous, she reluctantly conceded. And distracting as the devil. She closed her eyes to block out the sight, focusing once again on the business at hand. "You're Jonah Alexander? Eric's brother?"

"Yes. I shortened my name so you wouldn't recognize it."

She'd figured out that much already, but it still came as a distinct shock to hear the casually stated confession. She sank into a chair, staring at him in disbelief. "*Why?*"

A cynical light turned his eyes a chilly golden brown. "Can't you guess?"

With his standing there in nothing but a loosely knotted towel? Not a chance. "Maybe if you dressed," she suggested faintly.

His mouth curved in amusement. "I will—just as soon as the clothes I ordered from the men's shop downstairs are delivered. No luggage, remember?"

She bowed her head to avoid looking at him. "I still don't understand," she said through gritted teeth.

"What in particular is giving you trouble?"

She could hear the laughter in his voice and resented it passionately. "What's going on? Why were you at the Cinderella Ball last night? Why did you marry me?" A sudden thought occurred and her head jerked up, her hair spilling across her shoulders in a riotous tangle of sable brown and deep russet. "We are really married, aren't we?"

"Oh, we're legal all right."

"But you used a fake name—"

"I just used a nickname, same as you. If you'd bothered to look at our marriage license, you'd have seen Jonah Alexander spelled out in all its glory." His tone was dry, his gaze mocking. "From there it would have been a simple enough leap to connect me to Eric."

"If I had, I'd never have married you," she retorted bitterly.

"No doubt."

"And you still haven't answered my questions."

He ran a hand across his shadowed jaw and she remembered how his day-old beard had abraded her skin when he'd nuzzled her neck. Mild pain had melded with a more profound pleasure. The result had been electrifying and she eyed his jawline speculatively. What would it be like to feel that tantalizing scrape against her breast? An intense warmth unfurled in the pit of her stomach at the mere thought and she clenched her hands, fighting the unwanted sensation.

"Well?" she snapped.

He shrugged. "I came to the Montagues' to stop you from marrying Eric."

"*What*? I wasn't planning to—"

"I know that now."

"But you didn't last night," she stated with dawning comprehension.

"Not until after we'd conducted a rather lengthy conversation."

"The one outside in the garden." His strange behavior the previous evening began to make sense. Finally. "That's why you were asking all those odd questions and kept pestering me about my prospective bridegroom. You didn't understand the purpose of the ball."

"Not entirely," he conceded.

"What in the world did you think I was doing there?"

"Meeting Eric."

"I can't believe this," she muttered, dragging a hand through her hair.

"The evidence was damning," he explained without apology, "especially the part about you and Eric flying to Nevada on International Investment business—"

"We don't have any business interests here," she inserted automatically.

"I'm well aware of that fact." He waited a beat before adding, "And so is the rest of the office staff."

She couldn't hide her dismay. Apparently Eric's pursuit of her had left ample room for conjecture, not to mention gossip. "But we weren't traveling together," she argued. "I didn't even know Eric had followed me until he showed up at the Montagues'."

"The bottom line is that you both flew to Nevada. You both had reservations here at the Grand. And there'd already been talk of an affair. In this case, two and two may have added up to five, but to an outsider it sure as hell looked like an elopement."

"You were leaping to conclusions," she said dismissively.

"Was I? Don't forget one other detail—the Montagues' Cinderella Ball. The few facts I'd ascertained suggested it was some sort of gala for couples who wanted to marry. And when I called the Grand, they confirmed that most of their guests were attending and gave me directions. I'd have booked a room here, but they were full by then."

Her eyes narrowed suspiciously. "How did you find out about the Cinderella Ball?"

"You left the announcement on your desk."

"You searched my desk?" she demanded, outraged.

"If you're expecting an apology, you've got a long wait," he said with callous disregard. "I had a job to do and I did it."

"So you came out to Nevada believing Eric and I were going to marry and bent on stopping us, right? Why? What difference did it make if I married your brother?"

"Aside from the fact that I believed you were already married and that you have a few years on him?"

She lifted her chin. "Yes. Aside from those reasons."

"Your…relationship had begun to affect your work. You acknowledged as much last night. Why do you think Loren called me home?"

Her eyes widened in alarm. "The Sanderses—your parents—know?"

"What they know, or rather thought they knew, was that Eric was having an affair with an older, married woman. The affair had become common gossip among the employees and had distracted the principals involved to the point that they almost succeeded in losing the Dearfield account."

"Oh, no!"

"Oh, yes," he responded with brutal deliberation. "I recommended they fire you. If you hadn't been a nominee for the Lawrence J. Bauman Award, you would have been."

"Why?" she demanded. "Because I had the temerity to catch the eye of the boss's son?"

"No. Because you allowed your personal life to interfere with business."

"So it was Jonah Alexander, troubleshooter, financier extraordinaire and former LJB winner to the rescue. Is that it?" She didn't bother to hide her resentment.

"That's it."

"And your solution was to marry me?"

"Not by a long shot. You were the one who settled on that as a solution. I merely accommodated you."

"Why?"

For the first time, anger disturbed the even tenor of his voice. "What choice did I have? I couldn't change your mind about marrying and you wouldn't settle on an acceptable husband. Then Eric showed up and it was either marry or expose you as a liar.'' He stepped closer, his expression falling into grim lines. "But believe this, *Mrs. Alexander*, if I didn't think that revealing the truth might damage the reputation of International Investment, I'd have given you up in a heartbeat and damn the consequences.''

"I had to do something about Eric,'' she protested.

"You didn't have to lie. If you make such foolish decisions in your personal life, I have to wonder what the hell you're doing on the job.''

The criticism struck hard and cut deep. "My work is beyond reproach!''

"Except for the Dearfield account, you mean?'' came the harsh retort. "Well, we'll find out, won't we?''

"What are you saying?'' she asked apprehensively.

"I'm saying that I intend to analyze your performance over the past year. And if I find anything out of sync, LJB Award or no, you'll be out on that pretty little tail of yours.''

She leaped to her feet, her hands balling into fists. "If that's how you feel, why did you bother to marry me?''

"You think I wanted to?'' His anger erupted with tangible force, reflected in the taut line of his jaw and the hot sparks of gold flaming to life in his eyes. "Our marriage is an inconvenient means of salvaging an untenable situation. And you, my accidental wife, are a temporary encumbrance.''

"How dare—''

"Oh, cut the self-righteous indignation,'' he snapped. "You used me last night every bit as much as I used you. What did you say? It wasn't just Eric but some personal matter you needed to resolve, as well?''

His reminder stopped her cold. How could she have forgotten Krista and Keli? ''Yes,'' she conceded, her anger fading as swiftly as it had flared.

''Well, at least Eric won't be a problem any longer.''

She stared in confusion. ''Why not?''

''He won't poach,'' Jonah stated succinctly. ''After this morning, there won't be any doubt in my brother's mind that not only are we married, but we share a passionate relationship. If I read him right, he'll be furious at you for not telling him the truth about us. Any feelings he might harbor should die a swift and bitter death.''

She turned her back on him, blinking hard. She'd never wanted to hurt Eric, only ease an uncomfortable situation. But everything she'd done so far only succeeded in exacerbating matters. ''How do we explain our marriage to him?'' she asked quietly.

''We say that we became engaged before I left for London and we married a short time afterward on one of my trips to the States. We kept it quiet because we didn't want it to affect your position at work.'' His voice acquired a cynical edge. ''We'll tell him you preferred to make it on your own. He should buy that.''

Her mouth tightened. ''Go on.''

''We're celebrating our one-year anniversary by renewing our vows at the Montagues' party and had planned to make the big announcement to the family immediately afterward.''

"You have it all worked out," she said, unable to conceal her resentment.

"Somebody had to."

"I'll have you know I had complete control of the situation." She turned to face him. "Your interference wasn't necessary."

"You had it all under control?" She couldn't mistake his sarcasm. "Which part?"

"Once I married—"

"Fine. Let's start there. Never in my life have I heard of anything as crazy as this Cinderella Ball. You really intended to marry a complete stranger?"

"Yes." She strove for nonchalance. "What's wrong with that?"

"What—" He bit off a curse. "You knew nothing about me. Not even my real name. I could have been an ax murderer. Or worse."

"What's worse than an ax murderer?" she muttered.

"Don't tempt me to show you. How could you be so irresponsible?"

"I'm sure there were no ax murderers present," she argued. "The Montagues ran security checks. They had all the guests investigated before they authorized their invitations."

"A fat lot of good that did."

His voice had become dangerously soft, the bass tones rumbling with stormy threat. His hand closed around her arm and he tugged her close. She made a small sound of complaint, not that he noticed or cared. Instead, he secured her against him, the thin cotton of her nightgown providing as flimsy a barrier as his towel. She splayed her hands across his chest, her fingers sinking into the generous pelt of hair to the taut layer of skin and muscle beneath.

"Joe—Jonah, please. You don't understand. It was perfectly safe."

"Really? Well, for your information, *wife*, I didn't have an invitation. I walked right in the front door and no one made a move to stop me. Now tell me again how everyone was investigated and deemed safe. Am I safe? Well? *Am I?*"

She stared into blazing hazel eyes, the strength of his fury impacting with stunning force. More than anything, she wanted to look away. But she didn't, compelled to meet that impossible gaze while still retaining the tattered scraps of her control. "No," she replied tartly, remembering his attempted seduction once they'd returned to the hotel. "You aren't the least safe. Last night proved that beyond any doubt."

"Did it?" His eyes narrowed as he considered her comment and she regretted ever having made the dig. "After thirty-odd hours without sleep, some of it's a bit hazy. I don't recall much toward the end, except—"

"Nothing happened!" she broke in defensively.

A hint of jade green crept into his curious gaze, and a slow smile creased his mouth. His arms slid around her, his hands settling on her hips. "That's not quite the way I remember it," he said, easing her close.

Struggling was out of the question. She hardly dared so much as breathe for fear of the consequences. "I thought you couldn't remember anything."

A quiet laugh broke free. "I don't. At least not much. My last memory was falling asleep on the softest, fluffiest pillow I've ever set cheek to.'' Color flamed in her face, and his gaze drifted from there downward, settling on the agitated rise and fall of her breasts. ''I wouldn't mind trying it again.''

''Let go of me.'' If anything, his hold tightened and she was terrified that he might kiss her. If that happened, she'd be lost, just like every other time he'd touched her.

And he knew it as surely as she.

''I don't recall much after that.'' His brow wrinkled. ''I sure don't remember undressing. And yet when I woke up this morning, someone had taken off my shoes.'' He cocked a gold-tipped eyebrow. ''You?''

''I may have.''

''And my shirt?''

A sudden image of the night before came to her. Once she'd gotten over her initial shock and anger at his falling asleep, she'd been unable to just leave him sprawled on the bed, fully dressed. He'd looked too uncomfortable. The shoes had been easy. The shirt less so because he'd worn a cummerbund. Never having seen a man put on such a device, let alone attempted to remove one, she'd wrestled with it for endless moments before locating the hooks. Added to which, he'd been so huge, it had taken every ounce of strength to roll him over enough to take care of the problem.

''You haven't answered my question,'' he prompted.

''Once I figured out how your cummerbund worked, the shirt was a snap. I put your cuff links on the dresser, by the way.''

She didn't add how unnervingly intimate the pro-

cedure had been. Finding the buttons within the folds
of his dress shirt hadn't seemed so bad; his body heat
singeing her through the soft cotton, though, had
come as a distinct shock. He'd lain stretched across
the bed, his shirt gaping, hers to touch and care for.
She'd hurried initially, desperate to get the job done.
But as she'd worked the shirt off his shoulders and
arms, her movements had slowed. And heaven help
her, she'd been unable to resist caressing that incredible musculature. Did he know? Did he suspect that
she'd traced every hard curve—the deep furring of
his chest, the taut ripples of his abdomen, the beautifully sculpted biceps?

She risked a quick upward glance, but his expression told her nothing. He held her so close the crisp
hairs of his chest brushed the curve of her jaw,
swamping her with desires she'd never known she
possessed—desires she didn't dare communicate to
him. They were the same feelings that had spilled
through her as she'd unbuttoned his trousers. She'd
panicked then, just as she was almost panicking now.
Last night, she'd bolted from the bed and locked herself in the bathroom for a long, hot shower. Afterward, she'd thrown a blanket over his slumbering
form and crawled into bed next to him. Curling into
a tight ball as far to one side of the king bed as she
could manage, it had taken her a long, long time to
drift off to sleep.

"Where have you gone, Nikki?" he questioned
softly.

Her gaze flew to his and she shook her head, unable
to answer. For where she'd been, she didn't dare allow him to follow. To her eternal relief, a knock

sounded at the door, sparing her the need to invent a response.

"I think this conversation might be worth pursuing further," he said.

"I disagree." She stirred within his hold. "Aren't you going to answer that?"

"I'm debating."

"There's nothing to debate. We've been an awfully long time," she said, pulling free of his embrace. "Let's hope it's your clothes and not Eric."

It was clothing. After signing for the package, he glanced over his shoulder at her. "With any luck, Eric's put the appropriate construction on our delay and is busy inventing an excuse for being in Nevada." He tore open the package and his towel hit the floor. "You might want to get dressed, too."

With a strangled gasp, Nikki snatched up her overnight bag and flew into the bathroom, slamming the door. It took five minutes to calm down enough to dress, and a further five to dab on enough makeup to conceal the ravages of a restless night. Finally, she emerged, dressed in a businesslike fitted gold skirt and blouse, her hair thoroughly brushed and gathered at the base of her neck with a clip.

Jonah took one look at her and shook his head, his mouth settling into a grim line. "Not a chance."

"What's wrong now?" she questioned defensively.

"You look like my secretary, not my wife." He approached, flicking open the first several buttons of her blouse and removing the clip holding her hair. "Unless we're at work, you wear your hair loose."

"Why?"

"We're making a statement, remember, creating an illusion? That illusion is that we're married and can't keep our mitts off each other. When we walk into the dining room, the first thought that I want Eric to have is that we've just made love and then thrown on whatever clothes came to hand in order to join him.'' He examined her critically. ''No jewelry except your wedding band and wear your heels from last night.''

''But they're ivory. They don't match—''

''Exactly. We dressed in haste, remember? Come on. Let's go.''

Jamming her feet into the shoes he indicated, she snatched up her purse and followed him to the door. They accomplished the ride in the elevator in total silence. Just before the doors slid open, he cupped the back of her head and pulled her close for a quick, hard kiss.

''I hate it when you do that,'' she protested the minute he released her.

''If you hate it so much, stop clutching my shirt. And when we join Eric, follow my lead. Understand?''

''No.''

''Do it anyway. You ready?''

She nodded, dreading the next few minutes. He started toward the restaurant and she caught his arm. ''Jonah, wait.'' She moistened her lips. ''Please. Don't…don't hurt him.''

His gaze turned wintry. ''I think it's too late for that. Don't you? But if it makes you feel any better, I promise I won't give you the chance to hurt him anymore.''

With that, he snagged her elbow and led her toward what she suspected would be the most uncomfortable conversation of her life.

CHAPTER FIVE

"WHAT do you mean we're going to Chicago?" Nikki demanded as they entered the airport lobby. "I need to get back to New York."

"And you will," he retorted, joining the short line in front of the first-class passenger check-in counter. "Just as soon as we stop in Chicago and see my parents."

That didn't sound good. "Do we have to?" she asked faintly.

"Yes, we do." He glanced down at her, correctly interpreting her reaction. "Don't worry. I'll do the talking again."

And suffer through the accusatory stares and barbed silences she'd experienced with Eric? Not a chance. "That's what I'm afraid of. Last time you did the talking, I ended up appearing—"

"Heartless? Guilty as sin? A traitor?"

She shot him a sour look. "You do it deliberately, don't you? You twist everything I say to your own advantage."

"I don't have to twist a single thing. You've managed to tangle yourself in this little web of deceit all on your own. I'm just trying to straighten out your mess. If, in the process, you come across as less than sympathetic, it's not my fault."

"Oh, no?" She planted her hands on her hips. "For

your information, I wasn't the only one being deceitful last night, *Joe*. Nor would I be in this mess if you hadn't interfered. I had everything all planned.''

His eyebrows winged skyward and he made a small noise that sounded suspiciously like a snort. ''You call attending the Montagues' ball a plan?''

''Yes.'' She ticked off her points one by one. ''Go to the ball and find a husband. Make a big production out of introducing him at work. Take care of a personal situation. And let Eric down gently. *Gently*!'' She glared at him. ''Do you even know the meaning of the word 'gentle'? The man I intended to marry would have.''

''I see. Adding another player to the drama is supposed to simplify it. Especially someone unfamiliar with both the role and his lines. And a gentle man, no less.'' His voice dripped sarcasm. ''Now there's a contradiction in terms.''

She bit down on her lip to halt the impetuous rush of words. She knew when to beat a temporary retreat in order to salvage her pride. And that time had definitely arrived. Besides, their breakfast with Eric had gone precisely as Jonah had predicted and had been every bit the unmitigated disaster she'd feared. Eric had offered the transparent excuse of calling on a potential customer as his reason for being in Nevada. Jonah had repeated the story he'd invented surrounding their engagement and marriage. And she'd sat there gulping coffee and trying to appear madly in love with one brother while avoiding the hurt gaze of the other.

Taking a deep breath, she asked, ''What are you going to tell your parents?''

''The truth. It'll make a pleasant change, if nothing

else.'' The ticket window cleared and he crossed to it, dumping their luggage on the scale. ''Reroute these through Chicago for a one-night layover,'' he requested, slapping their airline tickets on the counter. ''And what's your first available flight from Chicago to New York on Monday morning?''

''No! I have to get home tonight,'' Nikki protested. ''I'm expected.''

''Change your plans,'' he said without a trace of sympathy. ''I've had to. There's a bank of phones behind you. I'm sure the incomparable Jan can reschedule your early-morning appointments with one hand tied behind her back.''

Realizing further argument would prove futile, she did as he suggested and crossed to the phones. She called her sister first, keeping it light and breezy. ''I won't be home until Monday, I'm afraid. My business took longer than expected. And…and I have a surprise for you.''

''For me?'' her sister asked. ''You didn't have to do that.''

''I mean…it's not for you precisely. It's—it's something I got for myself. But I hope you'll be pleased.''

''What is it?'' Krista demanded. ''Tell me.''

''I can't. I've been a bit impetuous.…'' Nikki glanced at Jonah's broad back and swallowed. *Very* impetuous might be closer to the truth.

''*You*? Impetuous? I can't believe it.''

''Believe it,'' Nikki retorted. ''I'll see you Monday, though I'm not sure when. And I'll bring my surprise with me. You'll love him.'' She groaned. ''*It*. You'll love *it*.''

A momentary silence greeted her statement. ''Oh,

Nikki,'' Krista said in a troubled voice. ''What have you done?''

''Something wonderful,'' Nikki insisted with a hint of defiance. She shut her eyes. Wonderfully terrifying. Terrifyingly wonderful. ''I'll see you tomorrow.''

''And we'll talk, right?''

Nikki winced. ''Right. All my love to you and Keli. I've got to run.''

''Nick, honey?''

''What?''

''It's not your fault.'' Krista's voice dropped, the words tumbling out in an urgent rush. ''You don't have to spend the rest of your life making up for one youthful indiscretion. You have to stop blaming yourself for what happened. It isn't worth ruining your life over—''

''I'm not,'' Nikki interrupted briskly. ''I'm just trying to take care of you and Keli. It'll work out, I promise.''

''Try taking care of yourself for a change,'' Krista shot back. ''That's all I ask.''

''I will.'' Eventually. Just as soon as she'd secured the futures of her various family members.

''Yeah, right.'' A sigh drifted across the line. ''I love you, sweetie.''

''Me, too. I'll talk to you soon.''

The tears pricking Nikki's eyes caught her by surprise and it took a full minute to collect herself enough to place the next call. Despite being disturbed at home on a Sunday, Jan took the instructions to rearrange Monday's schedule with her customary composure. Just as Nikki concluded the phone call, Jonah approached.

''Finished?''

"All set."

"Good. We'll have to hustle. The flight leaves in fifteen minutes."

"But…aren't you going to call your parents and warn them we're coming?" she asked in dismay.

"I'll do it on the plane. Let's go."

The flight lasted a torturous three hours, giving Nikki ample time for reflection—although she spent most of that time worrying rather than reflecting. She'd met Loren Sanders when she'd first been hired and only once or twice since. Though he seemed charming, she'd sensed he didn't suffer fools gladly. On the other hand, she'd never met Jonah's mother and knew little of her except what could be gleaned from office gossip. Stories of Della's immense charm and appeal circulated there on a regular basis. Which might be why the idea of confronting the Sanderses with her idiocy was sufficient to put Nikki in a total panic. For she knew without a doubt that that's how she'd be perceived—as an absolute idiot.

Jonah was right. She'd made a mess of this entire situation. She should have forced Eric to listen from the beginning. Instead, she'd compounded deceit with deceit until she'd compromised herself so thoroughly, it was a wonder Jonah didn't just let her choke on all the lies. But then, as he'd so nastily pointed out, if it hadn't been for the potential harm to International Investment's reputation, as well as her nomination for the Lawrence J. Bauman Award, he would have left her to her fate without a single qualm.

At least he couldn't fault her business decisions, she attempted to console herself. Despite what he'd threatened, when he examined her record, he'd be im-

pressed. Very impressed. And on that note, she shut
her eyes and willed herself to catch up on some vitally
needed sleep.

Jonah glanced at his wife. The instant she'd nodded
off, she'd snuggled into his arms as though she belonged. With her head tucked into the curve of his
shoulder and her fingers laced through two of his belt
loops, it would be understandable for a stranger to
think theirs a familiar position.

He should find it humorous, and he might have if
not for one troubling detail. Even in sleep, her features had a drawn appearance he didn't like. He knew
it was due to stress combined with exhaustion. Faint
purple bruises beneath her eyes emphasized her pallor
and a tiny line remained between her brows as though
even in her dreams she hadn't found surcease from
her difficulties.

He smoothed his thumb across the bothersome
wrinkle, pleased when he succeeded in ironing it
away. At his touch, she sighed and relaxed more fully
against him.

"Excuse me, Mr. Alexander," the flight attendant
paused to whisper. "We'll be landing shortly. Can I
bring you and your wife some coffee?"

"Thanks," he said with a nod. "Black for me. Two
cups with extra sugar for my wife."

He didn't bother to waken her. The rousing aroma
of the coffee did it for him. She stirred, her nose
twitching first, followed by the reluctant flickering of
her lashes. "Tell me I'm not dreaming," she murmured sleepily. "Is that really coffee?"

"You don't even have to open your eyes. Just hold
out a hand and it's all yours."

To his amusement, she did as he suggested. Halfway through her second cup, she straightened. From the flush tinting her cheeks, he gathered she was somewhat embarrassed to have awakened in his arms. And from the tightening of her mouth, he guessed she intended to pretend it hadn't happened. Unwilling to allow the episode to pass without consequence, he reached over and combed his fingers through the spill of russet hair caressing her cheek. If he'd hoped to disconcert her, it backfired. Badly. He'd heard of hair being compared to silk and always thought it a poetic exaggeration. Now he knew differently. Never had he touched anything so smooth and soft.

"Feel better?" he asked quietly, tucking the wayward strands behind her ear.

"Yes, thank you." She continued to avoid his gaze. "How much longer until we get there?"

"Fifteen or twenty minutes."

The faint line he'd smoothed away earlier reappeared. "We'll go directly to your parents' house?"

"It's an apartment, and yes, we'll go straight there. I don't expect the traffic to be too bad on a Sunday. It shouldn't take more than forty minutes."

"Oh." She moistened her lips, clearly working up the nerve to ask the question she'd been fretting about for the past five hours. "You said you were going to tell them the truth. What exactly do you plan to say?"

"That Eric's made an ass of himself. That you overreacted. And that if I'd had enough sleep before wading into the middle of things, I would have resolved matters with more finesse than I have."

She shot him a look of alarm. "You think marrying was a mistake, don't you?"

"It was an extreme solution to a not-so-extreme problem. Don't worry. I'll deal with it."

A troubled expression darkened her eyes. "I didn't marry just because of Eric, remember? I do have a secondary reason."

"So you said. Care to tell me about it now?" Her lashes swept downward, but not before he'd caught a telltale flash of violet. Whatever this reason involved, it visibly upset her. And for some reason, she didn't trust him enough yet to explain the details.

"I'd rather wait, if you don't mind," she replied. "It's—"

"Personal. Yes, I know." He lifted an eyebrow. "I hope you're not going to make me guess. With your propensity for chaos, I doubt my imagination is up to the job."

"I'll tell you—" her mouth firmed "—when I'm ready."

"I hope so. I may have difficulty resolving it otherwise."

"I don't want you to resolve it!" she retorted, stung. "I can take care of my own problems."

"So I've noticed." He cut her off before she could say more. "Fasten your seat belt. We're about to land."

By the time they'd collected their luggage and caught a cab to the Sanderses' apartment, the afternoon had all but vanished. Della answered the door to his knock, flinging her arms around him with customary enthusiasm.

"I'm so glad you're here. Dinner will be ready in half an hour, so there's plenty of time to freshen up." She smiled at Nikki and held out her hand, a slight reserve curbing her enthusiasm. "You must be Mrs. Ashton. Welcome."

"It's Nikki," Jonah interrupted lazily. "Nikki Alexander, to be exact. As in Mrs. Jonah Alexander."

"Oh, that just tears it!" Nikki turned on him, her taut control dissolving in the face of her fury.

As he'd hoped, the cool, reserved businesswoman vanished, replaced by an impassioned spitfire. He found the spitfire much more to his liking. Knowing his parents, they would, too. "Something wrong?" he asked innocently.

"You—you need to ask?" she sputtered. "You couldn't have broken the news to your mother more gently?"

"I don't do gentle, remember?"

Della's mouth fell open. "You're *married*?"

Nikki planted her hands on her trim hips, her fury a glorious sight. At least Jonah found it glorious. He slanted a quick look at his mother, relieved that she appeared more confused than shocked.

"It didn't occur to you to prepare her first instead of just nuking everyone in sight with your announcement?" Nikki demanded.

He shrugged, fighting to keep a straight face. "Don't exaggerate. The only everyone in sight is my mother. And I prefer speed to delicacy."

"Well, that's obvious." She shot him a reproving glance. "Although in your line of work, I'd have thought you'd have learned something about diplomacy."

"Not much," he confessed. "I've always found making money takes talent and intelligence, not tact."

Della glanced over her shoulder. "Loren, you better get out here."

Nikki's eyes glittered with ill-humor, the color as

vivid as a tropical sunrise. "That's beside the point. You told me you were going to call them."

"I did call—while you were asleep." She sounded a bit grouchy, Jonah decided. Perhaps he should have fed her three cups of coffee instead of just two. "I told them we were coming for dinner."

"What's all the yelling about?" Loren questioned mildly as he joined his wife.

"That's it? Just 'we're coming for dinner'?" Nikki stabbed a finger at Jonah. "You couldn't have added, 'And by the way, Nikki Ashton and I just got married. I'll explain when we get there'?"

"They're married," Della announced to her husband. "Jonah and Nikki."

"How can they be married?" Loren demanded. "She's already married to that Ashton fellow."

"See? This is why I waited." Jonah leaned against the doorjamb, confiding, "Getting married is the sort of happy news parents prefer to hear face-to-face."

"In the *hallway*?" Nikki questioned, infuriated.

"They want to share in our joy and happiness, no matter where we are."

"They don't look the least joyful or happy. They look…stunned."

"I'm not stunned. I'm confused," Loren grumbled to his wife. "I thought she was having an affair with Eric."

Della shrugged. "Well, now she's married to Jonah."

"You couldn't even wait until we were invited in?" Nikki folded her arms across her chest and glared at Jonah. "Maybe work it casually into the conversation over drinks?"

He fought to assume an appropriately contrite expression. "I must have gotten carried away in the excitement of the moment. It just came out."

"You, carried away?" She snorted. "My Aunt Fanny. You never do anything without a reason."

Loren looked from one to the other, his brow wrinkling. "Who the hell is Aunt Fanny? And while we're on the subject of relatives...what the dickens happened to Mr. Ashton? Have we ever figured that one out?"

"There is no Mr. Ashton," Nikki and Jonah said in unison.

Loren thrust a hand through his salt-and-pepper hair. "No Mr. Ashton? I don't understand any of this. Would someone please tell me what the devil is going on around here?"

"Maybe we should finish this discussion inside before the neighbors complain," Della suggested.

"Excellent suggestion, Mother," Jonah approved.

An awkward moment followed while they all filed from the entranceway into the living room. "What a gorgeous view," Nikki volunteered.

Della offered a strained smile. "You should see it when it snows."

"Yes, yes. The view is wonderful. Snow is wonderful. The whole damned world is just by golly wonderful!" Loren declared testily. "Now what the hell is going on here? Or is a reasonable explanation too much to expect?"

"It's all my fault," Nikki began.

"I believe I told you that I'd handle this." Jonah's tone didn't brook defiance.

She lifted her chin. "Fine. You handle it." Turning her back on him, she crossed to stare out at Lake

Michigan. What did it matter how he slanted the
story? His parents were going to be upset regardless.

"I'll see if I can't keep this simple. There is no
Mr. Ashton. Nikki isn't married and never was. She
pretended to be married because Eric was making inopportune advances." At Della's muffled exclamation, Jonah shook his head. "No, Mother. It wasn't
anything like that. He'd just allowed an understandable infatuation to get the better of his common
sense." To his amusement, both Della and Nikki
blushed.

Loren's brows drew together. "Let me get this
straight. In order to put Eric off, Ms. Ashton—
Nikki—invented a marriage?"

"'Fraid so," Jonah confirmed. "And that's when
matters got a little out of hand."

"I'd say matters were out of hand a good bit before
then," Loren inserted drily.

Jonah exchanged a silent look of agreement with
his stepfather. "No comment."

"Could we get on with this?" Nikki pleaded. "I
know I screwed up. It's no secret."

Jonah took up the story again. "When Eric continued to express his concern over the prolonged absence
of Nikki's husband, she decided to rectify the situation. Last night, she attended a marriage ball in
Nevada with the full intention of finding herself a
suitable husband to present at work."

Della sank onto the couch. "Oh, my dear child.
How could you?"

"It seemed like a good idea at the time," Nikki
whispered.

"The suitable husband she found was me." He
eyed his parents, his expression implacable. "Until

Eric is past this infatuation of his and we get the situation at the New York office straightened out, Nikki and I stay married. And we all treat it as if it were real and permanent.''

"Well, I think you have both lost your minds." Loren crossed to the wet bar and poured himself a Scotch. "And I want no part of it."

Jonah glanced at Nikki and his mother. "Give me a minute with him."

Della rose to her feet. "As much as it pains me to say this…" She smiled at Nikki. "Shall we check on dinner?"

"Do we have a choice?"

"I'm afraid not."

Jonah waited until the two women were out of earshot, then turned to confront his stepfather. "Whether you agree with my decision or not, I expect your support on this. And I expect you to treat Nikki with all the respect due my wife. If you can't, tell me now and we'll leave."

Loren's brows shot up. "You're serious?"

"Very. You called me home to take care of a situation, and that's what I'm doing."

"It's how you're taking care of it that worries me."

"Blame it on jet lag."

For the first time, a hint of amusement touched Loren's face. "I thought you didn't believe in jet lag," he said, pouring his stepson a drink.

"I do now," Jonah replied wryly.

"But marriage?" The older man shook his head. "You don't really expect me to endorse such a crazy scheme?"

"Look, Loren, we have to protect International

Investment at all costs, which means we can't fire her, and for the time being, we can't transfer her.''

"So, what do you propose?''

"Just this…'' Jonah took a healthy swallow of Scotch. "The LJB Award comes right before Christmas, so we hang tough till then. I have an excellent assistant in London who can take care of our overseas operation until after the holidays. In the meantime, I'll spend the next six weeks in New York playing the doting husband.''

Loren shot his stepson a shrewd look. "What will you really be doing?''

"Looking over Nikki's track record and making sure she and Eric haven't screwed up any other accounts. As soon as I feel matters are under control, I'll return to London. We give it six more months after that. Then we encourage the lovely Ms. Ashton to either transfer far from Eric's sphere of influence or find employment elsewhere.''

Loren lifted an eyebrow. "Your solution is a bit rough on your wife, isn't it?''

Anger lit Jonah's eyes. "My wife is directly responsible for this situation with Eric. If she'd told him no, or contacted any one of us when it became a problem, we wouldn't be in our current mess.''

"What happens once the situation with Eric is resolved?'' Loren asked.

"Nikki and I divorce,'' he stated baldly.

"Divorce? Don't you mean get an annulment?''

Jonah's mouth tugged to one side. "I believe that falls under the heading of none of your business.''

"Perhaps. But she is my employee. Come to think of it, she's also my stepdaughter-in-law. At least for the time being.''

"Point taken." Jonah finished off the Scotch and set the glass gently on the bar. "When the time comes, we'll divorce."

"This time, I'm doing the talking," Nikki stated firmly. At least she stated it as firmly as she could, considering Jonah's uncanny ability to get his own way. She found the knack quite disconcerting and suspected that not only did he know it, he took advantage of that fact.

"We'll see," he replied in a noncommittal voice. The cab pulled up in front of an attractive brownstone and he peered at it through the smudged passenger window. "Is this it?"

"Yes. I rent out the first floor and we occupy the second."

"We?"

"My…my sister, Krista, and her daughter, Keli. They live with me."

"Their picture is the one in your office?"

"How…?" Her eyes narrowed. "Oh, that's right. You searched my desk. Yes, that's Krista and Keli. The photo was taken last year when Keli was five."

Jonah unloaded the luggage and paid off the driver. "How long have you lived here?" he asked as they climbed the steps to the front door.

"Forever." Her response sounded short to the point of rudeness, but she was reluctant to trust him with even such a small piece of her privacy. "Krista and I grew up here."

He paused at the top of the landing. "I assume you haven't told her about us."

"No." She caught her bottom lip between her

teeth. "And fair warning, she may not take the news too well."

"No problem," he responded drily. "I'm getting used to that sort of response to our announcement. Is she the other reason for your decision to marry?"

"Yes." Taking a deep breath, she admitted, "I guess I should have explained earlier."

"That might have helped," he agreed blandly. "Although now works just as well for me. Does Krista know your first marriage was a fake?"

"Yes, but she's not to know this one is, too." Alarm flickered in her gaze. "Which reminds me, don't, under any circumstances, tell her you're related to Eric or she'll know for sure something's up."

His eyebrow notched upward. "I take it this is supposed to be a love match?"

"Yes, yes," she said with a nervous glance at the door. "We're in love. Madly, passionately in love."

"Got it." He tilted his head to one side. "Care to tell me why we're madly, passionately et cetera, et cetera? What are we trying to accomplish?"

"You don't need to know that. You just have to act the part of the love-struck groom." Impatience edged her voice. "Can you do it?"

"In spades."

Without warning, he wrapped powerful arms around her and yanked her against a granite-hard expanse of chest. Before she could catch her breath to protest, he nailed her with an all-consuming kiss. She should struggle came the dazed thought. She should give him hell. She should level him with a good, swift kick to the shins. Instead, she wrapped her arms around his neck and gave herself up to the illicit thrill of the embrace, only vaguely aware of his fumbling for something behind her. It took a moment to realize he was leaning on the doorbell. By the time it dawned on her, the door had been flung open.

"Aunt Nikki!" a childish voice declared. "You're home. I've been waiting and waiting— Oh!"

"Jonah!" Nikki whispered frantically, shoving at his massive shoulders. "Let go."

The little girl began to giggle. "Mommy! Come quick! There's a strange man kissing Aunt Nikki."

"My goodness! So there is." Another voice had joined the party.

Nikki managed to wriggle free of Jonah's hold. Turning, she offered her sister a flustered smile, then had the breath knocked out of her as the child launched herself at her aunt for an exuberant hug.

"What's your surprise?" Keli demanded, wrapping her arms around her aunt's waist.

"I think that's me," Jonah confessed, lowering himself to her level. "You must be Keli. I'm your Uncle Jonah."

Nikki watched as her niece peeped shyly up at him. Even in a crouch, Jonah's impressive size tended to overwhelm, and Keli studied him uncertainly for a long moment. Wisps of strawberry blond curls floated in a brilliant halo around her face, highlighting the doubt written all over her dainty features. Then, like a shadow floating clear of the sun, the doubt vanished and she grinned.

"Hi," she said. "I didn't know I had an uncle."

"Neither did I," Krista said in a confused voice. She offered a hand to Jonah as he stood. "I'm Krista Barrett, Nikki's sister. And you are...?" She lifted a winged eyebrow.

"Jonah Alexander," he said, accepting her hand. "Your brother-in-law."

"Oh, good heavens!"

"We are *not* doing this on the doorstep again," Nikki interjected.

He grinned. "I believe we just did."

"Everyone inside," Nikki snapped. "We'll talk there."

With a shrug, Jonah picked up the bags and stepped across the threshold. Keli trotted after him, studying her new uncle with unabashed curiosity.

Krista caught Nikki's arm as she started past. "What's going on?" she demanded softly.

"I'm married."

"For real this time?" Krista questioned, not bothering to conceal her concern. "This isn't another scheme you've dreamed up because of that Eric Sanders?"

"The marriage is real enough." Nikki took a deep breath and fought to put as much conviction and enthusiasm in her voice as possible. "And just so you know, I love him. In fact, we're both madly in love. And it's permanent. 'Til death us do part and all that."

Krista's brows drew together. "Uh-huh."

"I mean it!"

Nikki sent Jonah an uneasy glance. He stood with Keli, listening to her excited chatter. "And this is the living room," the child was explaining earnestly. "We keep it all picked up for Aunt Nikki. She works real hard and it helps her when I keep my toys in our bedroom."

"The one you share with your mom?" he asked.

"How'd you know that?"

"A lucky guess." An odd expression had crept into his gaze, Nikki realized with a tinge of apprehension. They'd taken on that autumn chill again, the brown-gold appearing rock hard.

"Well," Krista said in bewilderment, "I guess congratulations are in order. I'm sure we have a bottle of champagne around here someplace." She stared at Jonah. "Your name is familiar. Do I know you from somewhere? Do you live nearby?"

"No, you don't and no, he doesn't," Nikki answered with more haste than grace. "He's just come back from overseas. He doesn't have anyplace to live, which means he'll be moving in with us."

"That's going to make it a bit crowded," Krista observed, then offered, "Why don't I put out some feelers to some of my friends? I'm sure I could find another place."

Nikki wrinkled her brow in what she hoped was a thoughtful frown. "That's a possibility. But there's no hurry."

"No hurry at all," Jonah cut in coldly. "In fact, we want you and Keli to stay put. We'll be moving into my apartment."

Nikki's mouth fell open. "But—"

"I was keeping it as a surprise wedding gift, sweetheart. Krista, the place is all yours," Jonah stated in an intractable voice. "We just stopped by to give you the good news and to pick up some of Nikki's clothes." His hand clamped down on her arm as she started to protest. "Didn't we?"

"I'm so pleased you let me do the talking," she bit out, watching all her plans dissipate like smoke in a high wind. Aware of Krista's worried stare, she added a terse, "Darling."

"My pleasure." He bared sharklike teeth. "Honey."

CHAPTER SIX

"How could you?" Nikki demanded furiously.

"How could I? How could *you*?"

"You don't understand!"

"You're damned right I don't," Jonah snarled, tossing their luggage into the spacious elevator. Inserting a key in the floor-selector panel, he slammed his palm against the button for the penthouse. "Krista is a member of your family. Doesn't that mean anything to you?"

"Of course it does—"

"And yet you'd still toss your own sister and niece out of their home?"

He swiveled to confront her, and the spaciousness of the car instantly shrank. She felt as though she'd stumbled into a lion's den and found herself face-to-face with the top cat—a savage, ill-tempered beast only too happy to shred some flesh from her bones. It wasn't a pleasant sensation.

"I'd never force Krista to leave," she insisted.

"But you'd make it so uncomfortable for her, she'd vacate of her own accord, right?" The contempt in his voice ripped at her self-control. "I'll bet it's the only home those two have ever known, isn't it?"

She didn't dare answer that one, not when her response would further incite him. "Krista doesn't want to live with me anymore," Nikki attempted to explain. "She wants to move in with a friend. I'm just trying to give her a gracious way out."

His eyes flashed with gold fire. "Oh, you're giving her a gracious way out, all right. Right out the door and onto the street."

"That's not true! The problem is, she won't leave because she doesn't want me to live alone. She's got this crazy idea that she owes me."

He folded his arms across his chest, drawing her attention to the imposing width of his shoulders. Where once she took comfort in his size, now it only served to intimidate. "And who gave her that idea? You?"

She wouldn't explain, and no amount of baiting on his part could force her to. "I don't care what you think," she said tightly. "I told you from the start that I needed a husband in order to resolve two problems."

"Eric and a personal matter. I remember." He speared her with a flinty look. "If I'd had any idea what that personal matter involved or how you planned to rectify it, I'd never have married you."

"And if I'd known you'd end up interfering in something that's none of your business, I wouldn't have married you, either," she flashed back, her temper smoldering. "Krista and Keli are the two most important people in my life—"

He gave a short, hard laugh. "You have a funny way of showing it."

"I let you handle Eric the way you thought best. But you didn't grant me the same courtesy, did you?"

"There's one important difference. I had Eric's best interests at heart."

"Just as I had Krista's! If you'd let me do the talking instead of butting in the way you did, it would have all worked out fine. But now you've ruined everything I worked so hard to arrange. I went to all the expense and awkwardness of marrying for nothing. *Nothing!* And it's all your fault.''

He turned to stare at the elevator doors, the muscles of his jaw flexing. ''Fine. It's all my fault. I can live with that.''

Fury exploded to life with all the force of a wildfire. She fought to control the rage, to dampen it with cool, calming logic and reason. For the first time in recent memory, she couldn't. ''You had no right to interfere! None. I'd planned it so carefully, taken away every last excuse she could dream up. And thanks to you, my plans are ruined.''

''You think I give a damn about that?'' He turned sharply to face her. ''Don't expect me to apologize for protecting Krista and Keli from your machinations. I'm glad I interfered.''

''You don't understand.'' She closed her eyes to hide her frustration. Because of Jonah, Krista wouldn't be moving out anytime soon. That was quite clear. Why fly the nest when it was so convenient and safe to remain? Why risk the pain and sorrow of a cruel world when she could use Nikki as the perfect excuse for staying put? Nikki needed her. She owed Nikki. Nikki had saved her life. ''Now she'll never leave.''

''Tough.''

''Tough?'' She stared at him in disbelief. ''What am I supposed to do when our marriage ends? I can't move back in with Krista. She'll never get on with her life if I do.''

''All I've done is prevent you from throwing your

sister and niece onto the street.'' The elevator doors slid open and once again he picked up the luggage, transferring it to the door of the penthouse. ''Why not let your sister continue to use the brownstone? Kids should have a house to call their own. When we divorce, you can find an apartment. Something immaculate where you won't have to worry about a kid cluttering up your space with her toys.''

''You still don't understand,'' she repeated.

''You're right. I don't.'' He keyed open the door and swept her into his arms.

''What are you doing?'' she demanded in alarm.

''Carrying my bride over the threshold. Welcome home, Mrs. Alexander.'' Then he dumped her onto her feet. ''Don't get too comfortable.''

Nikki blinked hard, fighting the unexpected rush of tears. Turning away so he wouldn't see how much he'd upset her, she crossed the black marble entryway into the living room. A bank of windows lined one wall, offering a stunning panorama of Manhattan. It was clearly the focal point of the room. The furniture had been artfully arranged to take advantage of the view while still maintaining an air of intimacy. It was beautiful and expensive and chillingly cold.

''It must have been pricey maintaining this place while you were in England,'' she commented without turning around. Though she hadn't heard him enter the room, the shiver that slid down her spine gave her all the warning she needed.

''It's not mine. International Investment uses it for entertaining,'' he replied. ''Or we'll allow the occasional client to stay here when he or she flies in from out of town.''

''Won't Della and Loren object to our using it?''

"It's my decision. Why would they object?"

She turned around, regarding him curiously. "Isn't it Loren's call? Isn't he the CEO?"

"Don't you know?"

"Know what?"

"I'm CEO. It's a recent change, I'll admit. But still, a woman in your position should have made it her business to stay current."

"Eric never said and I assumed..." She shrugged. "My mistake."

"One of many, it would seem."

She refused to allow him to get under her skin again. "So what now?"

"Now we have lunch and then go to work. I expect Eric will have gone in bright and early this morning and leaked the news of our marriage. Once there, we introduce you as Mrs. Alexander. We accept the employees' congratulations, ignore their curious whispers and stares and get down to business."

"What about after we make the big announcement?" she asked. "I mean, what happens when you return to England?"

"I don't go back until some time after the holidays. We'll have plenty of opportunity to discuss our options."

Her eyes narrowed. "Why so long? At the Montagues', you claimed you'd only be in the country for a few weeks."

"My plans changed when we married."

"Why?" she repeated baldly.

"It would look strange if your husband missed out on your big night." At her blank look, he prompted, "You know. The LJB Award."

With all the furor of the past several days, she'd

forgotten about the award ceremony. But Jonah hadn't. And with sudden, devastating insight she realized that her nomination must have played an important part in his choosing to marry her when Eric made his unexpected appearance. "It wouldn't do for International Investment to lose an LJB nominee, would it?" she asked.

"I prefer not to."

"But if the nominee isn't a winner? What then?"

He tilted his head to one side. "I'm not certain," he admitted frankly. "I'd like to see the quality of your work before I reach that decision."

"You won't be disappointed," she informed him confidently. "I'm good at what I do."

He didn't appear convinced. "We'll see."

Krista hesitated in front of the reception desk of International Investment, not quite certain whether she had to check in before going in search of Nikki's office. But since the desk wasn't occupied, she couldn't ask for either directions or instructions.

She'd never bothered her sister at work before, but the past three weeks had been odd. Something wasn't right. The few times she'd been over to Nikki's new apartment, there hadn't been an opportunity for private conversation. So she'd decided to hold the discussion here. Noticing a small crowd clustered near a huge double door at the far end of the hallway, she decided to ask one of them for directions.

"Excuse me," she began, tapping the shoulder of a tall man with golden brown hair.

"Sshh." He waved her silent without turning around. "This is too good to miss."

"What—" And then she heard it—shouting coming from the far side of the door. Her eyes widened. Good gracious, that sounded like…

Nikki.

"What do you mean you've reassigned the Stamberg account?" her always-in-control, emotions-on-ice sister shrieked. "That's my account!"

"Well, now it's Meyerson's," a masculine voice roared back. Krista's mouth dropped open. If she wasn't mistaken, that sounded very much like the brother-in-law she'd gained three weeks ago. Her brow wrinkled in confusion. She hadn't realized he worked with Nikki.

"Meyerson? That idiot? He can't tell a put from a place, much less organize a portfolio as complicated as Stamberg's. I thought you wanted to improve business."

"I do."

"Well, guess what? This isn't going to do it."

"You seem to forget who's working for whom around here," Jonah snarled.

"I doubt that will be a problem much longer."

"And just what the hell does that mean?"

"It means that a few more asinine decisions like this one and you won't have to worry about impertinent employees, portfolios, accounts, or who's working for whom at International. Because we'll all be out of work!"

"You don't know what the hell you're talking about."

"I know one thing. Appointing Meyerson is the biggest mistake you'll ever make."

"Meyerson will double Stamberg's profits."

"Don't make me laugh. Meyerson couldn't double his own age."

''Shall we make a small wager about that? Or are you all talk and no action?''

''You want action? I'll give you action. Not only won't Meyerson double so much as one of Stamberg's stock picks, but he'll lose money on the few investments he does make.''

''And if you're wrong?''

''Then I'll…I'll…''

''You'll what?''

''I'll dance naked on top of your desk!'' Krista heard her sister declare rashly. ''But if you lose, you do the honors on top of mine.''

A collective gasp rippled through the crowd, and Krista leaned against the wall, torn between shock and amusement. This was a side of Nikki she'd never heard before.

''What I wouldn't give to see that,'' one of the men muttered.

''Shut up, Bently,'' the man she'd first approached growled.

''Oh, dear, oh, dear,'' a balding man groaned. ''What will I do?''

''You'd better win that bet, Meyerson, or Alexander will have your head on a platter,'' Bently warned.

There'd been several minutes of silence behind the door. Then Krista heard the sound of a chair being shoved back. ''You've got yourself a deal,'' Jonah said. ''Prepare to lose, wife.''

''Hah! There's not a chance in hell you'll win this bet.''

Her voice grew louder as she approached the door and everyone hastily dispersed. The man who'd told Bently to shut up turned, catching her off guard.

"Don't just stand there," he said, grasping Krista's arm. He thrust open the nearest door and practically shoved her over the threshold. "Nikki won't appreciate our eavesdropping on her conversation."

He crowded in behind her and Krista found it difficult to breathe. He couldn't be aware he still held her, she decided, closing her eyes against the unexpected warmth pooling in her stomach. Or that he'd molded her so tightly against his lean form. Feelings she hadn't experienced in almost seven long, lonely years stirred, disconcerting her. "Please—" she began.

"Wait a sec," he murmured close to her ear. Opening the door a crack, he glanced into the hallway. "Here she comes."

"Oh, really?" Nikki was saying, fury rippling through her voice. "Well, we'll just see about that." A door opened and then slammed closed. She swept by, rich color blooming in her face. Never had she looked so alive, or so beautiful, Krista thought.

The door opened once again and she caught a glimpse of Jonah. "Yes, we will see. And in the meantime, prepare to start stripping!" The door slamming punctuated his final taunt.

Krista wriggled. "If you don't mind," she said.

"Oh, sorry." He stepped back, his hands falling slowly away. Gazing down at her, he frowned. "You look familiar. Do I know you?"

"I don't think so." She held out her hand and gave a rueful smile. "I'm Krista Barrett. Nikki's my sister."

He blinked in surprise, then began to chuckle. "No kidding. I'm Eric Sanders. Jonah's my brother."

Startled, she stared at him. This was the man who'd

been infatuated with Nikki? The man who'd made her so uncomfortable she'd invented a husband? *And* he was the brother of Nikki's new husband? Something strange was going on here. This had to be more than a coincidence. Which meant that Nikki's marriage might not be a simple love match as her dear sister had claimed. Krista eyed Eric speculatively. Maybe he knew what was up. And maybe, just maybe, he'd clue her in.

"Listen, I know this is a bit unexpected, but...would you care to have lunch with me?" Eric offered.

"I don't know," she said. "I'd hoped to see Nikki."

He grinned, a charming, boyish sort of grin. "I don't think this is a very good time to talk to her, do you?"

"I guess not." She studied him, finding his gentle appeal impossible to resist. Besides, lunch might be the perfect opportunity to pump him for a little information. "Okay. Let's go."

"Great." Warmth gathered in his hazel eyes along with something else.... Masculine appreciation, she finally discerned with bemused astonishment. It had been so long since she'd experienced it, she almost hadn't recognized that sudden, explosive attraction. He reached for the doorknob, then hesitated. "I guess I should tell you that I used to be very attracted to your sister. Nothing happened, you understand," he added hastily.

She hid her amusement. "I understand."

"Besides, I just realized something."

"What did you realize?"

"That while Nikki's perfect for Jonah, she'd have

been a bit much for me. Besides, she's a career woman and I'd really like a more traditional wife." A slow smile lit his gaze and he opened the door. "So tell me, Krista. How do you like children?"

She laughed. "Funny you should ask."

Nikki entered her office and banged the door closed behind her. Never in the twenty-eight years of her existence had she been so furious. And it was all due to one infuriating, impossible man.

Her husband.

She paced the office, trying to calm herself, struggling to regain control. It didn't work. Nothing worked—not staring out the window and counting cabs, not reorganizing her well-organized files, not even tidying her already-tidy desk. Only one thing would calm her. Grimly, she crossed to her office closet and dragged out a large carton. After removing a huge tarp from the top of the box, she spread it on the floor. It was followed by a whole array of equipment—a special blend of soil, fertilizer, gloves, snippers, atomizer, an assortment of ceramic pots and an apron. She laid everything out with military precision, then crossed to the window to gather up her plants.

They'd been given to her by various staff members, all of whom had one thing in common—black thumbs. She took pleasure in nursing the plants back to full health before returning them. As always when she worked with her plants, the fury of her emotions eased, dissipating until she was once again in control. She worked straight through lunch, happily repotting.

An hour later, she finished. Feeling much more relaxed, she rocked back on her heels and tossed her gloves onto the tarp. She nodded in satisfaction as she gathered up her supplies. Two of her specimens could be returned by the end of the week, she decided. And undoubtedly, there'd be several others to replace the ones she gave back. She made a mental note to sweep the office for more casualties. With Christmas fast approaching, she didn't doubt she'd be kept quite busy. Just as she finished cleaning up the clutter, the phone rang.

''Nikki Ashton,'' she said without thinking, then made a face. ''I mean, Alexander.''

''Nikki, dear. It's Selma.''

''Hello, Aunt Selma.'' She tucked a strand of hair behind her ear and smiled in genuine pleasure. ''How are you?''

''Wonderful. Excited. In urgent need of advice.''

Nikki brightened. ''You know I'm happy to help.''

''I know you are, dear. That's why we always call on you.''

''So what's up?''

''Ernie and I have had the most delicious offer.'' Excitement bubbled in her voice. ''Of course, we want to discuss it with you before we act.''

Some of Nikki's pleasure faded. This didn't sound good. But then, Selma and Ernie's ideas seldom did. ''Why don't you drop by the office tomorrow? Is noon convenient?''

''No, no. It has to be tonight. We're much too excited to wait any longer. Besides, time is of the essence. We'll come to your place.''

Nikki straightened abruptly. ''I don't think—''

''Krista says your apartment is gorgeous and we'd love to meet that new husband of yours. Shame on you for eloping, by the way, and doing us out of the pleasure of a big wedding." There was a delicate pause and then Selma asked, "What time, dear?"

Nikki thought fast. "How about six?" she suggested, unable to dream up a reasonable excuse for changing the venue.

"Six it is. See you then."

Hanging up, Nikki leaned back in her chair. It would work out, she attempted to reassure herself. With any luck, Jonah would work as late tonight as he had every other evening this week and she could meet her relatives without his interference. At least he'd better not interfere. Not again. Not when Aunt Selma and Uncle Ernie required such delicate handling.

She closed her eyes, tension creeping back. Maybe she'd better sweep the office for more plants right now. Why repot tomorrow when she could repot today?

"All we need to do is put up fifty thousand and we'll have the exclusive franchise," Selma said, clasping her hands together enthusiastically.

"But it's a limited-time offer," Ernie added. "If we don't get the money together by the day after tomorrow, we're going to miss the boat."

"This is one boat it wouldn't be such a bad idea to miss," Nikki muttered beneath her breath.

"What's that, dear?" Selma asked anxiously.

"A note. I didn't want to miss making a note of the date. The day after tomorrow," she repeated, writing Wednesday in large block letters. "And what's the name of this man who wants you to invest?"

"Timothy T. Tucker. Such a delightful man, isn't he, Ernie?"

"Really knows his way around numbers. Had our heads spinning. Why the way he has it figured, we can triple our investment in under a year."

Nikki tossed down her pen. "Uncle Ernie, even I can't do that."

He patted her hand. "Yes, sweetheart. We know. But we won't hold that against you."

"You do your best, I'm sure," Selma maintained stoutly. "We're all very proud of you."

Nikki groaned. "How did you meet this man? What do you know about him?"

"He walked into our coffee shop right out of the blue."

"A red-letter day that was," Ernie pronounced, folding his hands over his ample middle. "Looked around and knew right off we ran a profitable business."

"I'll just bet." Nikki scowled. He'd probably watched the flow of traffic, made a few quick calculations and decided the shop kicked off plenty of disposable income. Then he'd have asked a few questions of her naive aunt and uncle and...*voilà*. The birth of a scam. "Did you tell him about your mortgage?"

Selma looked surprised. "But we don't have one, dear."

"I know that, Aunt Selma. Does this Mr. Tucker know? Did you tell him?"

"I think we may have touched on it," Selma confessed. "But it was all very innocent. He was interested in opening a storefront in our area and wondered what the rent might run."

"Of course we had to admit we didn't know," Uncle Ernie inserted. "Since we own the property outright, we aren't all that knowledgeable about what rents go for these days.''

"Why, if he's selling these franchises, does he need to rent a storefront?'' Nikki questioned in exasperation.

"To interest people in buying the Miracle Box, of course.''

"But that doesn't make any sense.'' Unfortunately, her aunt and uncle put little credence in logic and reason, much less common sense. "If you have the franchise to sell this box, why would *he* open—''

Selma reached over and patted her hand. "Don't feel bad, darling. We were confused at first, too. Dear Mr. Tucker was so patient with us, though. Wasn't he, Ernie?''

"Answered every one of our questions. Explained about the patents and our territory and made all that technical jargon sound quite sensible.'' He grinned proudly. "Why, I can talk about fax modules and cable companions with the best of them.''

"So I see.'' Picking up her pen and pulling her steno pad closer, Nikki started jotting down notes. "Timothy T. Tucker. The Miracle Box. Fifty grand. Wednesday. I don't suppose you have his business card by any chance?''

"Sure.'' Ernie plucked it from his wallet and handed it over. "Must be doing all right for himself. Cards of that quality are expensive.''

"I wonder where he gets all that wealth?'' Nikki asked, not the least surprised when they didn't pick up on her sarcasm.

"From ideas like the Miracle Box, I imagine,'' Ernie said thoughtfully.

"And how are you going to sell these boxes and still run your coffee shop?"

"Gordie and Cal are helping."

Nikki closed her eyes and sighed. She should have known her cousins would be involved. If it was an idiotic scheme and sure to cost a lot of money with little to no return, they'd be the first in line. Her aunt and uncle would be second.

"So what do you think?" Ernie asked anxiously. "May we have the money?"

"Not a chance," Nikki answered without thinking.

"Oh, Nikki. Please. It's not so much to ask. We really need the money, dear." Selma fumbled in her purse for a hankie, applying it to teary eyes. "If you won't do it for us, think of your poor cousins. It's an opportunity that will never come along again."

Nikki groaned. "I couldn't be so lucky."

"We have a CD coming due next week," Ernie reminded her. "Can't we borrow against that?"

"I have an investment lined up for that money already."

"What about our savings account?" Selma asked. "Isn't there enough in there?"

Nikki shook her head. "I thought you wanted that money so you could open up Ernie's Beanery 2."

"We can wait. Why, with the money we'll make selling—"

"No."

"But *why*?" Selma dissolved into tears. "I thought it was our money."

"It is," Nikki admitted uncomfortably.

"Then why can't we spend it the way we want?"

"You can," a new voice interrupted. Jonah stepped into the living room. "Can't they, Nikki?"

CHAPTER SEVEN

"No, THEY can't," Nikki retorted. "Stay out of it, Jonah. You don't understand."

"That doesn't come as any surprise." He tossed his coat and suit jacket over the arm of the couch and deposited his suitcase on the floor beside it. "I seem to have a knack for misunderstanding."

A hint of angry color washed into her cheeks, and her eyes flashed with violet warning. Jonah smiled in satisfaction. He knew what that meant. If he goaded her just a little more, she'd lose her temper as thoroughly as she had earlier that morning. He'd enjoyed their clashes over the past few weeks. He particularly enjoyed shaking her composure, watching as the icy facade melted enough to reveal the vibrant flame within.

"If you don't mind, I'm having a private discussion here."

"But I do mind, sweetheart. You haven't introduced us." Jonah approached and held out his hand, wondering who these people were and why they'd turned their finances over to his wife. "I'm Jonah Alexander, Nikki's husband."

"Ernie and Selma Crandell." They shook hands. "You sure are a busy man. We've been trying to arrange a little get-together ever since Nikki told us you two got married, but you've always had a schedule conflict.''

"Is that right? I wish I'd known.'' Jonah glanced at his wife and said with deceptive mildness, "Sweetheart, you should have nagged me more. If I'd realized that your—'' He broke off pointedly.

"Aunt and uncle,'' she whispered.

A deadly silence descended for an endless moment before Jonah picked up the slack. "If I'd realized your aunt and uncle had been serious about throwing us a party, I would have found the time.''

"Well, since we missed out having you for Thanksgiving, perhaps we can make a try for Christmas,'' Selma offered tentatively. "Or do you have another commitment? Nikki wasn't certain.''

Jonah's mouth compressed. Selma clearly wasn't aware that he'd never even heard their names before, let alone received any of their invitations. But Ernie didn't appear quite so obtuse.

"Maybe we've caught you at a bad time,'' he muttered uncomfortably. "Don't mean to be pushy relatives.''

"Not at all.'' Jonah shot a grim look toward his wife. She made a point of avoiding his gaze, but couldn't hide the guilty color staining her cheekbones. "I'll see if I can't arrange to be free. In fact, I'll make a special note of it on my calendar.''

Ernie gave a more enthusiastic nod. "Great. Since we're all the family Nikki and Krista have, we try to make the most of the holidays. My wife and their mom were sisters, you know.''

"Were?''

Ernie shot his niece a curious glance. "Did she forget to mention?''

"Apparently, there's quite a bit she forgot to mention," Jonah observed drily.

"Oh. Well, Nikki's mom and dad were killed eight years ago in a boating accident," Ernie explained. "She was just a teenager, poor mite."

"Hardly a teenager or a mite," Nikki corrected crisply, jumping into the conversation. "I was twenty and a very independent college student."

"Eight years ago." Jonah glanced thoughtfully at his wife. She sat in her chair, every muscle tensed. Where only moments ago, her color had run high, she now appeared pale as a winter moon. The urge to protect her from a topic that caused such obvious pain battled with his intense curiosity. He couldn't resist probing just a little deeper. "That would have made Krista…"

"Sixteen," Selma supplied, shaking her head. "That year and a half after their death was such a tragic time. Perhaps if Edward and Angeline had lived, things might have been different for the girls. But with Krista marrying so young and then Nikki involved in that terrible incident—"

"I think that's enough," Nikki interrupted tautly. "I'm sure Jonah doesn't want to hear all the boring details. Besides, it's ancient history."

He pinned her with a narrow gaze. It would seem they'd pushed an emotional hot button. Interesting. "I didn't mean to upset you. We can save this particular conversation for a more convenient time."

Alarm lit her expressive eyes. "There's no need."

If she'd hoped to discourage him, she'd failed. Miserably. Instead, she'd whetted his appetite to learn more. He suspected that whatever had happened seven years ago would shed considerable light on several aspects of Nikki's personality—such as the tight control she kept on her emotions. It might also explain her odd attitude toward family.

"She's right," Jonah conceded with an easy smile. "This isn't the appropriate time to talk about the past. I see I've interrupted an important financial discussion." He settled onto the couch and gestured for them to continue. "Please. Don't let me interrupt."

"I believe we've concluded this discussion," Nikki announced, thrusting back her chair.

"But what about the money?" Selma turned to appeal to Jonah. "The deadline's Wednesday."

"I'm certain Nikki won't want to disappoint you," Jonah assured her. "Will you, darling?"

Nikki gathered up her notes, her color riding high once again. "I'll look into it further," she offered through gritted teeth.

Reluctantly, her aunt and uncle stood. "Well, if that's the best you can do…" Selma murmured. She glanced at Jonah in desperate appeal. "It's just a small thing we're asking."

Jonah gained his feet and gathered up the coats and scarves tossed over the back of a nearby chair. "I'll see what I can do," he whispered as he helped Selma on with hers.

"Such a good boy," she said, giving him a delighted smile. "So reasonable. And by the way, welcome to the family."

"Why, thank you." He shook hands once again with Ernie. "I'm sure Nikki will be in touch soon."

"Excellent, excellent," Ernie replied in a hearty voice as he pulled on his gloves. "Took one look and knew you were the man to make her see reason."

"Uncle Ernie—" Nikki began.

"Now, now." He enveloped her in a fierce bear hug. "Don't be too hard on yourself, Nikki. You do your best. But it's clear this husband of yours knows a thing or two about finances. Can't hurt to have him take a look at Tucker's prospectus."

With a final goodbye, the two left. Jonah glanced at Nikki. She stood with her back to him, her vibrant hair restrained by a wide gold clip. She'd changed out of her office clothes. Gone was the stark gray suit from that morning and in its place she'd donned ivory slacks and an oversize cable sweater in a jewel-bright emerald. He could feel the tension emanating from her and stood unmoving, anticipating the explosion. He didn't have long to wait.

"How dare you?" she demanded as she swung around. She stalked toward him, her eyes blazing with amethyst fire. "How dare you interfere in a family matter?"

"I *am* family." He smiled blandly. "Or have you forgotten?"

She halted a few feet away. "I wish I could forget," she informed him passionately, tossing her notepad and pen onto the glass-topped coffee table. "But you make that impossible."

"Good. Impossible works for me."

He watched her frustration gather, watched the struggle to control her temper. And watched her fail. "Why are you butting in where you don't belong?"

"In case you weren't aware of the fact, that marriage license you were so hot to acquire came with a few strings. I'm family now, whether you like it or not. Family is allowed to butt in." He closed the distance between them, towering over her. He didn't care if she found his size intimidating. He hoped he intimidated the hell out of her. "And as long as I'm your husband, you'll treat me with the proper respect that entails. Is that clear?"

"And if I don't?"

"You don't want to know the answer to that." He thrust a hand through his hair and glared at her from beneath drawn brows, allowing a small measure of his own anger to show. "You allowed me to walk into that situation blind tonight. Do you have any idea how that felt? I didn't have a clue who those people were. Selma may not have realized, but Ernie sure as hell did. Nor have you bothered to inform me of their invitations, something else he picked up on."

She managed to meet his gaze this time, but a hint of her earlier chagrin still lingered. "I didn't think you'd be interested," she claimed.

"Don't lie to me, Nikki," he snapped. "I won't tolerate it. That's not the reason and you damned well know it. You wanted to keep me well away from your aunt and uncle."

"With good reason."

"Oh? And just what is that good reason?"

She folded her arms across her chest in a defensive gesture. "Our marriage isn't real. That's why."

He shrugged. "What difference does that make?"

She gave him an impatient look. "You know what difference. I don't want them to count on your being there when we both know it won't last. In case you didn't notice, they're a sweet couple whose affections are easily engaged."

"Mmm. I did notice," he admitted, remembering Selma's instant acceptance of him.

"Exactly. They're very trusting." She scowled at him. "Too much so."

"And I'm someone they shouldn't trust?"

To his amusement, she didn't give him a straight-forward answer. "Let's just say the jury's still out," she muttered. "But that doesn't change the fact that you're returning to London soon. By the time you do, they'll have become overly fond of you. They'll also assume you've deserted me and be hurt and upset on my behalf."

"And what about you?" he questioned curiously. "Will you be hurt and upset, too?"

"Not a bit," she stated with an interesting lack of conviction. "It'll be a relief to have you gone so I can get my life back to normal."

"Does that mean you'll move in with Krista and Keli again?"

"Absolutely not. I still have hopes of salvaging that situation, despite your interference. Which is an-other reason I neglected to introduce you to my rel-atives. You stuck your nose in where it didn't belong with Krista. I wasn't about to have you do the same with Uncle Ernie and Aunt Selma."

"I told you why I interfered in your business with Krista."

"You didn't have all the facts then, just as you didn't tonight. You had no right to tell Ernie and Selma I'd allow them to invest that money until you had all the information at your disposal."

"I agree."

"I—" She blinked in surprise. "What did you say?"

"You heard me. I spoke without thinking."

"Since you're being so agreeable, would you mind explaining why you jumped in?"

"Because I thought you were being unreasonable."

"*Unreasonable*? A fat lot you know!"

"Nikki…" He yanked irritably at his tie as he searched for an approach that wouldn't rouse her anger again. He shook his head at the irony. For such a cool, logical female, she sure had a hot temper. "They're your relatives, not your clients. Maybe if you stopped treating them as if it was a business transaction and started treating them like family—"

"I'm responsible for their financial stability."

"Maybe you shouldn't be."

"You don't understand."

"You know, I'm getting really tired of hearing that phrase." He shot her a penetrating look. "How can I understand when you won't explain? And don't tell me it isn't any of my business, because as of now I'm making it my business."

She lifted her chin. "And if I refuse to tell you anything?"

"I suspect your relatives will be more forthcoming. Of course, it might be somewhat embarrassing for you when I get my answers from them—answers my wife should have provided."

Agitation brought renewed color to her cheeks. "That's blackmail."

He tilted his head to one side in mock contemplation. "I believe you're right. It is."

"Why are you doing this?" she demanded in frustration. "What do you care? They're not your relatives."

He shrugged. "Damned if I know. I guess because I take my family obligations seriously."

"Then—"

"Enough, Nikki. Are you going to answer my

questions or do I have a man-to-man conversation with Ernie?''

Stubborn to the end, she stewed about it for a full two minutes. Since he considered the outcome inevitable, he gave her all the time she needed. He crossed to the liquor cabinet and removed a bottle of cabernet sauvignon. By the time he'd poured them each a glass, she'd reached her decision. He waited while she gathered her composure, understanding her dilemma better than she realized. To discuss family, she had to give up a certain amount of control and trust him. And for some reason—perhaps that incident seven years ago—control was everything to her; trust something to be avoided at all costs.

''Well?'' he asked, handing her the wine.

She took a disrespectful gulp and fixed him with a defiant glare. ''What do you want to know?''

''How old was Krista when she married?''

Nikki dropped onto the couch. ''Seventeen,'' she said bleakly.

He had suspected as much, but it still came as a shock. ''She was pregnant with Keli?''

''Yes, though it wasn't a shotgun marriage, if that's what you're asking. She and Benjie were very much in love. Krista gave birth two days before her eighteenth birthday.''

''That makes Keli, what? Six?'' At Nikki's nod of confirmation, he asked, ''And what happened to Benjie?''

''He died in a car accident four months after the wedding.''

Jonah sucked in his breath. ''Jeez, Nikki. I'm sorry.''

"We all were," she said with marked understatement. "It wasn't a good time."

"I'll bet. What did Krista do?"

Nikki shrugged, staring into the ruby depths of her wine. "Benjie's family wasn't in a financial position to help, whereas our parents had left us some insurance money. So, Krista moved in with me."

"And has lived with you ever since," he concluded. "You've supported them?"

"Krista has a part-time job. But I've encouraged her to stay at home with Keli. I earn enough to take care of them."

"What happened to change all that? Have you gotten tired of living in such tight quarters? Or is having a six-year-old around cramping your life-style?"

She set the glass on the coffee table with great care before turning on him with all the ferocity of a tigress defending her young. "Don't you ever say that again," she said harshly. "Ever. I love Krista and have adored Keli from the moment of her birth. If I had my preference, they'd never leave."

"Then why the hell are you throwing them out?"

Emotions chased across her expressive face—pain, sorrow, resignation. "I finally realized that Krista was using me to hide from life. She never dates, rarely goes out with friends. Her entire life revolves around Keli, and to a lesser extent, me. I overheard a phone conversation shortly before the Cinderella Ball. She was explaining to a friend how much she owed me, how she could never leave me because I needed her. And I realized that all these years..." Nikki snatched up her glass and drained the contents.

Without a word, Jonah refilled it. "All these years

you've protected her from life instead of forcing her to face up to it.''

''Yes.''

''So you've decided to set her free. In fact, you're tossing her out of the nest whether she wants to go or not.''

She nodded, tears glittering on the ends of her lashes. ''I've come home every day for the past six years to a hug from Keli, and now... And now—'' Her voice broke and she buried her face in her hands.

He was beside her in an instant, gathering her in his arms. ''Don't,'' he murmured. ''I'm sorry. You're right. I did misunderstand.''

''Keli should have a father. And Krista should have a husband.'' She visibly fought for control, but a stray tear escaped unchecked. ''But as long as I'm in the picture, that won't happen.''

''What about you?'' he asked quietly, rubbing her back in slow, gentle circles. ''You say that Krista's subconsciously used you as a shield, protecting herself from further pain. But haven't you been doing the same?''

She stilled. ''What are you talking about?''

''I don't think Krista was the only one hurt seven years ago. Selma implied—''

''My aunt talks too much.''

''There was a man, though. Wasn't there?''

''You don't under—''

He stopped the words with his mouth, tired of hearing them. She tasted of wine, the flavor far sweeter than anything he'd ever poured from a bottle. It would be all too easy to lose himself in the pleasure of the moment. But that had to wait. Right now he needed answers. ''Don't lie to me again. Not now,'' he muttered against her lips. ''Was there a man? Yes or no.''

''Yes.''

He cupped her chin, forcing her to meet his gaze. Her mouth was pink and damp from his kiss and distracting as hell. ''What happened? Did he desert you because of Krista?''

Her breath escaped in a harsh laugh. ''You're way off.''

''But you loved him and he left you.''

''Oh, yes. He left.''

''And for the past six or seven years you've remained as cloistered as Krista.''

''I've been pursuing my career,'' she retorted, stung. ''Not living in a convent.''

He slid his hand down the length of her neck to the fragile bones beneath the neckline of her sweater. ''Really? And how many men have there been since the one who deserted you?'' She attempted to pull free, but he tightened his hold, refusing to release her. ''How many, Nikki? One? Two? Or none?''

''None,'' she whispered, the fight draining from her.

''Because they all threatened to take something from you,'' he persisted. ''They wanted pieces of you that you weren't willing to give.''

''Isn't that what love is all about?'' she asked cynically. ''Giving up control to another person?''

''Is that how it is with Krista and Keli?''

''That's different,'' she denied instantly. ''They're family.''

''How is it different? You give pieces of yourself to them,'' he pointed out.

The tears had returned and she stared at him, her

eyes glimmering with jewel-like brilliance. "But they don't use up those pieces," she whispered. "They cherish them, make them more complete rather than less."

He'd never heard a more poignant description, a description that mated the ultimate joy love could bring with the devastating possibility of betrayal. Unable to resist any longer, he drew her close. Employing infinite tenderness, he captured her tremulous mouth with his, probing the moist warmth within.

The man who'd betrayed her had been a fool, Jonah decided in that instant. To have all this and use it so cavalierly was a crime. He might not have loved her, but he didn't have to destroy her in the process.

Jonah removed the clip confining her hair and lowered her to the couch cushions. It had been weeks since he'd had the opportunity to run his hands through the silken strands. He'd found that he wanted to do it at the oddest times—when they'd sat across each other at the dinner table, when he'd come into her office unexpectedly and caught her twirling a lock of hair around her finger. Even in the midst of one of their arguments, the temptation had struck. But not once had he given in. Until now.

Her deep russet hair spilled through his hands and across the white couch cushions, fire on ice. She was the most beautiful woman he'd ever seen. And as he held her in his arms, she responded so passionately to his kisses that her beauty took on a sensual wildness he found fiercely arousing.

"Jonah," she whispered, tugging at the buttons of his shirt. "Let me touch you."

He helped, yanking off his tie and ripping his shirt free of his trousers. Then he turned his attention to her, sliding his hands beneath the bottom of her sweater and along an endless expanse of baby-soft skin. Nothing hindered his progress, not even the expected scrap of lace and silk. With a husky moan, he cupped her breasts, his thumbs scraping across the sensitive crowns. The breath burst from her in frantic gasps and he drank in every minute sound.

But it wasn't enough. He wanted more of her.

Reluctantly releasing her mouth, he swept the bulky sweater over her head and tossed it aside. She froze beneath him, the chilly air momentarily bringing her to full awareness. He hesitated, reluctant to push her any further, ready to back off if she took fright. But far from panicking, she shivered at his touch, her spine arching reflexively.

"They're even softer than I remember," he commented, filling his hands with the abundance of wealth.

To his amusement, his twenty-eight-year-old wife blushed. "I thought your memories of that night were hazy."

"Not all of them. Of course, I was too tired to take advantage of my position then." He met her eyes with a determination she couldn't mistake. "But I'm not tonight."

Her eyes took on the most intense violet glow he'd ever seen and his gut clenched in reaction. He wanted her. Desperately. With a fierceness he hadn't felt with any other woman. The knowledge came as a distinct shock. He'd been aware of a nagging desire for weeks now. But he'd assumed it was a simple physical urge that would be satisfied with the inevitable bedding. After all, she was beautiful enough to attract any man worthy of the name. But this went deeper.

Curiosity ate at him, a need to see if she was as soft as he remembered, if her skin was as white, her legs as long and shapely. Like having a craving that demanded satisfaction, he found he had to explore the womanly secrets hidden beneath her clothing or go quietly insane.

He didn't just want to possess her body.

He wanted to lose himself in all of her—mind, body and spirit.

As a result, he'd pressed her hard tonight, forcing the issues she'd been using as a shield. Well, he'd stripped her of most of that armor and been pleasantly surprised by what she'd been hiding. Far from the cold, calculating creature he'd anticipated, he'd found a warm, generous woman, willing to sacrifice her own happiness for a member of her family.

She felt incredibly delicate beneath him, fragile and breakable. He took his time, warming her cool skin with his hands and mouth, lighting a fire that would burn bright enough to engulf them both. When she rewarded his patience with the sweetest of responses, he peeled away her slacks, uncovering legs that seemed to go on forever. He palmed the spot where delicate ankles met trim calves, and her eyes drifted closed, a soft sigh melting off her lips. His fingers danced higher, over her knee to the enticing curve of her thigh, pausing at the wisp of white that concealed russet-masked secrets. His breath grew harsh with need.

His control wouldn't last much longer, he realized, sparing her a brief glance. What he saw stopped him cold. Her violet-blue gaze met his with such a mix of need and anxiety, it threatened to unman him. And suddenly he knew he'd be making a terrible mistake if he didn't stop. Reluctantly, his hand slid away. "I won't take advantage of you like this. I'm not that other man."

"I know you're not," she whispered.

"I don't want any regrets come morning and if I'm not mistaken you already look like a woman with regrets."

She moistened her lips with the tip of her tongue. "No, really. It's all right."

But the anxiety remained and he saw it. "Well, it's not all right with me." He couldn't reach her sweater, so snagged his shirt instead, wrapping it around her. It didn't cover her completely, but it helped cool the fire to a manageable level. He pulled the collar tight beneath her chin and leveled her with a direct look. "In case you weren't aware of it, my sweet wife, making love—not having sex, but making love—means giving up a certain amount of control. But it's control freely given by both parties."

"I know that," she began.

"No. I don't think you do. I suspect you were forced to give everything while your partner took everything. I gather some men prefer it that way. I'm not one of them. I want the woman I'm with to be a full participant. And I won't take anything I'm not also willing to give. Until you realize that and trust me, I'll pass, thanks."

"Trust you," she repeated. Her bleak laugh was heartbreaking. "You don't ask for much, do you?"

He didn't answer, just kept looking at her with those calm, hazel eyes. She struggled upright, curling her legs beneath her. It was so tempting to tell him everything—about the Miracle Box, about her parents' deaths and the aftermath. It was especially tempting to tell him about that other humiliating incident.

But he was a temporary addition to her life and she an "accidental" wife, a choice he'd reluctantly made and within hours regretted. She couldn't depend on him. She couldn't depend on anyone but herself. She'd learned that lesson the hard way and spent the past seven years making certain she didn't repeat it. She'd also spent those years compensating for that one single blunder.

Still, for the first time, she wanted someone. Needed someone. The urge to trust trembled within, like a bird desperately seeking to escape confinement. "Jonah—"

"Don't force it, sweetheart," he said gently. "I'm not going anywhere."

"Not yet," she responded bitterly.

"Not yet," he confirmed. "Go to bed. We'll talk more in the morning."

"Maybe by then I'll have come to my senses," she muttered.

He merely grinned. "I couldn't be that lucky."

CHAPTER EIGHT

NIKKI awoke the next morning to discover Jonah waiting for her at the breakfast table. Over the past few weeks they'd been careful to time their comings and goings to avoid each other. Apparently, last night had changed all that.

He filled two earthenware mugs with coffee, added sugar to each and set them side by side in front of her. To her relief, he didn't say a word until she'd consumed the first cup. Then he poured some for himself, replaced her empty mug with a platter of toasted English muffins and joined her at the table.

"Don't think me ungrateful, but what brought on this sudden burst of domesticity?" she questioned cautiously, helping herself to a muffin. "Or don't I want to know?"

"You probably don't want to know."

"But you're going to tell me anyway, right?"

"Yes." He leaned back in the chair and folded his arms across his chest. The movement pulled his crisp white shirt taut across the generous spread of his shoulders. She had vivid memories of those shoulders in all their naked glory. Too vivid. "We neglected to discuss Ernie and Selma's dilemma last night," he reminded her.

"Mmm. We did get distracted, didn't we?" she

murmured, burying her nose in her coffee mug so she wouldn't get distracted again this morning.

"Pleasantly so, I hope."

She didn't dare answer that one, not when she caught a glimpse of green flame smoldering deep within his gaze. "What did you want to know?" she asked, hoping to move the conversation into safer channels. It would seem that talking about family now qualified as a safe topic. The irony of that fact didn't escape her.

A brief smile of awareness touched his mouth. "I want to know everything, of course. We can start, however, with your role as financial advisor. How did that come about?"

"I inherited it," she explained with a shrug. "My father was the family accountant. When he died, everyone turned to me because I was majoring in finance at the time."

He took a swallow of coffee and studied her with a thoughtful air. "You were a bit young to take on such a burden, don't you think?"

Privately, she was in complete agreement. Aloud she said, "They didn't trust anyone else."

"Ah. That old issue of trust rears its ugly head."

"Can we move this along?" she asked, reaching for another muffin to hide behind.

She wanted to get off the subject of the past. Badly. And since the future was just as uncomfortable a topic, that left the present. To her secret disgust, the idea of telling him about the Miracle Box actually held some appeal. Quite a change from how she'd felt before last night. If she wasn't careful, she really would start to trust him.

"I still have one or two questions about the past,"

he said, a hint of steel appearing beneath the congenial surface. "Your aunt made a reference to an incident that happened six or seven years ago and involved you. What was that about?"

"It wouldn't interest you," she replied with deceptive calm. "What's the problem, Jonah?" she couldn't resist taunting. "I thought you'd want all the gory details of how I'm being a coldhearted Scrooge and refusing to give my relatives their money. Instead, you're obsessing about a chapter of my life that's over and forgotten ages ago."

He didn't take the bait as she'd hoped. "Over, perhaps. But not forgotten." He allowed an uncomfortable silence to descend before adding, "You're not going to be able to duck a discussion of the past forever. You realize that, don't you?"

"I don't realize that at all." She fixed him with a determined look. "What I am willing to do is explain my current actions since they're of such importance to you. But my past and my future can't be of any interest."

He simply smiled. "You'd be amazed at what interests me."

Flustered, she made a production of dumping another spoonful of sugar into her coffee. "There's no point in getting too involved with each other's lives. Ours is a temporary arrangement, remember?"

"All too well." He leaned forward and caught her hand before she could spoon any more sugar into her mug. "I'll make you a deal. You stay out of the sugar bowl and I'll stay out of your past."

"Deal," she agreed instantly.

Amusement gleamed in his eyes. "At least I'll stay

out for now. In the meantime, tell me about this investment.''

''Right. The investment.'' Wriggling her fingers free of his hold, she stood and crossed to the sink, adding more coffee to her cup to dilute the abundance of sugar. ''My dear aunt and uncle have been offered the unbelievable chance to own the exclusive local franchise on something called a Miracle Box.''

''Never heard of it.''

''Really?'' she drawled in exaggerated surprise. ''But it's a brilliant invention. Absolutely everyone is going to want one.''

''What does this Miracle Box do?'' he asked warily.

''Let's see if I can remember it all....'' Turning to face him, she leaned against the counter and took a quick sip of coffee. She fought to hide her grimace of distaste. It needed more sugar again, but she'd cut off her hand before reaching for that bowl. ''It's part fax/modem, part telephone answering machine and part cable TV receiver and VCR all in one convenient, plug-into-the-wall device.''

''And I'll bet it washes dishes and gives change for a dollar, too,'' Jonah said drily.

''Not yet. But only because the inventor hasn't thought of it.'' She frowned. ''The problem is that this Miracle Box sounds just close enough to what's already on the market or soon to be available that to people like Ernie or Selma it appears quite believable.''

''Interesting scam.''

She gave a short laugh. ''Oh, but I haven't told you the best part yet.''

"Well? Don't keep me in suspense. What's the best part?"

"My aunt and uncle can have this exclusive franchise for the rock-bottom price of fifty grand."

She'd stunned him with that one. "You're kidding."

"I'm dead serious. Not only has he conned them into believing this box will make them a fortune, but he's buffaloed my cousins, as well. Which means that everyone will be so busy selling the Miracle Box, they'll neglect Ernie's Beanery."

Jonah shook his head in disgust. "By the time they realize it's all a scam, business will have bottomed out."

"And my family will be under investigation for fraud. If neglect doesn't succeed in destroying their café, lawyers' fees certainly will. But the bottom line will be the same. They will have happily paid fifty thousand dollars to put Ernie's Beanery out of business and themselves into bankruptcy."

"I'm sorry, Nikki. I should have—"

She cocked an eyebrow. "Trusted me?"

"Something like that," he conceded.

"That's all right. I have a bit of trouble in that department, too." She dumped the remains of her coffee in the sink and rinsed the mug. "Well, I'll tell you how you can make it up to me...."

"You want me to tell them they can't have the money," he said in a resigned voice.

She hid a smile. "Why, thank you. I accept. Shall we go into work now or shall I introduce you to the Beanery?"

"You say that as if I have a choice."

"The Beanery it is." She didn't bother to hide her grin. "Tell you what. I'll let *you* do the talking this time."

Jan opened the office door and poked her head in. "Sorry to disturb you, Nikki."

Nikki shoved aside the papers she'd been working on and glanced at her secretary. "What's up?"

"There's a man on line two who insists on speaking to you. He won't leave his name or number and this is the third time he's called. Do you want to talk to him or should I try to find out who it is again?"

Nikki shook her head. "No, don't bother. I'll take it, thanks." She reached for the phone and punched the appropriate button. "Nikki Alexander," she stated automatically. She'd certainly grown accustomed to using her married name, she realized with a bitter-sweet smile. She'd better hope she found it just as easy to get *un*used to.

"Ah, Mrs. Alexander. At last. You're a very difficult woman to get hold of."

"Who is this, please?"

"Timothy T. Tucker. I'm sure you've heard of me."

Nikki straightened in her chair. "I don't believe it. Mr. Miracle Box himself."

"The one and only. I spoke to your aunt and uncle this morning and there seems to be a small problem."

"Oh?" she drawled. "And what might that be?"

"Ernie's having trouble getting his hands on the money to invest in my proposition."

"And he gave you my number?"

There was a small pause. "Several of them," he said deliberately.

Her eyes narrowed. What did that mean? Had

Uncle Ernie been foolish enough to supply this man with her number at Jonah's apartment? She stirred uneasily. And what about the brownstone? The idea of Tucker having Krista's number was very unsettling. "What do you want?" she demanded.

"I want the money Ernie and Selma promised me. Fifty thousand to be exact."

"I'm sorry, Mr. Tucker. Perhaps my aunt and uncle neglected to mention it. They've chosen not to invest in your scam—" she deliberately paused before correcting herself "—I mean, in your invention."

"I don't think you understand—"

"No, it's you who doesn't understand," she informed him crisply. "My aunt and uncle may be gullible, but I'm not. I've examined your prospectus and plan to hand it over to the appropriate authorities."

"What the hell are you talking about?"

She swiveled in her chair to face the office window. "I'm talking about fraud. The technology you claim to have doesn't exist."

"My box—"

"Your box is as phony as you are. Goodbye, Mr. Tucker."

"I wouldn't hang up if I were you! You better give your uncle that money, or you'll regret it."

"I don't think so."

"Oh, no? Your aunt and uncle aren't just gullible. They're also very talkative. And I'm a great listener. In all my conversations with them, they were quite full of their brilliant niece." His deliberate pause was an exact copy of her own. "Brilliant *now*, that is."

She slowly straightened. "Get to the point, Tucker."

"You weren't quite so brilliant seven years ago,

were you? I think the LJB committee would be very interested in the details of that little escapade, don't you?''

Her hand tightened on the receiver. ''Are you threatening me?''

''Oh, no. I'm making you a one hundred percent guarantee. You ruin my deal with your aunt and uncle, and I expose that nasty little skeleton in your closet. Look at it as an investment in your own personal Miracle Box. Fifty grand in exchange for a box that does absolutely nothing. You have my personal guarantee that it won't make so much as a peep.'' He laughed raucously at his own joke. ''So, is it a deal?''

Nikki closed her eyes. All she'd worked for over the past seven years, all she'd done to try to make up for that one horrible disaster would be for nothing. She knew the interpretation people would put on that incident. Not only would the award committee take away her nomination, she'd undoubtedly lose her job, as well. But to pay this slime fifty thousand in the hopes that he wouldn't say anything?

''Not a chance,'' she whispered. ''I don't pay blackmail. Do your worst, Tucker.''

''I plan to,'' he snarled and slammed down the phone.

Nikki hung up, staring blindly out the window. So what did she do now? Without conscious thought, she crossed to the office closet and pulled out her box of gardening supplies. For the next hour, she worked and weighed her options. Briefly, she considered going to Jonah for help. It was possible he'd understand. After all, he'd understood about Krista. He'd also understood about her aunt and uncle. He'd even gone to them and explained that Tucker was a con man, all the while handling the situation with a diplomacy she couldn't have emulated on her best day.

Then he'd taken his assistance one step further. He'd supported her advice that they use their savings to open a second Ernie's Beanery and employ her cousins to run it. By the time he'd walked out of the café, they'd all fallen in love with him.

Just as she had.

The breath stopped in her throat and she closed her eyes, fighting the sudden and inescapable knowledge. No. She couldn't be that irresponsible. She couldn't truly love him. Love was for fools. Love forced a person to give up control. Love didn't work for her; she'd resigned herself to that fact. But she'd never lied to herself before and didn't intend to start now. Slowly, carefully, she searched her heart. And there she saw the truth.

She didn't know when or how it had happened. Perhaps it had come on her bit by bit without her even being aware. Still, that didn't change the fundamental truth. She did love him, with a bone-deep intensity. Where once she thought her heart and soul irreparably damaged, now she saw they'd been healed. And that healing was due to one man.

Jonah.

But to have fallen in love. She shook her head. How foolish of her. Because if she loved him, that meant she trusted him. And if she trusted him, she'd have to tell him about...

Tucker.

She shuddered. She couldn't dump this on Jonah, couldn't watch the green fire in his gaze turn to gold ice. Perhaps if he loved her in return, she'd take the risk of telling him about the past. But the painful fact of the matter was…he didn't love her. Oh, he wanted her. And he'd make sure she found their time together special, no matter how brief. But in the end, he'd leave and she'd be alone once again.

Which still left the main question unanswered.

What did she do now?

Nothing, she decided at last. She couldn't be certain that Tucker would make good on his threat. By doing so, he risked exposing himself. And slime like that preferred operating in the safety of the shadows. Too much light brought too much attention.

A peremptory knock sounded at her office door. "Nikki? I wanted to talk to you about—" Jonah stepped across the threshold and stopped dead, staring at her in astonishment. "What the hell are you doing?"

"Potting plants," she replied with a self-conscious shrug. "Or rather, repotting. I do it whenever I need to think."

His narrowed gaze swung to the empty windowsill and back again. "So, you weren't killing them. You were saving them."

She glared at him indignantly and started to put her hands on her hips. Just in time, she remembered she still wore her gardening gloves. "You thought I was killing plants?" she demanded, stripping off the gloves and tossing them to the protective tarp. "On purpose?"

"You'll have to forgive my ignorance," he said gently. "At the time I came to that conclusion, I didn't know what a maternal soul you had."

His assessment gave her an odd feeling. She'd never considered herself the least maternal. She was a career woman first and foremost. Any fleeting thoughts she might have indulged with regard to children had been just that. Fleeting. Besides, she had Keli. She bit her lip. *Had* being the operative word. Soon she wouldn't even have that, not if her plan succeeded.

"What are you thinking?"

She avoided his gaze. "Nothing important." Removing her apron, she began loading her supplies into the box.

"You were thinking about Keli, weren't you?"

His perception dismayed her. "Yes," she admitted, aware that denials were pointless.

"Haven't you ever considered marrying?" He edged his hip onto the corner of her desk, his trousers pulled taut across his thighs. "For real, I mean? Having children of your own?"

"Once."

"Ah. Seven years ago again. We really must clear the air about that."

"Did I mention? I'm beginning to like coffee unsweetened." She shoved the box in the direction of the closet, hoping that would close the subject. "I assume you came in here for some reason other than to annoy me."

"Not really." His large hands closed around her waist and he lifted her aside. "Allow me." With an ease she could only envy, he hoisted the box as though it were weightless and deposited it in the closet.

"Thanks," she murmured.

"No problem." Turning, he scrutinized her with unnerving intensity. Almost hesitantly, he reached out and swept a stray lock of hair from her temple. Then with a muffled exclamation, he thrust his hands deep

into her topknot. Her hair came loose, spilling in
heavy waves about her face. "Temptress," he muttered, drawing her close.

"Jonah—"

But his mouth stopped her incipient protest. And
then it stopped all thought. It had become easier and
easier to give in to him—especially when his demands so closely matched her own desires. She
wrapped her arms around him, not the least surprised
when he crushed her along his hard length, tugging
her between his legs and against the very heart of him.

"Am I interrupting something?" an amused voice
asked from the doorway. They both spun around. Eric
stood there, leaning against the jamb. "You took so
long getting that update on the Dearfield account,"
he addressed Jonah, "that I decided to come looking
for you."

Jonah swore beneath his breath. "Right. The Dearfield account."

Hot color swept across Nikki's cheekbones. "I
have the update with my files. Let me get it for you."

"I guess the honeymoon's not over yet, huh?" Eric
asked innocently.

Nikki stared at him in horror, unable to say a word.

"What the hell does that mean?" Jonah growled,
shooting her an uneasy glance. "We're not on our
honeymoon."

Eric shrugged. "That's not what it looks like to
me."

"You—you're wrong," Nikki managed to say.

"Of course I am." He stepped into the room, grinning. "Good thing I'm not a client, though. Not very
professional, you know, making love on the office
floor. Or were you planning on using the desk?"

"Go to hell, little brother," Jonah snapped. "The day I need a lecture from you about professionalism—"

Eric held up his hands. "Okay, okay. Though at least allow me to suggest you lock the door next time."

Jonah's hands balled into fists. "Why you—"

"Stop it!" To Nikki's horror, tears pricked her eyes. Stress. It had to be stress. Between her family problems, her marriage and Tucker, it was a wonder she hadn't gone completely insane. "Here's the update," she said, tossing the file onto her desk. "Now, if you'll excuse me?" She didn't give either man a chance to reply, but swept from the room before she disgraced herself completely.

Jonah started to follow, but Eric caught his arm. "She won't thank you for going after her. Women prefer to conduct these crying jags in private."

"What! She was crying?"

Eric shrugged. "I thought I caught a glimpse of tears."

"Damn." A resigned expression crossed Jonah's face. "Mind telling me what makes you such an expert all of the sudden?"

"Just using a little common sense for a change. And as long as I'm so full of it, so to speak, I'll offer you some more advice. Give her time." He paused a beat. "The first year of marriage can be tough on a couple."

"And I told you this isn't—"

"It's as good as. You can't count *your* first year. You didn't spend any of it together," Eric argued reasonably.

"I...she..."

"Yes?"

"Forget it!"

Eric slanted him a sly look. "Your wife sure was upset."

Jonah's gaze followed the direction Nikki had taken. "Bad, huh?"

"Has to be stress," Eric pronounced thoughtfully as he headed for the door. He glanced over his shoulder. "I mean, it can't be sexual tension. Now can it? Not after what I just saw." The door quietly closing punctuated his observation.

"It can't be sexual tension. Now can it?"

In the three days since Eric had made the comment, Jonah had been consumed by that thought to the exclusion of all else. *Sexual tension.* He pushed his fork around his dinner plate, cursing beneath his breath. Oh, he was tense all right. Very tense. Very, very tense and getting tenser by the minute. He scowled across the table at his wife. Not that she noticed.

Nikki stared at her plate, struggling to work up sufficient enthusiasm to eat. For the past three days, she'd been consumed with thoughts of her husband, and of love and trust and horrible men who made horrible threats. She'd also spent the time trying to decide how to handle the predicament she'd gotten herself into. In fact, it had become a daily battle— whether or not to trust the man she loved, despite the fact that he didn't love her. She peeked at Jonah from beneath her lashes. Not that he noticed.

Jonah threw down his fork. If his brother were here now, he'd strangle the smart-mouthed little—

"What did you say?" Nikki asked.

"I said, I've had enough."

"I'm sorry. Don't you like it?" She glanced down at her own plate of linguini. "Too rich, huh?"

"Actually, I've changed my mind. I haven't had enough." He shoved back his chair. "But I'm about to change that. Right now."

She tilted her head to one side, the candlelight catching in the ruby tones of her hair. "You want seconds?"

"No. I want firsts."

Her brows drew together in delicious bewilderment. "I don't understand."

"You will." He circled the table, and without further ado, lifted her into his arms. "Catching on yet?"

"Jonah! What—what are you doing?"

"What I *would* have done that first night if I hadn't been so tired. What I *should* have done three nights ago, if I hadn't gotten so involved in playing the noble husband." The bedroom door blocked his path and he kicked it open. "And what I'm *going* to do right now because it's what we've both wanted from the instant we met."

He tossed her onto the mattress, waiting for the inevitable argument.

She didn't say a word.

He waited for anxiety to turn her eyes the color of amethysts. They slowly changed color, but it was passion that lurked in the violet depths, not fear.

He waited for her to flee. Instead, she remained in the middle of the bed.

Her very inaction sealed her fate. He approached, unable to take his eyes from her. Her skin gleamed like ivory, while her hair was a vivid splash of darkest crimson against the black down comforter. His gaze never left her as he ripped off his shirt. His shoes came next, then his belt. Finally, he reached for the zip on his pants. Her eyes grew huge and the tip of her tongue appeared, skating across her bottom lip.

He wanted that lip, he decided. He wanted it for an appetizer. He wanted to nibble on it, to sink his teeth into its fullness before exploring within. And once he'd temporarily sated himself with her mouth, he wanted to taste his way downward, sampling every inch of her, course after delicious course. It would be the most magnificent feast he'd ever consumed. And for dessert, he'd return to the sweetness of her mouth.

"To hell with linguini," he muttered, settling onto the bed beside her. "Nothing can be more satisfying than this."

Nikki stared at him in utter astonishment. After three full days of endless confusion and doubt, it took a split second to realize the undeniable truth. Not only did she love Jonah, she trusted him. Totally. Implicitly. Without reservation. And with that knowledge came the most amazing sense of freedom. Joy welled within. She could tell him. She could tell him everything and he'd understand.

He gathered her close, resting half on top of her, his hands sinking into her hair. "Speak now, wife," he muttered, catching her lower lip between his teeth. "Or forever hold your peace."

"I'd rather hold you," she whispered. Wrapping her arms around his neck, she returned the passion of his kiss. Tomorrow they would talk. But right now, there were more important matters to take care of. They had the give and take of their latest merger to work out.

Removing her clothing became a serious negotiation. The zipper of her skirt voiced a loud argument as he drew it downward. Each button of her blouse needed to be coaxed free of its hole. Her lacy garters had to be convinced to release their tight embrace on her silk stockings. And the hooks and eyes of her bra had to be rescued from their enforced closure. But she found that having a brilliant negotiator for a husband had certain advantages. With due patience and diligence, he overcame every dilemma.

And the end result was the most satisfying she'd ever known.

She lay within the safe circle of his arms, coming alive beneath his touch, on fire for him and for him alone. And she discovered the unassailable truth of his earlier observations. Making love *was* a partnership. For everything she gave him, she received tenfold in return. The more she opened to him, the more he opened to her. To offer a delicate kiss had him returning it with a deeper one. Slipping her hands across the endless expanse of his chest led to his painting lazy circles around the rosy tips of her breasts. And when she shyly initiated a more intimate caress, he unlocked passionate secrets that had been trapped within her for years, giving her a pleasure she'd never before experienced.

"Do you trust me?" he demanded at one point.

Tears welled into her eyes and she visibly fought to control them. "I—I haven't dared to," she admitted in a broken voice. Slowly, she looked at him. "Until now."

He cradled her close. "Are you sure? Very sure?"

"Yes," she whispered. "I'm positive."

And with her words still lingering between them,

he mated his body with hers, taking her with exquisite care and tenderness. It was as though he sealed her pledge of trust with his body and offered her love's ultimate completion as his return promise. Without fear or hesitation, without thought to what the morrow might bring, she gave herself to him. She gave all of herself, holding nothing back, discovering the full height and depth of love.

And when ecstasy finally came, it was within the sheltering embrace of her husband, the one man she'd love to the end of time.

Nikki lay quietly as dawn lit up the sky with the promise of a new day. And in that moment of earth's gradual awakening, she listened to her inner voice, waiting for the doubt and uncertainty to return. But nothing disturbed the smooth tenor of her thoughts. She felt now as she had last night. If there was one man in the world she could trust, it was Jonah.

Rolling onto her side to face him, she discovered him already awake and watching her with an unnerving intensity. "Good morning," she whispered.

"Waking up with you in my bed is nice," he murmured in a sleep-husky voice. "The only thing better would be waking up with you in my arms."

She smiled and snuggled closer, happy to accommodate. He punched the pillows behind him, shifting to recline against them. She nestled her head into the crook of his shoulder and threaded her fingers through the thick mat of hair covering his powerful chest. His heart beat slow and steady beneath her palm.

Gently, he cupped the side of her face with his large hand, his thumb stroking across her cheekbone. She leaned into the tender caress.

It was time for the truth.

"Jonah?"

"I'm here, sweetheart."

She took a deep breath, awed at the ease with which the words came. "I need your help."

His thumb never stopped its calm, soothing motion, but the tiny tremor that shook his hand told her a very different emotion raged within. "How can I help?" he asked with gruff simplicity.

CHAPTER NINE

"NIKKI? Are you home?" Jonah crushed the paper in his fist, frustrated anger darkening his eyes. "Sweetheart?"

"I'm here."

She appeared in the doorway to the bedroom, dressed in a black silk slip and damned little else. If it had been any other time, he'd have snatched her into his arms and returned to the bedroom with her. There he'd have removed that bit of nothing and made love to her until they were both too exhausted to move, think or even speak. Especially speak. As it was, he brushed past her, grabbed a thick terry robe and held it out.

"Put this on. We need to talk."

A warm smile tugged at her full, kissable mouth, tempting him almost beyond endurance. "I can't talk to you wearing my slip?" she teased.

"It depends on the kind of talking you want to get done."

He tucked the newspaper beneath his arm and helped her on with the robe. Jerking the front closed over the plunging black neckline, his knuckles scraped over her full breasts and he stilled, caught between desperate desire and the need to give her the bad news. As much as he'd like to delay the inevitable, they had too much to accomplish if they were to avert disaster.

Sweeping her hair from beneath the collar of her robe, he gathered a handful of the silken tresses in his fist and contented himself with a prolonged kiss. Just like every other time he touched her, she melted into his arms, her lush curves settling against him in a way guaranteed to send his blood pressure through the roof. And just like every other time he touched her, she gave totally of herself, never holding anything back. Reluctantly, he ended the embrace.

She blinked up at him. Her eyes—as soft and velvety as pansies—expressed absolute faith and confidence. He stifled a groan. Heaven help him. When his wife decided to trust him, she didn't bother with half measures. It was all or nothing.

He wrapped an arm around her and headed for the kitchen. "Let's fix some coffee."

She lifted an eyebrow, a hint of concern creeping into her expression. "Coffee or something stronger?"

"I'd prefer something stronger. But we'll stick with coffee." Moving with brisk efficiency, he dumped ground beans into the filter, added the water and hit the start button. "You can even have sugar with it."

"So the worst has happened," she murmured.

"Yeah, it happened." He dropped the newspaper onto the tile counter. It was one of the more disreputable rags floating around the city. "LJB Award Nominee Swindled Family Out Of Inheritance!" the headline screamed.

She squared her shoulders and faced him. "Am I fired?"

"How can you even ask such a question?" he snapped.

"You have to protect International Investment. I understand that." She responded with such cool logic, he wanted to grab hold and kiss her until her teeth rattled. Or until she regained her senses.

He shoved his hands into his pockets to quell the impulse, settling for an unsatisfactory glare of annoyance to express his irritation. "International Investment will ride out this particular storm just fine without any noble gestures on your part."

She set her rounded chin at a stubborn angle. "I'll tender my resignation effective immediately," she said as though he hadn't spoken. "And as soon as I've dressed, I'll go in and clear out my desk."

"Stop it, Nikki."

"No, it's all right. I knew this could happen when I refused to submit to Tucker's blackmail scheme."

"Refusing to have any further dealings with that man was one of the few intelligent decisions you've made since we met. And before you ask, the other was confiding in me."

"It's not your problem," she insisted. "I'll handle it."

"You asked for my help the other night, remember? I told you then I'd deal with Tucker."

She bowed her head. "I know you did your best."

He bit back an exclamation of fury. She was determined to play the tragic martyr and he knew of only one way to snap her out of it. "What happened to all that talk of trust?" he questioned caustically. "Or was that all it was—just talk?"

As he hoped, her head jerked up, her eyes flashing with violet fire. "It wasn't just talk!"

"Then trust me, damn it. I'll stop that piece of slime if it's the last thing I do."

"But what about in the meantime? How long can you protect me if International Investment starts losing customers? What are you going to say to your clients? Yes, she swindled her relatives, but she won't do it to you?"

"You didn't swindle anyone!" he roared.

The momentary silence was deafening. Then the coffee machine gave a final, inelegant burp and she offered a watery laugh. "Thank you for your support."

"My pleasure." He filled three mugs, automatically setting two in front of Nikki. Shooting her an assessing glance, he wondered how best to break the next bit of news. "Sweetheart…"

She kept her gaze fixed on the sugar, determinedly spooning it into her mugs. "There's more, isn't there?"

He sighed. "I'm afraid so."

She took a fortifying gulp of coffee. "Tell me the rest."

"The LJB nomination committee has requested that you attend a special session to determine whether you should be dropped as a candidate."

"When?"

"Nine, Monday morning."

"Three days." She caught her lip between her teeth. "Who brought the charges? Or is that a ridiculous question?"

"They refused to say. But I think we both know who's responsible."

A fine line appeared between her drawn brows. "I can't do this, Jonah. I can't go before those people and talk about my past. It was difficult enough telling you.'' He could see the panic she fought so hard to suppress. "They're strangers. They'll never understand.''

"We'll make them understand."

She stilled. "We?"

"I'll be right there beside you."

He'd surprised her with that one. Hope dawned in her eyes. "You're going?"

"You're my wife. Of course I'm going. I wouldn't let you deal with this alone."

Words eluded her. She shoved her coffee aside and covered her face with her hands.

He slammed his mug to the counter and pulled her to her feet, catching her in a rib-cracking embrace. "I have it on excellent authority that women prefer conducting these crying jags in private," he murmured against the silky top of her head. "But I refuse to leave you alone right now. So I'm afraid you're stuck with me."

"I don't want to be left alone," she responded in a muffled voice. "Please hold me."

"I'm not going anywhere," he assured her.

"Yet."

His mouth compressed at the reminder. They'd both been careful to avoid a discussion of the future and he had no intention of correcting that oversight. At least, not now. "That's right," he said at last. "I'm not going anywhere. Yet."

"Jonah," she whispered, "I'm afraid."

He swung her up into his arms, cradling her close. Her head drooped against his shoulder like a delicate rose with a damaged stem. She felt so fragile, so vulnerable. The instinctive urge to protect gripped him—

the unshakable need to defend her from harm. And like a feral animal determined to keep his mate safe, he strode toward the sanctuary of his lair.

Monday arrived all too soon as far as Nikki was concerned. Choosing an outfit to wear before the committee—or "inquisitors" as Jonah insisted on dubbing them—became a major undertaking. The minute she plucked a garment from the closet, Jonah categorically rejected it.

"Too depressing," he pronounced, tossing aside the severe black suit she'd selected. "Besides, it makes you look guilty."

"What do you want me to wear?" she demanded in exasperation. "My wedding outfit? That's about all I have left."

"It's a thought. Wait a sec. Aha." He yanked a stylish ivory suit and matching silk blouse from the closet. "Here we go. This, gold jewelry and heels."

She stared at him in disbelief. "You're not serious, are you? Jonah, this isn't a business suit. I bought it to wear last Easter."

"Exactly. I want them to take one look at you and think, 'innocent'. And this outfit will do it."

"In case you've forgotten, I *am* innocent," she muttered.

He turned, the look on his face instantly silencing her. "I haven't forgotten a thing. And once the LJB committee has seen and heard you, they won't have any doubts, either." He handed her the suit. "Put this on. Oh, and leave your hair down."

"Anything else?"

"Yeah." His eyes blazed with suggestive green highlights. "Make sure you wear silk and lace underwear, stockings with those sexy little seams in the back, and garters.''

She planted her hands on her hips. ''That's supposed to make the committee think I'm innocent?''

''No.'' He dropped a swift, hard kiss on her mouth. ''The silk and lace is for me. The committee will just have to sit there and wonder what you have on under all that soft lamb's wool. But I'll know.''

A reluctant smile tugged at her lips. ''You're impossible.'' She found it incredible that she could find anything humorous at a time like this. Thanks to her husband, she had. She peeked up at him. He never ceased to amaze her.

''It'll be our little secret,'' he said, rubbing his hands together. ''Anytime I start to lose my temper, I'll think of popping those flimsy little garters. It'll wreak havoc with my self-control, but it should keep me from blowing a fuse.''

''Great. And what am I supposed to think about?''

He leaned down, nestling his mouth close to her ear. ''You think about what I'm wearing under my suit.''

Her eyes gleamed with laughter. ''You have something hidden in there I don't know about?''

''Could be...'' His grin was wickedly sensual. ''But I'm not telling. You'll just have to find out for yourself after the meeting.''

''You're going to make me wait that long? No fair!'' she protested.

''Ah, but there's method to my madness. Anytime you feel panicky, I want you to think about what it might be.''

''And that's supposed to calm me?'' He couldn't know how he affected her if he thought that. She couldn't look at him, touch him, listen to the deep, rough tones of his voice without a desperate need sweeping through her.

"If nothing else, it should distract you." He gave her a gentle swat on her backside. "Get dressed, wife. I'll fix breakfast."

"One cup of coffee this morning," she requested. At his questioning look, she added, "I'm jittery enough without the extra caffeine."

"Beauty combined with intelligence. We can't lose."

His comment helped her get through breakfast and the cab ride to the office complex where the nomination committee had scheduled the meeting. The first attack of butterflies didn't hit until they entered the elevator. To her surprise, Jonah must have felt something similar. Ignoring their fellow passengers, he reached out and captured her hand.

"White?" he asked.

She stared in bewilderment. "What?"

"The garters. Are they white?"

She blushed at the amused sidelong looks they received. "Ivory," she whispered. "With pink rosebuds."

He closed his eyes and grinned. "Oh, yeah."

She peeked over at him. "Boxers?"

"Not telling."

A picture of Jonah leaping into bed in a pair of Santa-festooned shorts flashed through her mind and she fought to suppress a giggle.

The elevator door opened just then, and squeezing her hand, Jonah forged a path from the back of the car. "We're on," he warned. "Be confident. We're in the right here."

"Okay." As they approached the reception area, she asked softly, "Bikini briefs?"

"Nope."

"May I help you?" the receptionist said with a congenial smile.

"Mr. and Mrs. Alexander to see the nomination committee."

"Yes, you're expected. Follow me, please." She led the way down a short hallway and paused to knock on a set of double doors.

A sudden thought occurred to Nikki and she caught Jonah's hand before he could walk into the conference room. "Wait! You do have on…? You're not totally…?" She couldn't say it, her gaze drifting downward in fascinated horror.

"Oh, no?" He gave her a slow wink, then thrust the doors open, stepping boldly across the threshold. "What do you say we get this show on the road?" he demanded.

Two women and three men were grouped at one end of the room. At Nikki and Jonah's entrance, the five swiveled in unison, like puppets on a string. A tall, gruff-looking man built on proportions similar to Jonah took the initiative and approached.

"Bill West. I'm the committee chairman," he said, shaking hands with each of them, before turning his attention back to Jonah. "We didn't expect to see you this morning, Mr. Alexander."

"No, I'm sure you didn't. But I'm here nonetheless." He cocked an eyebrow. "I trust you have no objections?"

"Would it matter if I did?"

"No."

A reluctant smile creased Bill's mouth. "I didn't

think so," he murmured drily. "Well, you're welcome to observe. But you do understand that the accusations have been leveled against your wife and the answers will have to come from her."

"What I realize is that we're here at your request to answer unsubstantiated allegations. We're doing it as a courtesy and without benefit of counsel. Should, in the course of this...*meeting*, I feel that situation should change, I'll inform you." His wintry gaze held Bill's for a long moment. "*Now* I believe we understand each other. Do you agree?"

"Oh, yes. We understand each other perfectly." The chairman gestured toward the conference table. "Make yourself comfortable. Can I get you anything? Water, coffee?"

"Three coffees. Two with sugar, one plain," Jonah ordered briskly. Turning, he escorted Nikki to the far end of the table, then held the chair for her.

"I didn't want any coffee," she whispered as she took her seat.

"I know. I just did it to tick him off. It's a power thing."

"Thanks," she said wryly. "I'm sure that 'power thing' will help the inquisition go much smoother." She folded her hands demurely in her lap. "By the way, did I mention that I have precisely five items on under my suit?"

She slanted a quick peek at him from beneath her lashes. As she'd anticipated, he was conducting a rapid-fire inventory and coming up precisely one item short. She smothered a smile. Jonah wasn't the only one capable of pulling a "power thing". Wondering what she'd left off should keep him busy for a while. At least she hoped it would.

"Your coffee," Bill announced heartily, as an underling scurried in, setting cups and saucers in front of them. "Now. Shall we begin?"

"You ready, Nikki?" Jonah asked.

"As ready as I'll ever be."

Bill joined the other four members at the opposite end of the table. "First let me say, Mrs. Alexander, that we apologize for the inconvenience." A deep frown creased his brow. "Unfortunately, it's important we clear this business up. Lawrence J. Bauman nominees must be above reproach. Companies who hire our candidates demand it. Why, a nomination alone can assure a position at the most select firms."

"I already have a position at one of the most select firms," Nikki inserted smoothly.

Jonah smiled in appreciation at her comment. "And the select firm in question supports Mrs. Alexander fully in this matter."

Bill sighed. "Yes, Mr. Alexander. We're well aware of your support. We're also well aware of International Investment's standing in the business world. Nevertheless, due to the seriousness of the charges, we're forced to investigate this matter to the fullest. We don't like it. You don't like it. But we have no choice if we're to survive public scrutiny."

"What would you like to know?" Nikki asked, taking a sip of coffee and struggling to hide a grimace at the lack of sugar. Without missing a beat, Jonah switched cups with her.

"I have information here from an unnamed individual—"

"Timothy T. Tucker," she interjected again.

"You know this man?"

"Yes. He attempted to sell my aunt and uncle

his…invention. When I recommended against it, he threatened to publicize details of my past.''

''Tell them the rest,'' Jonah prompted.

She didn't question his directive, but simply said, ''Tucker also offered to keep quiet if I changed my recommendation and authorized payment to him to the tune of fifty thousand dollars.''

The committee paused for a moment's discussion. Then Bill nodded. ''We suspected that Mr. Tucker's motives for providing this information were questionable at best. But that's beside the point. What we must ascertain is whether the information is accurate.''

''You'll have to be more specific,'' Jonah requested crisply.

''Very well. Let's get into specifics.'' Bill consulted his notes before fixing Nikki with his undivided attention. ''Did you take money belonging to your relatives and invest it in worthless real estate?''

''One moment, please,'' Jonah interrupted. He leaned close, gathering her hands in his. ''Give them the honest truth,'' he instructed calmly, his thumb tracing the outline of her wedding band. ''Don't hesitate in answering. Don't attempt to explain at this point. They don't want explanations, just an admission.''

Her fingers tightened on his. ''And you want me to give them that admission?'' The butterflies in her stomach had become a swarm of hornets.

''I want you to give it to them.'' He met her eyes unflinchingly, the utter confidence in his gaze easing her fears. How could she have ever thought those eyes resembled the bitter chill of autumn? she wondered in confusion. She must have been blind. They exactly matched the brilliant greens and golds of a warm spring day. "Trust me," he said.

"You know I do." She glanced at Bill West and flushed. "I'm sorry. Would you please repeat the question?"

He released an impatient sigh. "Did you take money belonging to your relatives and invest it in worthless real estate?"

She didn't look at Jonah. She didn't need to. "Yes," she said.

Her answer clearly surprised him. He referred to his notes again. "And did you then borrow money from the bank in order to finance an additional purchase?"

"I did."

The questions came faster. "And did you lose that money?"

"Yes."

"Did the bank foreclose on the original property when you were unable to make the monthly payments?"

"They did."

"And did the lending institute discover that the appraisal had been fraudulently obtained and that the property wasn't worth anything close to what you'd borrowed against it?"

"It was worth approximately half of what I'd borrowed," she confessed.

Bill tossed down his pen and stared in dismay. "Mrs. Alexander, I'm at a loss for words. These are very serious charges and you've admitted to each and every one of them."

"Yes, Mr. West, I'm well aware of that. But these

questions were asked out of context. I assume you'll permit me to put them in context?''

"If you can," Bill retorted.

She spared Jonah a brief glance. He gave her an encouraging nod, and drawing a deep breath, she began to explain. "Eight years ago, my parents died—''

The woman on Bill's left stirred, the overhead lights picking out the iron gray streaks in her hair. "I hardly see what the death of your parents has to do with these proceedings—''

"My wife has extended you the courtesy of listening and responding to each of your allegations," Jonah cut in, his fury barely held in check. "You'll do no less for her."

"He's right, Clara. Let her tell the story her way. It's the least we can do," Bill said reasonably. "We apologize, Mrs. Alexander. Please continue."

"Their deaths have quite a lot to do with this story," Nikki responded. "I'm sure you'll understand that it precipitated a major crisis in my family. Not only did we suffer from the emotional loss, but my mother and father were also the financial advisers for a number of my relatives. Because I was studying business at the time of their deaths, that burden then fell to me." A self-mocking smile flitted across her mouth. "Youth combined with an unfortunate arrogance allowed me to think I could handle the responsibility."

"I suspect we've all been there at one point or another," Bill murmured.

"I'm relieved to hear it. In my case, I had a college professor who'd become my mentor and encouraged me in my new capacity. Whenever I had a question, he'd advise me. About the time I turned twenty-one,

he left the university to pursue more lucrative opportunities.''

''Real-estate investment?'' Bill guessed shrewdly.

''The very real-estate investment for which I'm
currently under investigation,'' she confirmed.

Jonah spoke up again. ''I'd like to make it clear—
since I doubt my wife will—that at this point in her
life she was also supporting a pregnant younger sister
who'd just been widowed. Although Nikki's parents
had left some insurance money, I question that it was
sufficient to cover the expenses she was incurring at
that time.''

''No, it wasn't,'' Nikki admitted. ''I suppose that's
why I was vulnerable to Professor Wyman's offer.''

''Professor Wyman?'' Clara interrupted again.
''Professor Wilbert Wyman?''

''Yes. Although he preferred people to call him
Bert.'' Nikki looked at her curiously. ''Do you know
him?''

''My—my daughter did.'' Her hand clenched
around her pen. ''I'm sorry. Please go on.''

''Bert showed me a commercial property that he
felt would be a guaranteed money-maker. Funny...I
still remember the name. Sunrise Center. Anyway, he
was incredibly enthusiastic, said that if I didn't grab
it, he would.'' She shrugged. ''So I grabbed it.''

''You went to your relatives for the money?''

She nodded. ''We used everything we had—my
parents' insurance money, my aunt and uncle's nest
egg...'' Her voice grew husky with remorse. ''Even
the funds set aside for my cousins' college tuition.''

''Didn't you consider that risky?''

It took a minute to gather the emotional resilience
to respond. ''Not a day goes by that I don't regret

having taken that risk," she told them with devastating candor. "But you can't make money without risking money. Or so Bert said."

"What happened then?"

The words came more easily. "Once I'd finalized the purchase, he came to me with a second proposal. He wanted me to borrow money from the bank against the property I'd just bought."

"What did he want you to do with that money?"

"He suggested we invest it in what he called a short-term turnaround. We'd buy and sell this surefire money-maker within the space of a few months." She played with her coffee cup, remembering the naive fool she'd been. She started to pick up the cup, but her hands shook so badly, she returned it to the saucer. "I should have known it was too good to be true. Later, I learned that Bert had bribed the appraiser to grossly inflate the value of Sunrise Center. As a result, the bank loaned me over twice its value."

"And the money?"

"I handed the check over to Bert." She tried to smile. "Quite the brilliant young finance student, wasn't I?"

"I assume Bert promptly disappeared with the funds?" Bill questioned gently.

"Yes."

"What in the world did you do?"

She gathered the last of her inner resources, struggling to summarize the most difficult time of her life with as little emotion as possible. "I spent the next seven years working harder than I ever had before. I learned everything I could about the business world so I'd never be taken like that again. And I gradually paid back the money to the bank, to my aunt and uncle, to my cousins and to my sister. With interest. Last year, thanks to several legitimate investments, I was able to square all accounts.''

''And what happened to Professor Wyman?''

''I have no idea. I assume he went on to scam other gullible college students.''

''He did,'' Clara inserted softly. ''But not for long. He was sent to prison five years ago.''

Nikki stared at her, stunned.

Without further ado, Bill gathered his notes. ''Thank you, Mrs. Alexander. That will be all.''

''No, that damned well won't be all,'' Jonah bit out. ''We'll hear your results here and now. Is she still a nominee or do I contact my lawyers?''

''Don't, Jonah,'' Nikki whispered, slipping icy fingers into the welcoming warmth of his huge hand. ''And just so you know....I'm wearing two stockings, one garter, a slip and one more item.''

She'd managed to distract him. ''Which did you leave off?'' he demanded softly. ''Top or bottom?''

''You figure it out.'' She raised her voice. ''I don't intend to contest your decision. But in all fairness, I do think I deserve an expeditious finding.''

''One moment please.'' There was a hushed conference among the committee. ''We have no objection to giving you an immediate ruling. Assuming we find no discrepancy in the statement you've given, your nomination will stand.''

''And how long will it take to look for any discrepancies?'' Jonah questioned irascibly.

''The ceremony is Saturday. If Mrs. Alexander's status changes, you'll be notified by Friday.''

Afraid of what Jonah might say to that, Nikki stood. ''Thank you for the opportunity to answer your questions.'' She tucked her hand into the crook of Jonah's arm and, using every ounce of her strength, dragged him from the room. ''You are more stubborn than any mule,'' she muttered.

His hand coasted down her spine before settling in the small of her back. Abruptly, he stopped fighting. ''Come on. Let's go home,'' he said.

''What's the sudden hurry?'' she asked, eyeing him suspiciously.

He stabbed the button for the elevator. ''I think I know what that missing item is.''

She lifted an eyebrow. ''Oh?''

''Yeah.'' He grinned, tugging her into the empty car. ''If I'm right, it's the same item I'm missing. And I've decided I'd much rather find out for sure than argue with a bunch of stuffy committee members.''

''Me, too.'' She snuggled into the crook of his arm, sliding an experimental hand along his hip. ''Good grief, Jonah! You really aren't—''

The elevator door banged closed.

CHAPTER TEN

"AREN'T you nervous?" Selma questioned.

"Well, I—"

"Why should she be nervous?" Krista said dismissively. "She's a shoo-in."

Nikki gave a self-conscious shrug. "Oh, I doubt—"

"Damn that Tucker anyway." Ernie glared across the width of the huge stretch limo. "Why didn't you tell us about him, Nikki? I'd have strangled the little weasel when I had the chance."

"But I did—"

"Thank heaven for Jonah," Selma inserted, offering him a dazzling smile of unabashed approval. "I don't know what we would have done without his guidance."

"Yes. Thank heaven I was there," he agreed, draping an arm around Nikki's shoulders. "After all, it's a husband's duty and moral obligation to protect his wife."

"And the little woman's family, too?" she finally erupted.

"Yes, that, too." His grin flashed in the darkness. "Feel better now?"

She nodded, the momentary anger siphoning off some of her tension. "Much."

"Good." His eyes glinted from the shadows as he

shifted closer. "Have I mentioned how beautiful you look tonight, Mrs. Alexander?" he asked, nuzzling the spot just beneath her left ear.

"Hey, hey! None of that," Eric protested. "You can celebrate after she's won."

"*If* I win," she hastened to correct. "Which is doubtful. I hope all of you won't be too disappointed."

"No one's going to be disappointed," Jonah said as the limo pulled up in front of the hotel. He peered out the window. "Good. They're here."

Nikki strained to see past his bulky shoulders. "Who? Who's here?"

"Mom and Dad," Eric replied. "They decided to catch a cab directly from the hotel instead of taking the limo with us."

"I think I'm going to be ill," Nikki said with a groan. "You didn't warn me they'd be coming."

"They're here to support you, just like we are." Jonah caught her fingers in his, squeezing gently. "Ivory?" he whispered.

She sighed, relaxing against him. "Black. Boxers?"

"Thong."

A watery laugh shivered between them. "Don't tease."

"Who's teasing?"

The door opened, ending any further conversation. Loren and Della hurried forward to greet her with effusive hugs and kisses, acting as though she truly was their daughter-in-law. And she found herself wishing it was fact and not just a momentary fantasy. Once inside the hotel, they were directed to a huge, glittering ballroom where a table had been reserved for them close to the stage. Other nominees graced nearby tables. Dinner and speeches followed, dragging out the evening. By the time Bill West took the stage carrying the LJB Award, Nikki's nerves were stretched taut.

"Before I make the big announcement," he began, "I'd like to tell you a little about the winner of this year's Lawrence J. Bauman Award. The person we've selected epitomizes the standards for which the award was designed—brilliance, dedication, shrewd business acumen and, above all else, integrity. This individual possesses those qualities and a few more besides. It was those extra few qualities that allowed our committee to reach an immediate and unanimous decision."

"That's you, dear. It has to be," Selma whispered.

Tears gathered in Nikki's eyes and wordlessly she shook her head. The moment he'd used the word "integrity", she'd known they'd chosen someone else. Not that it came as any great surprise.

"This person has surmounted terrible adversity," Bill continued, "not just learning from and overcoming past mistakes, but benefiting from them, as well. No mountain proved too high, no problem slipped by until an honorable solution had been found, no moral dilemma went without the appropriate choice being made, no matter how difficult that choice might be. So, without further ado, it is my great honor and privilege to present this year's Lawrence J. Bauman Award to...Mrs. Nikki Ashton Alexander."

Nikki was so shocked, she couldn't move for a full minute. Jonah came to her rescue, sweeping her from the chair and into his arms. Giving her a hard kiss, he aimed her toward the stage. "You earned it, sweetheart. Now go get it."

She weaved through the tables, climbing the steps to the podium in a total daze. Bill West shook her hand, then held out the crystal-and-gold award. Accepting it, she stared blindly at the graceful design, fighting for control. After the scandal had broken, she'd counted herself fortunate to have retained her status as a nominee. But she hadn't expected to win. She honestly hadn't. She looked up, realizing in dawning horror that she would have to make a speech. But from the moment her name had been called, her mind had gone blank.

"I—I…" Her throat closed up, her self-control deserting her. Just as panic seemed her only remaining option, her gaze fell on Jonah. It only took one look at his calm, steadying features to quiet the inner tumult. Heaven help her, but she loved that man.

Taking a deep breath, she said, "My thanks to the LJB nominating committee for both this award and the opportunity to set the record straight." She glanced at Loren and Della. "To International Investment, I extend my deepest appreciation for their unwavering support in the face of overwhelming adversity. It was more than I expected and certainly more than I deserved."

Her hands trembled and she'd have given anything to flee the stage at that point rather than bare her soul to public scrutiny. But opportunities like this only came along once in a lifetime. And she owed some people. It was time they knew it. "I'd like to thank my family for their enduring love and faith in my ability. They deserve this award far more than I. For such intelligent people, they took some foolish risks with their continued backing.''

Ernie and Selma beamed. Krista just shook her head with a hint of exasperation. Nikki's gaze sought Jonah's once more. ''And, finally, I want to thank my husband, Jonah.'' She struggled to subdue the husky catch in her voice. But she couldn't. So she just said the words, allowing the emotion to spill free. ''You gave me something I thought lost to me forever. Thank you for proving it's possible to trust again. Because without trust—''

Her voice broke, destroying what little remained of her composure. The room grew hushed as everyone waited to see what she would do or say next. She caught her lip between her teeth. Never had she wanted so badly to cut and run. But she was determined to finish. Jonah deserved no less. Gripping the award so tightly she feared it would shatter in her hands, she spoke with heartfelt sincerity. ''Thank you for proving it's possible to trust again. Because without trust, you can't have love.''

She didn't remember much after that. Somehow she got off the stage and back to the table. There she endured a thousand hugs and handshakes. But all she really wanted was to walk into the protective warmth of Jonah's arms and never leave. Unfortunately, she couldn't even get near him. He stood off to one side, a cryptic smile on his face, watching as she accepted the unending flood of congratulations.

''I say we all go out and party,'' Krista suggested, once the room had begun to empty. ''Champagne, caviar, the works.''

Eric nodded in agreement. ''After all, we do have two reasons to celebrate. Nikki's award and...'' He grinned, holding up Krista's left hand. A huge diamond solitaire sparkled on her ring finger. "We're engaged."

Nikki stared in astonishment, unable to move, unable to even draw breath.

Krista giggled, snuggling against Eric. "Your expression is priceless, big sister. I guess you didn't see that one coming."

"Now you two don't have to stay married if you'd rather not," Eric added, his gaze moving from her to Jonah.

Nikki's mouth fell open. "What?" she managed to say.

"The Cinderella Ball," Krista explained. "Between us, Eric and I figured out the truth about that night. We also realized that you and Jonah must have married for our sakes—you know, so we'd get on with our lives."

Eric dropped a kiss on his fiancée's cheek. "And we have. Although I'll bet you didn't expect us to do it together."

Nikki darted a quick look at Jonah. If his expression had been difficult to read before, now it was utterly impossible. "I don't understand. How did you two meet?" she asked her sister.

"I came by the office to see you," Krista explained. "But you were busy. I bumped into Eric and he invited me to lunch."

"One thing led to another," he said, picking up the tale. "And here we are. So, although we appreciate what you've done you don't have to keep pretending." A wily grin touched his mouth. "Unless, of course, you've fallen madly in love and want to stay married."

"That's enough, Eric," Jonah cut in. He offered his hand. "Congratulations. And I agree with your suggestion. This does deserve a celebration." For the first time, he turned to Nikki. "Doesn't it? After all, you finally have everything you ever wanted. Right?"

Nikki tossed her coat onto the couch and carefully placed her award on the coffee table. "What are we going to do?" she asked without turning around. She was afraid to face him, afraid of what she'd read in Jonah's cool, remote gaze.

"I don't know about you, but I'm going to hit the sack," he replied with a shrug. "You're welcome to join me if you'd like."

"That's not what I meant."

His sigh held an impatient edge. "If you're referring to our future, I don't think this is the time for that particular discussion."

Dread ran an icy finger along her spine. "Why not?"

"Because I leave for London in the morning."

"*London*?" She sank onto the couch, staring in disbelief. "You never said…you never mentioned…"

"I didn't mention it earlier," he explained evenly, "because I felt you had enough to deal with."

She laced her fingers together to hide how badly they trembled. "Your return to London…is it permanent?"

He stilled. And suddenly he seemed larger, harder, tougher. "You have to ask?"

She bowed her head. "Oh, that's right. You promised Ernie and Selma you'd be here for Christmas. I assume you intend to keep that engagement?"

"What the hell do you think?" The words sounded

like they'd been torn from him. "Have I ever failed to keep a promise I've made?"

"No," she whispered. "You've kept every one. And you've done an excellent job of it, too. Thanks."

His coat hit the arm of the couch and tumbled to the floor unheeded. "I don't want your damned thanks," he said with barely restrained fury.

She lifted a hand in appeal. "Then what do you want?"

"The one thing it seems you find impossible to give, despite tonight's fine speech."

"You want my trust?" she asked in confusion. "You have it."

"Do I?" He ripped the bow tie from around his throat. "Prove it."

"How?" she demanded. "You don't have a family who needs rescuing. Your reputation isn't in jeopardy. Neither is your job. You don't have any deep, dark skeletons in your past that I can magnanimously overlook. I have no way of proving myself."

But she did, and she knew it. All she had to do was speak three simple words. Tell him what she'd kept so carefully hidden within her heart. Trust him with that final piece of herself. The words fought for escape, fought to wing free. But, in the end, fear kept them locked tightly away.

He stood mute and aloof, watching and waiting as she waged her inner battle.

Desperate to give him the proof he needed without having to surrender that final bit of control, she left the couch. Reaching for the side zip of her dress, she yanked it down, the black silk puddling at her ankles. She stepped over the inky pool and approached. To her dismay, he made no move to either accept or reject her overture.

"Jonah, please..." She slid her palms along the taut muscles of his chest, wrapping her arms around his neck.

His hands closed on her shoulders. For an instant, she thought he'd push her away. Instead, he pulled her close, holding her against him for several, silent minutes. Then he thrust his fingers deep into her hair and tugged her head back, gazing down at her as though memorizing each tiny detail of her face.

"Kiss me goodbye, Nikki," he whispered.

Tears gathered in her eyes. "Not goodbye," she insisted frantically. "You'll return for Christmas. You promised."

"Let's not drag this out. Kiss me, sweetheart."

"But your flight isn't until tomorrow. We still have tonight."

He shook his head. "I leave early in the morning, so I'll stay at one of the airport hotels for the remainder of the evening."

She moistened her lips, searching wildly for a way to delay him. "You—you still need to pack."

"I have a bag ready to go."

"This is it?" Her chin quivered. "You're just going to walk away?"

He lowered his head, the tenderness of his kiss almost destroying her. "What is there to keep me?" he asked.

He didn't wait for a response. Releasing her, he snagged his coat from off the floor. And moments later, he was gone.

Nikki awoke the next morning to a cold and empty bed. She also woke to discover that Jonah had kept his final promise. On the front page of the newspaper was an article reporting the arrest of Timothy T. Tucker for fraud. Credit for information leading to the arrest was attributed to an unnamed concerned citizen. But Nikki didn't need to question the identity of that "concerned citizen".

She knew it was Jonah.

The next several days were the most miserable of Nikki's existence. She'd thought signing the bank's money over to Bert Wyman had been the biggest mistake she'd ever made. But she soon discovered it didn't come close to equaling the one she'd made with Jonah.

The only excuse she'd been able to come up with to explain her idiocy was that she'd been caught off guard. The shock of Eric and Krista's announcement coming on the heels of her own emotion-laden win at the award ceremony had ended in sheer, unadulterated panic. Maybe if she'd had time to calm down, she would have been all right. Just a few days in which to get used to the idea that she and Jonah had precisely one reason left for continuing their marriage.

Love.

And she did love Jonah, despite being unable to tell him. It had taken hours of soul-searching, but she'd finally concluded that it wasn't saying the actual words she'd feared most. It was his response to her declaration. She was terrified that he didn't love her in return.

Yet he'd demonstrated over and over how much he cared. He'd helped her resolve her problems with Eric and Krista. He'd rescued her family from a con man and solidified their financial well-being. He'd salvaged her reputation, standing by her in word and deed when no one else would have.

And with each and every tender touch, he'd shown the depth of his feelings.

Prove it, he'd said. Prove she trusted him.

Prove that she loved him, was what he really meant.

Suddenly, she knew the perfect way. She could say the words, but somehow she suspected that wouldn't be enough. Not any longer. She reached for the phone, wondering if she'd have sufficient time to put her plan into action. It'd take a bit of work. Arranging for the fax and the plants would be the easy part. It was the Christmas gift she intended to have delivered that might take extra effort.

But if she could just pull this off, it would be worth it in the end.

Christmas Eve ended up being the longest day of Nikki's life.

She went into the office, running on sheer nerves. She kept wondering if Jonah had received her fax, worrying that she'd waited too long before contacting him, and panicking over whether or not his special gift would arrive in time. The only thing she didn't question was her feelings for him.

Or his for her.

By early afternoon, the last of the employees had left for the holidays. The building grew silent and vacant and vaguely cold. Reluctant to return to an apartment empty of Jonah's dynamic presence, she stood in the darkness staring out the window at the bustling crowd. A bittersweet smile touched her mouth. They were all rushing to get home, to share in the warmth and joy of the season. How she wanted that, too!

As she watched, the first flakes of snow tumbled through the inky night sky. Keli would be thrilled. She'd have a white Christmas. Nikki closed her eyes, desperately fighting to hold the tears at bay. But would all that beautiful snow delay Jonah?

She wanted him. Heaven help her, she needed his strength and tenderness and love. Why hadn't she just told him the truth when she'd had the chance? How could she have risked losing the single most important person in her life? She bowed her head, her breath catching on a sob.

Please, she prayed, *just let him get home safely*. It didn't matter if he was late. It didn't matter if his present didn't arrive on time. Nothing mattered, except that he return to her whole and healthy.

Behind her, something hit her desk with a soft thud. She spun around with a gasp. A file lay spotlighted in the middle of the oak surface—a file that hadn't been there moments before. Hardly daring to breathe, she crept closer, struggling to read the name through her tears.

It was the Stamberg account.

From the darkness, a shirt came flying through the air. Then a tie. And then a belt.

"Jonah," she cried, torn between laughing and giving in to her tears. "What are you doing?"

"Making good on our bet, of course."

She covered her mouth with her hand. Angels singing heavenly hymns couldn't have equaled the beautiful sound made by Jonah's rough, husky voice.

"You're going to dance naked on my desk?" she demanded.

"Unless you have a better place for me to dance naked."

Laughter won out. "I have a much better place." Impatience lent wings to her feet and she raced around the desk, hurling herself against the wide, comforting breadth of him. "Did you get my fax?"

"I got it. And I must say, it caused quite a stir at the office." He tilted his head to one side. "Let's see...how did it read?"

"'Jonah, please come home. Urgent. There's something I forgot to tell you,'" Nikki quoted softly.

"Everyone thinks you're pregnant." He snagged her chin in his huge hand. "You're not, are you?"

"No." A minute frown crept between her brows. "At least, I don't think so."

"Too bad. It would have simplified matters."

She rubbed her cheek against his palm. "I'm not very good at simple," she confided. "Somehow I always end up doing it the hard way."

"I've noticed," he said with unmistakable tenderness. "So what did you forget to tell me?"

She took a deep breath. "I forgot to tell you that I love you. In fact, I forgot to tell you that I love you very, very much."

A slow smile touched his mouth. From there, it expanded into his eyes, the autumn chill melting into a rich spring warmth. "I'm supposed to take your word for that?"

"Yes. Because—" she glanced swiftly at him from beneath her lashes "—I think you love me, too."

He cocked an eyebrow. "You think?"

"I know," she corrected hastily. "I know you love

me. And I thought of a way to prove my feelings for you.''

He was openly grinning now. ''And how's that, Mrs. Alexander?''

''Well...'' She tightened her hold on his neck, reveling in the delicious scent and sound and touch of him. ''You'll have to wait until tomorrow. But I have a few ideas that should tide you over in the meantime.''

''Do any of those ideas involve getting out of the rest of our clothes?''

She laughed. ''At least one of them does. But maybe you'd rather wait until we get home.''

He heaved a deep sigh. ''Haven't you figured it out yet? With you in my arms, I am home.'' His voice deepened, filled with a rich certainty, an unquestionable commitment to the future. ''And by the way, my sweet wife, I love you, too. Very, very much.''

And then he kissed her, proving beyond a doubt that Christmas was still a time of miracles.

When Christmas morning arrived, it proved to be the most joyous Nikki had ever experienced. Waking up in Jonah's arms, then to his hungry kiss and finally to his urgent lovemaking got the day off to a perfect start.

Once they reluctantly left the bedroom, she showed him the changes she'd made to the apartment. Plants filled every nook and cranny. And occupying one entire corner stood a live, potted evergreen covered in lights and ornaments.

''It wouldn't be a real home without your plants,'' he observed quietly.

''No,'' she disagreed, slipping into his arms. ''It

wouldn't be a real home without you. The plants are just to prove that I'm here to stay."

The relatives started arriving midmorning, adding their laughter to the apartment, along with an assortment of flavorful dishes. Nikki was on tenterhooks from the moment the doorbell first rang, rushing to peek into the hallway each time she thought she heard footsteps approaching.

"Who are you expecting?" Krista asked curiously at one point. "I thought everyone was already here."

"They are—"

A knock sounded at the door just then, and breaking off, she raced to answer it. Flinging it open, she called to Jonah, "It's for you. Hurry!"

He didn't come quickly enough to suit her and she rushed to his side. Grabbing his arm, she tugged impatiently. Curious, the rest of the family followed, gathering in a loose semicircle behind him. In the hallway stood a messenger dressed in the same white-and-gold uniform that the footmen at the Cinderella Ball had worn.

"I understood this was urgent," the messenger said with a broad grin. He handed Jonah a beautifully wrapped package. "Merry Christmas."

"Open it," Nikki urged the instant they'd closed the door.

With an indulgent smile, he ripped off the bright gold paper to expose a small rectangular box. He removed the lid and looked inside. Nervously, she awaited his reaction, his expressionless face worrying her. At long last, he looked up. Ignoring the eager questions from all the relatives, he closed the box. Catching hold of her hand, he towed her through the living room and out onto the balcony.

It was freezing cold, but she barely noticed. "Jonah?" she questioned anxiously. "Don't you like it?"

He dug a hand into his pocket and pulled out a small square package. "Maybe you should see what I bought you."

She ripped off the ribbon and wrapping paper and slowly flipped open the red velvet lid. Inside nestled a pair of wedding bands. Very unique, strangely etched wedding bands. "Oh, Jonah," she whispered, tears pricking her eyes. "They're made from the tickets to the Cinderella Ball."

"It was odd. The Montagues said we're the second couple requesting rings like these."

She shook her head helplessly. "It's a beautiful idea. Thank you."

"I thought it was time we had real rings and couldn't think of anything more fitting." For the first time, a hint of uncertainty crept into his voice. "I didn't want there to be any question as to my feelings for you."

"That's why..." She gestured to the box she'd had delivered to him, fighting to speak through her tears.

Huge, puffy snowflakes began to swirl downward, catching in her hair and on the ends of her lashes. He gathered her into his arms. "That's why you gave me tickets to the Anniversary Ball."

She nodded. "It's where it all began. It's where I fell in love with you. And where I first began to trust again."

He kissed the snowflakes from her lips. "I'll never give you reason to question that trust, Nikki. I swear it."

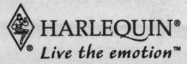

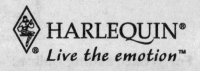

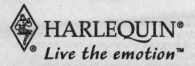